A HUNT RANCH SERIES

NIGHT RIDER

SLOANE FLETCHER

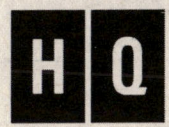

ONE PLACE. MANY STORIES

HQ
An imprint of HarperCollins*Publishers* Ltd
1 London Bridge Street
London SE1 9GF

www.harpercollins.co.uk

HarperCollins*Publishers*
Macken House, 39/40 Mayor Street Upper,
Dublin 1 D01 C9W8
This edition 2026

1
First published in Great Britain by HQ,
an imprint of HarperCollins*Publishers* Ltd 2026

Copyright © Sloane Fletcher 2026

Sloane Fletcher asserts the moral right to be identified as the author of this work.
A catalogue record for this book is available from the British Library.

ISBN: 9780008782337

Run
Words and Music by Anthony Smith and Tony Lane
Copyright © 2001 ALMO MUSIC CORP. and ENSIGN MUSIC CORPORATION
All Rights Reserved Used by Permission
Reprinted by Permission of Hal Leonard LLC

This novel is entirely a work of fiction. The names, characters and incidents
portrayed in it are the product of the author's imagination. Any resemblance to
actual persons, living or dead, events or localities is entirely coincidental.

All rights reserved. No part of this publication may be reproduced, stored
in a retrieval system, or transmitted, in any form or by any means,
electronic, mechanical, photocopying, recording or otherwise,
without the prior permission of the publishers.

Without limiting the exclusive rights of any author, contributor or the publisher of this
publication, any unauthorized use of this publication to train generative artificial intelligence
(AI) technologies is expressly prohibited. HarperCollins also exercise their rights under Article
4(3) of the Digital Single Market Directive 2019/790 and expressly reserve this
publication from the text and data mining exception.

Printed and bound in the UK using 100% Renewable
Electricity by CPI Group (UK) Ltd

(Weirdest dedication ever)

This book is for my horse, Cinder, who helped me through the most difficult period of my life by reminding me to just keep breathing.

Trigger Warning

This book contains descriptions of a single sexual assault and reference to sexual assault, rape, and grievous bodily harm. Please take care while reading.

PART ONE: ESCAPE

Prologue

Los Angeles, California – June 2, 2025

There was somebody in her house.

Nina Keller knew this absolutely.

She stood in her spotless kitchen, its big bay windows overlooking the Hollywood Hills, and stared at the three placemats sitting side by side on the counter. One was crooked, and though her militant organizational preferences would never have allowed such a small but glaring slip, that wasn't the entire reason she knew she was not alone.

Rather, she could feel him in the house with her.

She knew he was there in the same way she had known when to avoid one of her mother's 'friends' as a child.

She felt it in her bones.

In the hair on the back of her neck, which slowly crept to attention.

In the pit of her stomach – that anxious place where her childhood nightmares were stored.

The eighteen years she'd spent as the daughter of a whore had taught her many things. When to trust her instincts. When to hide. When to run. And when her only option was to fight.

Now, she held her breath as she strained to hear, listening for even the smallest sound that might give away the intruder's location.

She pressed her back to the cold glass window so that she could see in all directions, and quietly fumbled around in her purse for her phone.

She pulled it out, spared one glance at the screen so that she could dial her best friend, Markus, because in her fear, she forgot that she was no longer that little girl who had been systematically trained to never call 911.

Markus answered on the first ring. 'Baby girl, please tell me you've changed your mind about coming out with me tonight?'

Just hearing his cheery voice was enough to take the edge off her panic. Still, when she spoke, she whispered, 'Markus,' slowly, and when even that sounded too loud, she lowered her voice, and between deep inhalations, added, 'there's somebody in my house.'

Chapter 1

Hunt Ranch, Santa Barbara County – One Week Later

'I heard Farrah got out again.'

Maverick Hunt collapsed into one of the chairs in his sister's office and sighed, grateful to have thirty minutes off his feet. Even if it was for a staff meeting.

'Yeah,' he replied. The mini horse, who they'd rescued from auction and aptly named Farrah for her thick, blonde mane, was the cutest inconvenience in existence. She lived to wreak havoc – and did so often. 'And she let the goats and Babe out. By the time I got there, two kids staying at the resort were in the mix too.'

'Let me guess: the Carson twins?'

'Yup.'

'Nothing screams luxury resort like eight escaped animals running wild with the guests,' Sierra drawled sarcastically.

'I know. I don't even know how she did it this time. We'll add a padlock to the gate.'

'You got them all back in with no issues?'

'We did. Babe took some bribing. Benji had to rope Farrah to catch her.' Mav's grin was slow. 'He made a show of it to entertain the Carsons.'

Sierra had nothing to say to that. Instead, she sat at her desk and pointedly started organizing her paperwork for the meeting.

Maverick didn't say more.

His dog, Shadow – a faithful mutt of indiscriminate lineage that Mav had found on the side of the road six years earlier – lay at his feet and rested her head on the toe of his boot before closing her eyes and promptly going to sleep.

At this time on a Sunday, the Weekenders – guests who typically came from around California to stay at Hunt Ranch for a quick three-day getaway – had checked out already. Those few guests on an extended stay – a couple on a 'babymoon' from Oregon, a twenty-year-old socialite from New York, and an elderly couple from London celebrating their joint retirement by exploring the 'Wild West' – had come in for the night and were washing up from their trail rides or relaxing before the summer barbecue started in a couple of hours.

But it didn't matter that it was Sunday, or that it was five o'clock in the evening; there were two industries that never rested: ranching and hospitality, and the Hunts were buried up to the neck in both.

Mav surveyed his sister's domain as he waited for the weekly staff meeting to start. Sierra's office was pristine. As she'd undoubtedly intended, the room, with its oversized desk, heavy leather chairs, and contrastingly sleek Apple computer, looked like it had been staged for the centrefold of some fancy home catalogue. The selection of neatly framed, black-and-white photographs on the wall showed snippets from the 124 years of Hunt Ranch family history and added that touch of personality to an otherwise business-like room.

Maverick studied the photos as he mentally ran through the list of things he still needed to get done that day.

He could trust Benji, his best friend and Hunt Ranch's head wrangler, to see to the resort's seventy trail horses, but the forty or so rescue horses on the ranch were Mav's responsibility – for no other reason than he was the one who couldn't turn them away.

He would check in on a new rescue that had come in two days prior. The horse, a little palomino Quarter Horse mare, had been starved, abused, and then abandoned on a major thoroughfare in the middle of the night. Though Mav had technically promised his sister he wouldn't take in any more horses, not even Sierra had been able to turn away the downhearted mare when the sheriff had brought her by.

Mav figured by the time he was done with the staff meeting and the horses, it would be pushing six-thirty. He'd run home and take over from his nanny, make sure his five-year-old daughter, Poppy, was bathed, fed, and put to bed.

Once Poppy was down, he was technically on call. So that while he could shower and eat and go to bed, his phone would be on his nightstand, and any ranch calls were his to deal with, the same way that any resort calls the night staff and concierge couldn't handle would be his sister's.

After a – hopefully uninterrupted – night's rest, his day would begin again at four-thirty the next morning.

His schedule was gruelling. He routinely clocked fourteen-hour days before going home to try and sneak in some quality time with Poppy. He never stopped, most days even skipping lunch in the hope that he could save thirty minutes somewhere else. He worked physically all day, and at night he sat down with a single beer and the spreadsheets and accounts his sister insisted he keep for the ranch horses. When he wasn't working, he was a single dad, which was to say he clocked another three or four hours of work once his nanny left for the day.

It was hard.

It was thankless.

Mav wouldn't have changed a single thing . . . Well, except maybe the spreadsheets. He hated spreadsheets.

As he waited for the meeting to start, he covertly watched his sister, looking for signs of how she was holding up. Every time he asked her outright, she snapped at him and told him to mind his own business.

Today, she had twisted her long hair into some fancy knot at the back of her head. She wore a sleek black jumpsuit and a pair of break-neck heels. Her makeup, though immaculate, couldn't hide the dark shadows beneath her eyes.

Behind him, various management staff began filtering into the office. Mav nodded to Benji as he came in and leaned against the wall, keeping as far away as physically possible from Sierra.

Sierra didn't look up or otherwise acknowledge Benji, but the way her entire body tensed told Mav that she knew he was there.

Jordyn, their restaurant manager, took the seat next to Mav's. Without batting an eye, she kicked her feet, clad in bright pink Crocs, up and rested them on his knees. 'Please,' she said dramatically, and raised a hand to her brow, '*please* tell me we're done with bachelorette parties for the year.'

Exhausted nods of agreement came from just about everyone except Mav and Benji. They'd had a relatively quiet weekend despite the bachelorette party. The women had either been too intoxicated or too hungover to ride for most of the weekend. And though they had wandered down to the stables in small groups to pet the horses and ogle Benji, only two of the women had wanted to go out on horseback, which had given his staff some extra time to catch up on their ranch work.

'One more. But it isn't until early December, so we have some time to regroup.' Sierra looked up from her notebook. She did a quick head count, and then passed out the neatly printed notes she made before every staff meeting.

Mav took one and passed the stack to Jordyn.

Sierra didn't waste any time. 'We have sixteen guests checking in tomorrow morning. Two families taking advantage of our twenty per cent off "Weekday Summer Stay" discount – one family of four and one of six. Two couples, one on their honeymoon, one on vacation from Germany. A single woman who is "celebrating her divorce settlement" – that's what she wrote in the notes section of the online booking.'

Jordyn laughed.

Paul, the resort manager, sighed. 'The new divorcées are always so much work.'

'The last one tried to seduce Mav,' Benji added. 'Stripped to her lingerie and waited in the stables for him. What was her name, Mav? Margie or Meggie . . .'

A round of laughter followed.

Maverick only shook his head, refusing to comment.

'Her name was *Marcie*,' Sierra sighed. 'Now can we please—'

'I heard about that. José was the one who found her?' Jordyn asked.

Benji grinned. 'Oh yeah.'

'Poor kid got an education, that's for sure,' Jordyn commented. Turning to Mav, she asked, 'What was she? Like sixty? Sixty-one?'

Maverick didn't reply, but his lips fought a smile. *Marcie* had been a handful. Harmless. But a handful. And while it had been José who had found her, it had been Mav who had made sure the *very* drunk, very upset divorcée had made it back to her cabin safely – and fully clothed. Marcie was all right. She was just single for the first time in forty years. And upset. Add one too many margaritas to the mix and you had a dangerous combo.

But despite the awkward situation, she had come in to apologize the very next morning.

Mav had taken her riding and listened while she'd cried and talked about her ex-husband, a man who she'd loved for two-thirds of her life, a man who'd conveniently fallen in love with a woman thirty years younger and left Marcie in the dust with her broken heart.

Still, wanting to avoid any more talk of Marcie, he pointedly refocused his attention on the printed sheet.

There weren't any more guests listed. Only the names, lodges, and special notes for the fifteen Sierra had already mentioned.

'That's only fifteen.' Benji spoke Mav's thoughts.

'I'm *getting there*,' Sierra said slowly.

The room fell quiet as the tension ratcheted up a notch.

Benji didn't snap back as he once would have. He didn't say anything, only tipped his baseball cap over his eyes and looked back down at his printed notes.

'The sixteenth isn't listed for a reason,' Sierra continued. 'She's coming here to recuperate.' Mav's interest piqued at his sister's cautious tone. 'She's well known. I have NDAs for each of you to pass along to your staff.'

'Why NDAs?' Jordyn asked, frowning. She waved one hand in the air. 'We have celebrities come out all the time to get away from the public, and we haven't had any problems before.'

'This doesn't go beyond this office,' Sierra reiterated, looking at each of them in turn. 'If your staff have questions about the NDAs or refuse to sign them, then take them off the work schedule for the next month.'

A collective hush settled through the room.

Mav pondered the unusual request. Despite Jordyn's question, it wasn't *unheard* of for them to have to sign NDAs. Hunt Ranch was one of the few luxury guest ranches in California. They were located on two thousand acres in beautiful Santa Barbara County, less than three hours from Los Angeles. So, they had their fair share of photoshoots and film location bookings.

Their prices reflected the value of the amenities, which, at least in Mav's mind, included the guests' privacy. But the NDAs were usually only for those staff who would be directly working with the celebrity guests, not the entire staff, which included over one hundred full- and part-time employees.

'While we are not expecting any trouble, I need you to be aware of everyone coming and going while she's here.'

'Why?' Lucas, their event planner, asked.

'She was assaulted in her home last week.'

Lucas raised both brows. 'Well . . . shit.'

'I don't know much,' Sierra continued, 'but according to her agent, the police haven't identified her attacker yet. They suspect he might have been a stalker. Or just plain crazy. Probably both.

'If any of you feel uncomfortable with the situation, I need you to say so now. Otherwise, from the moment she arrives to the moment she leaves, you're all deaf and dumb.'

'We need to be able to tell the wranglers.' Benji didn't even bother addressing Sierra. He spoke to Mav. 'They're always armed. They know this land. And no city nutjob could one-up any of them.'

'This is not a protection detail,' Sierra argued instantly. 'We're only guaranteeing her privacy while she's here. Everything else, including security, is up to her—'

'Before you two start,' Jordyn interjected, 'could you wrap this up for the rest of us?'

Sierra didn't even bother denying it. She passed out the wads of printed NDAs. 'I need these back by tomorrow, prior to check-in. If any staff are off and coming in later in the week, get them to sign them the moment they step foot on the property.'

'Now I'm super curious,' Deb, Lucas's assistant, commented. 'Who is it?'

Sierra smiled. 'Nina Keller.'

Confused by the stunned silence that followed, Mav looked over his shoulder, and seeing the awestruck expressions on nearly everyone's faces, spoke for the first time since the meeting had started. 'What?' When no response was forthcoming, he added, 'Who is she?'

Jordyn slowly turned to gawk at him. 'You live under a rock?' She seemed to remember who she was talking to and added, 'You know what, never mind.'

'She's only like *the* Hollywood golden girl right now!' Deb exclaimed. 'Oh my God!' She clapped her hands together excitedly. Stopped almost immediately. 'Wait. You said she was *assaulted*?'

Sierra held up both hands. 'I don't know the details. But she's coming here to take some time off, *which means*,' she said, looking pointedly at Deb, 'no fawning, no gawking, no harassing for pictures or autographs. As far as we are concerned, she is just another guest, paying to stay at our luxury resort.' She zeroed in on Mav. 'I asked her to arrive around two-thirty so she could check in discreetly. She already signed the liability waiver via email, but if you could check her in, show her around?'

Mav nodded.

'That's it for today,' Sierra said, ending the meeting. As people started filtering out of her office, she called after them, 'Please read the notes on each guest! Jordyn! David Morgan is allergic to peanuts!'

'Got it!' Jordyn called back before disappearing down the hall.

Benji was last to leave, and it was only when he already had one foot out of the door that Sierra snapped, 'You don't want to discuss the wranglers?'

Benji stopped in the doorway. He turned slowly. He searched Sierra's face for a long moment, but when his look was met with cold, unflinching resistance, he turned to Mav. 'Let me know about the wranglers.'

Mav nodded. He waited for Benji's footsteps to sound down the hall before standing and closing the door.

This time, when he took his seat, Sierra dropped her head into her hands. 'I know,' she murmured. 'You don't have to tell me. I know. I'll try harder.'

There were so many things he wanted to say, so many things she needed to hear. Only, when faced with the burden of it, Mav couldn't bring himself to open the conversation. His own guilt weighed his tongue down, stopping those particular words in his throat. 'It's not a bad idea to bring the wranglers in,' he said instead. 'If this woman—'

'Do you really not know who Nina Keller is?' Sierra asked, her frustration as clear as her desire to change the subject.

'Does it matter?' Mav countered.

She ignored his question. '*Escaping Juárez*? *Killer Mistress*? *The Dogs of Despair*?'

'Movies?' he guessed.

'Very good, Mav,' she replied sarcastically.

'Sierra, the last movie I watched was *Barbie*. It was *two hours* long. And Poppy didn't even understand most of it. She just liked the songs and colours. So, unless this Nina Keller played Barbie—'

'Oh my God, you don't even know who Margot Robbie is.' She looked genuinely devastated.

'. . . Barbie?'

Sierra let her head fall back on a groan. 'I worry about you. Truly.'

Maverick pushed to his feet, Sierra's neat notes and the NDAs rolled in his hands. 'I'm going to ask Benji not to come to the meetings anymore,' he said, redirecting them momentarily. 'I think the distance will be good for you both.'

'It's been eight months.' Her eyes glassed over instantly. 'Time isn't going to fix anything. Just leave it alone.'

Mav didn't walk around her desk and hug her as he might have once, knowing Sierra wouldn't have welcomed it. She wanted – needed – to pretend that everything was fine. But pretending only got a person so far. Sierra was a dam wall in a flood; she was just waiting to break.

Still, because he would always be on her side, he asked, 'Do you want me to tell him to leave?'

'No. I wouldn't do that. To him. Or to you.'

'I would understand. Shit, so would he.' But his heart broke for her. For both of them. Sierra might have been his little sister, but Benji was his brother in every way that counted.

He and Benji had been best friends since first grade. They'd laughed together, cried together, bled together. A decade ago, when Maverick had decided to diversify the ranch after his parents' death, it had been Benji who had come back to help him build. When his ex, Shannon, had left him with a newborn, it had been Benji who had been the first to come and help, even though he'd known as much about babies as Mav had – zero.

So, while Mav's loyalty belonged to his sister, his heart had torn equally in two when they had broken up.

'Was there anything else?' Sierra asked, but she turned back to her computer and began clacking away without waiting for a reply.

Anything else? Mav thought. There was *everything* else. But one glance at his sister's rigid posture and tightly composed face had him replying, 'No. Nothing else. I'll see you at home later.'

He whistled, waking Shadow and calling the dog to his side. And he left.

Needing to get away from the tightness in his own chest, Maverick went straight to the barn.

The familiar smell of the horses was enough to ease some of the pressure, as always. Mav, who wasn't very talkative or very social, had always preferred animals to people. Animals only gave. And if you understood them and were kind to them, they gave you their all, always.

He watched as the horsemen – women included – worked, cleaning out hooves, brushing out coats, manes, and tails, and stalling and feeding those horses that were on grain or various supplements. He joined in, working alongside them wordlessly until the last horse had been seen to, and only then did he detour to the new rescue.

The mare had been stalled to keep her fed and safe from the other horses until they could figure out which of the various herds she could be turned out with. There were bound to be some bites and kicks as the animals reconfigured their pecking order to accommodate her, but Mav wouldn't put her through it until she could hold her own.

The mare stood in the corner of the stall, her head hanging low, her bony hipbones nearly poking through her skin. Her pale coat was covered in mud, her white-blonde mane and tail knotted in ugly bunches. Superficial slices and gouges marred her, and

Maverick knew he would only find more once he eventually got her clean. Her eyes . . .

Her eyes were so soulful and sad – until she saw him. Then she arched her neck back, moving her face as far away from him as she could, even though he hadn't opened her stall door yet. Her eyes rolled back until he saw their whites. It was pure, wild terror.

Looking at her didn't even make him sad. It made him angry. He knew that pain begot pain and that some people were never given the chance to be kind, and still, he didn't understand how anyone could break a spirit so routinely, so thoroughly.

'No need to be dramatic,' he said at plain speaking volume.

He talked to her while he mixed her food and supplements. When he was done, he opened her stall door. He stepped inside, all the while breathing deeply and audibly, and without looking at her, emptied her grain into the feeding tray.

He stood with his back to her as he mixed it with his hands, but it was only when she edged closer to him and snorted that he angled his body, creating a wide opening for her to access the grain. Maverick talked to her the entire time, saying useless things like, 'I know you're hungry,' 'You're so pretty.' And when she took that last step and came abreast of him to eat, 'Good girl.'

He saw Benji standing at the stall door out of the corner of his eye, said, 'She's not feral,' as he reached out one hand and patted the mare's neck. 'Someone loved this horse once – before she got passed down the line.'

'Yeah,' he agreed. 'She's only hurting.'

'Did you manage to do her hooves yet?'

'Cleaned them myself. Took me a goddamn hour, even with the sedative.'

'Are they in bad shape?'

'Mostly looks like a bit of overgrowth. No bad chipping or abscesses.'

Maverick nodded as he continued to stroke the horse's neck. 'We should name her at some point.'

'Let one of the guests do it,' Benji suggested. 'They always get a kick out of it.'

'Yeah. Good idea.'

A silence followed, and Mav, knowing that Benji was very rarely quiet, calmly stroked the horse as his friend figured out what he wanted to say.

It didn't take him long.

'I'm moving on, Mav. She needs space, and I can't . . . I can't be close and not reach out.'

Maverick nodded slowly, though the pain came back in full force. 'Where will you go?'

'I don't know. Haven't figured that out yet. But I have enough saved up to get by for a long while. Figured I'd travel, maybe wrangle a few temp jobs along the way to keep Diablo in work.'

At mention of his name, Benji's dun Mustang, Diablo, poked his head over his stall door behind them. He snorted.

Benji turned to face him. 'I wasn't talking to you. Don't be nosy.'

Diablo stared at him for a long moment before turning his butt pointedly in Benji's direction.

Maverick laughed. 'That horse has you wrapped around his hoof.'

Benji only shrugged. 'He always has.' He dusted the stall door distractedly. 'Anyway, I figured I'd work through the summer. Give you time to find my replacement. Head out at the end of August.'

'I hate to see you go.'

'Yeah.' Benji glanced away, cleared his throat. 'But we both know I can't stay.'

'I think you and Sierra need to sit down and talk. Fight. Just speak to each other! It might help.'

Benji only shook his head. 'Our kid died, Mav. Nothing is going to help.' He tapped the door once before stepping back, repeated, 'August,' before turning and walking away.

Chapter 2

By seven o'clock the next morning Maverick had fed the horses and updated both the trail riding and lesson sign-up sheet for the day. He had helped muck out the stalls and then made it back in time to watch the sunrise, a cup of coffee in his hand, his dog at his feet.

Over at the resort, guests would be starting to stir, wandering down to the dining room for coffee and breakfast, or ordering it up to their rooms. The folks staying in the lodges might be putting a pod in their coffee machines or ordering a fresh one, maybe a French press or pour over, from the main lodge.

The well-trained staff on both the resort and the ranch would already be well into their own routines.

Everyone had their schedules, and for the most part, things ran like clockwork. But the horses and the sunrise were Mav's. One little moment in time he took for himself every day. Because in the early hours of the morning, when all the guests were still asleep and the animals were just beginning to stir, Mav remembered why he had kept Hunt Ranch when his parents had died.

He could have sold. He knew the value of the title deeds, knew that if he had sold, he and Sierra, their children, and their grandchildren would never have had to work again. And he'd considered it seriously. Both he and Sierra had.

But then he'd asked himself what he'd do if he had all that money and the time to do anything he wanted, and the answer had been simple: he'd buy a goddamn ranch. Maybe he wouldn't have so many cows or horses. Maybe he wouldn't have the resort and the guests. Maybe he wouldn't work so hard. But he had 124 years of family history proving otherwise.

So, the choice had been easy for him.

Less so for Sierra, but even then, Mav knew she only struggled with all her memories. His sister had seen a lot of heartache at Hunt Ranch.

The sound of the front door opening had him turning in his chair as Poppy came out, dressed in her PJs, a matching shirt and pair of shorts in pink that Sierra had undoubtedly picked out. Her tiny feet were bare. Her hair, the same dark brown as his, was a wild tangle that Mav took one look at and sighed. Her eyes, brown like Shannon's where his were blue, were still half shut.

On the floor, Shadow's tail thumped loudly.

'Good morning,' he said quietly.

'Hi, Daddy.' Poppy smiled and walked to him, pausing on the way to pat Shadow.

She crawled onto Mav's lap, rested her head against him, and yawned.

Maverick inhaled her familiar scent, vaguely resonant of Johnson & Johnson shampoo, and his heart settled. His mind quietened. And when Poppy looked out at the ranch, saw the horses grazing, and whispered, 'Pretty,' Mav reminded himself that he was exactly where he was meant to be.

He kissed her head, asked, 'Did you sleep okay?' though he knew the answer already. Poppy had two modes: awake and dead to the world.

'Yeah. I slept good.' She reached for his coffee mug and gripping it with both hands, raised it to her mouth when he released it.

Poppy took a single sip, scrunched her face up as she swallowed, and then passed the mug back to him without a word.

'Still don't like it, huh?'

She made a gagging sound. When he laughed, she did it again.

Mav ran his hand over her hair, covertly trying to see what he was in store for. 'Want me to make you breakfast before daycare?'

It might have been mid-June, the first full month of summer for most kids, but Poppy was still too young to be left alone on the ranch for full days, and her nanny couldn't spare the extra time from her part-time job. So, daycare it was. At least until she was old enough to hang around the ranch without slowing him down or getting hurt.

'Eggs and toast,' came the succinct reply.

'Okay.' Mav helped her down, groaned as he pushed to his feet. 'Why don't you go and get changed, and I'll start breakfast.' As she ran inside, letting the door slap closed behind her, he called out, 'You have to hurry! Jenna is picking you up soon!'

''Kay!'

He almost shouted back *No rain boots!* but thought better of it, knowing how proud Poppy was that she could dress herself now.

Last week she had insisted on wearing her rain boots with every outfit, despite there being no clouds in sight. And she was starting to get picky with her hair, insisting on something called a French braid when Mav only knew how to do a ponytail and a regular braid. An American braid? He didn't even know. The only reason he knew how to braid at all was because his father had taught him how to do it in horse manes and tails to prevent breakage.

But such was the life of a girl dad.

With one last swig from his coffee, he let himself inside. Poppy's footsteps sounded above his head.

Inside the kitchen, Mav took out his supplies and placed them on the countertop. He bent down to take a frying pan out of the cupboard.

Upstairs, something crashed.

He paused what he was doing and listened, but when no call for help sounded and the footsteps resumed, he walked to the base of the stairs, the frying pan in hand, and shouted up, 'What was that?'

After a moment, Poppy replied, 'The lamp.'

He could hear the quiver in her voice, decided on nonchalance before the situation escalated. 'Don't worry, I'll get another one. Don't touch it! And put shoes on before you do anything else, please!' Mav didn't get flustered or mad, knowing it wouldn't solve anything.

''Kay!'

Mav fought his need to go check that Poppy did what she was told. She might have been five, but she was a five-year-old on a working ranch. Following orders was the first thing she'd have to learn, and things like broken lamps were the safest way he knew how to teach her.

He sighed, forced his feet back in the direction of the kitchen, and mentally added cleaning up a broken lamp and ordering a new one to his list as he went back to the stove.

By the time he got to the resort at eleven, the lamp had been long cleaned up and Poppy's entire room vacuumed in case of any glass he couldn't see. The task had taken him thirty minutes he hadn't had to spare, so he was running behind on everything else.

Check-in time, occurring between eleven and two, was sacred. Each guest who arrived was given a refreshment as their bags were covertly taken to their rooms by staff dressed in western gear – jeans, boots, and a Hunt Ranch work shirt. They were presented with 'The Welcome Speech' and the associated liability forms, which outlined the rules of the ranch and prevented any run-ins with one of their thousand-plus-pound animals. And then those guests who wanted to settle in, could, while he and some of the wranglers alternated taking the rest of the new arrivals on a walking tour of the resort property before showing them to their rooms.

Now, at a few minutes past eleven, the resort lobby was brimming with people already. The family of six seemed to have arrived first. The parents held one kid in each hand like seasoned pros, forgoing refreshments in order to keep their children close and out of the surrounding chaos.

Mav greeted them. 'Morning, folks.' A round of cheery replies followed. 'My name's Maverick.'

'Mine's June Morgan!' This exuberant declaration came from the youngest, a little girl with blonde curls who couldn't have been more than three.

'Well, howdy, June Morgan!' Mav greeted her enthusiastically. 'I like your cowgirl boots,' he said, tapping her brand-new, bright pink boots with the toe of his scarred leather ones. 'Did you bring your hat too?'

Her smile faded. She shook her head and turned to look accusingly at her mom. 'Mommy, you didn't get a hat?'

Mav bit back his smile and replied before Mrs Morgan could. 'Hmm, we'll have to fix that,' he said. 'Can't be a cowgirl without a cowgirl hat.' He turned back to the check-in desk, plucked a hat from the pile, craftily labelled with the Hunt Ranch brand, off the counter. He plopped one on June's head himself before passing the rest out. 'There you go.'

'I'm a cowgirl now!' June chirped.

'I'm a cow*boy*!' her brother, who was maybe closer to Poppy's age, stated seriously and craned his head back so that he could see out from under the hat's brim.

'You sure are,' Maverick affirmed. 'How about we go wrangle some horses, pardner?' he drawled.

He ushered them towards the door, past a couple, sitting in the lounge, side by side on one of the huge leather sofas, waiting to check in. The woman was as slender as a willow sapling, with long black hair that fell in a curtain, concealing the side of her face. She was wearing baggy forest-green linen overalls with a white top underneath. Mav couldn't figure out why she didn't look ridiculous in the strange outfit. She certainly should have. Instead, she somehow managed to look bohemian.

The man was a statuesque, athletic Black man wearing all-white cowboy attire, including a Stetson.

Mav took stock of all the white fabric just waiting to get dirty, figured they were city folk here to play for the week. Maybe the honeymooners?

As he moved past, the man accidentally dropped his phone on the floor by the woman's feet.

Maverick smiled and bent to retrieve it. 'Here you go.' He looked up, the phone in his hand.

And then simply stared.

The woman looking back at him had big, dark eyes that were completely oversized in her pale face. They were so intense, so sad, that for a full three seconds, he didn't see the bruises beneath the expertly applied makeup.

When he did, the sight of them, the unexpected whip of anger that slashed through him, kick-started his brain. Not the honeymooners, he realized. The actress.

He had been told she'd be arriving later in the day, and taken off-guard, at a loss for what to say, he only smiled and quietly tipped his head in greeting. 'Ma'am.'

The actress – Nina Keller, he remembered – returned the smile politely but she didn't reply, only angled her face away, hiding the bruises once again.

It was her friend, or boyfriend, maybe, who leaned forward and took the phone he held.

'And *you are*?' he practically purred, batting his eyelashes exaggeratedly.

Okay, not *her boyfriend*, Mav deduced. 'Maverick.' He stood and stepped back, out of her space. And because he had already moved to help the Morgans, he didn't change course. 'Welcome to Hunt Ranch, folks. I hope you enjoy your stay. If you need anything, don't hesitate to flag down any one of our staff.'

He caught up with the Morgans outside, began his tour with: 'We have over one hundred horses here . . .' But as he talked, gave the tour he'd given countless times before, his mind kept wandering back to Nina Keller.

He didn't know why he'd been expecting some vivacious blonde who would need to be pampered. But he had been. So, the quiet, Bohemian woman with the sad eyes had surprised him. Intrigued him. But even as he thought of her, he remembered what she had been through and he reminded himself to keep his distance. He'd check in with Sierra, maybe have Riley or another one of their female staff check Nina Keller in for her stay.

He waited for the Morgans to get sidetracked by the horses, and as they stood at the fencing *oohing* and *aahing*, he pulled out his phone, shot a text to his sister.

Actress arrived early. I was already checking in the Morgans, but I'll send Riley up to check her in instead. Make sure she has female staff when possible. She's spooked.

It wasn't exactly poetry, but he knew Sierra agreed with him when she replied only moments later with:

Will do.

'You did that on purpose,' Nina accused Markus the moment the cowboy walked out the front door.

'Damn right I did.' Markus raised one hand dramatically to his heart. 'And this is the thanks I get?' He leaned close, stage-whispered, 'Did you at least benefit from my efforts?'

Nina only tipped her head, but she wouldn't deny that she'd noticed the cowboy. Anyone would have.

She'd seen him the moment he'd walked in, his long-legged stride determined, his dark brown hair sticking out beneath an old LA Dodgers baseball cap, his blue eyes a little harried. She'd been helpless but to watch as he'd greeted the family. She'd even smiled when she'd overheard his conversation with the little girl, who had declared to the entire lobby that her name was June Morgan.

And Markus was right about one thing: the man – Maverick – certainly filled out a pair of old blue jeans. Still, she knew better than to encourage Markus, and so replied, 'He has lovely eyes.'

'I didn't notice,' Markus quipped, making her smile. 'Did you see the stretch in those blue jeans though?'

Nina had. But, on principle, denied it. 'No.'

'They must have been a polyester, Lycra, denim blend. Hmmm.'

Nina knew that exact look. 'Let me guess. A spring photoshoot. Cowboys. Denim. Horses.' She swiped her hand across the space in front of them as if painting the picture. 'A lone cowboy carries his saddle across a golden field in search of his trusty steed.'

'Hell yeah. I can see it now, Neens.' He pushed to his feet, all sense of playfulness gone. 'I can convince one of the big brands to bite on this. Maybe Levi's. Or Wrangler.'

Nina was half convinced he wanted to do it. Markus was one of the most sought-after photographers in LA, so he could pick and choose his clients. The other half of her knew: 'And then you can get paid to check up on me.'

Markus patted her on the head. 'Small perks, honey.'

On a mission now, he flagged down a passing staff member. 'Excuse me!'

Nina groaned as the girl, whose name tag identified her as 'Debbie', stopped. She shot Nina an anxious glance, murmured, 'Hello. Welcome to Hunt Ranch.'

Markus didn't notice, and even if he had, he wouldn't have cared. His philosophy in life was to go after every opportunity with both hands and then hold on to it in a vice-like grip until he'd sufficiently conquered it. 'Who's in charge here?' he asked now.

The girl looked around uncertainly. 'The Hunts – Maverick and Sierra. If you have a complaint, I'd be happy to find one of them for you.'

'Oh no! No complaints!' But Markus raised one eyebrow. 'Maverick, you said?' At six feet, Markus might have been only one or two inches shorter than Maverick, but he held one hand a foot above his head, said, 'About yea high? Rugged? Handsome? Dodgers fan?'

Debbie laughed, immediately relaxing. 'Yes. That's Maverick.'

'Thanks, girl.' He winked at her. 'I know where to find him.'

Markus took Nina's hands and gently helped her to her feet. 'Come on, baby. Let's go.'

'Markus, they asked us to wait a few minutes.'

'This can't wait.' He started walking. Nina followed. 'These things are always easier in person, and if I can sort it before I leave later, we'll have the ball well and truly rolling by the time I need to pitch it. I could be back with you in under a week.'

'Markus—'

'How did I not know this was right here?' he asked, deliberately steamrolling her. 'Cowboys! Only three hours away!'

Nina struggled to keep up with his big strides. Her attacker had cracked her eighth and ninth ribs when he'd kicked her, and too much movement was excruciating. 'Markus, I don't want you to put your life on hold for me.'

Markus heard the pinch of pain in her voice and slowed his pace. He jammed his hands in his pockets, but only because she had started snapping at him every time he fussed. 'Why not?'

'Because you have a life,' she responded immediately. 'A job you love. A boyfriend who has already been entirely too accommodating of me. I'm here now. I'm safe. You need to go home.' And even though she didn't actually want him to go, Nina added, 'I'll be fine.'

Because she had to be. If she was ever going to get back to the woman she had been, the woman who had clawed her way up in the world using nothing but her brain and a God-given stubborn streak, she needed to start working on it.

Markus closed his eyes and mumbled something incoherent.

'What are you doing?' she asked.

'Praying for patience.'

'Markus—'

He held up one finger. 'Almost done.'

And damn him because she truly laughed for the first time in over a week. And *it hurt*.

Markus opened his eyes, but he didn't smile. He said, 'We're going to tackle that horseshit chronologically. One—' he held up his index finger again '—you are one of the most important people in my life. Two—' his middle finger joined his index one '—my boyfriend loves you, and if he doesn't understand why you are my priority right now, then he's not the man I thought he was and he's certainly not the man for me. Three, you are here now, and you are safe but I'm not going home until you're settled in, and I am one hundred per cent certain you're okay to be left alone. And four—' his pinkie joined the rest '—I genuinely love this concept, I'm in demand enough as a photographer that I think I could arrange it, and then *I* could worry less because I could be closer to you. It's a win-win.'

Nina's tears welled before she could bank them. 'I just want to move on. And I feel like I won't be able to do that if I get used to leaning on you too much.'

After her three-day hospital stay, she had moved in with Markus. She had slept in his bed with him while Juan took the couch because she kept having nightmares about the attack. She had started waking up in full fight mode, her arms and legs thrashing.

She hadn't been out alone since the attack, even with her customary baseball-hat-and-sunglasses disguise. The one time she'd tried to go to the grocery store, only a few days prior, she'd driven all the way there and then descended into full-blown panic.

She'd sat in her car and cried for an hour before finally calming down enough to drive back to Markus's.

'It's just a bump in the road that's slowed you down for a while,' Markus insisted. 'Neens . . . You suffered something horrific, and it's not just going to go away because you want to move on.' He held out both arms, and she walked into his hug. He sighed and added, 'It's going to go away because I carried you for a bit while you rested and recharged. And it's going to disappear forever when I find the bastard who hurt you and show him that this queen has balls.'

Overwhelmed by guilt and shame and love and gratitude, Nina choked on a laugh-sob. But she took a moment to rest against him, drawing from his strength. She whispered, 'I love you.'

And she smiled when he only sniffled and replied, 'Don't make me cry. I didn't bring my makeup.'

Chapter 3

They found Maverick just as he was herding the Morgans into the barn to show them where they would meet up with the wranglers if they signed up for any riding lessons. They waited on the peripheries, listening as his deep voice explained, 'Once you fill out the sign-up sheet at the front desk and schedule a ride, we'll know which horse will suit you best—'

'Which one will I ride?' June squeaked.

Maverick didn't repeat his instructions. He only smiled and crouched down to the little girl's level. 'I'm thinking Spirit for you.'

Mr and Mrs Morgan laughed.

'Which one is she?' June asked seriously.

'He's that big one over there.' He pointed to a stall behind where Markus and Nina were standing and saw them for the first time. 'If you go with your mom, you can have a look at him.' Maverick pushed back to his feet. 'Excuse me for a minute, folks.'

Nina hated that her muscles tensed as if preparing – just in case. She despised the fact that she couldn't fake a smile. She was an actress, goddammit! But the grimace she plastered on her face felt tight, forced. Wrong.

'Everything okay?' Maverick asked as he approached, but Nina noticed that he stopped a good five feet from them.

Embarrassed by her obvious anxiety, she only looked to Markus, who immediately stepped in to say, 'I was hoping to sneak in a quick chat about booking a photoshoot here.'

As Maverick moved closer, Nina turned away. It wasn't that she was scared, necessarily, but she had seen the moment he'd noticed her bruises in the lobby; she'd recognized the anger that had turned his blue eyes dark and killed his kind smile. And it had embarrassed her, that a stranger could feel so much rage on her behalf when she couldn't summon the emotion for herself. All she felt was sad and scared. And *so tired*.

So, she avoided Markus's concern and the cowboy's anger and let them talk business as she wandered off to peek in the stalls.

She moved slowly, making sure not to make too much noise or alarm any of the horses. June Morgan's mother smiled at her in that oddly intimate, exuberant way that people did with celebrities, as if they knew them well when, in fact, they only knew the characters they'd played. 'Hi! It's so amazing to meet you! I'm a huge fan!'

Nina returned the smile, and although she was too aware of her bruises to stop and make conversation, she replied, 'Thank you. It's lovely to meet you too,' as she continued walking past the stalls.

A few of the horses nickered. One particularly curious one, a black-and-grey horse whose name, Zephyr, was tacked above her stall, came forward and snorted at her.

Nina sighed and, reaching one hand forward tentatively, stroked the horse's silky black nose.

She moved on after a few minutes, walking slowly, taking her time as she absorbed the smells and sounds. There was something so visceral about the earthy, heady smell of horse and hay and manure, as if there were some biological mechanism at play that compelled her curiosity, perhaps some evolutionary awareness of how much humans had depended on them at some point. Being among them felt natural, she supposed, as if she'd done all this before when, really, Nina rarely spent time in the country.

She came to the last stall and looked in.

Her heart stopped beating for one long moment as she took in the defeated creature inside. She didn't have to know anything about horses to see one that had been grossly mistreated and malnourished. She could count the poor thing's ribs over her oddly barrelled stomach. And her eyes . . . Her eyes brought tears to Nina's own.

'Hello,' she whispered, and took a step closer.

The horse jerked to attention.

Nina's heart lurched.

She stopped moving as the horse shied away and began to pace anxiously.

Nina took a few hurried steps back – straight into a solid chest.

She jumped just like the horse had, spun around clumsily, her hands raised instinctively.

Instead of reaching out to steady her, Maverick held up both hands, his palms facing forward, and in a voice that was so low, so quiet, said, 'Easy.'

'I'm so sorry!' Nina placed one hand over her pounding heart, begging it to settle. 'I didn't see you there,' she explained breathlessly.

'No harm done.' He smiled gently, looked past her to the horse. 'She's a new rescue. She only came in a few days ago, so she's a little worse for wear.'

He stepped past Nina and, raising his voice, said, 'She's a little spooky still.'

'I think I scared her,' she replied. 'I didn't know. I just wanted to say hi and—'

'Miss Keller—'

'Nina.'

Maverick ignored that. 'You didn't do anything wrong.'

The horse continued to pace. 'Don't you think we should be quiet?' she whispered.

'Stop looking at her.'

'What?' Nina frowned at the gently issued command, but she looked away from the horse to focus on Maverick.

He smiled, softened his tone, but it seemed to be more for Nina's benefit than the horse's. 'Horses are prey animals. Predators have eyes that face forward, so if you're looking at a horse straight on, sometimes they feel threatened. Horses that have been around good humans a lot might not have the same fearful response. But in her current state, and trapped in the stall as she is, she can't handle it.' He leaned his back against the stall, deliberately ignoring the horse.

Nina shouldn't have noticed the span of his broad shoulders or the way his shirt contoured to muscles well used to physical labour. She shouldn't have noticed his gentle blue eyes, or the laugh lines around them. But she did. And she begrudgingly acknowledged that Markus might have something for his shoot.

Maverick kept his tone even when he continued. 'Horses can also hear human heartbeats within four feet of them. So, if your heart was racing and you approached her straight on, she wouldn't have thought you just wanted to say hello. She would have thought "Danger!" and reacted appropriately.'

Nina took stock of her heart, still beating frantically, and then moved back several steps, putting herself well over four feet away from the horse. 'I'm sorry.'

'Don't be. She needs to learn that she's safe; otherwise, she won't be rideable. And she won't find a home. The only way she's going to learn is by exposure. Or *desensitization* as we call it in the horse world.' On the other side of the barn, the Morgans moved closer, and Maverick lowered his voice just for her. 'I'm not telling you all this to make you feel guilty. I'm telling you so that you understand she's having a very normal response. She only needs to work through it.'

Nina glanced at the horse, noticed that she had already stopped pacing. Now, she stood stock-still, her ears twitching, her eyes focused on Maverick's back. 'She seems calmer.'

'Yeah.' Maverick tipped his head in the horse's direction. 'Wanna come try again?'

Nina hesitated. She didn't want to cause any more harm than she already had . . .

Maverick saw her hesitation. 'I wouldn't offer if I thought either of you couldn't handle it.'

Nina didn't move, but she did ask, 'What do I do?'

'Take a huge breath in, hold it in your lungs for two seconds, and then exhale it loudly.' He demonstrated, filling his lungs with a big breath and then releasing it slowly.

Nina's skin prickled as the Morgans' attention fixed on her. She looked for Markus, hoping he'd intercede, but he was distracted, taking photos of a horse further down. Seeing no way out, she took a deep breath, quietly asked, 'Is this where you make fun of the city slicker?'

'No, ma'am.' When he grinned, Nina felt a tiny responding nudge low in her stomach. 'We save the line dancing for that.'

When she still hesitated, Maverick didn't push, only waited quietly.

It was Nina who took the first breath. She inhaled deeply, held it, and then exhaled in one huge whoosh.

'Good. Keep doing that.'

She breathed five more times before Maverick waved her forward, and when she took a tentative step, he said, 'Don't be so cautious. She'll think she has something to worry about. Just do everything normally. As if you were talking to a friend or working on a film.'

Nina approached more confidently, though it was a lie. An act. She felt unsure and anxious, even a little scared.

'Keep breathing.'

She exhaled the breath she had been holding in another loud whoosh. Inhaled again as she touched the stall door.

Maverick slid the lock out and slipped inside. 'You ever meet Margot Robbie?'

'No. Why? Is she good with horses?'

'No idea.' He shrugged. 'I just watched *Barbie* with my daughter the other day, and my sister told me the actress was Margot Robbie.'

'You didn't know who Margot Robbie was?'

'I do now – keep breathing.'

'What are we doing here exactly?' she asked, but she did as she was told.

'Talking. Breathing.'

Nina took another pointedly exaggerated breath in and released it.

Only this time, the horse behind her did the same thing. Nina heard it – the long exhalation, almost a sigh. 'Did you hear that?'

Maverick grinned. 'How's that heart of yours?'

Nina focused on her heartbeat, realized that he had completely distracted her from her anxiety. 'Huh.'

'Breathing,' he said simply.

'Now what?'

Maverick turned. He reached over the stall door and into a nearby bin, pulled out a scooper filled with pellets.

The horse perked up at the sound.

'Come stand this side of me,' he told Nina. 'I don't want you between her and the wall.'

Nina followed orders, and when the horse took one step closer and her heart started thumping excitedly, she resumed her deep breathing.

'See, you're a natural.'

'I feel like an idiot.' She laughed. 'Breathing for a horse.'

Those blue eyes flickered over her, assessing. 'You don't look like one.' Before Nina could make sense of the compliment, he passed her the handle on the scooper, stepped back. 'Here. Pour it into her tray, and when she comes for it, don't hesitate. Stroke her neck. Firmly. Like you know what you're doing and aren't scared of anything. Breathe. Be confident. I'm right here.'

Nina didn't question why she trusted that Maverick Hunt

would never endanger her, and she didn't waste time either. She poured the grain into the tray and held her breath as the horse blew a breath on her elbow.

'Breathe.'

She exhaled loudly. 'I keep forgetting.'

'You're doing great.'

Nina breathed deeply as the horse came closer, and the moment she lowered her head to eat, Nina reached out her hand and patted the matted coat.

The horse paused at the contact, but before she could snatch her hand back, Maverick said, 'Don't stop.'

And she didn't. Nina kept moving, gliding her hand firmly down the horse's neck while she ate. At one point she looked up and saw that Markus was watching. He gave her a thumbs up.

Maverick leaned one shoulder against the wall of the stall, watching the situation closely.

Nina felt his gaze, heavy on her skin. 'Is this covered by that liability form I signed?'

He laughed, and the sound was lovely. Deep and rolling. The lines around his eyes and mouth deepened. 'Yes. Though a fancy lawyer could make a solid case for reckless endangerment if anything were to happen.'

Nina smiled. And it was genuine this time. She felt it move upwards from her heart, which was momentarily at peace after a week of turmoil. 'Worth it,' she whispered.

They made a pretty picture, the tiny, dark-haired woman and the small, palomino horse with her white-blonde mane and tail, and Mav had to wonder if it was their contrasting colouring or because their eyes carried that same quiet devastation.

He heard her whispered 'Worth it' and though he didn't say anything, he couldn't help but internally agree with her.

He had seen her face the moment she had made contact, seen the relief and wonder and joy. Just as he saw the sadness creep in again now, when she looked down at the horse's neck and saw the gouges that had been stripped from her.

Nina blinked rapidly and angled her face away, but not before Mav saw the glistening tears in her big, dark eyes.

As the father of a five-year-old, he was used to tears of all kinds, but these . . . These ones felt too personal. And he didn't know what to say, other than, 'She's going to be fine.' And even he didn't know which he was talking about: the horse or the woman.

Nina nodded, but she didn't reply. Only kept her face angled away from him as she continued to stroke the horse.

'She needs a name,' he said, trying to give her something else to hold on to. 'You're the first guest to make contact with her, so it seems only fair you choose it.'

She looked down at the horse's neck. 'Really?'

'Yeah. Think on it. Let me know, and we'll have her tags made for her halter and her stall door.'

'I don't need to think on it.'

Maverick only raised his eyebrows.

'Barbie.'

Mav looked at the palomino horse, with her blonde mane and tail, decided, 'Perfect.' And he meant it. 'My kid is going to get a kick out of that.'

But noticing that the food was nearly gone, he made space for Nina to pass and said, 'Let's give her some time to think about how nice that interaction was.'

Nina moved past him immediately and exited the stall. Maverick followed and slid the door closed behind him.

For the first time since she'd arrived, the mare – Barbie, he reminded himself – poked her head over the door. She didn't stay long, simply looked around before receding back inside.

And when Mav turned and saw the glow in Nina's eyes as she

approached Markus, her quiet: 'Did you see that?' reaching his ears, he smiled.

'Hell yes! I got the whole thing on camera!' Markus slung one arm over Nina's shoulders.

Mav saw the way she flinched at the contact before settling into the embrace, and he wondered if she was in pain or if she was scared – both, maybe?

'You're welcome to come back and see her anytime. I'll introduce you to my head wrangler, Benji. Just make sure that one of us is with you before you go into her stall.'

Nina raised both her hands to her heart. Those eyes, already so big, widened. 'Really?'

'Yeah. Sure. She needs a lot of attention. We haven't even been able to groom her properly yet, but today you got closer for longer than any of us have. And you're smart – cautious. Gentle. If you want—'

She didn't let him finish. 'I do.' She looked at where Barbie had receded back into her stall. 'I want to help.'

'It probably won't be much more than spending time desensitizing her to humans for the first week. And not alone, given that liability issue you brought up. But between Benji and me, we'll find the time to help you.'

'Can I pet Barbie?' This question was asked by June Morgan, who had been picked up by her dad so that she could see into the stall.

'How about you pet the horse you're going to ride?' he asked, easily appeasing her.

'Spirit?'

'Yeah, you remembered.'

'He's mine.'

'He's the horse you're going to ride,' Mrs Morgan corrected.

Maverick turned to Markus and Nina. 'You're welcome to join the tour or wander around and discover things yourselves – seeing as though you signed your lives away already.'

'We'll wander around,' Nina replied.

Markus only pointed his cell phone in Mav's direction. 'Photoshoot?'

'Yes, to booking it. Text me the dates once you know them and I'll coordinate with my sister. Maybe, to hiring horses and a few wranglers for the day, but I still have to see which staff might be interested once we have dates. And *hell no*, to me being one of them.'

Nina laughed. Her dark eyes lit up.

As Mav watched her face transform beneath the bruises, he saw it, that *thing* some people had. It wasn't charm. Charm was too practised. Too rehearsed. It was pull. *Magnetism*. Like a horse kick to the gut when you were least expecting it.

Markus only narrowed his eyes at Mav and tapped his phone against his palm. 'I don't give up easily.'

'And I'd rather ride naked through Nevada in the height of summer than be in a photoshoot,' Mav countered. He wasn't a model. He was a horseman.

'Wait.' Markus made a stopping gesture with one hand 'Is that an option?'

Maverick only shook his head. But he took one last look at them standing side by side, Markus grinning outright, Nina quietly studying his face, gauging his reaction. 'You two . . . You two are trouble.'

Markus laughed.

Nina smiled.

But what Mav couldn't quite figure out as he walked back to the Morgans was that he hadn't been joking. Markus might have been a tornado in human form, but Nina Keller was more dangerous. A man didn't see her coming. She was quiet but devastating, her sad eyes drawing you in before that flash of a smile knocked you off your feet entirely.

Maverick tried not to think anything of it. He had eyes, he rationalized, and Nina Keller was a beautiful woman. Which made him want to look. She was hurt, which made him want to help. And Mav had never been one to turn his back on suffering.

Those were just facts.

Chapter 4

'So, this is pepper spray.' Markus held up a black spray bottle no larger than a lipstick. 'It might not look dangerous, but this baby has a ten-foot range. It's compact, so you can take it anywhere. It's safe – you just slide your thumb under the doodad, point, and shoot.'

'The doodad?'

He ignored her raised brows and cynical tone. He leaned over the small arsenal on her bed and picked up a stun gun, this one in bright pink. 'Stun gun. If you have to use this, things are bad. Because the perp's already too close to you.' Markus pressed the button on the side and demonstrated.

Nina took a step back as the Taser made a zapping noise. 'The perp?'

'Yes, the perp.' He nonchalantly waved the Taser. 'The lunatic. The bad guy.'

'Stop pointing that in my direction.'

Markus turned it off. But he flipped it over and said, 'Look. It has a flashlight too.'

'Very cute.'

'Next—' he picked up a small rose gold device that looked like a USB drive '—we have the Birdie.'

'The Birdie?' Nina crossed her arms, cocked a hip.

'Girl. Don't give me that sass. This baby only cost me twenty-three dollars on Amazon. *Twenty-three dollars!* It clips onto your clothes, and when you press this button, it emits a siren that could blow the clothes off a man at twenty feet. *And it has a strobe light!*' He turned on the strobe light, raised his hands in the air and made an 'intz' sound as he danced as if he were in a nightclub.

Nina tried her damnedest to smile, knowing he was trying to make a seriously depressing conversation light-hearted and fun. But she couldn't quite manage it, even for Markus.

She looked down at the items on the bed. The pepper spray, stun gun, and Birdie were just three from the pile. There was also a folding knife, a first-aid kit, another flashlight with extra batteries, a period kit (tampons and chocolate included), a box of thirty granola bars, and a twenty-four pack of bottled water.

'This is like a full earthquake preparedness kit,' she argued.

'No. This is a self-defence kit for the girl who never took Tai Chi with me.'

'I thought it was stretching.'

'It's. A. Martial. Art.'

Nina let it go, knowing that Markus was legitimately serious about his Tai Chi, but she did wave at the twenty-four pack of waters. 'What am I going to do with those – throw them at him?'

'No. *Those are for drinking,*' he said, enunciating each word slowly. He tapped her on the nose with one finger. 'We might look twenty-three, but my knees know we're a decade older than that. And hydration is the only thing all the health quacks agree on. And sleep,' he sighed, 'but we both know you aren't going to get enough of that anytime soon. But—' he picked up a bottle of pills off the bed and rattled them '—I'm leaving my prescription hydroxyzine here for you, just in case.'

'I can't use your prescription, Markus.'

'It's only illegal if you get caught.'

'No. I mean, I need to be lucid in case . . .' *In case what?* she thought. Her attacker almost certainly wouldn't be able to find her, and even if he did, she doubted he'd risk coming to Hunt Ranch. And, still, there was that little voice in her head telling her she needed to be lucid. Ready. 'I can't take the risk of being drugged if he comes back.'

Taking both of her hands in his, Markus bent his knees until they were at eye level. 'He has no way of knowing where you are. This,' he reassured her, 'this is just my way of giving us both peace of mind.'

She pulled her hands out of his grip. 'I know. I do,' she insisted when he raised a hand to frustratedly rub his forehead. 'But I just I want to move on. I want to forget.' She didn't say it aloud but pretending that nothing had happened felt like the only way she'd ever truly be able to live again.

'Always carry one thing on you. Please.' When she still didn't reply, he added, 'For me.'

'Fine.'

'Promise.'

'I promise.' She would, too. Markus never asked for promises unless he absolutely believed he had to, and Nina respected that. He was trying to help in the only way he knew how, but instead of comforting her, his concern only made everything worse.

When tears burned her eyes for the millionth time in only seven days, Nina blinked, refusing to let them fall. It didn't matter that she never cried them, though. Markus knew her, sometimes too well.

He took a step back and ran both hands over his head. 'I don't feel comfortable leaving you alone right now.'

'Markus, I'm putting my foot down.' She smiled, though it cost her immense amounts of what little energy she had left. 'Look around,' she insisted. 'This place is perfectly safe.'

Markus did look, and she knew he saw what she did.

The cabin Alison, her agent, had reserved for her for the month was gorgeous. It was furnished luxuriously while somehow maintaining the rustic aesthetic. Thick, off-white knitted rugs lined the floor, heavy wooden furniture had been strategically placed to create a cosy atmosphere, and clever lamp stands sculptured from horseshoes added a homey touch. The kitchen, though she didn't plan on using it, was fully serviceable. The bedroom was big and airy, with a California king bed she desperately wanted to sleep in – but wouldn't. And the en-suite bathroom had a ginormous egg tub right by the floor-to-ceiling window – which she sincerely hoped was made from one-way glass.

Best of all, dozens of horses grazed in the pasture right outside her door. Nina could see them even then, outside her bedroom window, their heads down as they ate, tails swishing, ears twitching as they listened for any signs of danger.

'It's the safest you can be for now. Until they find him.' He pulled her into a hug. 'And they will.'

Nina didn't bother arguing. What was the point?

She returned the hug.

Then she stepped back and said, 'I'm fine.'

'You're a shit liar.' But he tipped his head towards the door. 'Walk with me.'

Nina started for the door.

Markus didn't move.

He pointedly cleared his throat.

Nina sighed. But she went back to the bed and picked up the Birdie, slid it into the pocket of her overalls. 'Happy?'

'Appeased,' he corrected.

He slid his arm through hers as they walked outside.

It was nearing five o'clock. A light breeze had picked up, causing Nina's long hair to dance around her face.

She took a deep breath as she looked at Hunt Ranch under the glow of early evening. The irrigated horse pastures, bright green and lush with grass, faded into the rolling golden hills in the distance. Horses grazed. A flock of birds arrowed through the blue sky overhead. Somewhere close by, a child laughed.

'Could you imagine living here?' she asked. 'Just waking up to *this* every day?'

Markus shook his head instantly. 'Vacationing, yes. Working, absolutely. But living . . . No way. This boy needs city amenities.'

'But it's so quiet,' she observed. 'Peaceful.'

'I live downtown.' Markus shrugged. 'Ambulance sirens literally lull me to sleep. And what would I do without bars and clubs? And restaurants. Oh, God, I'd have to learn how to cook.' He patted her hand with genuine concern. 'Are you sure you're gonna be okay here for a whole month?'

'Yeah . . . I think I'm going to enjoy it. I need it. Time away from everything.'

Although Markus couldn't know how true that was, Nina meant it. She needed time away from her house and the memories there, time to decide if she could ever live there again. She needed time away from work, from the new fear that followed her. Because now that she understood real terror, she wasn't sure she could act it anymore. And as much as she hated herself for it, she needed time away from Markus and his constant concern.

The exhaustion and shame weighed her down, and every time he tried to help, or tried to comfort her, she felt it rise in her throat, suffocating her.

'Alison said the team is holding off on filming your last scene in *Shadowlands* while you're recuperating,' he reminded her.

Nina laughed bitterly at that. 'Oh, I bet they are.'

He frowned at her tone. 'What's that supposed to mean?'

'I'm contracted, and I've filmed ninety-nine per cent of it already. They're hardly going to restart filming now. If anything, they'll scrap my last scene. Or use a body double to film it. And that's *if* they don't cause drama over the fact that I've breached my contract.'

'Nobody with a brain would ever scrap you. Your name is literally selling that movie.'

He was right. But more than her name, Nina had thrown her

whole heart into making the film. *Shadowlands* was supposed to have been the one that made her career. And then in one night, everything she'd ever deemed important had been cut down. Ruined. Questioned.

And now she didn't know if she would ever be able to do it again. 'I've worked so hard for so long, and do you know what I've only just realized?' Nina asked quietly.

'What?'

'If acting doesn't work out, I would have given the best years of my life to millions of strangers for nothing but money.'

'Nina, baby, you're thirty-three.' He kicked a stone in his path and sent it bumping ahead. 'The best years are yet to come, and, though I shouldn't have to remind you, this guy—' he pointed to himself '—was promised the honour of being your plus-one when you're nominated for an Oscar. It is going to happen.'

Nina thought it was so strange that an Academy Award had seemed like the most important milestone of her life only a week ago, and now . . . If she didn't have acting, she wasn't exactly sure what the hell she did have. No family. Few friends. 'Do you know that I've never had a boyfriend?'

'Not technically true. Chad Hardy was your boyfriend.'

'Chad Hardy and I were set up by our agents to attend six events together and "avoid any comment on the status of our relationship". That's not dating.' Nina looked up, towards Markus's sleek Jaguar, so out of place in front of the untamed, rolling hills. 'If I decide not to go back after *Shadowlands*, I'll have to start my life from scratch.'

Markus pulled her up short as they reached his car. 'Okay, what's going on? Seriously. I know you. You *love* acting.'

She did.

Absolutely.

She loved the stories, loved the filming, loved seeing her fragmented scenes get stitched together to create something wonderful. And, still, she couldn't voice her darkest fear to

Markus, couldn't tell him that she worried she might never act again. So, she fell back on an easy half-truth. 'Do you know how many people visited when I ended up in hospital?'

Markus sighed. 'No.'

'Four. Four people in the three days I was there. You. Alison, Val, who wanted to know when I could be back on set. And Alex, the producer of the film I was working on.' Only talking about it made her want to weep. Her stomach roiled with nausea.

'You didn't tell anyone what happened,' Markus argued. 'Luigi and the gang would have shown up. Michael definitely would have come.'

'He's my publicist, Markus. He literally works for me.'

'Still, that's another six or seven people right there.'

He was right, of course. She had worked at Luigi's Italian Restaurant for years as a kid, and Luigi and the staff had become her default family of sorts. But Nina hadn't called Luigi for one simple reason: she didn't want anyone to know what had happened. Because then she'd have to explain *everything*. And she wasn't ready. She probably never would be . . .

'Who else?' she asked instead. 'If people had known, who else would have shown up for me?'

Markus's silence was deafening.

'I'm not feeling sorry for myself,' she said, though she was. 'I'm just trying to figure out exactly when I gave up everything else to pursue acting. God, Markus, it's been *fifteen years* of hustling roles and scavenging the rent money.'

'Baby, you haven't scavenged in at least five years,' he reminded her. 'And you've kept your circle small for a reason. You don't trust people. And all that aside, rather a few good friends who truly care than a posse who shows up to take pictures of your trauma for their Instagrams. God, Neens, do you know how many people in the world don't have what we have? And I'm not talking about our fabulous jobs – although God knows that's enough.' He tucked an errant strand of hair behind her ear. 'I'm talking about this.'

Taking her hand, he placed her palm over his heart, kept her hand covered with his. '*Us*. Yes, you might not have a giant family and a swarm of friends who show up when shit goes south, but you have me. And I better be enough for you, biatch. Because you've always been enough for me.'

Nina swallowed the emotion, the shame, in her throat. She'd hurt him, she realized. Really hurt him. 'You're enough. I'm just panicking. Without acting I don't have much of a life . . .'

Markus smiled. 'You still have acting. You always will. But for now, just rest. Take some time for you.' He released her and opened the car door. 'If you need anything – anything at all – you call. I'm close.' He waved his phone. 'And I have Maverick's number now, so if I can't get here quickly, he can.'

Nina groaned. 'Markus, do *not* text him.'

'Sorry, baby. I'm not promising anything.' He slid into his car, started it and rolled down the window. 'If things go my way, I'll be back before you can miss me.'

'I miss you already,' she said, and even though she needed him to leave, there was a conflicting anxiety thrashing around in her stomach at the sight of him preparing to actually go.

Markus reached one arm out his window, cried, 'Wanda, save yourself!'

It was their ritual instead of saying goodbye, something that had started when they'd met on the set of *Zombie Bride*, fifteen years prior. They had been extras, actors paid a menial amount to die horrendous deaths on screen. Markus and Nina had been paired together, and when the camera had swooped down on them, Markus had ad-libbed. As he'd been taken down, he'd flung out an arm, pushing her away while screaming, 'Wanda, save yourself!'

And having not expected the words, and in a completely impulsive moment, she'd replied, 'All right!' And she'd run away, leaving him to die.

The crew had laughed, and the director had included the scene, thus giving Nina her first two seconds of face time.

She put the fear and grief in her voice and cried, 'All right!'

But as she watched Markus zip away, down the shaded drive, very real panic stuck in her throat.

Maverick watched Nina Keller from the hitching rail outside the resort lobby as she said goodbye to Markus, her arms wrapped around her midriff, her shoulders rounded. She looked so small and alone, so terrified.

She stood there, watching the road for minutes after the car disappeared from view, and when she finally turned around to head back to her cabin, he noticed the tears streaming down her face.

When she saw him, she hurriedly swiped her flushed cheeks, and sent him a shaky smile as she passed.

Mav returned the smile, and though he wanted to, he didn't speak. He didn't ask if she was all right when she so clearly wasn't.

He let her go.

She was a celebrity, as used to being in the public eye as he was being alone and working with the horses, and – unlike everyone else – he would give her the privacy she had come to Hunt Ranch to find.

The other truth was that Maverick hadn't realized just how big a deal she was until he'd resumed his tour with the Morgans, only to have them completely ignore the remainder of it to gossip over Nina Keller and the bruises under her makeup. He hadn't minded, had found himself listening as he'd shown them to their cabin.

Given all the tidbits the Morgans had known about her, Maverick figured Deb had nailed it when she'd announced in the staff meeting that Nina Keller was Hollywood's current golden girl.

He couldn't imagine what that must be like, never being able to go out in public – to the store or a restaurant or the beach – without everyone recognizing you, stopping to talk to you as if they knew you. And after seeing the Morgans' reaction to her, Mav was concerned.

Not about the Morgans, though Mrs Morgan was going to cave and ask for an autograph and a photo by tomorrow. But about everyone else. The NDAs took care of the staff, but he and Sierra could do nothing about the other guests, who could total nearly thirty at any time.

He sighed and angled his head to watch Nina Keller as she walked back to her cabin, her arms still hugging her stomach, her head lowered, and he wondered how the hell they were going to give her the peace and quiet she needed for her entire month-long stay.

Hunt Ranch had gates, but they stayed open all day so that people could mosey in and eat at Stagecoach or grab a coffee from the little café, the Hitching Post, and explore the gift shop and the petting zoo. And while the buildings were quite a ways from her cabin, once a person was on property, Nina wouldn't be hard to find – especially if someone was looking.

And he wondered: why wouldn't a woman, a wealthy celebrity who had been assaulted in her own home, bring private security with her on vacation? It might not have been any of his business, but that didn't mean he didn't think about it. It confused him. Worse, it worried him.

Chapter 5

The first thing Nina did when she got back to her cabin was check the locks on her door and windows, something she hadn't wanted to do in front of Markus.

The door also included an interior security chain. Though neither was failproof, she knew somebody would have to be exceptionally committed, enraged, and powerful to actually kick the door in.

But the windows . . . The cabin windows, four at the front of the house and two in the bedroom, were big casement windows that opened outwards. They were beautiful, made from the same dark wood as the rest of the cabin, and they opened to views of the horse pasture. But Nina's heart sank when she saw the flimsy brass sliding locks, made more for aesthetic purposes than anything else. They looked lovely but she had no need for pretty window treatments.

She needed to feel secure.

She slid the lock into place and walked outside, following the porch until she came to the same window. Raising both her hands, she pushed where the wooden frames met in the middle. The lock slipped out of place immediately, the window popped open, giving her a full view of her small lounge area and, further towards the back, her bedroom. Worse, the sill was only waist-high, so that all she had to do was sling one leg over to hop inside.

She momentarily considered asking if they could move her inside the resort building where every room undoubtedly had standard keycard security, but then immediately decided against it because she didn't want to be so close to all the other guests at Hunt Ranch.

It wasn't that Nina didn't typically like people or enjoy the attention that came with her fame. But at the moment, she was tired. Too tired to fake a smile and pretend she was having a grand time talking to a bunch of strangers about acting. Too tired to lie about the bruises on her face. Only the mere thought of all that speculation, rumours, and questions was enough to exhaust her.

Instead, she went back inside, walked through the bedroom to the bathroom.

The only window in the bathroom was the floor-to-ceiling one by the tub. It was a single pane of glass, fixed in place. It didn't open. Still, Nina skirted the sleek egg tub and stood in front of the glass. She pressed around the edges, testing the strength of it, and only once she was satisfied that it was sturdy did she turn to assess the lock on the bathroom door.

It was a single-sided deadbolt. Strong enough.

She turned around, taking in the bathroom. It was big. The floors were wood, the tile on the walls and in the shower a soft green. The white monogrammed towels, neatly folded over the rail, were big and thick. It certainly wasn't the bedroom with its luxurious California king bed, but it would have to do.

Nina walked back through the cabin. She rechecked that the door and the windows were locked, opened a bottle of wine and grabbed a wine glass and a bag of chips from the fully stocked bar in the kitchen. She headed back to the bathroom, set everything up on the ledge of the tub before walking back through to her bedroom.

She stripped the bed and carried the comforter through with a single pillow before going back for pyjamas and her laptop.

She locked herself in the bathroom.
Showered.
Changed.

She turned off the lights and crawled into the bathtub, which she'd turned into a makeshift bed, picked up her wine, and opened her laptop to find a movie.

Her absurd attempt at security wasn't lost on her. Nina was fully aware that she was suffering for no reason. She could have asked to be moved to the resort. She could have asked for sturdier locks to be installed on the windows and knew, given the price she was paying, it would be done. But she also understood that any hypervigilance on her part would only raise additional questions – questions she wasn't prepared to answer.

So, instead of all the things she could have done, she opened Netflix and chose *How to Lose a Guy in 10 Days* because in the past week even the anxiety of a new movie plot had become too much. And nothing comforted her more than rewatching a low-stakes romcom, one where she could just follow along without stress or fear or uncertainty.

Nina hit play and settled back against her pillow. She took a sip of her wine as the opening credits rolled, tried to ignore the setting sun outside the window, and promised herself, 'Only for tonight,' even though it was just another lie.

She started fighting sleep during the first season of *Bridgerton* close to one o'clock in the morning.

Outside, the darkness was thick around the cabin, so that Nina couldn't see anything but the glare of her laptop reflected back at her.

As the violins played on screen, she stared at the glass window, narrowing her eyes on a slight movement outside, only a hint of movement in the darkness.

Someone was outside.

Her heart began to thrash, each heavy *da-dum* ricocheting in her ears so that all she heard was her fear. Through the mayhem, her brain screamed at her to get up and run, even as her legs locked with panic, refusing to budge. Sweat surfaced on her skin.

She hit the space bar, pausing the show.

She stared at the glass for a long, taut moment.

Waiting.

Watching.

Praying.

And when the shadows didn't flicker again, she tentatively sat up in the bathtub. She slowly, *so slowly*, leaned forward, almost pressing her face against the glass in an attempt to see into the blackness.

She jerked back, a rabbit in a trap, as he slammed himself against the glass outside, hands and face plastered as if he could simply pass through.

His eyes, bloodshot and crazed, stared at her.

His mouth curved in a knowing, mocking grin.

Nina dropped the laptop. She scrambled back and out of the bathtub as an otherworldly scream was ripped from her throat.

She tripped and landed on her ass, didn't have time to stand, only faced the window as she scurried backwards like some lesser life form. A crab. A mouse. Something small and easily consumed.

Her back hit the bathroom door with a solid *thwack*. She stopped, curled into the corner. Her mind flicked through her options. *Run* – but he would be faster. *Fight* – but he would be stronger. *Call for help* – but he would have her by the time help arrived.

Knowing the advantage he had, he laughed, and it was not a monster's cackle but a deep, smooth chuckle that fogged the glass in front of his mouth.

Bile rushed her throat as he began to write in the condensation, the sound of his excited breathing reaching for her through the glass. Though she knew it was impossible, his cologne stung her sensory memory. There were only three letters that Nina read backwards. **RUN.**

She woke up in a full panic.

She gasped deeply, trying to inhale through the suffocating tightness in her chest. Each breath sawed out of her, sounding painful even to her own ears. Her sweat turned cold on her skin, making her shiver. Tears of frustration streamed down her face.

She lay stock-still and focused on breathing as she took in her surroundings. *You're safe*, she reminded herself. *No one knows you're at Hunt Ranch.*

Outside, early morning light was just starting to creep into the darkness, easing some of her claustrophobia. Nina closed her eyes and took deep, deliberate breaths as she tried to calm herself.

Slowly, her heart stopped racing, her tears dried. But as the adrenaline began to drain from her system, all she felt was deeply, unmeasurably empty.

On the computer screen in front of her, Netflix wanted to know if she was still watching, and because she desperately wanted to click 'Continue' and then curl up and stay right where she was, Nina, on principle, shut the laptop and sat up. She wrapped her arms around her legs and rested her forehead against her raised knees for a moment as she composed herself.

She wasn't entirely sure how it had come down to this, wasn't quite certain how a life could be so drastically altered in only one night.

The despair and hopelessness threatened to take her back under, but this time Nina did not allow it. She needed to find her way back to the woman she had been only a week ago. She needed to take control of her life again, needed to stop being so afraid. Of everything.

Only seven days ago she had been a successful, famous, wealthy woman who had started from nothing – less than nothing. She had been the most unlikely of statistics. The American dream.

But as she had discovered, the problem with dreaming is that at some point you had to wake up.

'Get up. Move on,' she told herself, and when the suffocating despair didn't dissipate, she repeated it like a mantra. 'Get up. Move on. Get up. Move on.'

She pushed up out of the bathtub, wincing slightly as her ribs protested the movement, and cautiously let herself out of the bathroom. Her eyes scanned each room before she entered, checking that nobody was there, but she tried not to internalize it too much. After being assaulted in her own home, Nina wasn't sure any room would ever feel safe again, and she could allow herself that so long as she could still force her feet to enter them.

She decided, 'Coffee,' and after only one look at the sun just starting to peek over the mountains, added, 'outside.' She might live in the Hollywood Hills, but not even she had a view like this.

She didn't bother changing, only picked up the red and tan striped blanket off the back of the sofa in the lounge, threw it over her shoulders, and padded barefoot to the kitchen.

Four minutes later, she unlocked the front door and stepped onto the little cabin's porch, a cup of coffee in one hand, her cell phone and the *Birdie* from Markus in the other. She ignored the way her heart started that incessant anxious tick at simply walking outside and forced her feet to move forward. She padded to the porch swing and curled up on it, tucking her feet beneath her as she took that first sip.

The view was incredible. As dawn crept over the mountains, painting the sky in blues and golds, Nina looked out at green pastures. Horses of different colours grazed, their heads down, tails flicking.

Unable to resist, she put her coffee on the seat beside her and picked up her phone. She numbly dismissed the seven missed calls from Alexander Cane, the *Shadowlands* producer, and snapped a picture of the sunrise. Though she knew he would be fast asleep for hours yet, she sent it to Markus, captioned it with: *Are you sure you couldn't live here?*

And then she simply sat there alone, curled up on the porch swing, comforted enough by the unfurling day and stretching sunlight to fall back into an exhausted slumber, her coffee forgotten beside her.

⊍

Maverick saw her immediately. Or, rather, saw her head of glossy black hair immediately. The rest of her was cocooned in one of the fancy resort blankets.

He was surprised, too. If he'd had to guess which guests might be up before sunrise, Nina Keller wouldn't have been one. But only because he figured a woman with a face like that got beauty sleep in epic proportions.

Still, he raised a hand and waved.

She didn't respond.

At all.

With any other guest, it wouldn't have bothered him. But given that Sierra had told them all to have their eyes and ears to the ground during Nina Keller's stay, his compulsion to check on her won out over his rational mind, which told him she had probably just dozed off.

Maverick cued Zephyr into a brisk walk in her direction with a subtle shift of his lower body. He crossed the large pasture quickly, only slowing his horse when he was close enough to notice that she was, in fact, fast asleep.

He stopped Zephyr about thirty yards from the cabin's porch, and though he knew he should have turned and walked away, he didn't. Couldn't. He looked at Nina, her skin clear of any makeup, and saw the patchwork bruises spreading over the entire right side of her face, from her hairline to chin. They were starting to fade. A week old, he reminded himself. But that meant that the reds, purples, and blacks were fading to that sickly yellow, which somehow looked so much worse.

He took in her size, so small and delicate, maybe five-four and a buck ten, and couldn't quite fathom the type of person, the type of man, who would raise his fists to someone so much smaller than himself.

Fights happened. Mav understood that, accepted it. But any man who raised his fists to a woman, to someone who had no chance of an equal fight was the worst type of coward.

So many thoughts crossed Mav's mind. He wondered if it had been a break-in, and if anything valuable had been taken. If it had been a random attack, the man had certainly possessed an unholy amount of rage. To hit a woman was bad enough, but to hit one you didn't know, repeatedly . . .

He wondered if, instead, her attacker had stalked her, and if Nina had crossed paths with him at one time, maybe rejected his advances? That would explain, though not justify, the rage – and it would give Maverick more to be concerned about.

The little he did know about stalkers indicated that they weren't rational. They were obsessive and disillusioned, which typically equated to dangerous. A random attack wouldn't have concerned him so much, but a stalker . . . If she had a stalker, there was no telling when he would try to find Nina Keller again. But it didn't take a genius to figure that, statistically, he would.

Still, knowing that he had no right to ask, and that he was intruding, Mav leaned his weight back in the saddle and extended his legs slightly, silently telling Zephyr to back up.

The horse got five steps before snorting – loudly.

Chapter 6

Nina popped awake with a loud gasp.

Zephyr spooked and danced to the side. Mav kept his seat easily, issued a long, deep, 'Whoa.' Beneath him, the horse settled.

Nina, on the other hand, had one hand over her heart. She took deep breaths as if she was on the verge of a panic attack. Her eyes darted about like ping-pong balls.

'Apologies,' he said quietly. 'I didn't mean to startle you.' And in lieu of telling her he had been checking up on her, added, 'I was just rounding up the horses for the day.'

She managed to focus on him through the panic. Recognition dawned slowly. She closed her eyes, took one last audible breath, and said, 'That's okay.' She turned her face away from him, clearly embarrassed. 'I must have dozed off.'

Mav deliberately looked out over the pasture, giving her time to compose herself. 'It's as good a spot as any.'

'Yeah. Yeah, it is.'

She got to her feet, which, he noted with some surprise, were bare, and padded across the deck to the porch rail. Gripping the blanket with both hands at her collar, she indicated to his horse, asked, 'Is she yours? I saw her yesterday . . .'

'Yeah.' Mav sent Zephyr forward with the tiniest roll of his calf until the horse stood directly in front of Nina. She raised one slender hand and stroked the mare's face. 'She was born in a kill pen. One of their staff, an eighteen-year-old kid who was new to the job, stole her. He and a buddy accessed the property at night, put her in his truck, brought her here.'

Nina didn't look at him, only watched the horse as she continued to stroke her. 'That's a good origin story.'

Maverick smiled when he remembered the rusty truck bumping down the Hunt Ranch drive and the shock of surprise he'd felt when José, just a kid himself, had hauled the tiny, sickly foal out of the back seat of his Ford. 'Kid quit the next day. Came to work for me. That was about six years ago now.'

'She's only six?' Nina asked. 'She's so grey.'

'The black and grey is her natural coat colour. We call it "blue roan".'

Nina stepped back. 'Watching you up there makes me wish I had learned how to ride.' She shook her head. A soft, sardonic smile teased her mouth. 'Though I don't suppose I'd look as natural as you do.'

Mav thought about that for a moment. 'There's not much opportunity for horseback riding in LA.'

'Some. But it's rare for inner-city kids, and my mother . . .' She seemed to rethink what she was going to say, finished with: 'She could never have afforded it.'

There was something in her tone, something sad and resigned. Bitter, maybe. He didn't pry. Only said, 'It's never too late to learn. And the basics of horse riding are simpler than most things.'

'Oh?'

'Yeah. Don't fall off, for starters.'

Nina smiled. She looked at his saddle, almost mistrustfully. 'Something tells me it's a little more complicated than that.'

'Not on Zephyr,' he insisted.

She took a step back, but she looked straight at him for the first time when she replied. 'Maybe, I'll sign up for a riding lesson while I'm here. See how it goes . . .'

'How about now?'

'Excuse me?'

Mav told himself that the only reason he offered was because she looked so small and forlorn, so lonely, up there on the porch, and he didn't want to leave her. But it was more than that. He hated suffering, tried his hardest to ease it wherever he could, be it in an abused horse or, as it were, a woman. He had always been like that. As a man who had been raised tending animals, his prime directive had always been to guard and nurture. He didn't know any other way.

But his own pain had amplified his need to protect others too. When his parents had died, he'd thought nothing would ever hurt as much. Then Shannon had decided that being a rancher's wife wasn't going to be as easy as she'd thought it would be and she had left, and that had hurt even more because it had been his fault, his shortcomings that she had thrown in his face as she'd packed her things. As it were, she barely even checked in on Poppy. Oh, there was the rare phone call and even rarer visit, but only when Shannon needed to relieve her own guilt a little bit. And even then, it was *Mav* who felt guilty. As if his inability to make Shannon happy had deprived Poppy of the chance for a family – a family like the one he'd grown up with.

Then Sierra and Benji's baby girl had died and that had been the hardest. He'd arrived at the hospital filled with joy and excitement, and left with a broken heart, the flowers he'd carried with him becoming morbid in a single moment. And then afterwards, he'd had to watch his little sister and best friend live with a degree of suffering he couldn't even fathom, let alone do anything to ease.

Mav never wanted to feel any of that pain again, and he couldn't help but try to reduce it as much as he could for others, too.

'Put some jeans on,' he said to Nina. 'I'll give you your first lesson and then source you a decent cup of coffee.'

Nina tightened the blanket around her shoulders. 'I don't want to get in the way . . .'

He considered being gentle, settled on directness instead. 'Is that true?' He leaned one forearm on the horn of his saddle. 'If you don't want to ride, I'll understand. You're a guest, here to relax. But if you're genuinely worried about getting in the way – don't be. Ms Keller, I'm not the type to offer when I don't mean it.'

She blinked once as if he'd shocked her.

'You have a pair of boots?' he asked.

She nodded.

'Well then.'

Gripping the blanket with one hand, she raised the other to her mouth, nibbled on her thumbnail as if the decision was giving her genuine anxiety.

Maverick didn't push, though he found himself surprised at how much he wanted her to say yes.

She didn't maintain eye contact, rather turned to study Zephyr, her eyes wide with a mix of anticipation and uncertainty. 'Five minutes,' she said finally. She turned to go back inside, looked over her shoulder at him, but only to repeat, 'Five minutes.'

The moment he nodded, she dropped the blanket on the porch and ran inside, but not before giving him an eyeful of barely there pink silk pyjamas and slender legs.

Mav exhaled one tight breath, looked away, out over the pasture, and reminded himself that while noticing wasn't a crime, he could – *would* – be professional. And nothing more.

Nina was famous, and he wouldn't be one of the sad millions who treated her differently because of it. She had just been hurt irreparably by a man and didn't need to ward off another. Hell, even if she had been interested, he didn't do casual. At the rate he was going, he didn't do serious either.

He had dated in the five years since Shannon had left, sure. He loved women, missed having one in his life. But even though he had been attracted to more than one of the women he'd gone out with, he hadn't felt anything more than that little spark and certainly not enough to introduce a single one of them to Poppy.

He didn't consider himself overprotective. But he knew the agony of being abandoned, of being found lacking, and he wouldn't risk Poppy's heart by introducing her to anyone he wasn't certain would stick around.

So, he ignored the pleasure he'd felt when Nina had agreed to the lesson, pointedly eradicated the image of her pink silk pyjamas from his mind, and reminded himself that it was his job to ensure guests enjoyed their stays. Nothing more.

He figured she'd take twenty minutes, so was genuinely surprised when she ran back out not even seven later. She was dressed in jeans, boots, and a pretty white blouse that was just begging to get ruined. She had covered her bruises with light makeup, hiding the worst of them, and hurriedly braided her hair so that it fell in a long tail down her back.

'Record time.'

'I would say that I didn't want to keep you waiting, but the truth is that I hate to primp. It wastes so much time. And for who?'

Maverick swung his leg over the saddle and dismounted. He wanted to say that, with a face like that, she had no need to primp anyway. But didn't.

He sized her up, guesstimated the length of her legs and adjusted the stirrups accordingly.

Nina approached Zephyr cautiously, less confident now that she realized she was going to be sitting on top of the horse. Maverick noticed her slow movements, asked, 'Remember what we went through yesterday?'

'Yes.'

But he summarized the lesson anyway. 'Breathe deeply. Approach with confidence.'

'She doesn't seem anxious,' Nina observed. 'Not like Barbie was.'

'She's not. But you are.'

'Oh.' She laughed lightly, raised one hand to her heart as if she needed to feel it beating. 'I suppose I am.'

'Look at me.'

She raised those fathomless eyes to his.

Maverick felt the pull of them immediately and took a deep inhalation to steady his own pulse. 'I'm not going to let anything happen to you.' When she only nodded uncertainly, he added, 'This is the horse I teach my five-year-old to ride on. She's what we call "bomb-proof". That's not to say she doesn't get scared – she's still an animal. But at her most terrified, she might spook a tiny bit. It'll feel like a little lurch beneath you, and I'll be right at your side to steady you in the unlikely event that she gets a fright. All right?'

She exhaled her first audible breath. 'All right.'

Maverick waved her over, and when she approached to stand beside him, he asked, 'May I touch you?'

Nina jerked to attention.

Her head snapped back.

Those enormous eyes, full of questions and fear, searched his face.

Mav only raised one hand to the saddle. 'You're a little short to reach the stirrups and we don't have a mounting block,' he explained. 'I'll need to help you up.'

She flushed, opened her mouth to speak, to apologize, but Mav beat her to it. 'Don't,' he said before she could talk. 'Don't apologize. Not for that. Never for that. If you don't want to be touched, you tell me. We'll find another way to get on.' He looked around, saw the porch railing and figured he could make it work.

But Nina only stepped closer. In what he knew was a deliberate act of trust, she placed her hand lightly on his arm. Only for a second. But Mav felt that faint pressure like a hot iron. 'I don't mind,' she said. 'And I appreciate the fact that you asked.' She shook her head quickly. 'Most people don't understand . . .'

'I don't either,' he said quietly. 'How could I? But that's why you're going to have to be vocal about what you're comfortable with. And what you're not.'

Without another word, he interlocked his fingers, forming a

little step, and bent down. 'You're going to face the saddle, hold on to it with both hands, and then put your left foot here.' He indicated the little platform he'd made with his hands. 'You pull upwards. I'll boost you slowly until you can swing your right leg over the saddle and take a seat.'

'Do you think I'm strong enough?' she asked sceptically.

'Absolutely.'

She nodded, looked down at his interlocked fingers one last time before following his instructions.

He boosted her into the saddle easily, stepped back, and then immediately reached out to grip her calf, steadying her in her seat when he saw her face, leached of all colour.

'What's wrong?'

She released a wheezing laugh. 'Cracked ribs. Just give me a moment.'

Mav tried to ignore that same whip of anger he felt when he'd first seen her bruises. Though he wasn't aware of doing it, his hand on her calf gentled, then began to soothe in long, calming strokes.

In the saddle, Nina took a deep breath and opened her eyes to look down at him. For a moment when their gazes met, he knew she saw all the things he wanted to say but didn't know how to communicate. Things like, *I'm sorry*, *That should never have happened to you*, and *I wish I could make it go away*.

'Do you need me to help you down?' he asked instead.

'No. I knew it would hurt.' She unconsciously raised a hand to her ribs. 'But I'm not going to put my life on hold anymore. And *this*—' she reached the same hand forward to pat Zephyr's neck '—this is something I refuse to let him take from me.'

She shifted her leg slightly, making him aware of his hand, which had come to rest around the back of her calf.

Mav calmly moved it away.

Nina didn't seem to notice. She grinned and reverently whispered, 'Holy cow, I'm on a horse.'

'Easy-peasy?'

'So far.'

He stepped back. 'Let your legs dangle for a minute. I want to take a look at your stirrups.'

As soon as she complied, Mav double-checked the length, making sure that the bottom of the stirrup fell just below her ankle. He held it at an angle and waited for her to put her foot in, then did the same to the other side. Everything looked good, but he still asked, 'How do you feel?'

'Amazing. This is—' she shook her head, settled on: '—so freaking cool.'

The certainty she said it with made him smile. He reached up, pulled his rope from the saddle horn in lieu of a lead rope.

'What do I do?'

'Zeph is very well trained and very responsive,' he said as he looped his rope through the underside of the bridle's noseband. 'All she needs are a few voice and leg cues. I'm going to teach them to you, and then let you take over.'

Her face fell. 'You're not going to leave me though – right?'

'No ma'am.'

'Okay.' She nodded rapidly as if trying to convince herself. 'Okay, I can do this. Tell me.'

Mav didn't give her time to doubt herself. 'Anytime you want her to move, it's two clicks. That's it.' He took two steps back, clicked with his tongue twice, and let Zephyr close the small space to him. 'It's the same to make her back up, but you're going to keep a tight rein.' He reached up, gathered the reins, showing her how much tension to apply. 'Horses have very sensitive mouths, so just keep the pressure firm but gentle. Consistent.' He waited for her to do it. 'Click twice.'

Nina made a clicking noise, and Zephyr immediately took two steps back. 'Oh my God!' Zephyr kept moving backwards. 'Oh my God,' she repeated.

'She'll keep moving backwards until you release the pressure,' Mav calmly told her, and watched her hands instantly slacken on the reins.

Zephyr stopped immediately.

'You remembering to breathe?'

Nina exhaled in an exaggeratedly loud whoosh of air, making him laugh.

'Okay, so, you've got forward and back. Now steering. In western-style riding and with a horse this well trained, most of your control is going to come from your legs. Keep the reins loose and use them for subtle corrections or if you miss a cue and need to quickly get her back on track.' He talked her through readjusting her hands until the reins were slack. 'To drive her body right, you're going to apply your left leg. It seems counterintuitive but think of it as gently pushing her body in the direction you want her to go.'

'What do you mean by *apply* my left leg? Like a kick?'

'Nope. Just roll your calf a little.' He reached out to adjust her leg, stopped.

Nina caught the movement, and this time she didn't hesitate to say, 'It's okay. Show me.'

He took her calf in one hand, tried not to focus on the slender shape of it beneath the denim, and gripped her booted foot in the other. 'You're just going to rotate your toes outwards until your calf makes contact and then slowly increase the pressure until she does what you want her to do – in this case, go right. The moment she turns, you remove the pressure.' He let her leg go. 'It's the same on the other side, to make her turn left.

'And the last thing you need to know for Lesson One is the word "whoa".'

'Not "*stop*"?'

'Nope. She doesn't know that one. *Whoa*. She's got the verbal cues down, but if she needs some help, sit back in your seat and extend your legs forward before repeating the cue.'

He made her demonstrate, nodded with approval when she got it first time.

'Okay. Are you ready?'

'Yes.' She nodded firmly.

Mav didn't move. 'You know what to do now.'

'That's it?' she asked, looking slightly dumbfounded. 'I just go for it?'

Mav held up the rope. It didn't matter that Nina could have walked Zephyr for days without the horse taking off; he understood that she needed to feel safe and knew from experience to always prepare for the worst when it came to inexperienced riders. 'I'm not letting you two make a run for it just yet,' he said gently. 'But you ride. I'll just be along for the walk.'

Nina sat down in the saddle, gripped the reins until her knuckles whitened. She urged Zephyr forward with two wavering clicks.

The horse moved forward instantly. Mav moved several feet off to the side and walked in line with Zephyr's shoulder, the rope in his hands.

After only twenty yards, he turned to look up at Nina on his horse. Her grin was a mile wide and nothing, not even the bruises under her makeup, could detract from how genuinely happy she looked just then. It was her eyes, he realized, eyes that had looked so sad but were now lit with awe and wonder in that moment.

Mav figured he didn't have to have seen any of her movies to know that those eyes had made Nina Keller a movie star. Everything she felt was amplified for the world to see, and Mav had front-row seats to witness the raw joy in her as she experienced a new first.

He ambled at their side and deliberately pushed all thought of the work he still had to get done to the back of his mind. When Zephyr whinnied upon seeing Spud, a little pony who was often stalled next to her, grazing, Nina laughed, and Mav decided right then that showing this beautiful woman how to ride a horse first thing in the morning might have been even better than his usual routine of watching the sun rise with his first cup of coffee.

Chapter 7

Nina felt her muscles slowly slacken as her body adjusted to the odd rocking motion of the horse beneath her. Her hands gradually loosened on the reins, and for the first time since the attack, she felt truly relaxed.

Maverick walked at her side, close enough to intercede if he needed to.

She had been so embarrassed when she'd startled awake, and then again when she'd been overcome with the pain from her injured ribs, but there was something so kind and non-judgemental about Maverick Hunt, and it had quelled her humiliation almost as soon as it had arisen. He didn't hover, or give her pretty, empty sentiments. He just trusted her to make her own decisions and silently helped when she needed it. She liked that.

He wasn't hard to look at either.

Nina peeked down at him, taking in his broad shoulders and tapered waist, and while she wouldn't ever admit it to Markus, he had been right about the stretch in those blue jeans. Overall, the hulking frame was a beautiful contradiction to the quiet, gentle temperament.

When he'd stroked her calf earlier, trying – she knew – to soothe, Nina had been taken aback by the contact. Because she'd been acutely aware of his big palm running over her leg, and she hadn't wanted him to stop.

She might not have considered herself a prude, but she wasn't exactly experienced either. Living with her mother had made her mistrustful of men, so that when she'd been younger, she'd avoided them completely. Then she'd been so busy working that she'd only had time for occasional dates, and though she'd had sex, she'd only really done it to see if it would make her feel something more for the men she'd been dating. And it hadn't. Instead, it had only left her feeling more disappointed and alone than before.

And then once she'd started to become better known, time had been the least of her concerns, because then she had also had to sort through men who were interested in *her* and those who were only interested in the perks of dating Nina Keller.

The last date she'd been on had been over a year ago. She had met Alexander Cane, a well-known and respected producer, while auditioning for *Shadowlands*, the movie she was currently working on. Nina had liked him well enough, but not enough for anything serious, so she'd balked when he'd started to press for sex.

The memory left a bitter taste in her mouth now.

But not even an inexperienced woman could have missed that zap of awareness she'd felt when Maverick had touched her. It had shocked her, that little zing. But not more than the sense of calm that had quickly followed.

She wondered why that was, wondered what it was about this particular man that was so grounding.

As they walked, Maverick didn't ask her about acting like most people did. In fact, he didn't seem to feel the need to make small talk at all. It was Nina who opened the conversation, and not, she realized with some surprise, because the silence was awkward – it wasn't. She was genuinely curious. 'Do you ever get tired of this?' she asked. 'Teaching city slickers how to ride horses day in and day out?'

He didn't reply right away; rather he seemed to think about it for a long moment. 'It depends on the city slicker,' he said finally, making her smile. His blue eyes, made more intense beneath the blue Dodgers cap, glinted with humour. 'But no. Watching peoples' faces the moment they take those first steps on a horse is magical. Especially the kids – they don't regulate their joy like adults do. They just feel it.'

'You said you have kids?' she remembered and glanced down at his ring finger. No ring. Though she wondered what the story was there, she didn't ask.

'Just one. A little girl – Poppy.'

'I bet she's the happiest kid in the world.'

Maverick laughed at that. 'Kids don't tend to notice how lucky they are. They're just in the moment, but Poppy . . . I really hope she looks back one day and realizes how extraordinary her childhood was.'

Nina noted the unashamed love in his voice, told herself that, regardless of how young his daughter was, Poppy already knew she was lucky. As someone who was raised – if you could call it that – by someone so uninterested, Nina could barely fathom what it was like to have a parent who was so shamelessly attached to her.

'She will,' Nina said with vindication. She looked out over the pasture, towards the resort. 'How could she not?'

'Yeah.' Maverick followed her gaze. 'It took a lot out of us – opening the resort when we did. We had to sell some land to cover the start-up costs,' he explained. 'It hurt some, selling our legacy to guarantee that we could keep the rest of it afloat.'

'You didn't always do this – the resort?'

'No. We started construction on the resort about a decade ago but have only been fully operational for about eight years now.' He laughed. 'Turning a profit for less, maybe six years.'

'What was it before? A farm?'

'Ranch,' he corrected. 'Cattle.'

'That's a big change.' But she could see it, could envision the rolling hills dotted with fat cows, could easily picture Maverick on the back of a horse, rounding them up.

'It was.'

'Why did you do it?'

His smile softened, turning sad. 'My dad and I had been talking about it for a while. California's regulatory environment is getting increasingly difficult to navigate, especially if you're keeping animals on valuable land. And God forbid you have access to water.'

'I didn't realize.'

He shrugged. 'It's become a hard life. Even the cows we have now are more to lend the resort authenticity than to turn any significant profit.' He stepped out in front of the horse to open the pasture gate. 'Once my dad passed, it seemed like the right time to diversify. He was the last true cowboy in the family.'

'You're not a cowboy?' She pointedly looked him over, from his scuffed cowboy boots, up jean-clad legs and his long-sleeved work shirt, to his ratty baseball cap. The man had a rope attached to his saddle – and not for aesthetics, but because he genuinely used it. 'Coulda fooled me.'

Maverick grinned. 'Not really. I mean, I know how the ranch works, and I can keep it going. But I've always been more invested in the horses. My dad . . . He knew we had to make some changes, but I think he didn't want to be the first Hunt in over a hundred years to sell. He was too proud. Me . . . I'd rather keep a smaller slice of it forever than lose all of it, no matter how much money I could get for it.'

'I'm sorry – about your dad.'

'Yeah, me too.' He let her urge Zephyr through the gate before closing it behind them. 'But he and my mom died together, just like they always said they would. So that's something.'

It felt too personal to ask how it had happened, so she didn't. But Nina wouldn't deny that she was curious. Instead she said, 'They would be really proud of what you've built.' Because how could they not have been? She didn't need to have stayed more than one night on the Hunt Ranch – in a bathroom, nonetheless – to know that it was one hell of an operation.

It said something about his parents that Maverick didn't deny it. He said, 'Yeah, they would have been. Absolutely.'

They started down the dirt road in the direction of the barn in silence. Nina, who hadn't been able to go out in public for years without being recognized and stopped for an autograph or picture, loved that he didn't seem to care about the fact that she was actually quite famous.

She hadn't forgotten what it was like to just be normal, to be treated like a regular person, to be spoken to and to speak back without any veneers, without having to guard her every word and action in case it ended up in print. But she did miss it. Markus and Luigi's gang were the only ones who knew the Nina Keller she was behind closed doors. Every other person she interacted with knew her as a movie star and treated her as such.

When they came to the barn, Maverick took over, leading Zephyr to one of three concrete mounting blocks. He patted the horse's neck. 'Coffee time?'

'Amen,' Nina replied.

'You're going to dismount the exact opposite way you mounted. Right foot out of the stirrup first, right leg over the saddle to the mounting block, and then left leg last. Try to focus more on rotating your hips and keeping your torso as still as possible to help with those ribs.'

Nina gripped the saddle and followed his instructions until she stood on the mounting block.

'All good?' He held out one hand to help her down.

Nina took it, tried to ignore how aware she was of that huge, rough palm against hers. 'Yup.' She craned her neck back to look up at him as she stepped off the mounting block. 'That was amazing. Thank you.'

'Anytime.'

'What now? Do I unsaddle her? Or groom her?'

'Not with broken ribs you don't,' he responded immediately. He tipped his head in the direction of a closed door that read: STAFF ONLY. 'Get yourself some coffee – we have the full set-up in there. Wander around, check in on Barbie. Relax. Get breakfast up at the resort. You're on vacation.'

'Mr Hunt—'

'Maverick,' he corrected.

'Only if you stop calling me *Ms* Keller. Or ma'am. One makes me feel like a spinster, the other like an old lady.'

He tipped his head at that. 'Seems fair.'

'I have some questions.'

'Shoot.'

Nina checked them off her fingers. 'Are you saying the coffee is behind the door clearly labelled: STAFF ONLY? Will anyone mind me going in there and helping myself? And will I get in the way if I stay down here?' She looked towards the resort, where the early risers might just be starting to wake. 'I'm in a stage of life where I prefer animals to people.'

In a gesture she found completely endearing, he mimicked her, counting off his fingers. 'The coffee is behind the door labelled STAFF ONLY,' he replied. 'Nobody will mind you going anywhere you want, and if that happens to be the stables, then it's the stables. And I didn't know that preferring animals to people was a stage. Here I thought it was just fact.'

Nina laughed, but she turned in the direction of the coffee. 'Can I get you a cup?'

He roped one arm over his saddle, leaned against Zephyr, his eyes intensely focused on her. 'I would have really liked that, but I can't just yet. Gotta head home quick, get Poppy ready for daycare. But if I see you around here later, I'll help you with Barbie.'

Nina wasn't entirely sure why she was disappointed, or why, as she watched him fluidly mount Zephyr, she felt like he was taking her safety net with him. Suddenly, the barn felt too big, too dark, too unfamiliar.

She stopped walking and looked around, searching the quiet.

'Nina.'

'Hmm?' she replied distractedly.

'Listen,' he said.

'What?'

'Listen,' he repeated, and tapped his ear.

She strained to hear over the sound of her racing heart and managed to pick out the talking and laughing, punctuated by the occasional whistle.

'You hear that?'

'Yes.'

'The wranglers are bringing the pastured riding horses in for the day. In thirty seconds, this place is going to be teeming with people, not one of whom would let anything happen to you.'

Even as he finished talking, a man rode in.

Nina blinked once as she took in horse and rider and tried to decide which one was more beautiful. The man was tall and lean with blond hair the colour of antique gold and piercing green eyes. Like Maverick, he wore a ball cap over his shaggy hair.

The horse he was on was champagne coloured with an impossibly long black mane and a tail that, even braided, dragged on the ground behind its hind legs.

'Morning.' The stranger sent her a megawatt smile. 'Didn't know anyone was up yet. Early riser?'

'Bad sleeper,' she replied.

'Benji, Nina. Nina, Benji.'

The man – Benji – only rolled his eyes. 'Unlike you, Mav, I know who Nina Keller is.'

Nina's eyes swung to Maverick.

He legitimately blushed. 'I don't watch many movies,' he explained, 'and when I do, they have to be suitable for a five-year-old.'

'Hence *Barbie*,' she replied, unoffended.

'Yeah.'

Benji watched the back-and-forth with interest. 'You two get a ride in, then?'

'Yup,' Maverick replied. He nodded in Nina's direction. 'Girl can sit a horse.'

Benji seemed genuinely surprised. 'Really? She sure looks like a city slicker with all those pretty clothes.'

Nina looked down at her jeans and flimsy white blouse, both of which were covered in dust and black horsehair.

'She'll be riding circles around you by the time she leaves.' Maverick shifted slightly, sending Zephyr forward without so much as a click. 'She's going to hang around, have some coffee and see to the new rescue – Barbie. Show her the ropes.' He looked at Nina, nodded once, and though his last words were directed at Benji, Nina knew they were meant to remind her that she wouldn't be left alone. 'Don't let her out of your sight. It's bad publicity if a celebrity gets hurt.'

Benji caught on fast. He turned a killer grin in her direction. 'Ma'am, did you sign the liability waiver?'

Nina replied, 'On the dotted line.' But she watched Maverick ride out of the dark barn and into the sunlight, his posture relaxed, natural, and thought she might just team up with Markus to try and convince him to be in the photoshoot. Not only for womankind everywhere – but for her.

She'd have Markus sneak her a one-of-a-kind shot. She'd have it blown up, printed, and framed, so that years from now, when people saw the rugged cowboy with gentle eyes looking at them from her living-room wall and asked her who he was, she could say, 'The man who taught me how to ride a horse.' And though she wouldn't say it, she felt the first flickers of her old self pushing through the numbness and knew he was also the man who had reminded her that kindness in small gestures mattered.

Maverick had had no obligation to waste his valuable time teaching an unscheduled ride but he *had*. And in doing that one small thing, he had given her something she hadn't been able to muster in over seven days.

He'd given her hope.

Because while she'd been up on that horse, she hadn't relived the attack or the after-effects. She hadn't suffered the extreme anxiety over her career ending or what she would do when it did. She had thought about nothing but staying in the saddle, had done nothing but focus on steering the horse and listening to Maverick talk about his home and his family. And it had been so lovely, to just be present.

Nina hadn't realized before the assault how important it was to simply exist in time and space without the trauma from the past dragging you back and the anxiety for the future pulling you frantically in the opposite direction, without the worry that what you had suffered had permanently altered who you were and what you were capable of becoming.

But she knew now.

So, she appreciated Maverick Hunt's small gesture. He had reminded her that somewhere, deep inside, the woman she had been still existed.

By the time Maverick had gotten Poppy up, dressed, fed, and to daycare, he was running behind on almost everything he was supposed to have done that morning. But even though he was pushed for time, he couldn't bring himself to regret his impromptu decision to take Nina for a ride.

He'd meant what he'd told Benji: she could sit a horse. She had a natural seat, her hands and hips following the horse's movements instinctively. Once he'd given her basic instructions, she'd run with them and hadn't needed his help once. And perhaps the biggest point in her favour, she seemed to genuinely love the horses. Maverick would remember the way her face had lit up when she'd taken those first steps on Zeph for a long time.

He thought about her as he walked back to the barn to check

in on everything, hoped in the back of his mind that she would still be there when he got in.

She wasn't.

But he found Benji in the tack room, setting aside the saddles and bridles for the eleven o'clock lessons and trail ride. 'I already told June Morgan she could be on Spirit,' he said.

Benji didn't pause in what he was doing. 'I had him brought in for one of the kids anyway. I'll make sure she gets him.'

'Nina Keller do okay this morning?'

Benji shot a grin over his shoulder. 'I figured it would take you longer to work your way back there.' He waggled his eyebrows. 'If it makes you feel all warm and fuzzy inside, she looked at you plenty too.'

Maverick didn't take the bait. He couldn't hide anything from Benji, so denying he was attracted wouldn't work. He didn't even try it. He simply ignored it.

Mav sat down in a nearby chair, taking the five minutes to be off his feet. 'Found her sleeping on the porch just after five. She woke up gasping for breath like a fish outta water. And those bruises . . . I couldn't leave her there.'

'You're a bleeding heart, son.'

No point in denying it. 'Yeah.'

Benji looked at Mav, frowned. 'You're genuinely worried?'

'Sierra said they didn't catch the guy.'

'I know.'

Mav leaned back in his chair. 'It's been bothering me. I mean, she gets beaten within an inch of her life and is here a week later without a single bodyguard, even though we all know she could easily afford it. She's still scared – anyone can see that. So, why no protection?'

'I don't know.' Benji took Spirit's bridle from its hook, placed it on the table with the rest. 'Maybe she figures it was just some crazy, and that we're too remote. I checked her Instagram. The last post was a month ago, on the set of the new film she's working on. *Shadowlands*. There was no news on her or the assault, so she hasn't told anyone she's here.'

'Hopefully none of our guests do either.' But he also had to ask, 'Why were you checking her social media?'

'Relax, Cassanova,' Benji teased. 'It's how modern human beings satiate their curiosity. If you'd ever had even a Facebook account, you'd know this.' When Mav had nothing to say to that, Benji added, 'Could you just open an Instagram account so that I can send you socially relevant memes instead of trying to explain over a decade of internet history to you?'

'Negative.'

Benji sighed. 'Well, could you at least watch *one* of her movies?'

'She any good?' Mav asked, though they both knew he would have watched one even if she wasn't.

'Incredible.'

'Which one should I watch?'

'Oh, *Dogs of Despair*. Definitely.'

'Gonna guess that's not suitable for Poppy? I'll fit it in,' Mav replied, and turned the conversation back to the problem at hand. 'I can't keep an eye on her twenty-four hours a day. But when she's here and I'm not, I'm making her your responsibility.'

'You're that worried?'

'Yeah, I am. Something doesn't sit right. And all I know is that she definitely got hurt, she's definitely famous, and she definitely doesn't have security.' Mav pushed to his feet. 'You don't have to baby her. I don't want her to feel like she's being watched. Just keep one eye on her.'

'Sure thing, boss. But you realize, you could just ask her about it?'

Mav assessed the bridles on the table, cross-referencing each with the horse it belonged to and the list of guests from that day's sign-up sheet. Benji had things under control – as always. But it didn't quite ease Mav's mind; it was just another reminder that Benji would leave Hunt Ranch soon. He didn't bring it up, knowing that Benji was doing what he had to to survive. 'I thought about it. But I don't want to put her through it again. She's here to recuperate.'

'You don't have to ask her for the intimate details,' Benji argued. 'Just ask her how vigilant we need to be.'

'Maybe.' But it didn't sit well with Mav. Pain should be shared willingly, otherwise it was just prying. 'There's one other thing I wanted to talk to you about.'

'I'm listening.'

Mav shifted. 'I'm going to start looking around for your replacement soon. That way you can train them before you go.'

Benji's grin faded instantly. 'Yeah,' he said regretfully.

Maverick hated to bring it up. He would rather have cut out his own heart than hurt either Sierra or Benji. Still, Hunt Ranch had to run, and Mav was the one responsible for making sure that it ran smoothly. 'When I do, Sierra is going to have questions. Do you want me to tell her? Or is that something you want to do yourself?'

'I should do it. God knows if I don't, it'll just be another thing she blames me for.'

Maverick didn't even deny it. 'I won't advertise for the job until you give me the green light then.'

'Thanks, Mav.'

'Don't thank me. If it was up to me, you wouldn't be going at all.'

'But you understand why I have to.'

Mav sighed sadly. 'Yeah. Yeah, I do.'

With a final nod, Benji got back to work. 'I'll keep an eye on Nina when she's around.'

'Thank you.'

Benji only pointed at him. '*Dogs of Despair*.'

'I'll watch it,' Mav promised.

Chapter 8

Over the next few days, Maverick tried not to worry about Nina and whatever had happened to her. Which should have been easy enough, except for the fact that she spent most of her mornings down at the barn, helping with the horses, taking lessons, and spending time with Barbie, so she was always in his line of sight and always in his thoughts.

He told himself it was none of his business, and then found himself talking loudly every time he approached her so that he didn't startle her. He told himself that she would have hired security if she'd thought she'd needed it, and then wondered why the hell she hadn't when she was still so clearly terrified. He reminded himself that she wasn't there for him to ogle, but kept finding his eyes turning in her direction.

Maverick couldn't help it. He really liked the way she moved, like a butterfly, all dainty and quick, and the way she mindfully slowed her fluttering when she was working with the horses. He liked that she had traded her pretty blouses for Hunt Ranch T-shirts she had bought in the gift shop, and that she didn't seem to care when she left the barn covered in dust and hair and sweat.

But the fact that he noticed her, the fact that he knew that she was intelligent and capable of making her own decisions, didn't automatically stop the worry. Even at that moment, he was sitting on the picnic bench in the guests' waiting area in front of the barn, cleaning tack in front of everyone instead of doing it in the tack room because he wanted to keep an eye on her.

He saw the way the other guests whispered and fawned over her, watched them as they summed up the courage to ask her for a picture or an autograph. And instead of admiring the way she always seemed so happy and flattered to be talking to them, he noticed the way her smile dimmed and her shoulders rounded the moment they walked away.

And in those quiet moments when she didn't realize that he was watching her, he saw the defeat and devastation in her. And it crushed him.

Maverick knew what it was to feel that way, as if the weight of your everyday had become too heavy to carry.

When Shannon had left, he'd felt that gaping emptiness and, worse, guilt. As if the pain of abandonment hadn't been bad enough, every time he'd run into an acquaintance and they'd asked him to give his best to Shannon, he'd had to explain, repeatedly, that she'd left him, and telling people *that* had felt like sharing his shortcomings with the world over and over again. He'd only been saved by Poppy, who hadn't given him the opportunity or, quite frankly, the time, to focus on his pain so much.

And, still, despite Nina's sadness, on the rare occasion she laughed, all he could do was stop what he was doing and listen. Maybe because she seemed so sad all the time, so her laugh, which was bright and quick, threw him off. Maybe because he liked the sound of it, almost as if she had surprised herself with it too. Whatever it was, Mav tried not to overthink it.

As his thoughts circled around her, he raised his eyes and saw her standing in the stall with Barbie, one hand firmly stroking the horse's neck as she whispered something to the animal.

'Think she'll take that horse with her when she leaves?'

Maverick went back to cleaning and oiling the tack as his

sister took a seat on the bench opposite him. 'Maybe. She's got a soft spot for her.'

'God knows she has the money to board her in LA.'

Maverick didn't have anything to say to that. When he looked at Nina, he didn't see her wealth.

'Did you need me?' he asked, knowing Sierra didn't willingly come down to the barn much anymore.

'It's about Nina, actually,' she replied, lowering her voice.

Mav went on alert instantly, but he didn't speak, only waited patiently.

'She's been putting the "Do Not Disturb" sign on the door every day, so housekeeping hasn't been into her cabin since she arrived.'

Maverick considered that for a moment. 'It's not completely unheard of. People like their privacy.'

'I wouldn't particularly care if she went the entire stay without changing the sheets once,' Sierra said. 'But yesterday she didn't put the sign on the door. I'm assuming she forgot.'

'Okay . . .'

'Housekeeping said she's been sleeping in the bathtub, Mav.'

He put down the bridle he was cleaning, angled his head to look at Nina, who had picked up a brush to groom Barbie. In that moment, she looked at peace. Happy. 'You think she's afraid?'

'I do. The bathroom is the only room with a secure lock. The others are more for display . . .'

It crushed him to think about how she must look every night as she curled up in the bathtub, so small and alone and scared. 'You sure?'

'Carmen told me the comforter and pillow were both in there, and that her laptop was shut on the ledge.' Sierra let that sink in. 'After Carmen spoke to me, I asked around. Do you know how many times she's made it up to the resort to eat?'

'I'm guessing zero?'

'She's ordered food to her room three times. That's it. Three meals total – in five days.'

Maverick sighed. That worry he'd been harbouring reared its ugly head. 'What do you want me to do?'

'I need you to talk to her, see if there's anything we can do to make her feel more comfortable. Christ, Mav, for the price she's paying for that cabin we could hire an armed wrangler to stand outside at night if it'd make her feel safe.'

'Yeah.' But he thought about the impending conversation. 'You don't think she'd feel more comfortable talking to you?'

Sierra only raised both her eyebrows. 'Being a woman and all?' she drawled sarcastically.

'It matters,' he countered quietly. 'Given what she's been through, it matters.'

Sierra sighed. 'Maybe. But rumour has it you two have been spending a lot of time together, and if I were in her position I'd prefer it to come from someone I was at least acquainted with.'

'Yeah, I've been worried about her,' he admitted.

'You think he'll come back?'

'I don't know. That's why I'm worried. If we had more information, we would know what additional security measures we'd need to take, if any. But as it stands, she's here completely alone.' Mav sighed deeply when he thought about the impending conversation. 'That doesn't sit well with me.'

'Well, if you have the conversation, I'll have concierge sort whatever she needs.'

'I'm shit with words.'

'No, you're not. You just don't like to talk. There's a difference.'

'Fuck.'

Sierra gave him a double thumbs up before pushing to her feet. She checked her watch, sighed. 'I better get back. But let me know what she says.' She turned to go.

'You don't want to say hi to Ty?' he asked.

Sierra stopped. Her spine went rigid. But she didn't turn around. 'I don't have time today.'

'It's not the horse's fault he was a gift from Benji,' Maverick reminded her, gently pushing even though he'd known she'd refuse.

'I know,' Sierra replied. But she didn't say more, and she didn't look back towards Ty's stall either even though the horse had popped his head over the door at the sound of her voice.

Maverick watched her go, and instead of feeling angry, all he felt was regret.

He waited for the twelve o'clock lunch break before approaching Nina because he wanted privacy for the conversation and because it had become somewhat routine for them to be the only ones left in the barn when the wranglers went to the staff quarters to eat.

Nina stood alone by the main arena, one booted foot on the lowest rung, looking out at the ranch.

'I saw you finally managed to groom Barbie,' he said loudly as he drew closer to her.

She still jumped. Only a bit. But he saw it, that quick jerk in her muscles before she realized it was him and calmed. She looked over her shoulder at him. 'Yeah.' A ghost of a smile haunted her lips, though her eyes stayed *so* sad. 'It took me most of the morning and she somehow still looks dirty, but Benji said it was still good progress.'

'It is.' Mav stopped a few feet from her. 'Her wounds are mostly superficial, so we can give her a bath as soon as she's feeling more at home. Maybe in a day or two after the vet comes.'

'Why hasn't the vet been already?'

He didn't hear judgement, only curiosity. 'I won't ask my vet or farrier to come see rescues I haven't had time to settle. It's not their job to try and calm or manage feral animals. It's mine. Barbie needs to be calm enough to be handled safely by a stranger.' He leaned his forearms on the rails, placed his own foot on the rung out of habit. 'You did that,' he said. 'You spent time desensitizing her to humans, and you relieved me of a lot of work. Thank you.'

Nina rested her chin in her hand. She smiled. 'I'm enjoying myself. It's cathartic.' Her smile dimmed. 'It's helped to keep my mind occupied . . .'

Mav held his breath, hoping that she'd share more, but she seemed to catch herself, and when she fell silent again, he used it as a segue. 'I've been meaning to talk to you about that . . .'

Nina turned those dark, wary eyes on him.

Christ, here we go, Mav thought. But he jumped right in. 'Yesterday you forgot to put the "Do Not Disturb" sign on your door.'

He didn't have to say more. Nina shook her head on a sigh and turned away as if she'd known her slip would come back to haunt her.

'If you want me to shut up at any time, you tell me.' When she didn't reply, didn't even look at him, Mav took two steps closer. He reached out and gently turned her face back in his direction. The tears in her eyes devastated him, but he pushed, knowing that he wouldn't find the courage to attempt the conversation a second time. 'But until you do tell me to shut up, I have some things to say. Okay?'

A tiny nod was the only indication that she was listening.

'You're paying through the teeth to be here. Hunt Ranch isn't just a dude ranch, it's a luxury resort with a twenty-four-hour concierge, and if you don't feel safe here, that is a problem for us.'

'It's not the ranch,' she rasped. 'I . . . I don't feel safe anywhere anymore. And I know that's irrational, but it's like my body won't listen to my brain.'

Her reply confused him. Christ, anyone would be afraid. 'I think that's going to be your new normal for a little while, all things considered. But there are things we can do to help.' He didn't reach out and touch her again, though he wanted to. He kept it transactional in the hope that a business conversation would ease her embarrassment. 'Option one, we post a wrangler outside your cabin at night.'

'No.' Her reply was instant. She shook her head vehemently. 'I don't want to be a burden. And I don't want people asking questions.'

'They already are, Nina,' he said quietly.

She had to be prepared. How many photos had she taken with fans over the past few days? How many of them had already posted those pictures to social media? In how many of those posted photos were her bruises faintly visible beneath her makeup? 'At least if we had someone posted outside your cabin, we could guarantee your safety and privacy.'

'I'm safe.'

'Your vindication only worries me more,' he countered quietly. Because it didn't make sense. How could she be so certain that people wouldn't figure out where she was? Or that her attacker wouldn't come for her if news of her whereabouts spread?

She wrapped her arms around her stomach, lowered her eyes to the ground. 'You haven't asked . . .'

'I want to.' He let that sink in for a moment. 'But I figured you'll tell me if and when you're ready to. Otherwise, it's none of my business.'

She didn't go into the attack. 'I still see him in my sleep,' she whispered, giving him that much. 'Which is why I've been staying in the bathroom. It . . . I guess, it helps me feel safe enough to fall asleep eventually. But I can tell you with certainty that I don't need security.'

'How can you possibly know that?'

'He wouldn't risk hurting me again.'

The confidence with which she said it only confused him. 'If you don't want security, we could move you up to the resort.'

She shook her head. 'Too many people. The crowding—' she brought both hands to her neck '—it makes me feel like I can't breathe, like I'm being suffocated by my own anxiety. Always watching. Waiting for someone to come up to me or touch me or hug me without warning.'

Mav understood. But he was about out of options. There was only one other solution he could think of, and he knew he should have run it by his sister before he offered. And yet, the words came out of his mouth anyway. 'The only other option I have is that you come stay in the ranch house.'

She frowned. 'The ranch house?'

'It's about a mile up that way.' He pointed towards where the house sat, nestled in a little valley and completely obscured by trees. 'We have two spare rooms. And Shadow would bark like crazy if any stranger came within a hundred feet of it.'

'Your house?' Her eyes rounded in surprise. 'No. I couldn't do that.'

'At some point you're going to have to realize that I wouldn't offer if I didn't mean it.' And because she only stared at him, he kept going. 'It's private. Secluded. Nobody who found out you were staying here would think to look there. You could still participate in all the ranch activities but save money on the cabin. You could stop sleeping in the bathtub and rest in an actual bed again. And Poppy's only five, so she doesn't really understand the celebrity thing.' He tipped his head. 'But I should warn you too, with my kid in the house, you'd never have a moment's peace. Only exhaustion – but the good kind.'

And because it would be a weight off his shoulders, he took a low shot. 'It would also put my mind at ease because then I could stop worrying, too.'

Though she knew it wasn't what he had intended, Nina was mortified.

She'd known when she'd gone back to her cabin and seen the bed neatly made and the room tidied that she'd made a giant mistake in forgetting to hang the 'Do Not Disturb' sign, but beneath the humiliation she had convinced herself that nobody at a five-star resort would pry. Only, Hunt Ranch wasn't just a luxury getaway. She knew that now more than ever. It was a family-run enterprise, a place founded on over one hundred years of roots and cowboy ideals.

'I'm not some poor, helpless damsel in need of rescuing.'

Infuriatingly, he only nodded, said, 'No, ma'am.' And then, damn him, he made her smile by adding, 'Those tubs are pretty comfy too. They cost an arm and a leg, so I'm glad they're earning their keep.'

Nina considered the offer.

She hated how appealing it sounded. Because the truth was, as safe as she was, *knowing* it and *feeling* it were two separate issues, and she knew beyond a doubt that sleeping in the same house as Maverick Hunt would make her *feel* safe. Wasn't he the entire reason she made her way to the barn each morning and spent way too much time there?

The horses – particularly Barbie – were a part of it, sure. Nina genuinely enjoyed spending her time with them, but as a guest, she shouldn't have been grooming, feeding, and caring for them until her damaged ribs spread fire through her side. She knew that. But the moment Maverick had left that first day, she'd realized that he was what had made her feel safe. And, since then, she'd stayed at the barn far longer than was normal so that she could rest her own vigilance, even for a little while. Because knowing that her attacker wouldn't hurt her again didn't mean that her body or mind would ever forget the damage he'd already done.

'Why do I feel that this isn't a normal offer?'

'It's not. But that doesn't mean it's not a genuine one.'

She tried to remind herself that he couldn't protect her. Maybe he could stop anyone else from physically hurting her, but her career was almost certainly over, and she had no idea what she was going to do. And, still, every time Maverick was kind or gentle with her, Nina felt herself relaxing, opening up to him in a way that terrified her.

And she couldn't afford to grow lax. She couldn't ever grow comfortable enough to share the truth because, while it might make her feel better in the moment, once unleashed, the truth would destroy her. Of that she was certain.

Wasn't that why she'd run?

Maverick Hunt was so clearly an idealist, and if he found out what had happened, he wouldn't understand why she'd done what she'd done. How could he? He didn't know what it was to have to fight tooth and nail for every rung of the ladder you climbed. He didn't know what it was like to get to the top of that ladder and then have somebody else kick it out from underneath you.

'You can't help me,' she said quietly, wanting to warn him away from her.

Maverick didn't agree. He looked her right in the eye, replied, 'Wanna bet?'

His assurance, his absolution, had a completely unprecedented effect on Nina, and the moment the words left his mouth, a half-sob left hers. She slapped a hand over her mouth, physically trying to stop the tears of embarrassment and guilt and *relief*. 'Oh, my God,' she managed even as tears blurred her vision. 'I'm so sorry.'

Mortified, she turned to go. She didn't even know where. She just needed to get away from her own humiliation.

But Maverick caught her hand in his, holding her where she was, her back still to him, her arm outstretched behind her.

Nina instinctively braced against the restraint, twisting her wrist in his large hand even though he held her gently. 'Please,' she croaked, refusing to face him as hot tears streamed down her face.

But instead of letting her go, Maverick said, 'Nina, look at me.'

His voice – the deep, gentle tone of it – soothed her. It broke through the panic in her brain, reminded her who she was talking to. But she still couldn't turn around, couldn't act her way out of the emotions she knew he'd read in her eyes. They were too real to smother, too raw to hide. She only shook her head.

From behind her, Maverick said, 'I would *never* hurt you.'

She shook her head, embarrassed all over again. 'I know,' she managed.

'Do you?'

'Yes,' she said the single word firmly.

'Good.' Without another word, he turned her around, manipulating her weight as if she were a child. He tugged her forward and settled her against him before wrapping both of his arms around her.

Nina tensed for a single moment before relaxing into the embrace. Even as she told herself that she was making a fool of herself, she tucked her arms in and sank into his strength. She buried her tear-streaked face against him and inhaled his smell – deodorant and horses and male. She closed her eyes, giving way to her exhaustion, and she let her circling thoughts rest. Just for a moment.

Maverick's heavy palm traced circles on her back.

He didn't say anything. Not one word. He held her, providing comfort without expectations.

Nina, who had never been embraced quite like this before, wasn't entirely sure how she was supposed to feel.

Her own mother had never been affectionate, choosing to go off with her latest boyfriend instead of staying in her dilapidated shoebox apartment with her only child, and while she had never physically harmed Nina, Lulu Keller had done much more damage with her words, and as Nina had grown up and started attracting looks from men, even looks she hadn't wanted, Lulu had only become worse.

On the day her mother had found Nina's acting headshots, taken by Luigi against the white wall in the restaurant kitchen, she had laughed herself to tears. She had torn the pictures up. And, worse, she had told Nina, 'You think you're so special. But just you wait. You'll end up on your back, just like me.'

So, Nina wasn't sure how she was *supposed* to feel. But it was as if his big body could shelter her from anything. His warmth seeped into her numb, cold heart, making it beat again. And, shockingly, there was a kick of lust, low in her belly, and because *that* terrified her, she took a moment to rest her forehead against his chest and breathe him in one last time, and then she stepped back. 'I'm sorry.'

He didn't touch her again, only quietly studied her tear-streaked face. 'Why?'

She laughed quietly, fully aware that most people would have been mortified by her breakdown. 'I'm not in the habit of breaking down in a stranger's arms.'

'Are we strangers?'

Nina was slightly taken aback by the question.

Maverick didn't give her much time to mull on it. 'I don't think we're strangers. A stranger is someone you pass on the street, someone you don't know at all. I know you.'

'You do?'

He turned back to look out at the mountains, rested both arms over the top rung of the fence. 'Maybe not all – but enough. I know you have a soft heart. I know you work hard, like animals, and have a stubborn streak wider'n any mule's. I know that you attract good people because I met your best friend, and friends say more about a person than anything else. I know that you're a beautiful woman who doesn't think much about the way she looks. And I know that you're scared, but that you've got thick skin protecting that soft heart.' He shrugged. 'So, not all – but enough.'

Nina wasn't sure what to say. Nobody had ever summed her up quite so simply. Or accurately. And because he had thrown her off, she tried for nonchalance. 'Stubborn streak wider than any mule's?'

'Oh yeah,' he replied decidedly.

'Because I slept in the locked bathroom?'

It was supposed to have been funny. Dark, but funny.

But instead of laughing as she'd wanted him to, Maverick's eyes dampened. 'No. Not because you refused to ask for help. That's not stubborn, that's proud. Which is a good trait to have until it starts stealing your sleep.'

He nudged her gently with his shoulder. The gesture was friendly, comforting, intended, she knew, to take the sting out of his words. But Nina liked the familiar way he touched her.

'I know you're stubborn because even though you're scared and sleeping in the bathtub, you get up every day, you come down here, and you work like I'm paying you overtime instead of relaxing like the Hollywood star everyone keeps telling me you are.'

'I like the horses.'

'I know it. But you also refuse to wallow and be self-pitying. And working with the horses has given you a reason to get up in the morning even when you'd rather not. You refuse to let him win even though I can see you're still terrified. That's stubborn. In damn spades.'

His words, though kindly intended, eviscerated her. They were as true as they were the greatest lie she'd ever heard. And as much as she wished things were different, and as stubborn as she admittedly was, she had let her attacker win. She had let him take everything from her.

'I ran,' she admitted quietly, saying more than she had to anyone else. 'I lied to the police. And I ran.'

She saw the moment that Maverick put the pieces together. His eyes narrowed. His jaw clenched. But instead of pushing for more, he replied, 'You ran to the right place, Nina.'

Seeing Benji and Riley coming back from lunch, she turned to walk away. Nina would later wonder why she'd done it, what had possessed her to be so sure of herself when she'd angled her face over her shoulder and said, 'I don't come here every day because I'm stubborn. Or, not only because I'm stubborn. I come here because I feel better – safer with myself – when you're in shouting distance.'

PART TWO:
REST

Chapter 9

Los Angeles, California – June 2, 2025

'Neens?' She heard the frown in Markus's voice. 'I didn't quite get that.'

How could he not have heard her when her voice had been so loud? '*Someone is in my house,*' she whispered again, becoming frantic now.

'*What?*'

She caught the faintest sound, coming from her lounge maybe. Or the attached conservatory. Wherever it was coming from, it was all the confirmation she needed.

She gripped her phone to her ear, trying to hold it in place as her hand began to shake uncontrollably.

'Nina, hang up.' On the phone, Markus began to panic. 'Call 911. Go wait outside. I'm on my way.'

His fear drove hers. 'Don't hang up,' she begged hoarsely.

But she took one step away from the glass window, one step toward the front door.

It was a straight shot. Fifty feet to the door, maybe eighty to the narrow, winding street that passed through the hills.

She heard Markus's car start over the line. 'Shit.' He was panting for breath. 'I think I should hang up. I have to call 911.'

'Please don't leave me,' she begged *so quietly* as she crept to the kitchen island. 'Please.'

'Fuck. Okay.' A horn blared. 'Stop talking. Is there a weapon you can grab? Somewhere you can hide?'

A weapon? Stupid. She should have thought of that. She looked around her kitchen, saw the knife block to her left by the stove and hurried to it. She chose the smallest knife, something she could wield easily, and lifted it from its resting place. Though she wasn't aware of it, she kept the phone in her right hand, choosing the person who made her feel safest over the option of violence.

Footsteps sounded in the next room.

Nina stopped moving.

She didn't dare breathe.

Her heart pounded in her ears, screaming for her to inhale. But she couldn't.

Her legs shook, but she locked her knees, refusing to curl up into a ball and hide behind the cabinets until help arrived.

'Just get outside.' On the phone, Markus sounded as if he was on the verge of tears. 'Wave someone down. Nina, make them wait with you until I get there. Okay?' There was a pause on the line, and when Markus's voice sounded again it was distant. 'You! Call 911!'

She passed the kitchen sink as she listened to Markus rattle off her address to a stranger.

She took one step into the foyer with its beautiful hardwood floors and the cherry blossom wallpaper she'd laboriously hung herself, wondered, in the back of her mind, how she had never noticed that the bright pink flowers made the little entryway seem *so small*.

Nina stopped before passing the spot where the foyer opened up. On the right, the stairs led to the bedrooms. On the left was the lounge. Behind her now, the kitchen.

She heard breathing, tight and restrained, and vaguely

wondered if it was her or Markus making so much noise. She wanted to tell him to keep quiet but couldn't summon the courage to open her mouth.

Her palms were slicked with sweat, loosening her hold on both of her lifelines.

Her vision narrowed on the door handle, only fifteen feet away.

On three she would run. There was no time to get to her car or wait for her garage to open. But Nina promised herself she would not look back, that she would not stop running until she had flagged someone down.

One.

She exhaled a quiet but deep breath, trying to slow her racing pulse.

Two.

She took a single step forward, preparing to run.

Her muscles shortened.

Her breathing stopped altogether.

Three.

In a burst of fear, with adrenaline coursing through her veins, Nina ran. She reached the door, gripped the handle in the same hand as the knife, and yanked it downward.

The door opened.

She had one perfect moment where she saw the 'Welcome' sign on her open door before somebody lifted her off her feet from behind . . .

Hunt Ranch, Santa Barbara County – Present Day

Nina had only to go back to her cabin at the end of the day and see her little bathroom set-up again to realize how ridiculous she was being in the face of Maverick's offer. The man had offered her a bed in an environment that would make her feel safe, and here she was choosing the cold, porcelain bathtub.

Stubborn, he'd called her. And he had been right, but that wasn't all of it either. It was instinct.

She had learned to be self-sufficient from a young age. And, now, it wasn't that she didn't ever need help or rely on other people, but, rather, that it wasn't in her nature to ask for help until it was offered. And, even then, she never accepted it unless she was in dire need of it.

So, she didn't call concierge or the stables or try and otherwise track Maverick down. She simply packed her bag and wheeled the bright pink suitcase down the dirt road to the barn.

When he saw her coming, Maverick stopped what he was doing – lunging a horse in the round pen – immediately. He stepped wide, moving in the direction of the cantering horse, and raised one hand. The mare came to a halt and turned to face him, and Maverick rewarded her by bringing her in and rubbing her face before he stepped away and passed the long lunging whip to Benji, who had been leaning on the rails, watching the session.

He said something to Benji as he climbed through the side of the pen, and the other man turned to glance in her direction.

Benji waved.

Nina returned the wave, but she stopped about fifty yards away and waited for Maverick to come to her because she didn't want to answer any questions just then. She didn't want to tell people that she was being moved to the owner's house because she'd been caught sleeping in the bathtub; that would only prompt more questions.

She watched Maverick's face as he approached, looked into those kind, blue eyes and tried to decipher his reaction. He didn't seem inconvenienced or resigned. He looked relieved.

He didn't ask her any questions, only reached down, lifted her suitcase, and headed in the direction of a Hunt Ranch Jeep, leaving her and Shadow to follow.

Nina stayed out of the way as he put her suitcase in the back seat, but when she moved to open her door, Maverick beat her to it.

'Thank you.'

He nodded and waited for her to climb in before gently closing the door and walking around the hood.

He opened the back passenger door for Shadow, who jumped in and settled on the back seat, her tongue lolling. Nina reached back to pet the dog as Maverick slid into the driver's seat.

'I won't get in your way. Or your sister's.'

He started the Jeep, put it in reverse. 'I can't promise the same for us. Sierra is a devil in the morning. She snaps and growls, and God forbid you approach her before she's caffeinated. And Poppy . . . Poppy has no concept of personal space.'

That had a little kick of anxiety kindling in her stomach. 'I have no experience with young kids,' she warned him. 'The only time I've ever interacted with one was in a diaper ad in my twenties. And all I had to do was hold out my arms and "laugh lovingly" until the toddler walked to me.'

'You're an actress.' He took his baseball cap off and threw it on the dash before running the same hand through his thick, dark hair. 'Just pretend to be sufficiently enthused over everything she says and does, and you'll have a new best friend.'

'That's it?' she asked doubtfully.

'Yup.'

'It's that simple?'

Maverick turned those lake blue eyes, glinting with humour, on her. 'Simple? You only say that because you've never had to pretend to be excited for mud pie.'

'Mud pie? What is that?' she asked. 'Chocolate?'

'Nope. It's mud, made from garden soil and hose water and garnished with one of Sierra's prized roses.'

'Mud?' Nina frowned. 'You let your kid eat mud?'

Maverick laughed and turned the Jeep down a short, shaded drive. 'No. She only had to put it in her mouth once to realize that real food was better. But she still likes to bake mud pies – and she still tries to convince me to eat them.'

'Huh.' Nina wondered what she had walked into. She was a good actress – she knew that. But how exactly did one pretend to be enthused about mud pie? 'Do you sling it over your shoulder when she's not looking?' she asked, because she genuinely wanted to know what the protocol was.

'Sometimes. But she's typically happy if you just pretend to eat it. You're a city girl, so think tea party – but outside and with mud.'

Nina smiled grimly at that. Tea parties had been about as foreign a concept during her childhood as mud pies, and the only tea her mother ever drank was the Long Island variety.

He pulled the Jeep into a shaded spot beneath a huge oak tree and parked. He turned off the engine. But he didn't get out right away. He asked, 'Why does this worry you?'

When he only waited in silence, giving her the space to continue, she said, 'I . . . I suppose I don't really have any family experience. I've never even lived with anyone else, really. And after everything you've done for me, I don't want to be a burden.'

'Only child?'

'Only child,' she confirmed. 'No father. And my mother wasn't exactly winning any awards in the parenting department.' She raised her thumbnail to her teeth in an anxious habit she'd thought she'd kicked but had recently fallen back into. Then, lowered her hand again as soon as she realized what she'd done.

'You're overthinking this,' he said gently. 'Poppy's five. She's young, but also precocious and self-sufficient. If she gets in your space, just gently redirect her. Ask her to find me. Or if I'm not there for some reason, put the TV on for her. It'll keep her occupied until I get there.' He shrugged. 'The only time she's ever alone is for a few minutes or so when she's sleeping in the morning and Sierra is heading to work as I'm heading home. I'm not saying she won't get in your way – she's five. But she's not your responsibility. She's mine.'

Nina thought about that. He had said something similar when he'd been talking about desensitizing Barbie before calling the vet and farrier to look her over. And while being responsible for one's child was the most basic of metrics for parenthood, she was beginning to understand that Maverick Hunt accepted responsibility for a lot of things. His child. Forty rescue horses. The ranch and resort. His staff. And now, Nina.

She would have felt guilty had she not been so relieved. Even sitting in the confined space of the Jeep with him made her feel safe.

'I've seen you with the horses,' he added. 'You're kind and gentle. Stop worrying. Poppy will love you.' And with that, he climbed from the vehicle and walked around to get her suitcase out.

Nina took a moment to look at the beautiful white ranch house with its wide porch and big windows before following Maverick up the three front steps and inside, Shadow on their heels.

The moment the door slapped shut behind them, a happy 'Daddy!' rang loudly through the house, followed by the sound of little feet on hardwood.

Poppy came running out, her face lit with unbridled joy as she made a beeline for him.

She was adorable. She had Maverick's brown hair, big brown eyes, and she was dressed in yellow *Beauty and the Beast* pyjamas. Nina watched as Poppy threw herself at Maverick, wrapping both arms around his knees in a hug. 'Daddy, I made dinner with Sisi!'

Maverick reached down and lifted her up in a quick hug, but he shot Nina a wink over his daughter's shoulder. 'Mud pie?'

'No! Pasta!' Poppy chirped. 'With 'matoes!'

Maverick put her back down. 'Yum,' he replied, sounding genuinely enthused. 'But you forgot your manners in the kitchen.' With one hand on each of Poppy's shoulders, he turned her around to face Nina. 'Did you say hi to Nina?'

Poppy angled her head. Those eyes sized Nina up openly, and a little sceptically. 'Hi!'

'Hi, Poppy.'

'Who are you?'

The question, the direct manner it was asked in, had Nina searching her mind for an appropriate response. 'I'm a friend of your dad's,' she said finally, choosing the path of least resistance.

'Oh.' Poppy laughed. 'I have friends too. Lots.'

'I bet you do,' Nina replied, genuinely amused.

Before she could defer or escape, Poppy came forward and took her by the hand. 'I made dinner. Come see!'

'Oh.' Nina let herself be led. 'Okay.' She cast one slightly panicked glance in Maverick's direction, but he only grinned and followed close behind them.

They walked down a wide hallway that was lined with dozens of framed family photographs. Nina caught glimpses of a young Maverick and Sierra and even Benji before she entered the kitchen slightly bent over, Poppy's tiny hand encased in hers.

Sierra Hunt stood at the stove, a white chef's apron over her pristine black pencil skirt. She didn't turn around, only asked, 'How did it go with Nina?'

Knowing that she had been a subject of concern to them had Nina flushing in embarrassment. But when Sierra turned, a spoon in her hands, and saw Nina standing in front of her, her dark eyes widened in surprise for only a moment. 'Oh. Hi,' she said, recovering quickly. 'I guess this answers my question.'

'I'm so sorry for imposing,' Nina began.

But Sierra only waved away her concern. 'It's no imposition.'

'I offered Nina a more private place to stay in lieu of the resort.' Behind them, Maverick spoke up. 'Figured it would be a weight off all our shoulders.'

Sierra didn't miss a beat. 'Absolutely. We've been worried.' She pointed the spoon in Maverick's direction.

'Please keep billing me,' said Nina. 'I wouldn't feel right staying here otherwise.'

Sierra nodded slowly as she thought it through. 'We'll bring it down to our bunk rate and apply the summer special,' Sierra said.

'That way you're still in our system as a guest and can access all the resort's amenities even though you're staying with us.'

Nina was instantly appeased. 'Thank you.' She consciously refrained from wringing her hands. 'I know this isn't exactly normal—'

'Your situation's not either,' Sierra said simply. She turned to her brother. 'Could you put Nina's bag in the second spare room – the one next to yours? It was cleaned recently, and I've been storing some of my boxes in the other one.'

'Yup.'

As Maverick disappeared around the corner again, Sierra walked to the fridge and pulled out an open bottle of white wine, held it up for Nina's inspection. 'Riesling?'

'That would be great. Thanks.'

'Come see,' Poppy said, and tugged Nina's hand again.

Nina followed. She watched in amusement as Poppy released her to pull one of the chairs from the kitchen table over to the stove. The five-year-old climbed up and peered into the pot of bubbling pasta sauce. 'I made it,' she said proudly.

'I heard,' Nina replied, but she couldn't quite relax with Poppy standing so close to the bubbling pot. Maybe she just had an overactive imagination, but all she saw were the numerous ways things could go wrong. 'Hold on,' she said, and when Poppy gripped the back of the chair with both hands, Nina pushed the entire chair a good foot off to the side of the stove.

Poppy looked at the stove, then back at Nina. She frowned. 'But now I can't stir.'

'How about I stir?' Nina offered.

Poppy seemed to genuinely consider the pros and cons of allowing Nina to intervene before nodding slowly. "Kay.'

Nina picked up the wooden spoon from the side of the stove and stirred the marinara, but she was very aware of Poppy's hawkish gaze. 'This smells really good,' she offered. 'What did you put in here?'

'"Matoes and . . . stuff."

'You don't remember what we put in?' This came from Sierra, who walked to them and passed Nina the glass of wine before taking a seat on the chair Poppy was still standing on.

Poppy roped her arms around her aunt's neck. 'I forgot.'

'Onion, garlic, oregano, basil, and salt and pepper.'

Nina smiled as Poppy repeated the list of ingredients as if Nina hadn't just heard Sierra rattle them off herself, and the moment she was done, Nina said, 'Wow, that's a lot to remember.'

'Yeah. We use a book.'

'A recipe book of my mom's,' Sierra clarified. 'She handwrote the recipes she liked her entire life, so every now and then we try to do one of the recipe books justice.'

Nina nodded, but she wondered what that must have been like, growing up with a sibling and both parents. *Stable* parents. Parents who ran a successful ranch and handwrote recipes and tucked you in at night. To Nina, the Hunts' lives may as well have been a movie. 'How many recipe books are there?'

'Seven.'

'*Seven?*'

'Yeah, but her recipes always end up stressing me out. Mom was really disorganized,' she explained, 'so her only rule was that she started a new recipe on a new page.' Sierra stretched to reach a notebook that sat on the kitchen table. She passed it to Nina.

Nina put the spoon down and took the notebook. She opened it randomly in the middle and found herself smiling as she read both pages. The first, neat handwriting, read: *Mav's Favourite Chocolate Cake*. The second page's title was: *Cream of Artichoke Soup*. 'I see what you mean.'

'I keep telling myself to scan all the pages onto my computer so that I can reorganize and sort them, maybe print them and have them book-bound in some coherent categories, so I don't have to flip through forty pages of random recipes to find the one I need.'

Nina couldn't imagine having something so special and

choosing to digitize it, even if it was for convenience. 'Don't do that.' She passed Sierra the book back. 'Or do it to preserve the recipes, maybe have them copied for when Poppy leaves home one day. But those shouldn't be digitized.'

Sierra smiled. 'Yeah. It's funny how many of our memories are linked so closely to a person's physical things. Every time I take one out, I hear my mom's voice in my head, saying "Now where on earth did I write that recipe down?"'

Nina chuckled, but she couldn't help but think that memories of her own mother hid in darker places. In a stranger's cigarette smoke. In old bars that had that stale booze smell. In instant ramen noodles and boxes of Cheerios, neither of which she could stomach anymore.

'Was your mom a cook?'

Nina laughed outright at that. 'No. I don't think I ever saw my mom cook anything. She . . .' Nina thought about how to explain, while being sensitive to Poppy's young ears. 'She wasn't like your mom.'

She didn't realize how bitter she was and how it bled into her tone until Poppy looked up at her, and in a voice so blunt, so accepting, said, 'I don't like my mom too.'

Nina didn't know what to say to that. She was so astounded by the child's astuteness, so shocked at the transparency, that for a long moment, she simply stared.

Poppy kept right on talking. 'She doesn't know what I like to eat. And she always makes my dad sad.' Poppy's lower lip trembled.

Oh, God. She'd made Maverick's child cry in her first hour. Nina didn't know what to say. She didn't know Poppy's story, so couldn't tell her that some women shouldn't be mothers, or that she was better off without a mother like that in her life. The only truth she absolutely knew was, 'But you don't need your mom because you got the best dad in the world.'

Poppy seemed to like that. Her eyes brightened immediately. 'Yeah!'

And perhaps wanting to push them all back to their previous happy chatter, Sierra roped her arms around Poppy's waist and pulled her onto her lap. 'What about the best aunty in the world?' she asked and started to tickle Poppy.

Poppy squealed, clearly used to the game. 'You're the best, Sisi! You're the best, Sisi!'

Sierra stopped tickling her as soon as she got what she wanted. But she finished with: 'Damn right, I am.'

Maverick heard the entire conversation. He had paused around the corner when he'd heard Nina talk about her mother, and not because he didn't want to interrupt, but because he wanted to know more about her.

Only, he hadn't expected the conversation to turn back on him quite so quickly.

He heard the long silence after Poppy's declaration that she didn't like her mom, followed by Nina's sweet reply.

Her words humbled him. He wasn't the best dad, not by far. He tried his best, and maybe that counted for something. And he would have taken a bullet for his kid, but most of the time he felt like a fish out of water. There was so much he didn't know, so many things he did terribly, and as much as Sierra was playing when she declared herself Best Aunty in the World, Mav wasn't entirely sure how he would have survived without her and Benji in those first few years. And Marisol, José's mother, who had come and helped him at nights. And Jenna, Poppy's nanny of almost four years . . . It truly took a village.

Despite the beautiful life he had been given, Maverick had seen plenty of hardship. But nothing came close to the difficulty of being a single parent. The highs were incredible. The lows . . . the lows could drag a person into the deepest despair.

Still, he plastered a smile onto his face and walked into the kitchen. He stopped just inside, as surprised by their tight circle as he was by the warmth that spread through him as he took them in.

Nina stood at the stove in a Hunt Ranch shirt, stirring the pasta sauce. Sierra sat in a chair nearby with Poppy on her lap. The three made a pretty picture, he thought. They might have been related.

Until a person looked closely.

Sierra and Poppy were darker, like him, compliments of his and Sierra's Chumash great-grandmother. Nina Keller, with her pale skin and pin-straight ebony hair, was all Black Irish.

'I could eat a horse,' he said, knowing it would get a reaction out of Poppy.

'No, Daddy!' She giggled. She climbed off Sierra's lap to run to him. 'We made pasta,' she said again.

'We still need to cook the pasta,' Sierra interrupted. 'Mav, why don't you show Nina to her room, and then get cleaned up?' She turned to Nina. 'No offence, but you both smell like the barn.'

Nina only laughed and held out her arms as she looked down on her dirty clothes. 'I don't even smell it on me anymore.'

'Come on.' Mav shucked his head in the direction of the stairs.

'Poppy, you stay here,' Sierra said as Poppy started to follow Nina. 'I need your help, little chef.'

''Kay,' Poppy said. But she turned to Nina and very seriously added, 'I'm making dinner, but I'll be here once you've had a shower.'

'Okay,' Nina replied, matching Poppy's tone.

Maverick was intensely aware of Nina behind him.

At her last birthday, Mav had shown Poppy static by rubbing a balloon against her hair until it had stood up on end and they'd both laughed hysterically. That's what it felt like to have Nina so close. As if there was a constant hum of energy between them, pulling the hair at the nape of his neck to attention.

'I'm sorry about that. Kids don't really filter the way we do.'

'Don't apologize,' Nina said from behind him. 'I should be the one apologizing. I almost made her cry.'

'She's five. If you're here for three weeks, I guarantee you'll see tears eventually.'

Maverick opened the door to the spare room. It was a large, airy bedroom with big windows that looked out over the tree-lined driveway and an en-suite bathroom. Though they rarely had guests, their cleaning staff deep-cleaned the ranch house once a month, including the guest room. 'It should be stocked with everything you need but just shout if something's missing.'

'Thank you, this is great. I would be more embarrassed if I didn't feel so much better already.'

Maverick liked that she felt safer, so all he said was, 'It's our pleasure.'

He started to go but stopped on the threshold when she said, 'Poppy's incredible. You should be proud, Maverick.'

Mav turned to face her again.

'I don't need to have had kids to know you're doing a great job.'

He leaned against the doorframe, hooked his thumbs in his belt loops. He took her in, the tiny woman sitting on the large bed, her hands twisted anxiously together in her lap, her black hair falling down to her hips. He had a need to go to her, to wrap her in his arms again, but he fought it, knowing that nothing good could come of it.

'Thank you,' he said. 'Most of the time I don't know what I'm doing, so that means a lot.'

'Trust me when I say this, you're off the charts on the parenting scale.' She looked away from him, shook her head. 'I never really thought about how much I still resented my mother. But Poppy . . . She saw straight through me.'

'Kids have a way of doing that,' Mav said. 'They're intuitive, even if they can't always understand the information they're processing.'

Nina raised her hand to her face, her fingers unconsciously tracing the faint bruising. 'It's strange for me, to see how natural you and Sierra are with her. Comparing you both to my own mother has me wondering if some people just don't have it in them.'

'You're not close – to your mom?'

'No. I walked out when I turned eighteen. Never saw her again. The last time I heard from her, she called to ask me for money, and when I said no, she sold my childhood pictures to the tabloids with some sob story about how I'd abandoned her.'

'I'm sorry.' Mav knew the words weren't quite right, but he didn't know what else to say.

'It was a long time ago.' She walked to the window and looked out at the ranch. 'The craziest thing is that even knowing she was a terrible mother and a horrible person, sometimes I still want to call her, you know? See how she's doing.' She laughed quietly. 'Pathetic.'

'I think that says a lot more about you than it does her.'

Maverick thought about Shannon, remembered how astounded he had been when she'd insisted he could have full custody of Poppy as long as she could keep her visitation rights. He'd been preparing to go to court, to fight it out, and instead, Shannon had just walked away.

He blamed himself. He shouldn't have pushed marriage just because she'd fallen pregnant. He should have worked less and tried to make her feel more at home on the ranch. He should have given her more attention because if she'd been happy, maybe she would have stayed. 'I don't know. I think life's just so hard for some people already, and the more it takes out of them, the less energy they have to expend on everything else.'

'And, still, some people never even try.'

'True,' he replied cautiously, and again he thought about Shannon. Irrespective of how much it had hurt, he could have forgiven her for leaving him because he had known she had been miserable. But leaving Poppy . . . In his mind, there was no excuse for that.

'I could forgive my mother for the life we'd led if I had seen her get up and go to work. Try. Pick up double shifts. But she never did. All she did was complain about how hard her life was, how unfair.

'I still remember getting my first job.' Nina smiled even though her eyes were distant. 'It was as a waitress in an Italian restaurant: Luigi's. I was terrified. I had grown up listening to my mother talk about having to work like it was this terrifying ordeal to be endured. I remember listening as my boss had described what I'd have to do, and thinking, that's it? Just show up, do the work, and get paid? It was so easy, so simple. And, yet my mother always made it seem so impossible.'

Maverick didn't interrupt. He listened intently.

'I worked so hard. I'd work doubles, and Luigi would let me even though he had enough staff to cover the shift and probably would have preferred not to pay me overtime, and the day I got my first paycheque . . .' She laughed lightly.

'Did you buy something ridiculous?' he asked, and he hoped that she had, that she had bought something just for herself.

'I did. It was so silly, but I had always wanted a fancy makeup box. You know, one of those ones with all the neat compartments and cubbies for your brushes.' She frowned. 'I don't even know why I wanted it. I didn't own any makeup, wouldn't have known how to put it on if I had. But that was the first thing I ever bought just for me.'

'Did you fill it with makeup?'

'No.' She laughed softly. 'My mom . . . She, ah, found it before I had a chance . . .'

She didn't have to say more. Mav exhaled a tight breath. 'Well. Fuck.'

Nina sighed. 'She stopped working completely, started taking my paycheques. But it didn't matter. Because every time she did, I'd watch her, and I'd promise myself that on the day I turned eighteen I'd leave and never look back. And I did. And my mother sobbed hysterically. And I didn't feel a single thing. No guilt. No regret. No love. Because I knew in my heart that she wasn't crying for me, only for herself.'

'How did you go from waitressing to acting?'

She shook her head on a laugh. 'Luigi had a love for old films. He'd play them on this tiny box television in the restaurant kitchen. *Meet me in St Louis*, *The Maltese Falcon*, *His Girl Friday* . . . And one day – I was about sixteen – I happened to be coming off a shift as *Casablanca* was starting. And the next thing I know, it's an hour and forty minutes later and I'm still there, watching the credits, tears streaming down my face.'

'And that was it?'

'No. Acting didn't even cross my mind. But Luigi was there, standing beside me. And he looked down at me, and he asked, "You ever thought about acting?"'

Maverick laughed at her Italian-American accent.

'And when I said no, he shrugged, said, "You got a face on you. And I've seen you sell a two-day old cannolo to a lady from Beverly Hills. Don't figure it takes much more than that."'

'I started thinking about it. Soon, I couldn't get it out of my head.'

'That's pretty incredible,' he said. It was a huge understatement. He didn't know why it mattered so much, but Maverick appreciated that she had worked like a dog for what she wanted. Maybe it was because he had done the same? He might have been born with more, but when you lived on the land you owned it was only as valuable as the work you put into it. Not very many people understood that. They didn't see the sweat and blood and uncertainty. All they saw was the value of the square footage to a developer.

Maybe it was because her story affirmed everything he already thought about her? Nina Keller wasn't someone who was afraid to get her hands dirty. She was a beautiful woman who was down to earth because she knew what it was to come from nothing, to work for what she wanted every day, and to make sacrifices to realize her dreams.

'It's certainly worked out for me so far,' she said. But her eyes changed, becoming so sad again. 'And I always have waitressing to fall back on.' She cleared her throat, turned to look around the room. 'I better get cleaned up.'

Maverick hesitated. He wanted to ask her what she'd meant by that. He wanted to tell her she could trust him. But then Nina stood and started unzipping her suitcase, and Mav lost his courage. 'See you down there,' he said, and with one last tap to the doorframe, walked away.

Chapter 10

Though she slept for what felt like the first time in days, early the next morning, Nina woke in a panic from another nightmare, her hands raised to protect her face.

Her own breathing sawed through the room, and the moment she heard it, she rolled over and buried her face in the pillow, trying to muffle the sound. She didn't want Maverick to worry. She didn't want Poppy to hear her and resultantly test that innocent curiosity on this particular matter. How did one explain, to a five-year-old nonetheless, that you had traded your peace of mind and your pride for an Oscar?

The moment she was able to get her breathing back under control, Nina rolled over and picked up her phone. She checked her texts, saw that she had two. One from Markus.

Should be back at the ranch around four p.m. tmmrw! X

One from Alex, the producer of *Shadowlands*, who'd also been calling her every day even though she never answered. Nina's heart crept into her throat as she opened the message. Her hands trembled as she read it.

Hi Nina. Missing you on set. Alison said you were taking a few weeks to rest before we wrap up your last scene. Hope you're not gone too long. Let's win that Oscar.

The message was perfectly polite, the subtext so clear.

Nina wondered what would happen if she breached her contract and simply refused to go back and finish *Shadowlands*. She wondered if Alex actually had the balls to tie her up in court or if he'd just have the last scene rewritten for a body double to shoot.

Anxious and exhausted, Nina rolled out of bed. She pulled a pair of oversized sweatpants and a baggy sweater over her slinky pyjamas and quietly let herself out of the room.

Though the hallway was quiet in the early morning, she could hear a white noise machine coming from Poppy's bedroom opposite Maverick's. A faint pink glow crept from the same bedroom into the hallway through the door, which Maverick had left ajar.

Nina was so terrified of waking Poppy up that she took minutes just to get to the staircase, her every footstep exaggeratedly silent on the hardwood. Every time the house creaked beneath her, she froze on the spot and listened.

When she came to the stairs, she took them slowly in the hope that she wouldn't make a sound. It was only when she got halfway down and heard a noise that she glanced up and saw Poppy standing on the landing.

Nina jumped. 'Poppy!' she gasped. 'You scared me.'

Poppy only tilted her head. 'What are you doing?'

Nina supposed she looked like a real idiot. Still, she explained, 'I was trying to be quiet, so I didn't wake you up.'

Poppy frowned. 'But I'm awake.'

'I see that.' Nina hesitated for only a moment before asking, 'You wouldn't know where your dad keeps the coffee, would you?'

'Yeah.' Poppy started down the stairs. She paused on Nina's step, craned her head back to look up at her, and said, 'I forgot to pee.'

Nina blinked. Was a five-year-old potty trained? She didn't even know. Poppy seemed pretty independent. Still, unsure of what to do, Nina simply replied, 'Okay . . .'

'Wait here for me to come back.'

The demand was issued in such a serious tone that Nina barely refrained from smiling. 'You betcha.'

Poppy hurried back up the stairs, only pausing to look back and check that Nina had stayed where she said she would.

Nina leaned her back against the wall as she waited and thought about the day ahead.

Markus would be arriving that afternoon.

Although they had been texting back and forth the entire week, Nina had purposefully refrained from telling him about her move to the ranch house yesterday. Markus was many things, but he would always be a worrier first and foremost, and if he received news like that via text, he would have panicked. And he would have come right away, even though Nina was enjoying the space.

So, she had refrained. And when he arrived, she would have to tell him that she had been caught sleeping in the bathtub, and she would have to convince him all over again that she didn't need security, and that knowing you were safe and *feeling* safe could be two completely different issues.

She groaned aloud at the thought. She was so tired of the guilt and the fear, and although Markus had the best of intentions, his hovering only served to remind her of everything that had happened.

''Kay, I'm ready now.' Poppy hurried back down the stairs until she was at Nina's level again. Without pausing, she grabbed Nina's hand and started tugging her down the stairs towards the kitchen.

'My dad likes coffee, too.'

'Oh, yeah?'

'Yeah. He drinks lots of it.' With barely a breath, she continued with: 'I don't like it. It tastes funny.'

Nina thought about that. 'It *does* taste funny.'

'I like juice,' Poppy offered.

'Oh, me too.' As Poppy led her to the full pot of coffee and showed her the mugs on the mug tree on the counter, Nina kept the conversation going. 'What's your favourite juice?'

'Apple.'

'Apple juice is good.' Nina poured herself a cup from the pot, took the first sip black to kick-start her brain before walking to the fridge to search for some milk.

Poppy watched in silence as she added milk to her coffee. Her gaze was so intent on Nina's face that she explained, 'It makes it taste better.'

But instead of acknowledging the comment, Poppy asked, 'What happened to your face?'

Nina's hand shot up immediately, covering as much of the yellow bruising as she could. She had been so consumed with thoughts of Markus's arrival, so ingrained in her morning routine and sourcing coffee, that she hadn't even stopped to consider her bruises, or how they would stand out under the bright kitchen lights.

What the hell did she say? Poppy was five. She was so sweet and innocent and free, and Nina didn't want to be the one to indoctrinate her into the real world.

For a long moment they just stood there, staring at one another, Poppy's eyes full of curiosity, Nina's full of doubt and pain.

That's how Maverick found them. Standing in the kitchen, staring at one another, Nina's hand covering her face.

'Good morning,' he said tentatively.

'Daddy!' Poppy ran to him.

He scooped her up instantly, planted a noisy kiss on her cheek. 'What were you guys talking about?' he asked, more concerned by the look that had been on Nina's face than Poppy's.

'I just wanted to know how she got her ouchie.'

'Ah.' Maverick put her down.

'Ouchie' was a word he thought Poppy had grown out of, but he supposed she might not have the vocabulary to describe the yellow mottling on Nina's face.

Nina herself was eerily silent, and unwilling to share her story without her permission, even with a child, Mav tried to generalize. 'Nina got hurt.'

'How?' Poppy asked.

He groaned internally. For a moment he considered lying, considered telling Poppy that Nina had fallen down the stairs or something similar. But before he could give life to the words, Nina intervened. She walked to Poppy, crouched down to her level, and in a voice that was so quiet, said, 'I got hurt by a bad man.'

Mav watched Poppy's face, and he wondered if it was ever too early to explain to a little girl that the world was full of predators? Was it ever too early to try and make them understand why they had to be careful all the time even though it wasn't fair?

Poppy's eyes widened. She didn't ask 'Why?' or 'Who?' She knew that bad people existed in the world, even if it was only through Disney. She looked at *him* and she said, 'But you won't let him hurt her again.'

Mav's heart softened at the absolute faith she had in him. But he angled his face to look at Nina, said, 'No. I won't.'

Nina seemed to be struggling with the emotional exchange. Her lips wobbled, and even as she fought her tears, he saw the way they filled her eyes, making them look like two black, inky pools.

Mav wasn't sure what to do. He wanted to go to her, to hold her, even as he told himself that she wouldn't welcome the touch and that he needed to keep his distance.

It was Poppy who reached up one tiny hand to trace the bruises on Nina's face, and when Nina smiled shakily at the sweet gesture, Poppy stood on her tippy toes and kissed Nina's face, whispered, 'All better.'

Instead of falling apart as he'd expected, Nina pulled herself together. He watched as she engaged that part of herself that had made her famous, saw her eyes dry and her smile brighten even though he knew it cost her. She said, 'It *does* feel better. Thank you, Poppy.'

'Poppy, why don't you go get your hairbrush,' he suggested, pushing them into safer territory. 'We can get a head start while we have coffee on the porch.'

"Kay.' She paused on her way out to remind him. 'But I don't want coffee.'

'I know, baby.'

He waited until her little feet sounded up the stairs before turning back to face Nina.

Before he could say anything, she pushed to her feet, whispered, 'I'm so sorry. I froze. I didn't know what to say.'

'Neither did I,' he admitted. He went to pour himself a cup of coffee from the pot behind her. 'But we figured it out.'

She raised that hand back to her cheek. 'That might have been the sweetest thing anyone has ever done for me.'

Because her voice shook, he nudged her arm with his elbow. 'You okay?'

'Not really.' She laughed tiredly and turned those sad eyes on him. 'But I'm trying really hard not to fall apart after everything you've done for me. And Poppy . . .'

'Nobody does emotions like kids. They don't regulate their own, and they don't judge other people for having or expressing them.'

Nina didn't shy away from the personal topic or change the subject as he'd expected her to. She said, 'I'm terrified that if I let too much of it in, I won't be able to pull myself out of it again.' She stared into her coffee mug. 'I just want to go back, you know – back to who I was ten days ago. It's hard to explain . . .'

'Hey . . .' Maverick waited for her to look at him again before he spoke again. 'You were seriously hurt. It's gonna take a while. It's *supposed* to take a while . . .'

She didn't reply. But she was standing so close that every one of her soft exhalations whispered across his throat at his open collar. She sighed softly, and his concern started shifting, started taking on a sharper edge.

Her eyes darkened and lowered to his lips as if considering . . .

Christ, he wanted her.

Feeling the pull of those huge, dark eyes, he lowered his head, moving closer. Though he wasn't aware of doing it, he put his mug on the counter.

Nina didn't shy away. To his absolute shock, it was her who rose onto her toes and kissed him gently. It was only one kiss. A sweet, soft meeting of lips that should have been innocent but that tore through him in a river of black greed.

Knowing what she had been through, Maverick tensed against it, against the urge to pin her hips against the counter and hold her in place as he took her mouth.

Nina felt it, and she misinterpreted his tension. She broke away immediately. 'I'm sorry. That was an accident. I—'

'Do it on purpose this time.'

She stopped moving and stared up at him. 'What?'

'If that was an accident, do it again. On purpose this time.' The request came out as a demand, but only because he desperately needed to know if he'd imagined that rush of need.

Nina seemed unsure of herself for only a moment, but one look at his face seemed to fill her with enough courage to close the small space she'd put between them. She rose up on her toes and roped both of her arms around his neck. She stared up at him, those big eyes wide and uncertain. 'I'm not good at this,' she whispered.

Astounded by her insecurity, but too afraid he might scare her, Maverick didn't pull her against him as he would have liked. She only needed to feel how impossibly hard he was to know that she was doing just fine. Instead, he raised one hand to her face. He gently tilted her eyes back to his and let his own barriers down, showing her the intensity of his need. 'There's nothing you could do that I wouldn't find impossibly sexy.'

Nina nodded uncertainly, but she took a deep breath, pressed her lips to his, and when he opened, welcoming her, she sighed into him as if she hadn't known something as simple as a kiss could be so consuming.

Mav wasn't entirely sure he had known either, but when Nina Keller kissed him, the world fell away. It was just the two of them, spinning into eternity, together.

Bending a little to compensate for their height difference, he took them deeper, and when Nina didn't shy away but pressed her lithe body against his, he cautiously placed his hands on her narrow waist.

She trembled, and instead of moving away, he broke the kiss to trail his lips down her neck as his hands ran up and down her sides in soothing strokes. But when the trembling didn't stop, Mav wrapped both arms around her and held her gently against his chest. 'Are you scared?'

'A little,' she admitted. 'But not of you.'

'I'm a little scared too,' he said. Half of him regretted that he'd told her such a personal truth, while the other half of him had known it was coming and had started to prepare for the fact that this woman would turn his careful life upside down.

Nina was an odd combination of vulnerable and tough that he found intensely attractive. Her stunning face and willow-neat figure didn't hurt either, of course. But it was her, the way she constantly fought for herself, that appealed to him. Because even as he worried that they led completely different lives and that he didn't do casual, he *wanted* her, desperately.

He now knew that her kisses knocked him as flat as her big eyes first had. But it wasn't enough. It would never be enough. Because now that he'd kissed her, he only wanted more. He wanted to know what her naked body would feel like in his hands and if her taste would drive him wild. He wanted to take her higher than she'd ever gone and then watch her shatter. And, surprisingly, he wanted those quiet moments after too. Those moments when she was soft and sleepy and vulnerable – and in his bed.

His need for all of her just then was so overpowering that he felt he had to warn her. 'You know where this is going.' It was pointless trying to deny it. And when he looked down at her, her eyes told him that she knew it too.

For one long moment, neither of them said anything.

But it was Nina who spoke first. 'I know where this is going.' And there was no doubt in her voice. 'But I . . . I need time, I guess . . .' she admitted quietly. 'I don't want you to think I'm not . . . *aware*.' She flushed. 'Or that I'm weak for being scared.'

'I don't think you're weak.' Reaching out one hand, he cupped her chin and brushed her cheek with his thumb. 'Christ, I think you might be one of the strongest people I know.' But because knowing that she was afraid was all the information he needed, he broke contact and, moving to the counter, picked up his coffee again.

Nina smiled. 'I'm going to regret how honourable you are later.'

'I'll still be around later,' he said, and although it was meant to make her laugh – and did – he shocked himself by how serious he was.

From the first moment he'd seen her, he'd had to remind himself that she was a paying guest, here for a month-long retreat. Nothing more. But his attraction had only grown as he'd started getting to know her. And now, when his logic was put up against that same attraction, it almost didn't matter that they were from separate worlds with nearly no hope of anything serious ever developing between them. The pull was that strong.

Overwhelmed by the kiss, Maverick picked up the thread of their previous conversation. 'I know what you mean – when you say you're scared to let go.'

She didn't push, only waited.

He wasn't even sure why he chose to share. Maybe it was

because he wanted her to understand that everyone went through it, and that there was no shame in being vulnerable. Maybe it was because he liked talking to her, liked getting to know her. 'When my ex left, it took a lot out of me. Poppy was only a few months old, and the resort was the busiest it had ever been . . .'

He thought back, felt exhausted at the memory of the long days followed by the sleepless nights with an infant. 'It felt like Groundhog Day in hell. Over and over. I would work all day and then put Poppy down, and by the time I fell into bed I was so exhausted I couldn't sleep. And then as my eyes were closing, she'd wake up for the first time.

'It was the lowest I'd ever been in my entire life. But I refused to admit it because I was so ashamed. Ashamed that Shannon had left me, ashamed that I couldn't care for my child.

'I just kept going. For months on end. Until, one day, I lost my shit down at the barn.'

Nina smiled. 'Over what?'

'Nina, I swear to you, I can't even remember. It was something ridiculously small, like a broken bridle or a stall that hadn't been cleaned perfectly. I just lost it, started screaming and shouting. And then I turn the corner, and Benji, José, and Riley are all just standing there, staring at me. And José asks, "Everything okay, boss?" And I just broke down.'

'Cried like a baby?'

'No, ma'am. Babies are supposed to cry. I cried like a grown man having a mental breakdown.'

She gave him that small half-smile. 'Not very rugged of you.'

Maverick grinned. He appreciated her sense of humour. It kinda came out of nowhere when a person least expected it.

'Nope,' he agreed. 'It was humiliating. But it might have been the best thing that ever happened to me, because then everyone else knew how deep in it I was. By that evening, José's mom, Marisol, had moved into my spare room to help with the night shifts – I didn't even know that a night nurse was a thing. Sierra covered the early morning shift for me so that I could catch up on the sleep I'd lost. Benji picked up my lessons when he could. And, slowly, I came out of it. But it took a really long time and a lot of help, and even then, there are still days where it all feels like too much.'

He looked at her. 'So, even though I haven't lived through what you have, I know what you mean when you say you're worried about not being able to pull yourself out of it. But you will. And you don't have to do it alone.'

'You've helped me so much already,' she said immediately. 'I don't want to be a burden.' The denial, the refusal of any help he might have offered was instant and instinctual.

But Maverick didn't let her get away with it. 'You're not a burden. I've enjoyed every minute I've spent with you.' When she blushed, he only tipped his head, added, 'Clearly.'

He watched her face as she processed that, saw the hesitation and pleasure warring for the upper hand in her dark irises.

She didn't acknowledge it though. She asked, 'Can I ask you a personal question?'

Maverick could have laughed at her blatant redirection. 'I think we're about at that stage.'

'Why did she leave? Your ex? I keep looking at you, waiting for that big red flag, that ah-ha moment that clues me in as to why any woman with half a brain would leave. But so far, I haven't figured it out.'

The question, the reminder of Shannon, was like a bucket of cold water to the face. It doused the last of his lust and sharpened his mind, reminding him why he'd promised not to cross that line with Nina even as he watched it disappear behind him.

But he answered her truthfully. 'My sister thought she might have had some postpartum depression . . .'. He shook his head. 'But Sierra didn't know Shannon like I did.' Mav remembered how upset Shannon had been when she'd told him she was pregnant. 'I think we fell pregnant when she didn't want to, and she panicked. She made decisions that took her further and further from her modelling career.'

'She's a model?' Nina asked. Before Mav could reply, recognition dawned in her eyes. '*Shannon*? Shannon Carlyle?'

'Yeah.'

'I didn't even know she had a kid.'

'Not many people do. According to Sierra, she'll occasionally screenshot a Hunt Ranch photo of Poppy and share it with a caption about how big her baby's getting, but other than that, she's largely out of the picture.'

'Why don't you hate her?' Nina asked. 'When you talk about her, you sound sad. But not angry.'

'I didn't help her enough,' he admitted. 'I tried. But I always seemed to fall short. I never really saw myself having kids with her specifically, but from the moment she told me she was pregnant, I was—' he shook his head, searching for the right word before settling on: '*thrilled*. And I don't know . . . Maybe I pressured her. That's what she said, right before she left. That I had pressured her into having Poppy, into getting engaged . . .

'But Shannon had never wanted that future. She wanted the city penthouse and glamorous modelling career and late nights at cocktail bars. I wanted the exact opposite – the ranch and the work and the big family.

'And, yeah, I think she struggled as much as any new mom those first months.' He had to catch his own shudder. 'It's a rough time, for anyone. But I think, for Shannon, more than that, those first few months showed her how much you have to give once you have a kid. She panicked. She couldn't look at it as a temporary stage, the newborn stage. Couldn't imagine a future where Poppy would be old enough to be in daycare and she could get back to her career . . .'

'So, she filed for divorce?'

Mav took a sip from his own coffee. 'We were never married. We had only been dating about six months when she fell pregnant.

We got engaged,' he offered. 'But marriage was my idea of trying to fix everything. I wanted her to know that I'd always stick, you know.'

'Did you love her?'

Mav thought about that. He wasn't sure anymore. They had said the words to each other, and at the time he had thought he had. 'I'm not sure,' he admitted finally. 'I wanted to, especially after I had proposed. I'm the result of one of those age-old romances,' he explained, 'and I always wanted the marriage my parents had. But I didn't feel heartbroken when she left. I felt ashamed. And embarrassed. Hurt. Lacking.'

He took a moment to process that, to think about how much of his grief and pain had been shame and pride rather than true heartbreak or betrayal. 'And Poppy barely gave me time to focus on it.'

'I'm sorry. That sounds rough.'

'It was,' he admitted. 'Sometimes it still is. But it was also the best thing that ever happened to me. Because I got Poppy without a messy fight.'

As if their conversation had summoned her, Poppy's feet sounded on the stairs again.

'Does she ever call? Or visit?' Nina dropped her voice.

Mav was too busy watching her as she took a glass down from the cabinet and filled it halfway with apple juice from the fridge to give her a proper answer, and only managed a distracted: 'Not really.'

'I found it!' Poppy came in wielding her hairbrush like a sword. 'I thought it was lost. But it was in my Dreamhouse.'

Maverick distractedly held out his hand for the brush, but Poppy didn't even notice. She went straight to Nina and passed it to her.

Nina took it without a word and passed Poppy the glass of apple juice in exchange.

'Thanks,' Poppy chirped. But she turned serious eyes on Mav.

'Am I allowed the glass?'

'Oh.' Nina turned concerned eyes on Maverick. 'I didn't realize...'

As they both stood there, staring at him, Maverick felt a pinch in his chest. It was so strong, so tight, that he chose to ignore it. 'It's okay,' he said, knowing that Poppy would have to transition from her plastic cups sooner or later. But he reminded her, 'Be careful, okay?'

''Kay!' Poppy took the apple juice in one hand and Nina's wrist in the other.

Maverick watched them go in stunned silence. He wasn't exactly sure what had just happened but figured at some point he'd have to deal with the fact that after just twelve hours, Nina Keller already knew more about Poppy than Shannon ever had.

It disconcerted him. He and Nina getting to know one another was one thing but inviting her into Poppy's life might have been a mistake, especially when she was only at the ranch temporarily.

Unsure of the new territory he was navigating, Mav pushed it from his mind for now.

He picked up his coffee and followed them outside.

They were sitting side by side on the steps, looking out at the ranch by the time he got there. While Nina's pin-straight hair fell almost to her hips, Poppy's was a wild tangle that had Mav wincing.

Luckily for him, the first thing he heard was: 'Nina, do you know how to do a French braid?'

'I sure do,' Nina replied.

'Can you do one in my hair?' Poppy asked and raised one tiny hand to her tangled hair. 'Daddy only knows how to do the American one.'

Nina turned to him, dark eyes glinting. 'The American one?'

He shrugged. 'It seemed fitting.'

She turned back to Poppy. 'Come sit here.' She tapped the stair below her and waited for Poppy to sit between her knees before starting on the bird's nest of hair.

'Mind if I watch?' Mav asked. 'I've been promising to get to a YouTube tutorial for about six months now.'

Nina only patted the space beside her in reply.

Mav sat down, his coffee in one hand. He sat close enough to watch but kept enough distance between them to make Nina comfortable.

And as she painstakingly brushed and then *perfectly* braided Poppy's hair, explaining each step to Mav as she worked, he decided that kissing Nina had been a terrible mistake. Because even though he knew they were from opposite worlds with little chance of anything serious developing between them, he was desperate to kiss her again. As soon as possible. She could choose the time and the place and how far it would go. But the only thing he knew with certainty was that if he didn't, he would regret it for the rest of his life.

Chapter 11

'I leave you alone for five days and this is what I come back to?'

Markus heaved his suitcase onto the bed in the Hunts' second guest room, which Sierra had cleaned out for him. Although he was only staying through Sunday morning, his brown leather suitcase was as big as Nina's.

'What's in there?' she asked, eyeing the straining zipper. 'You're here for *two nights*.'

'Only the essentials. And don't change the subject. Five days, Neens. I leave you alone for five days and you move in with the cowboy and his family?'

'It's not like that,' Nina insisted. Because it wasn't. Technically. . . . Yet.

'I know it's not like that,' Markus stated. 'I'm your best friend. I know you. And you barely date. You don't do relationships – especially after five days. Which means that either something is wrong, or something bad has already happened and you never told me.'

'I knew you would stress. I knew you would drop everything to be here, and . . .' Nina sighed. She wasn't sure how to tell him he was worrying needlessly and smothering her in the process. 'I don't need you to worry. I'm doing fine, Markus.' She thought about the time she'd spent with the horses and with Maverick and Benji and José, and added, 'I'm good.'

Markus knew her better than anyone, so he knew that she was telling the truth. But he still asked, 'So, why are you staying here? If you were warming the sheets with Maverick, I would be all for it. But seeing as though you're not . . .'

Nina couldn't quite contain her blush. The whole truth was that when Nina had told Mav that she was afraid, she had been talking about her inexperience.

She wasn't exactly the siren her films made her out to be.

Markus saw her blush as it spread fire across her pale cheeks. '*Oh. My. God. Are* you banging the cowboy?'

'Shhh!'

Markus gasped dramatically. 'You are!'

'No.' Nina cast a panicked glance at the door. 'And keep your voice down. There's a five-year-old in the house.'

Markus lowered his voice to a dramatic whisper. 'Are you banging the cowboy?'

'No,' she hissed back.

'Oh.' Markus's face fell. 'Boo.'

And because he was her best friend, she admitted, 'But I want to.'

'Yas!' Markus started happy dancing right there in the Hunts' guest room.

Nina watched him, and she couldn't help but smile at his antics. 'I missed you,' she said loudly, trying to get his attention over his bopping and weaving.

Markus stopped dancing. 'I missed you too, Neens.' He tapped her on the nose. 'But don't think you're changing the subject on me.' He sat on the bed, crossed one leg over the other. 'Spill!'

'There's nothing to tell really. Nothing much has happened yet.' It wasn't technically true, but Nina wasn't ready to share the details of the kiss. She wanted to hold on to it, to keep it for herself, just a little longer.

'*Yet?* All I'm hearing is that you *want* something to happen!' He clapped his hands excitedly. 'Nina, in all the years I've known you, you have never, not once, thought about jumping into bed with a man. Especially one who is so clearly relationship material.'

'That's not true.'

'It is,' Markus argued immediately. 'You've hooked up a few times, sure. But you only ever chose men you wouldn't miss. And once you landed *Camelot* and people started recognizing your face, you pulled back completely. I mean, you know I don't usually snoop in this area, but when was the last time your girl got some exercise?'

Nina groaned aloud, anxious all over again. 'Since about a month before *Camelot* came out.'

Markus was speechless.

'It's hard,' she said, feeling the need to justify her actions, or lack thereof. 'If I go on a date, do I have them sign an NDA beforehand, or do I just not tell them anything I don't want the world to know? And if I do that, are they really dating me or Famous Nina Keller? And if I have sex with a date, do I have to worry that they'll brag about it because I'm famous? Do I have to worry that they'll tell all their friends what my body looks like naked or if I'm bad in bed?'

Markus didn't focus on any of that. He said, '*Camelot* was . . . four . . . Are you telling me it's been *four years* since you got laid?'

'Shhh! *Markus!*' Nina cast an anxious glance at the door.

'Okay. Okay.' But he still shook his head one last time as he came to terms with her celibacy. 'Also, the world knows what your glorious body looks like since you did the nude scene in *Dogs of Despair*. Your problem,' he told her, 'is that you don't trust men in general.' Before she could argue, he held up both hands, raised his voice. 'I'm not saying I don't understand why. Lulu did a number on you in that department, so it's allowed. But not all men are untrustworthy.'

'I know that,' she insisted. 'I trust you.'

'Oh, baby. That's only because I'm your soulmate.'

'I trust Maverick Hunt.'

'Well. Shit.'

'He's *different*, Markus. Really, truly different. But he is so clearly a long-haul kind of guy. He has a kid, for Pete's sake! And his ex really hurt him.' Nina thought about what Maverick had told her about Shannon, and added, 'He's *so good*. And I don't want to hurt him.'

'Nina, I say this with all the love in my heart and the carnal motivation of a male sex drive: he's a single man with a kid. The dude is probably in desperate need of a lay. You'd be doing him a favour, really.'

Nina laughed even though she knew it wasn't that simple, that Maverick wasn't that simple.

'Good Lord, baby. Go for it! If you're that scared about hurting him, just be clear from the start. Maverick is a grown man who is perfectly capable of making his own decisions. And I don't have to remind you, you are seriously smart. And you're cautious. You don't fuck around, so if you feel like you wanna do the dance with the cowboy, then do the damn dance! We are thirty-three years old,' he said, his tone turning serious. 'Life isn't going to slow down for us to live it anymore.'

'I'm thirty-four,' she reminded him.

'Not for another five days,' he countered immediately. 'And, even then, you're only proving my point.'

'I'll think about it,' Nina promised. Because as much as Markus was right about Maverick being a grown man, capable of making his own decisions, Nina knew that he never made any decision lightly and so she worried about that pull between them. If she thought it would just be sex, she would have been more confident.

But she already knew it wouldn't just be sex.

Yes, she liked the way he looked. Yes, she felt that same heat. Of course she did. But it was more than that. She was an actress, as used to working with handsome, charismatic men as she was brushing her teeth, which is how she knew that Maverick Hunt was different.

She liked how strong but quiet he was, how competent. If a problem arose, Maverick handled it without a word of complaint. She loved watching him with the horses. He was so openly gentle and caring. And she'd only had to see him once with Poppy to know that he was a great dad.

'See that you do—' Markus's words were cut off by a timid knock on the door.

Poppy's little voice followed. 'Nina?'

'Come in, Poppy,' Nina prompted gently.

Poppy opened the door and walked in, a hairbrush in her hand. Her big brown eyes narrowed in on Markus sitting on the bed, close to Nina.

'Is she gonna laser vision me to death?' he whispered.

Nina introduced him. 'This is Markus.'

Poppy didn't say hi. She asked, 'Is he your boyfriend?'

'No. He's my *best* friend,' Nina replied, hoping to ease Poppy's mistrust. 'He came to visit me for the weekend.'

Poppy stopped a few feet in front of them, but she didn't take her eyes off Markus. 'Do you know the bad man?'

'The bad man?' Markus looked at Nina in question.

'Oh.' Nina's heart hurt at Poppy's anger on her behalf. 'Markus is the one who saved me from the bad man,' she hurried to explain. She turned to Markus. 'The attacker,' she explained.

Poppy seemed to consider this new information for a moment before nodding. 'My dad's not gonna let the bad man come here.'

Markus only raised both his brows in Nina's direction, said, 'Girl.'

'I know,' Nina replied.

'If I don't have ovaries, I just grew a pair,' he muttered. But he turned back to Poppy. 'Lady, I like your outfit.'

Poppy looked down at her white dress and brown cowgirl boots. 'It's my favourite.' She shook her long hair back, said, 'I dressed myself.'

'Okay, diva. You have style.' He made a twirling gesture with his finger, and when Poppy instinctually twirled, Markus clapped his hands. 'Gorgeous!'

Nina looked down at her phone, noted it was near six o'clock. 'Where are you going all dressed up?'

'Oh, yeah.' Poppy laughed. 'I was supposed to ask you if you wanted to come to the barbecue with us.'

Nina opened her mouth to refuse. Just the idea of all those people made her feel queasy.

But Markus didn't give her a chance. 'We would love to! Especially if we get to dress up too!'

Poppy beamed at him. 'It's fun. And there's dancing and music and food,' she added in her sing-song voice.

'My three favourite things,' Markus declared.

'Mine too!' Poppy laughed, immediately forgetting her initial scepticism.

Nina sighed and resigned herself to the fact that she would be attending her first resort event. She saw the hairbrush in Poppy's hand, noticed that her hair was still slightly damp from being freshly washed. 'Did you want me to re-braid your hair?'

'Yeah. The French braid.' Poppy passed her the brush and knelt on the floor between Nina's knees without being prompted.

Nina stoically ignored Markus's shocked silence and instead focused on Poppy. 'What about a waterfall braid?'

Poppy angled her head back. 'What's that?'

Nina pulled up a picture on her phone and showed it to Poppy.

The five-year-old stared at her with big eyes. 'You can do that?' she asked, her tone reverent.

'I usually only do it in my hair, but I can try if you want?'

Poppy nodded eagerly.

'Okay. Look forward for me.' As soon as she complied, Nina began brushing out Poppy's hair, but because Markus hadn't stopped staring at her, she explained, 'Maverick only knows how to do a normal braid.'

'The American one,' Poppy chirped over her shoulder.

Markus held a hand to his heart and rolled his eyes dramatically, clearly as enamoured by Poppy as Nina was. And when he spoke, he said something she hadn't expected. He said, 'Okay. I get it now.'

Nina only nodded. Because *wanting* and *needing* could be two separate matters entirely. She wanted to test the waters with Maverick. But want was simple. Nina was terrified that her want might turn into need, and she couldn't start needing someone else. She *needed* to get back onto her feet. She *needed* to be independent again, strong without Markus and Maverick's strength holding her up.

And Maverick had needs too, she reminded herself. He might *want* Nina, but he *needed* someone who could eventually make a commitment, to him and to Poppy. He needed someone who wouldn't choose her career over them like Shannon had, and – if she still had a career to go back to – like Nina would.

For the last fifteen years her career had been everything to her. In fact, on most days, it was all she had.

So, want was simple. But they would both have to think through what they *needed* before they acted on that want. In Nina's mind, that was just the reality of two adults who were attracted to each other but lived complicated lives.

Poppy came down the stairs at a full-blown run. 'Daddy! Daddy, look at my hair!' She skidded to a halt right in front of him and then spun in a circle, showing him her fancy braid, which formed a tiara around her head before spilling down her back.

'That is seriously cool,' he said. But internally, he panicked just a little because he hadn't even managed to get the French braid yet. Despite Nina's patient instruction, he had only managed to irritate three horses that morning with his fumbling attempts to French braid their tails.

'Nina did it!'

'She did a good job.' Maverick looked up the stairs. 'Did you ask them if they're coming to the barbecue?'

'Yeah. They're coming. Her friend—'

'Markus.'

'Markus said he had to glam up.'

Behind him, Sierra, who had caught the last snippet of the conversation, said, 'If you need to get down there, I'll bring them when they're ready.'

Maverick looked down at his watch. 'Yeah. That would be helpful.' He looked at Poppy, all dressed up and ready to go. 'Do you want to ride with me?'

'No, I want to wait for Nina.'

Maverick hesitated to leave her, and not because there wasn't space, but because he wanted to be cautious. 'Poppy, Nina's on vacation,' he said gently. 'She's only here for a short while, so you have to give her a little space to relax, okay?'

Poppy's big eyes turned sad. She looked so downhearted, and it crushed him. But she whispered, 'Yes, Daddy.'

His gentle redirecting ended up turning to dust anyway. The moment Nina appeared at the top of the stairs, she asked, 'Are you guys leaving?'

'Poppy and I figured we'd head out, let Sierra bring you and Markus,' Mav replied.

Nina started down the stairs, dressed almost identically to Poppy in a white dress, her working cowgirl boots, covered in dust, and the same fancy tiara braid in her long, black hair. 'Are you sure you don't mind waiting for Markus, Sierra? He takes a while to get ready,' she warned.

'Not at all. I could really use a glass of wine before heading back to work anyway. You three go.'

'Nina, you look like me!' Poppy exclaimed.

'I know!' Nina twirled, making her long, black hair fan out around her with the skirt of her dress. 'I thought we could twin.'

'Daddy,' Poppy turned those big eyes on him. '*Please* can Nina come with us?'

'Sure, kiddo,' Mav said. Relenting was easy. But it didn't stop the worry.

The closer the girls got to one another, the more he worried that Poppy would get hurt when Nina left. Because while Maverick was a grown man who understood what he was getting into and had his eyes wide open, Poppy was only five. When she loved, she loved instantly and with her whole heart. And it was his job to protect her from pain until she could learn to do it herself.

Nina clearly sensed his hesitance. She cocked her head slightly, asked, 'Everything okay?'

By way of answer, Maverick said, 'Not at all.' And when she only raised both brows, he added, 'You ladies don't have your hats.'

'Our hats?' Nina asked.

'Our dancing hats!' Poppy chirped. She ran to the hall closet.

'Poppy, get my red one for Nina!' Sierra called after her.

''Kay!'

Poppy returned a moment later, two cowgirl hats in her hands. Hers was pink suede with a single faux pink rose in the hatband. Sierra's, the one Poppy passed to Nina, was red leather.

'You don't mind?' Nina asked Sierra as she took the hat.

'No. I haven't worn one in years, and your black hair is just begging for that red.'

Nina plopped the hat on her head, tipped it back. 'How does it look?'

Sexy as hell, Mav thought, but because his mouth had gone dry, he just nodded like an idiot.

Sierra said, 'Movie worthy.'

Poppy gushed, 'We're so pretty!'

Nina held out her hand, and when Poppy took it unquestioningly, she said, 'Heck yes, we are.'

He watched them walk to the front door hand in hand, waited for them to amble outside before turning back to his sister. He had been meaning to check in with her one last time, but the look of wry amusement on her face stole his words. Was he that obvious?

Sierra started for the kitchen and her waiting glass of wine, but she tossed, 'You're in trouble, Mav!' over her shoulder as she left.

Maverick only sighed, muttered, 'I know it,' and followed them outside.

He loaded Shadow into the back seat of the Jeep and then climbed into the driver's seat. Poppy climbed through and perched on the armrest between him and Nina, something he allowed when they were on ranch property.

It was only once they were on their way that Nina asked, 'Are these barbecues a regular occasion? I haven't really explored any of the ranch activities yet.'

'We have some sort of outdoor event every night,' he replied, 'but it's not always barbecue.'

'*Every* night?'

'Yup. The schedule is posted in the lobby and on the website. We have guests checking in and out almost every day, so there has to be something happening every night. Sometimes it's just cocktails and appetizers by the lake. Sometimes it's a barbecue with live music – like tonight.'

'Daddy sings!' Poppy offered.

Nina didn't seem surprised. In fact, she sent him a comical look, said, 'Of course you do.'

'Not often.'

'But you'll sing for me sometime?' she asked, and when he groaned, she shot him an exaggerated version of puppy-dog eyes that made Poppy giggle.

'One time,' he decided. 'And I choose when and where.'

'Deal.' She turned back to the road and the approaching resort building. 'I suppose I never thought about how exhausting it must be, planning this all, day in and day out.'

'Yeah – but not so much for me anymore. We have an event planner on staff. He and his assistant do almost everything without any hand holding. The only time they need us anymore is if their budget isn't sufficient or if somebody makes a complaint.'

'Does that happen often?'

'Oh yeah. You can't charge the prices we do and not have people nitpick every detail. But for the most part, they're easy to appease.'

'The customer's always right?'

'Something like that.'

'I hate people like that,' she said. 'The level of entitlement always astounds me.'

'It doesn't bother me anymore. Used to, back when we first got started. But it helped us smooth things out.'

'What is the most ridiculous thing a person has ever complained about?'

Maverick thought about it. 'I don't hear about all of them anymore. We have a concierge who deals with those things, typically with Sierra's buyoff. But back in our first year, we had a woman complain that her towels weren't soft enough.'

Nina turned to stare at him. 'Please tell me you're joking.'

'Nope.' Maverick grinned. 'She had sensitive skin.'

'Bullsh-nap,' Nina caught herself before the word left her mouth.

But Poppy tucked her head and giggled anyway.

'I swear.' Maverick laughed. 'The funniest thing about it is that our resort towels are imported from Turkey. They're top of the line. Cost an arm and a leg. But when she complained, the only place open at nine p.m. was Target. The ones I replaced them with cost me like thirteen dollars.'

Nina laughed. 'What did she say?'

'She thanked me, gave me a long lecture about quality, and how if we wanted to make it as a resort, we'd have to up our game.'

'She did not.'

'Cross my heart.'

She shook her head. 'Unbelievable.'

Poppy saw the gesture and mimicked it. She shook her head

seriously, said, 'Unbelievable,' making Mav laugh out loud.

He chanced a glance at Nina.

She smiled back at him. It might have been the first full smile she had ever given him. Her dark eyes lit with it, stunning him senseless.

It shocked him that something as simple as a woman's smile could take him out. It worried him for so many reasons, least of all that he had only known her a week. It terrified him, because even as he told himself she was heartache waiting to happen, Maverick burned for her.

Chapter 12

When Markus came down, dressed in taupe pants, a white linen shirt, a Stetson, and snakeskin cowboy boots, he found Sierra alone in the kitchen, drinking a glass of white wine. He'd met her only briefly the day he'd checked Nina in, but their short acquaintance didn't detract from the fact that Sierra Hunt probably knew more about Nina's new living situation than he did. And Markus needed to know how Nina was really doing and why she'd been moved into the Hunts' private home. If he'd thought it was just because of the blatant attraction between Maverick and Nina, he wouldn't have worried so much. But Markus sensed there was more to it than that.

Still, he took his time, started with: 'Where is everyone?'

'They got a head start. Figured I'd wait for you and sneak an unofficial glass of wine before heading back.' She swirled her glass in his direction. 'Want one?'

'Always.'

Markus watched her as she went to the fridge and pulled out a bottle of Chardonnay. He figured good looks ran in the family. While Maverick and Poppy had dark chocolate hair, Sierra's was closer to honey-blonde in colour. But their skin was that same warm tone he thought of as Perpetual Tan in colour. While the strength in Maverick's body and the gentle wear on his face matched the fact that he worked outside and with his hands, Sierra had a tall, slender figure and smooth, unlined skin that hinted at a woman who looked after herself militantly.

'Do I have something on my face?' she asked, catching his direct perusal.

'Who does your Botox?'

'Au naturel.'

He might have called bullshit had he not seen the smirk on her face, so settled for a pout instead. 'I hate you.'

She shrugged. 'Good genetics.'

'That's for damn sure.'

He thanked her when she passed him the glass of chilled wine, took a small, deliberate sip, sighed in pleasure, and then pushed the conversation in the direction he wanted it to go. 'Okay. While I have you alone. Tell me everything about your brother.'

Sierra didn't shy away. She grinned wickedly. 'You see it too?'

'See it? The pheromones slapped me in the face the moment I walked in.' Sierra laughed, as he'd intended, but Markus reminded himself of what Nina had been through, and sobered. 'I'm not snooping,' he said.

Sierra leaned both elbows on the kitchen counter. 'Coulda fooled me.'

'Okay. I'm not *only* snooping,' he corrected. 'I'm really worried about her.'

Sierra tipped her head. She took a moment to think through it before replying, but when she did, the first thing she said was: 'He's been hurt. And he's closed that part of himself off since. I can count the number of dates he'd been on in five years on one hand – and I use the word "date" generously. But he's interested in Nina.'

'All that tells me is that he has eyes.' Markus took a bigger sip of wine. 'Have you *seen* my girl? Every man is *interested*. I want to know *who* he is and if he's worthy.'

Sierra ceded his point with a small nod. 'After his ex walked out to pursue her modelling career, he put everything into raising Poppy. And say what you want, but you only have to watch him with his kid to answer any question you have about his character.'

'Give me the SparkNotes anyway.'

Sierra shrugged, but she complied. 'Unfalteringly loyal. He'll stick, even when people don't deserve it.'

Markus noted the bitterness in her tone, and though he wondered over it, he didn't comment.

'Kind. Gentle. Patient. He saves and trains rescue horses, and he supplements the funding for them with his own paycheque when he thinks I'm not paying attention. He's stubborn. He can fight for what he wants, but he has to want it enough.

'Incredible singer,' she continued. 'Terrible cook unless it's scrambled eggs. Aquarius. And the fact that he's even looking in Nina's direction means he already cares.' She tipped her glass in his direction. 'Your turn.'

Markus didn't hesitate. 'She's nervous of men – even before the assault. Which is why I tend to be a little overprotective on this one issue.'

'Define *nervous*.'

'She's never dated seriously. Ever. Which, incidentally, means she already cares too.'

Sierra exhaled a surprised breath.

'She's fierce and determined. Hardworking. The best friend.' He grinned. 'Loyal. Stubborn. Also, can't cook. Gemini. And despite his gorgeous face, if your brother hurts her, I will eviscerate him.'

Sierra tapped her glass to his. 'Same goes, honey.'

Markus threw back his head and roared with laughter, making Sierra chuckle, and when he finally piped down enough to talk, he asked, 'Are we friends?'

Sierra nodded. 'Looks like.'

'Good.' He didn't waste any time. Leaning forward, he asked, 'So tell me, how did my girl end up moving in so fast?'

Sierra narrowed her eyes on his face, fully aware that she had been neatly trapped. 'Nina is still a paying guest at the ranch.'

Before she could add more, Markus held up one hand. 'Something happened. I know that. But she won't talk to me about it, and I'm terrified because ever since the attack, I've sensed . . .' He thought about how to explain to a virtual stranger that he knew in his heart that something was very, very wrong. 'I don't know. Something. Like she's not being entirely honest with me. And I'm really worried. She was hurt, Sierra. Badly. And even though she's still terrified, she's refused every attempt I've made to hire her protection. It doesn't make sense.'

Sierra didn't shrug off his concern. 'Yeah. Maverick's worried too.'

'So?'

'I don't know much. She hasn't offered, and I haven't asked. She only moved in last night, which coincidentally is the only time I've spoken to her for more than five minutes.'

'But *why* did she move in?'

'If you tell her I told you, I will deny it. And I will terminate this newfound friendship immediately,' she warned.

'I won't say anything – but I need to know.'

'She had been locking herself in her bathroom at night and sleeping in the bathtub.'

Markus swore.

Sierra continued cautiously. 'We only found out because she forgot to put the "Do Not Disturb" sign on the door one morning so housekeeping went in and found her bedding inside the tub.'

Markus scrubbed both hands over his face. 'Fuck.'

'Do we need to be concerned for her safety?'

'I don't know,' he replied honestly. 'I know she has some past trauma with this kind of thing – her mom was a junkie who let her Johns get too close a few times. But none of her behaviour since the attack has struck me as *normal* – if there is such a thing.'

'Yeah. We've been wondering too – about why she didn't bring close protection . . .'

'She told me it would just attract attention and that she wanted to get back to the way things were. I insisted. She pushed back – there's that stubborn streak. But, yeah, it's weird. I don't know if she's in denial, and I need to be here to protect her. Or if she's not telling me everything. Or both.'

'What are you going to do?' Sierra asked.

There was nothing he could do. Markus wasn't delusional, and there was a reason Nina was one of the few women who had actually made it in Hollywood. She was strong and independent but that didn't make him wish she'd lean on him a little too. 'Trust,' he said slowly, 'that she knows her own mind and knows what she needs to heal. Worry, because she's the other half of my heart and I can't just turn that off. Hope, that I'm just being paranoid and that your brother keeps an eye on her anyway.'

'He will.' Sierra reached out and squeezed his hand. 'As long as she's here, we all will.'

'Thank you.' Markus returned the squeeze. But because things had gotten far too serious far too fast, he threw back the last of his wine. 'Now, are you gonna show me a good time or what?'

Sierra held up her index finger, finished her own wine, and replied, 'Let me go put on my lipstick.'

'Blood red,' Markus told her.

Sierra pointed at him and nodded as she rounded the kitchen counter and hurried upstairs.

The Wagon Train at Hunt Ranch was a beautiful outdoor eating area by the lake. Three ancient oak trees circled the grassy lawn, the paved dance floor, and the small stage, forming a natural boundary. Two restored and outfitted wagons, one on either side of the clearing, served as bars. And, at least for tonight, a huge barbecue rig smoked happily away next to tables where staff were busy setting up a series of chafing dishes in preparation for dinner.

Nina, Maverick, and Poppy had claimed a cluster of wicker chairs right beneath one of the oak trees. As the band finished setting up, tuning their instruments and testing the mic, Maverick sipped a beer, Nina, a blended margarita.

It was a perfect June evening, the warm day cooling down to the mid-seventies. All around them, guests dressed in western attire formed little groups. Laughter rang through the air.

Nina was thinking how beautiful it was when she saw Markus and Sierra arrive, their arms linked, their heads bent together as they walked over.

In the big wicker chair next to the love seat she sat on, Maverick followed Nina's gaze. 'I haven't seen Sierra smile like that in a while.'

'Markus has a way about him,' Nina said fondly. 'He cares about making people happy. And he tries really hard – with everyone.'

Maverick didn't have a chance to reply as Markus and Sierra reached them. But he stood up immediately, asked, 'Can I get you two a drink?'

'I'll stick with Chardonnay,' Sierra replied and slipped onto the settee with Poppy.

'Markus?' Maverick swung his gaze to Markus.

'Uh, I'll have the same. Thanks.'

The band started playing and Sierra and Markus picked up their conversation, Nina covertly watched Maverick as he walked up to the bar. Whatever he said to the young bartender had the man grinning openly.

As the bartender turned to pour the wine, Maverick turned too. He leaned back against the bar and crossed his arms over his chest, surveying the crowd, Nina knew, observing, judging. Working.

He never stopped.

As he scanned the crowd of assembled guests, his eyes met hers. Held. That same message passed between them: *You know where this is going.*

Nina felt heavy, languid pleasure unfurl low in her belly. If they had been anywhere else just then, instead of surrounded by people who knew both of them, Nina would have risen from her chair and gone to him. Despite her inexperience and shyness, she *wanted* to be close to him.

Instead, she smiled.

Maverick winked before turning to pick up the two glasses of wine. He carried them back and this time, he didn't reclaim his empty chair but sat down on the love seat next to Nina.

He bumped her knee with his. It was just a quick touch, a lightly flirtatious gesture, but that didn't stop Nina's heart from tapping excitedly in her chest. Heat flooded her.

He was giving her the space to make the next move – she knew that – but because she didn't want to be overt in front of Poppy, Nina reached forward and picked her drink up off the low table in front of her, but this time, when she sat back again, she deliberately shifted closer, placing her thigh directly against his much larger, firmer one.

Only that small contact was enough to have her body pulling tight with anticipation. The flush of awareness running through her intensified, searing the blood in her veins until she knew her cheeks must be bright red with it.

Maverick didn't overtly react, instead he asked Markus, 'How was the drive up today?' and pressed his thigh more firmly against hers.

'Fine. It's one of those drives that's just long enough to be inconvenient.'

As they talked, the band started playing. They didn't waste time either, but jumped straight into a song even Nina, with her slight knowledge of country music, knew: 'Highwayman'.

Nina could barely focus on the music over the feeling of Maverick's leg against hers. Strangely, it reminded her of when she had been an extra in a movie in her early twenties. The screenplay's action had read, *In the seat next to Joe, a pretty teenage girl, giddy with the first flush of love, holds her boyfriend's hand.*

It might have been one of the smallest roles Nina had ever played. She hadn't even had a line. But she still remembered it as one of the most difficult she'd ever had to act for one reason: she'd had no personal reference for 'giddy with the first flush of love'.

But now, she thought she might understand what the writer had been trying to convey. She felt warm and flustered and weirdly shy even as her heart tapped with excitement.

She didn't fight it either. Nina tried to hold on to it, tried to sear the memory – the exact pressure of his leg against hers, the heat between them, the excited thrum of her own pulse – into her mind and heart, knowing that while this was a first for her, it might very well be a last too. Because once she left Hunt Ranch there was no guarantee that she'd ever meet someone like Maverick again, no guarantee that she'd ever feel this dizzying excitement and anticipation over something as small as a man placing his thigh against hers.

Slowly, as the band moved on to 'Last Night' by Morgan Wallen, Nina relaxed. She swayed gently to the music and when Poppy looked across at her, she did a small eyebrow wiggle and lip-synced the lyrics, making the five-year-old laugh.

Nina didn't pause to think that, right then, she wasn't fixating on the past or the future. She wasn't worrying about her career or the fact that it was probably over. She was present. And for the first time in weeks, that woman who had loved life peeked through the grief and the pain.

As the night progressed, people filtered onto the dance floor, taking advantage of the good music and free-flowing liquor. The sound of laughter was constant. The air tasted sweet with happiness. Children, dressed in their western gear, ran around, laughing and playing in a way she'd always associated with pre-television days but that seemed to be normal out here, in the middle of thousands of acres.

Markus dragged Sierra and Poppy onto the dance floor; she

knew to give her and Maverick a moment alone.

Nina didn't waste it. 'This is really special, Mav,' she said, the sudden emotion in her voice making it impossible to meet his eyes.

'It is,' he replied. He sat back in the seat, pulling Nina back with him so that she was nestled against him, his arm over her shoulders.

She relaxed against him, absorbing his strength and the sense of complete safety he provided. And when he placed his lips on the side of her head for one long moment, she sank into the sweet gesture.

'If we weren't in front of your staff right now, I'd kiss you back,' she whispered.

Maverick's thumb brushed her upper arm. 'It's not them,' he said. 'It's Poppy.'

Nina turned to face the dance floor again, and saw that Poppy was completely distracted, dancing between Markus and Sierra.

'I want you, Nina. I couldn't hide it, even if I tried to.' His voice was low, and despite the heavy topic of conversation, he never stopped that gentle, soothing touch. 'But I can't let her get used to you being in our lives.'

'I understand.' She really did. After what Maverick had been through with Shannon, Nina was glaringly aware of the fact that she would have to be careful. Honest. Open. Because it wasn't just him. It was Poppy too, and she would cut off her own arm before hurting a child, especially Poppy, who was so sweet and loving and innocent. 'But I need you to know: I can't promise more than casual.' Summoning her courage, she met those gentle blue eyes. 'I want you to know that before we . . .' She trailed off, embarrassed.

'Have sex,' he offered gently.

Nina flushed brilliantly. She couldn't quite reply through the sudden block in her throat, but she nodded.

'I know.' He smiled slightly. 'I've thought about it – and not lightly either. But every time I run through it, I arrive at the same conclusion.'

'Oh?'

'Yeah.' He grinned outright. 'I figure we're not compatible. I know you need to go back and pick up your life and the career. But the only thing I'm certain of is that if I don't take what I can of you while you're here, I'll always regret it.' Raising his hand to her face, he brushed his fingertips down her cheek, sending rivulets of need through her. 'I have plenty of regrets already, Nina. You're not going to be one of them.'

Seeing the others approach out of the corner of her eye, she nodded and slipped out from beneath his arm.

'Daddy!' Poppy ran to him and threw herself into his arms. 'Come dance!'

The band smoothly transitioned into Tracy Chapman's 'Fast Car'. As couples started swaying together and others started heading to the dance floor to join them, Maverick pushed to his feet, Poppy in his arms.

He put her down on the dance floor and bent down to take her tiny hands in his.

Nina watched them as they danced, the huge cowboy in his faded blue jeans, button-down, and baseball cap, and the little girl in her white dress and cowgirl boots, and she was reminded that life could be *so* beautiful.

Still, knowing what lay ahead for her made her eyes sting, and not wanting to ruin a near-perfect night, Nina took a sip of her drink, leaned back in her chair, and laughed when Markus caved to his need to photograph Maverick and Poppy and pulled out his iPhone.

As her friend took a zillion pictures, Sierra came and sat next to her. 'How are you doing?' she asked.

Nina thought she could happily stay in that moment for the rest of her life. She replied, 'Good. Really good, actually.' She waved one hand, encompassing the Wagon Train. 'This is incredible.'

She tilted her head back, closed her eyes. 'I swear the air tastes different out here.'

Sierra laughed lightly. 'It does. I always thought it was just my imagination . . .'

'No.' Nina inhaled. 'It's almost *sweet*.'

'Yeah. When I lived in New York and LA, I would forget what clean air tasted like, and then every time I would come home, I almost couldn't believe the difference. Nothing beats the smell of the valley.'

'Especially in the morning,' Nina said, thinking of those early mornings, sitting outside. 'When the sun is just rising and everything is a little dewy from the night before . . .'

Sierra studied her in silence for a moment.

Nina caught the look. 'What?'

'You're close to hooked,' Sierra teased gently.

Nina didn't deny it. Just because she hadn't known this type of life before didn't mean that she couldn't recognize it as extraordinary. Perhaps more terrifying than that, she could picture herself here or, if not here, somewhere similar, in the future. Maybe she'd buy a little plot of land somewhere remote and quiet. She could get a dog and a couple of horses, hire a full-time manager so that she didn't have to worry when she was away filming . . . *If* she was filming, she reminded herself.

The thought dampened her mood instantly. She had a lot to deal with before she'd even know *if* she'd act again.

Sierra looked out over the assembled guests. 'Most people who come here are looking for novelty. A few days to dress up and play cowboy for their Instagrams – so long as there are full amenities, of course.'

Nina laughed. 'I can't judge in that particular arena. I'm not outdoorsy. To be honest, I'd be hard-pressed to even glamp.'

'Oh man.' Sierra shook her head. 'You only say that because you haven't been out for an overnight in the valley.'

'Do you guys do that?' Nina had been so content to stay at

the stables near Maverick that she really hadn't explored much of what else Hunt Ranch had to offer.

'Yes. But don't do it guided. Ask Mav to take you to Wrangler's Clearing.'

'Wrangler's Clearing?'

'It's a family spot,' Sierra explained. 'Every time we talked about adding it to the trail ride, we backed out. It's *magical*. We decided to keep it a secret.'

'I don't know . . .'

'It has an outhouse,' Sierra offered. 'And I promise it will be worth it.' Sierra looked up at the blanket of stars above them and sighed. 'There's nothing like lying underneath the stars in your lover's arms. Absolutely nothing.'

Nina wasn't sure Sierra was even aware that her gaze shifted, finding Benji where he sat with a mix of ranch staff and guests. Nina didn't know their history, but when Benji looked up and found Sierra's eyes immediately, she knew that they had one.

Sierra turned away from him, giving Nina her full attention again.

And unsure what to say when she saw the deep grief that had suddenly appeared in the woman sitting next to her, Nina simply murmured, 'I'll think about it.'

Chapter 13

Maverick was drinking coffee on the porch swing on Sunday morning, Shadow at his feet, when Nina let herself out of the house, a cup of coffee in her own hand. 'Good morning,' she said quietly, and turned to guide the door closed so that it didn't bang.

'Morning.' Though he didn't say anything or close the distance as he would have liked, he felt deprived when she took her coffee to the top step and sat down, her slender legs stretched out in front of her, her back against the porch railing post.

Shadow immediately stood up from where she lay and stretched, and then walked over to Nina and plopped back down. When Shadow placed her head on Nina's thigh, she absently raised one hand to stroke the dog's ears.

'Did you sleep okay?'

She made a so-so motion with that same hand, and when Mav only waited patiently, she turned to look out over the ranch, avoiding his gaze. 'Nightmares,' she explained. 'I can't seem to fall asleep, and then when I do, I imagine variations of the attack and wake up with the feeling of his hands around my throat.' One of her own hands unconsciously rose to lightly grip her neck.

'Have you tried taking something? We have some sleeping pills lying around here somewhere. I could ask Sierra . . .'

'No.' Nina shook her head firmly. 'I'd rather be tired but aware of my surroundings, you know. Cognizant. Just in case . . .' She resumed stroking Shadow without finishing her train of thought.

Maverick leaned forward and placed his forearms on his knees. He thought about what to say to that but couldn't find anything that was quite right. He couldn't ask her what she meant without snooping. He couldn't offer comfort though he wanted to. There was only one thing he could promise her. 'I know it's not my place to demand the details. But I'll be here – when you're ready.'

Nina smiled sadly. 'You'll think less of me when you know everything.'

Her despair was so great, so suffocating, that Mav had to force himself to stay put when, really, all he wanted to do was wrap her in his arms. Instead, he reminded himself that if she'd wanted to be touched, she would have sat down next to him. 'I could never think less of you.' He said it with the vindication he felt coursing through him.

'How can you say that?' she asked, and this time her eyes burned into him, *through* him. 'How can you say that when you don't even know what—' she took a moment to recompose herself, finished with: '—what happened?'

'Because I know you.' She shook her head, denying it. But he only repeated. 'I know you. I've watched, Nina, and though I sure like looking, it's obvious. You're a Night Rider. You're running from something. Or, in this case, some*one*.'

Her gaze snapped, but not with anger. With panic.

Mav gentled his voice, but he didn't stop. 'But instead of figuring it out, I've come to know you. I've seen you spend endless hours trying to help a rescue horse that nobody else has cared for in a long time. I've seen you groom her and love her and sneak her extra grain when you thought nobody was looking.' Nina blushed, but Mav kept going. 'I've seen you muck stalls and clean tack, even though you're on vacation. I've seen you sing to my kid at a barbecue and braid her hair. So, I know that whatever happened wasn't your fault. And that isn't saying anything for the bruises you arrived with because even if I didn't know you, it is inexcusable for anyone to raise their fists to someone that doesn't have an equal chance of laying them flat. So, unless a five-four woman put those bruises on your face . . .'

He waited, and when Nina shook her head, he only said, 'Well then.'

'I'm not pushing,' he told her. 'But I am reminding you that I don't care what happened, and that I am one hundred per cent in your corner. And when the time comes for you to face whatever it is you're running from, you call me.'

She angled her face away, so he said, 'Nina. Look at me.'

When she did just that, slowly brought her eyes to his, his heart broke at the tears streaming down her cheeks. 'I don't care how long it takes. But whenever you're ready, you call me. Okay?'

She didn't speak. But she nodded and sent him a small smile that he instinctively knew was all the thanks she could manage just then.

Nina had never felt such an intense mix of emotions. It was as if a tornado was whirling through her, flinging them all together so that, combined, they were unstoppable and destructive. She felt so safe and warm, and because she knew he absolutely meant every word, she felt comforted. Because she *would* need him. And that terrified her, considering she had promised to brave it alone. And even then, when put up against her guilt and shame, she couldn't quite embrace all the good Maverick offered her.

She wanted to.

Desperately.

And when she had calmed enough to meet his eyes again, and saw the quiet rage he held, for *her*, she pushed up from the top step, dislodging Shadow, who watched her curiously as she approached Maverick.

He didn't reach out to her even though she wished he would, and she knew it was because he was too conscious of everything he didn't know and, so, erred on the side of caution.

It was Nina who took that step. She moved to him, and when he sat back and opened his arms, waiting for her to decide, she didn't hesitate. She crawled onto his lap like a hurt child might. She tucked herself against him, rested her head against his chest, and felt that solid, dependable heart beat furiously beneath her cheek.

His strong arms wrapped around her, holding her close, in safety. His familiar scent surrounded her, calmed her. He set the swing into motion, controlling the gentle sway of it with his feet firmly planted on the ground.

Nina had climbed out of her spacious bed with her heart racing and panic crawling up her throat. So, it was the oddest thing that her pulse steadied and her panic calmed the moment that she was in Maverick's embrace.

She didn't cry. She was too tired, too dried up inside. She sighed, closed her eyes. And fell asleep instantly.

She didn't sleep long. Only deeply. And when she woke up forty minutes later, Maverick's arms were still around her, but there was a blanket thrown over both of them. Markus sat on the bottom porch step, his camera and a huge lens set up on a tripod in front of him.

She should have been embarrassed. But she wasn't. She should have climbed off Maverick's lap and made some excuse for going inside. But she didn't. And when Maverick saw that she was awake and gently stroked her bare waist where her pyjama shirt had risen, she snuggled back against him beneath the blanket, welcoming his touch.

'Are you thinking sunrise for the shoot?' she asked, loud enough for Markus to hear her.

He turned from his tripod, a huge grin on his face, and even though he didn't say anything about her on Maverick's lap, she could see the gentle teasing and blatant approval in his eyes. 'We arrive Thursday morning, but I'm thinking most of that day will be spent prepping. Locations, lighting, models, fittings, props. Then Friday we shoot. Start early enough to capture the sunrise, finish after we get the sunset shots. You should come watch.' He sounded giddy with excitement. 'It's going to be a lot of fun.'

Beneath her, Maverick had tensed up. 'I don't think that's a good idea – all those people knowing you're here.'

Before Nina could reply, Markus said, 'I've got all the signed NDAs back.'

Mav sighed, but Nina heard it and knew that it was more resigned than relieved. Still, when she kept pointedly quiet, he changed the topic. 'My sister said they're planning a party for your team Friday night?'

'Yeah. Figured we could wrap up with a small celebration, since I'm missing my girl's birthday.'

Maverick looked down at Nina, but he didn't stop his gentle stroking or pause the porch swing's motion. 'It's your birthday?'

Those blue eyes seared into her, searching. Nina nodded slowly. 'Wednesday. But I don't usually celebrate,' she hurried to say. 'And this isn't a big one.'

'I'm almost afraid to ask . . .'

'Thirty-four.'

She felt him relax beneath her, teased him by asking, 'Were you worried about my age, Mav?'

'No. It wouldn't have mattered how much younger you were; this is happening anyway. But I would have guessed there was closer to a decade between us.'

'It's our skin regimen,' Markus offered.

'It's working.'

Nina shifted so that she could see his face. 'How old are *you*?'

'Forty.'

'Too close in age to be called a sugar daddy,' Markus teased.

And to Nina's surprise, Maverick teased back, drawing Nina back into the conversation. 'We can still role-play that if you want.'

Markus hooted with laughter.

Maverick grinned.

But Nina stunned them both when she finished the conversation with a casual shrug and: 'I might be into it.'

There was a long pause where they both stared at her. Markus started laughing first – not quietly either. 'Baby's back!' He whooped and pumped both fists in the air.

Maverick's grin was ridiculously adorable. It spread across his face until a dimple Nina hadn't known existed popped in his right cheek. Bringing his lips close to her ear, he kissed the side of her head, whispered, 'You better climb off.' He shifted.

She could feel him, of course. He was thick and hard beneath her. And even though she felt some anxiety, it was smothered by her lust. Nina didn't get off as he'd suggested. She settled her weight down on him, deliberately torturing both of them.

Maverick exhaled a winded, 'Fuck,' beneath his breath.

Nina might not have been the one to say it, but she shared the sentiment. It was too much. They had been dancing around one another for days, which might not have felt so long had they not been spending every hour together. It was time, and, still, she knew he would wait for her to take that next step. But how?

It would have been simple had she not been staying in his house with his sister and daughter across the hall.

Markus, half focused on shooting the sunrise, half focused on petting Shadow, asked, 'Maverick, have you watched any of Nina's films?'

'Not yet. But I want to. Benji says *Dogs of Despair* is the one I should start with.'

Nina blushed.

Markus grinned wickedly.

Dogs of Despair included her first and last nude scene, and although it was a good scene, one she was proud of, she hadn't felt the need to do another. Being naked on camera had made her feel too vulnerable. Even though the director had kept the crew to necessary folks only for that scene, being naked in front of them had made her feel helpless. It had reminded her of when she'd been young and would lock herself in the tiny apartment bathroom when one of the men her mother brought home had looked at her in that way that made her skin crawl.

Thinking back on it now made her realize how often she'd found sanctuary in a locked bathroom. And, still, the idea of Maverick Hunt watching her nude scene was a complete turn-on. It didn't make her feel shy or unsafe or vulnerable. She could imagine him once he realized . . . 'It's one of my better performances, actually,' she said, and God help her she had to engage her acting skills to level her tone and sound serious. 'But it's pretty violent so don't watch it with Poppy.'

Markus had to turn away to cover his laugh.

'I'll watch it.'

Nina nodded seriously, said, 'Let me know what you think?'

'I'm pretty sure I don't have to watch any of your films to know you're fantastic.'

Nina smiled sweetly.

Markus, bless him, was overcome by a coughing fit that almost sent him to his knees.

Chapter 14

He put the movie on that night as a reward for getting his spreadsheets done ahead of time. Maverick showered and changed into a pair of ancient sweatpants. He settled on his bed with his beer and turned on the television, making sure to keep the volume low so as not to wake up Nina, who shared a wall with him.

He found *Dogs of Despair* on Prime, offhandedly noted that it had an almost five-star rating, as he purchased it and pressed play.

Around him, the house settled for the night. As the opening credits rolled, he slipped off his bed and snuck across the hall to check in on Poppy one last time. She was sleeping on her stomach, one arm beneath her, the other flung across her bed.

Mav closed her door with a quiet click and backtracked to his room. On screen, a beautiful blonde woman with a chic, chin-length haircut and glamorous aviator sunglasses walked into a bank. Dressed in a short black skirt and a long black jacket that was open at the front, putting her impossibly perfect legs on display with every step she took in her sky-high boots. She carried a black leather suitcase.

When she reached the bank teller, she removed her sunglasses.

Mav slowly lowered his beer as Nina's big, dark eyes punched through him. He hadn't even recognized her – and it wasn't just the wig and the sunglasses. Everything about the woman on screen exuded sex and power, and though anything had yet to happen to prove it, violence.

He supposed that's what acting was, by definition. Yet it was strange, he realized, to see Nina play someone who may as well have been her antithesis.

The heist scene started so suddenly and occurred so quickly that Mav found himself completely immersed in the film in under a minute. He watched as it continued, as Nina – or 'Saskia' – covertly took out the bank's cameras and then opened fire on the floor-to-ceiling windows.

The glass shattered.

Unsure of what was happening, seeing an escape, the hostages started to flee *en masse*, pushing and shoving each other through the broken windows until people fell over one another in their haste to escape. And in the chaos, right as the police cars arrived, the camera panned to Saskia as she stripped her wig, removed her coat, and joined them, the briefcase, now full of money, in her hand.

She clutched it to her and rushed out onto the street, pointing and crying, 'He just started shooting! Oh, my God!'

The officers swarmed past her.

Saskia continued down the street unhindered. The next shot was a brief close-up of her face, and instead of the smug expression the viewer would expect, she looked devastatingly sad a moment before she put her sunglasses back on.

The plot progressed, as a blackmailed Saskia became more and more volatile and the police protagonist, Jude, started closing in on her, Mav's beer sat forgotten on his nightstand. He no longer saw Nina in a wig, playing somebody else. He saw Saskia, the ex-military single mom, working against the clock to save her daughter from the men who'd kidnapped her.

Approximately halfway through the movie, Saskia and Jude's paths crossed, and while Saskia knew him, the cop still had no idea that the victim from the bank robbery he was interviewing was actually the robber herself.

Their chemistry was undeniable.

The attraction raw.

And by the time Jude left the interview, his last words to Saskia were: 'I'm not supposed to do this, but is there any chance I could see you again sometime? Unofficially.'

Saskia slowly nodded.

Jude grinned at her. He tapped his phone once against his palm and said, 'Ah, I have your details. I'll call.'

Maverick didn't hold his breath that it would end happily as Saskia started plotting how she could use Jude, but when she met him for dinner to set her plans in motion and then invited him back to her place, Mav's heart started to tap.

On screen, Saskia poured Jude a drink and excused herself.

Maybe because he had half been expecting her to shoot the poor bastard, Mav was shocked when she reappeared on screen, this time nude but for a sexy-as-hell, high-waisted thong that defined her subtly curved hips. But the moment she did, he didn't see Saskia. He saw Nina, her small breasts gloriously naked.

Maverick didn't look away. He couldn't have, even if he'd wanted to. He did release an agonized 'Fuuuuck,' as, on screen, she sauntered over to an equally stunned Jude and then slowly removed her underwear.

Mav exhaled a tight breath as Saskia and Jude tore frantically at each other, their passion clear in their absolute abandon. But all he could think was that the woman completely naked on screen just then, the same woman who he had started something with, had told him to watch this movie.

Maverick looked down at his painfully hard erection beneath the fabric of his sweatpants. He could have finished himself using nothing but a few strokes of his hand and the rest of the scene. But it felt odd, even dirty, when Nina was right next door.

Taking his phone off the nightstand, he shot her a text.

About two-thirds of the way through Dogs of Despair . . .

He thought she might have been sleeping, but she replied right away.

Oh? What do you think so far?

Maverick grinned at the nonchalance, but he decided to play along.

Great acting. Gotta love a heist movie.

The little typing bubbles appeared and then disappeared. Appeared again.

Glad you're enjoying it!

Maverick looked down at the text. 'Glad you're enjoying it?' he whispered to himself. What the hell was he supposed to say to that?

He sat down on his bed and stared at his phone, suddenly unsure of himself. Maybe she hadn't meant anything by it? Maybe this was her best movie, and she had genuinely wanted him to watch it.

It *was* a damn good movie.

He decided he would go speak to her and got all the way to the door before he simply stopped and banged his head gently against it. 'What are you doing? Idiot.'

He had promised himself that he would give her the time and space to take that next step, and though he was pretty sure she'd wanted him to watch that scene, it didn't mean anything until she told him it did.

Because that felt right in his head, he turned towards his shower. He'd take it ice cold and then he'd finish the movie, this time fast-forwarding through any scenes where Nina wore anything less than jeans and a long-sleeved T-shirt.

He got halfway to his bathroom before a quiet knock sounded.

He knew it was her.

He could feel that static attraction pulling at his skin.

He exhaled one deep breath before backtracking.

He opened the door.

She stood a few feet back, dressed in those little silk pyjamas he'd seen her in that first morning. She shifted anxiously and clasped her hands together. Those dark eyes pulled at him. 'Based on all the rom-coms I've watched,' she whispered, conscious of Poppy across the hall, 'this is kinda the part of the movie where you're supposed to knock on *my door* . . .'

Maverick's heart thumped erratically. He took a single step towards her, watched as those eyes steeled with determination. She was still afraid, he realized. She was afraid and trying not to be. 'I won't hurt you.'

'I know. It's just . . . I'm not exactly *experienced* in this department.'

That gave him pause, but only because he wanted to know how gentle he needed to be. 'What do you mean by that?' he asked quietly. And when she didn't reply right away, but blushed furiously, he added, 'I want to know how to touch you without scaring you.'

She broke his gaze. 'I've had sex three times,' she said *so* quietly. 'And no, not three partners. Three times *total*. And mostly because I wanted to test myself, see if I could feel any deeper emotional connection to the men I was with after sleeping with them . . . And I didn't,' she said in a rush. 'And I'm kinda freaking out. Because I already like you so much, and what if I can't . . .' She dropped her gaze.

'Can't what?' he asked quietly.

'Enjoy it,' she said simply.

There was so much for him to process. To say he was surprised by her inexperience would have been a huge understatement. Nina wasn't just a beautiful, famous woman. She was sweet and gentle and kind and wrapped in a killer body. She was irresistible, so it was hard to imagine that more men hadn't broken their backs trying to woo her. And even over that, he couldn't quite reconcile that the three men she *had* been with hadn't seen that anxiety and inexperience and gone slowly, taken the time to show her how that fire could be kindled.

'I'll show you,' he promised. 'We'll go as slow as you need.'

When she nodded, Maverick closed the small distance between them – finally. When she didn't move, he gently guided her arms around his neck, and the moment she tightened them, he reached down and lifted her.

Her legs wrapped around his waist instinctively and squeezed, sending all the blood in his head to his crotch. As he turned and carried her into his bedroom, closing the door with a kick, he said, 'Anytime you want me to stop, you tell me. Okay?'

She nodded.

It was enough. Still, he silently promised himself that he'd take care of her, and that he'd show her what her body could do and that a man could be gentle and thoughtful.

'Mav . . .'

'Yeah.'

'No fingers inside . . . Please. I don't like it . . .'

Maverick stopped walking. He wondered over that. He worried, because she sounded scared. He wanted to ask her for more information but wasn't sure how, so settled on, 'Nina, are you sure this is what you want?'

'Yes,' she replied firmly. 'Absolutely. It's just . . . He—'

'He touched you.' It was not a question. But as he carried her, so light, so small, to the bed, he promised himself that if he ever met the man who had hurt her, he would break those fucking fingers.

Nina's eyes glassed over, and she nodded. 'I fought, and then he heard Markus on the phone, and he couldn't . . .' She placed her forehead on his chest, hiding her face from him. 'He couldn't . . .'

'Shh, baby.' He sat on the bed with her. 'You don't have to tell me if you don't want to.' His hand stroked her back beneath her pyjamas, soothing her the only way he knew how.

'I don't want it here with us,' she whispered. So saying, she raised both her hands to her hair and pulled as if she could simply rip it from the roots. 'Make me forget, Mav. Please.'

♘

Nina had never told a bigger truth. Sitting on Maverick's lap, pressed intimately against his bare chest as he rubbed her back, was the most beautiful moment of her entire life. And she didn't want to ruin everything she was feeling if he touched her intimately, which was the only reason she'd told him about the assault. She didn't want any part of it in the room with them. She just wanted to keep this immense intimacy between them alive for as long as possible.

'I know I'm supposed to be this . . . *siren*.' She pointed to the television on his wall, where *Dogs of Despair* was frozen in a blur of indistinguishable colour. 'But I'm not.'

'You are to me,' he said quietly, and trailed his lips gently over her bare shoulder. 'The first time I looked into those big eyes, I felt like I was drowning. It wasn't reasonable or logical, and I tried to fight it. But it was no use, the draw was too strong. Those first few days, I looked for you everywhere.' His lips moved, whispering up and over her jaw, making her tremble. 'And that first morning when I saw you sleeping on the cabin porch, all I wanted was a few more minutes with you.'

'You . . .' Nina was shocked by his confession.

'Do you think I offer every guest six a.m. riding lessons?'

'I thought you were being kind.'

He shrugged. 'I was being kind. I didn't want to leave you alone when you looked so sad. But I'd be lying if I said that was the sum of it.'

Nina's heart raced at his words, even as his lips caught hers in a gentle embrace. It was barely a kiss, just the softest touch that left her aching for more. She closed her eyes and welcomed him, sank into the kiss as he took them both deeper.

His tongue brushed seductively against hers. Those big, rough hands settled *so* gently, like butterflies, on her hips, not squeezing or groping, only gently holding her in place.

Nina wasn't sure how only a kiss could set her on fire, but it did. Her body felt like a livewire – erratic and uncontrollable and dangerous. Her pulse skittered and jumped. Her breath started to come in small pants. And though she might have been mortified by her drenched underwear with another man, she couldn't summon the emotion through the immense sense of pleasure. It had never been like this for her before.

The few times she had had sex, it had been awkward and uncomfortable. She'd been more scared than turned on, and, so, she had been unable to get her body to lie to each of the men she'd been with. They'd known as surely as she had that it hadn't been pleasurable for her, and not one of them had called after, reaffirming her own sense of failure.

But here, now, with Mav . . . She was a goddess.

Beneath her, his hard thighs pressed against her intimately. His thumbs brushed against her hips where he held her, always soothing, she thought, always caring. He said, 'Are you sure you're ready for this?'

A moment of doubt filled her. But not because she didn't want him. She had felt those first tugs of attraction that very first time they'd met, too, when he had crouched to pick up Markus's phone off the floor. But she doubted her own readiness because Nina knew, unequivocally, that if they took this step, things would change.

'It's not smart,' she said.

Maverick sighed, but he surprised her by agreeing. 'No, I don't suppose it is. But I'm too selfish to deny myself you – *if* that's what you want too.'

'I hate to ruin the moment by being the voice of reason, but maybe we should come up with a few ground rules,' she said.

'Ground rules?'

Nina nodded, but she didn't climb off his lap. 'We keep this a secret so that you don't get harassed by the media and so that Poppy doesn't get the wrong impression. She needs to think I'm only a guest.' When Maverick smiled, Nina raised one eyebrow. 'Why is that funny?'

'Oh, it's far from funny,' he replied. 'I'm laughing at myself. Because here you are, coming up with ground rules, but the fact that the first one involves protecting my kid just makes me want to keep you more.'

A skitter traced her spine, but Nina was very aware that it wasn't all fear. It was pleasure too, pleasure at the thought of Maverick wanting to keep her. No man had before . . .

Knowing that was dangerous territory, she didn't let it play out in her head. She said, 'We do this while I'm here. But when I leave, we sever all contact.' It was an odd ground rule, but somehow Nina knew she wouldn't move on if he was still in her life.

He tensed beneath her. But he didn't object. He resignedly said, 'That's probably for the best. I hate it,' he insisted, making her smile. 'But, yeah, if we stayed in touch, it'd complicate things for both of us.'

She didn't ask him what he meant by that. She was too afraid she'd be pleased by the answer. Instead, she was filled with sudden urgency because she knew that their time together was slowly ticking down.

She scrambled off his lap, asked, 'Do you have any to add?' as she hurriedly stripped her pyjamas, her inexperience making her rush through the motions.

When she looked up at him again, he shook his head and rasped, 'Nope.'

She stepped towards him then, wanting to hide her nakedness in the shelter of his big body.

But he held up one hand, stopping her.

Nina paused a few feet away from him. While his eyes, dark with lust, drank her in, his obvious pleasure eradicating her self-consciousness, she looked her fill too. Maverick was so big, so tall and strong. Sculpted. His broad shoulders were straining with well-defined muscle, his abs clearly defined above his low-slung sweatpants. That dark brown hair, such a beautiful contrast to those piercing blue eyes, and when he looked at her like that, it made her feel like the only woman in the world.

'I have to taste you, Nina.'

It wasn't technically a question, but she sensed he was still asking for permission. She nodded, almost cautiously.

He slowly lowered himself off the bed and knelt on the floor in front of her.

He held out one hand for her and waited for her to take it before tugging her closer. 'How's your balance?'

'My-my balance?' she asked uncertainly.

He gently tapped her leg and, when she raised it, guided it over his shoulder, exposing her completely.

Her balance was excellent on any normal day, but with Maverick Hunt on his knees in front of her, one of her legs draped over his shoulder, his face inches from her, she felt a little weak in the knee. And when he didn't touch her with his fingers as she'd asked, only brought his face closer and blew a cool breath over her damp flesh, that same knee threatened to buckle at the intimacy.

Desperate for him to make contact and eradicate her nerves, Nina gripped both hands in his hair. 'Mav . . .'

He didn't have to be asked twice. Both of his hands steadied her from behind. He licked through her once, slowly, his eyes closed as if he wanted to savour the taste of her.

Nina's entire body shuddered at the wet, firm contact. She braced herself, tightening her hands in his hair, and though she wanted to close her eyes and enjoy it, she couldn't look away. She watched as he drew closer again, felt her core liquify completely as he used his tongue to furrow deeply into her, and when he worked his way up and gently flicked her clit, she lost the battle. She closed her eyes, arched her back, and sighed.

She pressed her hips forward, begging for more even as her stabilizing leg trembled beneath the weight of the sensations pummelling her.

'Your taste was made for me, Nina,' he said roughly. He momentarily rested his forehead on her pubic bone. 'I can feel you entering my bloodstream, taking over every cell.'

He didn't sound very pleased by it, but Nina didn't have time to think much about that as he held her hips and pivoted her so that her back was to the bed. He sent her backwards with the smallest nudge. Nina fell onto the bed, one leg still draped over his shoulder.

She easily ignored the ache in her ribs as he strung her legs over his shoulders. And this time when he lowered down to slide his tongue over her, he didn't stop.

He ravished her. Every stroke of his tongue savouring, every flicker meant to entice, every pull of his lips pushing her higher and higher, inch by inch.

Nina hadn't known that her body could feel so many sensations at once. Her bones were heavy, her heartbeat light and quick. Her heart at peace, her blood at war as it pumped fire through her.

Her hips moved with him, grinding in the tiniest of thrusts as if begging for more even as he tore her apart. Her legs trembled violently. Her hands in his hair tightened, holding him to her even though she knew he wouldn't be the one to leave.

The orgasm rose in her like a massive ocean wave, collecting size and momentum as it approached. She held her breath as the wave pummelled her, taking her under. And when Maverick sensed the change and gently slid his tongue deep inside of her instead of using his fingers, her back arched off the bed. She closed her eyes as that wave mercilessly tore through her, tumbling everything she'd thought she'd known and rearranging it into something entirely new.

And when she couldn't stop the loud moan that tore from her lips, she slapped her own hand over her mouth, muffling it against her palm as she rocked against Maverick's tongue, riding out the pleasure until she collapsed back onto the bed, exhausted.

She stared up at the plain white ceiling in stunned disbelief as the little aftershocks left her body in ripples of awareness. Her legs fell open as her muscles slackened. Nina might have been embarrassed had she even been aware of doing it.

Maverick shifted, trailing his lips from one thigh to the other and leaving little fires everywhere.

She shivered and closed her eyes as she tried to sear the moment to memory, because right then, basking in the afterglow of her first orgasm that hadn't come from a vibrator, she understood that she had been acting passion wrong this whole time too. It wasn't frantic and rushed and scary. It was heavy and huge and so, so consuming.

Nobody had ever told her that you weren't supposed to feel alone afterwards . . . But now, with Maverick, she didn't – feel alone. She felt entwined. As if they were the only two people in the ether of the universe.

When the first tear fell, Nina hurriedly swiped it away, embarrassed.

Maverick didn't ask her what was wrong, he only crawled up the bed to her and, propping himself up on one elbow, brushed them away himself. He touched his lips to hers, whispered, 'I'm here.'

Nina was old enough, and had been in therapy long enough, to understand that she had some major trust and intimacy issues. Her mother's numerous betrayals throughout her childhood had made her suspicious of everyone, but especially of men. She didn't welcome people into her life. In fact, she consciously avoided it, knowing the pain and uncertainty they came with.

The three times she had taken a man to her bed she hadn't

felt anything except vaguely scared, and then disappointed when the experience had left her feeling more lonely, more lacking.

But here, now, with Mav, she finally understood what she had been missing, and it was so simple, so obvious. It was *trust*. And it was the loveliest realization to know that she wasn't damaged beyond repair, that someone – Maverick – fit, like a key in a lock, opening that part of herself she had kept sealed away from everyone else.

Wanting to share it with him, wanting to keep trusting him, she snuggled back into him, pressing her bare butt up against the soft fabric of his sweatpants and his hard length beneath them.

He nuzzled that delicate spot behind her ear. 'I wasn't prepared,' he said quietly. 'I'll go into town tomorrow.' But he rolled her onto her back, lowered his mouth to her breast.

He pulled her nipple into his mouth and swirled his tongue around the sensitized peak.

Nina arched into him as that need started building again. But it wasn't enough. 'Mav . . .'

His big palm rose to stroke her hair immediately. 'What's wrong?'

'I haven't had sex in four years,' Nina said. 'I'm clean. And I'm already on the pill – to time my periods for filming.'

'I don't mind waiting,' he assured her. 'This . . .' He lowered his head to lavish her other breast with attention. 'This is still the best fucking night of my life.'

She loved that he genuinely would have waited, even as she hated how her body ached to be filled. Unsure of herself, unsure of him, she ran her hands through his hair, pulling his gaze to hers. 'Are you worried? That what happened to Shannon might happen to me?'

'No.' He shook his head vehemently. Then stilled. Paled.

'What?' she whispered, alarmed by the shock on his face.

He slowly met her eyes again. 'I don't want to scare you.'

'You won't.'

Taking her hand in his he placed it over the impossibly hard ridge in his sweatpants and pressed her palm down. 'It turns me on,' he said gravely. 'It's new, but yeah . . . Fuck.'

He expelled a huge breath and buried his face in his comforter.

She heard his muffled groan. But Nina knew he wasn't lying. She had felt him twitch beneath her palm as the words had left his mouth.

It shocked her, and it scared her a little. But only because it excited her so much too.

She wouldn't dare say it aloud. It was too much, too soon. It was a future that couldn't be hers, a movie she hadn't been cast in. But she cautiously slid her hand beneath his grey sweatpants to find him hot and hard.

Maverick hissed, almost as if he were in pain. He opened his eyes to stare at her.

Nina gently slid her hand up and down his length, marvelling at the heat and silky softness over iron. Placing her other hand on his face, she drew him to her and took his mouth. 'Please, Maverick.'

'I'll pull out,' he promised. When she nodded, he rolled off the bed and removed his sweatpants. 'It's been a long time for me too,' he said. 'Almost five years.'

'*Five?*'

He grinned. 'I'm not a casual guy.'

His words hung in the air between them for a moment, almost in warning to both of them that they were moving too quickly, but then he was climbing over the bed and kneeling between her legs, and Nina couldn't focus on anything but him.

She had never been turned on by only looking at a man's penis before. In fact, she typically felt only fear. Not now though. Maverick was big and thick and impossibly hard – for *her*. And, right then, she wanted him inside of her like she had never wanted anything else.

He gripped her thighs and hauled her closer. Nina's laugh died on a sigh as she felt him notch at her entrance, and when he reached down one hand to touch her and quickly caught himself, snatching his hand back, she whispered, 'Do it.' And when he still seemed unsure, she insisted, 'I want you to.'

Gently, as if she were made of glass, he slid a single finger through her wet heat. His breath caught audibly.

Nina didn't think about the assault or the last time a man had touched her there – without her permission that time. She couldn't.

All she felt was Maverick.

Everywhere that he touched burned.

He kept his gaze locked on hers as he slid his finger out of her and into his own mouth.

'Mav,' she begged, impossibly turned on.

He grinned wickedly, and lowering both hands to her hips, held her in place as he slowly sank into her.

She moaned.

Maverick stopped moving.

He looked down at her, that same slightly stunned expression on his face.

And then everything exploded. They took each other in a frenzy, a mating, hands never resting, legs tangling, breaths sawing through the room, and this time, when Nina gave herself to the wave passing through her, Mav didn't wait. He gripped her hips, thrusting into her in three quick pumps, and then pulled out, and followed her over the edge.

Chapter 15

The first half of the week passed in a blur as Nina and Maverick settled into a new routine that involved long days at the stables and around the ranch, followed by dinners at the ranch house, and then long, secret nights wrapped in each other's arms.

After that first night, Nina, not wanting to overstep, had been too self-conscious to go to him, but once the house had settled, Mav had knocked on her door, and when she had opened it for him, he hadn't said a single word, only swung her over his shoulder, carried her back to his bedroom, and gently thrown her on his bed.

Though they kept each other awake long into the night, now, when Nina slept, she slept deeply, the knowledge that she was safe in Mav's arms following her into sleep, so that on Wednesday morning, she woke up in her own bed, disoriented. She looked around and frowned once she realized that she was back in her own room. She didn't even remember leaving Maverick's bedroom the night before.

She rolled over, yawning as she stretched, and sighed when she saw that it was still dark outside. She reached for her phone on the nightstand, habitually bypassed the missed calls from Alex, and read the single message Markus had sent at midnight the night before.

I wanted to be the first person to wish you happy birthday! Can't wait to celebrate with you tomorrow! X

Nina replied and then flopped onto her back.

Another year gone, she thought. She knew she wasn't 'old' by any means, but at thirty-four she was starting to feel it. Throughout her twenties, it had seemed like she'd had all the time in the world. Time to work more, time to win an Academy Award, time to get that next big role. But now, with her career on the brink of implosion, it was the strangest thing to realize that she didn't have much else to show for her thirty-four years. Worse, had she never been assaulted, she might never had realized it. Relationships had never been part of her plan.

She had Markus, and God knew she would always be grateful for him. He had stuck with her through everything. She had Luigi and a few others from the restaurant, but Nina was ashamed to admit that she hadn't been good about staying in touch with them through the rigours of her work.

It was humbling to realize that she had spent her entire life frantically striving for something to judge her worth by – something, she knew, to prove her mother's prophecy wrong. It was embarrassing to realize that in that frantic search, she had somehow managed to avoid forming relationships at all.

From the moment she had stepped onto the red carpet for the *Camelot* première and felt the warmth of those camera flashes like a thousand brilliant suns, Nina had thrown her entire self into becoming someone.

And for what? For *whom*?

Because it was only now, with everything she'd worked for at risk, that she realized she'd somehow missed the big picture. She'd never been in a romantic relationship. Until Maverick, she'd never been held by a lover until she fell asleep in his arms, and that feeling of being cocooned in safety was so beautiful it made her think she'd probably missed out on quite a bit. She'd never even had a girls' night – though Markus would disagree with that – because she'd never had a female friend she'd been close enough to suggest it to.

Because it bothered her immensely, Nina promised herself that she would make more time for people going forward, no matter what happened with her career.

She was so busy mulling over her interpersonal shortcomings that she didn't hear the faint scuffling and hushed giggles coming from outside her bedroom. But when Poppy knocked and called her name, Nina sat up in bed and turned on her side lamp.

'Come in, Poppy,' she said, knowing that Maverick was probably out with the horses already.

The door opened, but it wasn't just Poppy standing outside. It was Poppy, Mav, and Sierra.

It took Nina a second to register what was happening. She stared at the brightly wrapped gifts Maverick and Poppy held and the birthday cake in Sierra's hands, and when they started singing 'Happy Birthday', she wasn't entirely sure what to do.

They came into her room as a unit, their singing loud and a little off-key. Nina found Mav's gaze, laughingly said, 'This doesn't count as you singing to me,' to try and downplay the immensity of her own emotion.

Mav just smiled. And when Poppy scrambled onto the bed, threw her arms around Nina's neck, and whispered, 'We made you a cake,' Nina's heart melted completely.

She wrapped both her arms around the five-year-old and returned the ferocious hug. 'Thank you, Poppy.'

'And I made you a present!'

'You did?' Nina said brightly, though her eyes burned with tears.

'Yeah.'

'Poppy, let Nina blow out her candles first,' Sierra instructed and held the cake closer.

'Don't forget to make a wish,' Poppy said solemnly. 'And don't tell anyone.' She stood on the bed and wagged a small finger in

Nina's direction. 'If you do, it won't come true.'

Nina's laugh was slightly watery, but she tugged Poppy onto her lap and wrapped her arms around her again. 'Want to help me blow them out?'

Poppy seemed unsure. She looked across the room to where Mav stood, a little out the way, two huge presents in his arms. 'Can I?' she asked.

Nina followed her gaze, but when she saw the slightly stricken expression on Mav's face, her own smile dimmed.

He cleared his throat. 'Yeah, baby. If Nina says that's okay.'

Nina tried not to worry too much about his look. She looked back at Poppy and smiled. 'On three, okay?'

Poppy nodded.

'One, two, three!'

Together, they blew out the candles, and even though she knew that hard work far surpassed the power of a wish, Nina closed her eyes and made one. It was spontaneous, the words flowing through her overwhelmed heart and into her thoughts so quickly that she had no time to reconsider or think of something more realistic.

The moment it had been made she opened her eyes again, slightly panicked by what she'd asked for in an unguarded moment. She looked straight into Maverick's eyes, then quickly away again.

Her heart lurched.

Her panic reared.

But before it could grip her and pull her under, Poppy jumped off the bed and retrieved the haphazardly wrapped gift she'd dropped on the floor. She passed it to Nina with a megawatt smile.

'You made this?' Nina remembered.

Poppy nodded, said, 'At school,' and then climbed back on the bed to sit beside her.

Nina turned over the gift and started on the mess of tape. 'Did you wrap this all by yourself?' she asked.

'No, Daddy did.'

'Oh.' Nina tried her damnedest not to smile.

But when Poppy added, 'He didn't do a very good job,' the smallest giggle escaped from between her lips.

Maverick caught it, and this time when Nina met his eyes, he was grinning. 'It's hard,' he insisted. 'The paper never stays put. And the tape always gets stuck everywhere.'

'Get a gift bag,' Sierra said.

'Wrapping paper shows that you put more time and thought into it,' Mav argued.

Nina kept unwrapping the gift and listened as they continued their back-and-forth. It was the strangest thing, to listen to grown siblings bicker like children, over something as small as gift wrapping. Nina loved it. They were so comfortable with one another, so *themselves*. She'd never really had a family, and loved experiencing all those little nuances that made one now.

She tore off the last bit of paper and opened the recycled Amazon box Mav had put the gift in. It took her about five seconds to figure out what it was, but when she did, Nina gushed, 'A flower!'

It was a craft project, one of Poppy's little hands stencilled, cut out and coloured, and then glued upright onto a painted kebab stick like the head of a flower. Leaves, coloured in bright green crayon, had been glued onto the stem.

She took it out of the box and held it up for everyone to see.

Poppy beamed. 'It's for your garden. You stick it in flowers.'

'I love it,' Nina said, but she knew she'd never put it outside for the sun and rain to destroy. Maybe she'd frame it. Or put it in an indoor potted plant. But not outside. She gave the five-year-old one last hug, whispered, 'Thank you, Poppy. This is the best gift I've ever gotten.'

'Welcome,' she chirped.

'You're welcome,' Mav corrected.

'You're welcome,' Poppy parroted.

Maverick didn't give Nina time to get emotional. He handed

her the next one, a huge, flat, rectangular gift wrapped in gorgeous linen cloth with a white silk bow. 'Sierra?'

'I wish,' she said. 'Mav and I split our gift – *unfortunately*, he wrapped it.'

'You—' he pointed at Sierra '—need to go and get your coffee.' But he turned back to Nina, explained, 'Markus left that with me over the weekend. He didn't want you to wake up without it on your birthday.'

'He's thoughtful like that,' Nina commented as she undid the bow. The linen cloth fell away easily, revealing the back of a photo frame. 'Oh, a photo!' She used both hands to hurriedly flip it over.

And then simply stared.

She wasn't sure how Markus was so easily able to capture the essence of a single moment, but the photo did just that. It was of her and Maverick on that first day, standing in the stall with Barbie. He had somehow managed to pick a second in time when they had been looking at each other, Mav smiling softly, Nina trapped by his gaze. The photograph was in contrast, with her and Maverick in a patch of filtered sunlight, the horse and the dark stall behind them.

'That's Daddy!' Poppy said and touched Maverick's face in the photograph.

'Wow.' This came from Sierra, who had come around the bed to look, the cake still in her hands. 'That's legitimately incredible.'

'It is.' Nina ran her fingers lightly over the frame.

Maverick was being polite, or, maybe, conscious of how he behaved in front of Poppy. He hovered at the foot of the bed, so Nina flipped it around and held it up for him to see.

'It's a great shot,' he said.

'Yeah.' But because she heard the caution in his tone, she added, 'Markus always frames his best ones for my birthday.' It wasn't true. It was an outright lie. But she didn't want him to worry, didn't want him to read too much into it. After all, they had come up with ground rules for a reason.

'While you open that last one, Poppy and I are going to cut this cake,' Sierra said.

Poppy, in her excitement for cake for breakfast, didn't argue. She hopped off the bed and ran after Sierra, her happy little voice chatting all the way down the stairs.

The moment they were out of earshot, Nina said, 'Don't overthink the photograph. Markus sees people as art, and sometimes he forgets . . .'

'I wasn't overthinking it. I was wondering if I could ask him for a copy.' He walked around the bed and put his own wrapped gift on the mattress next to her. Before she could move to open it, he leaned down, placed his hands on either side of her face, and brought his lips to hers.

The kiss was as quick as it was hot, over before she could right her addled brain let alone return it. But it still spread through her like wildfire, burning with no thought as to what walls it destroyed.

He straightened, nudged the last gift towards her. 'Happy birthday.'

'You guys really didn't have to go to all this effort,' she said as she ripped the mangled tape off with quick fingers. 'I typically don't celebrate.'

'At all?'

Nina shrugged. 'Markus usually forces me to go out. Or, if I refuse, he and Juan come over and harass me into a movie or pizza night.'

Maverick sat on the edge of her mattress. 'I'm glad he's there for you. Birthdays should be celebrated.'

'I don't know. Celebrating getting older doesn't always feel fun.'

'It's not only a celebration of age. It's a celebration of *you* and what you bring to the world. It's one day where other people have an excuse to show you how much you mean to them, and the value you add to their lives.' He reached out one hand to tuck her hair behind her ear, repeated, 'Birthdays should be celebrated.'

Nina felt a little choked up, not necessarily because she disagreed, but because his words only proved her earlier thoughts. She had one friend who celebrated her birthday – who celebrated *her*. One.

But because she didn't want to be self-pitying on this, the best birthday, she laughingly asked, 'Oh? And what do I bring to your life, Mav?'

He waggled his eyebrows suggestively, making her laugh.

Nina tore the last of the paper away, but this time, when she saw what the gift was and the emotion clawed up her throat, she had to grind her teeth together to stop it from coming out. Because there, in her lap, was the most beautiful makeup box she'd ever seen.

The wood was dark and smooth beneath her fingers. The box was long, maybe two feet, and had been designed to sit on a bathroom counter. The back opened to little compartments meant to hold brushes and eyeliners or mascaras. The front contained one long drawer beneath which four smaller ones sat. Two little brass hooks for jewellery were on either side, and when Nina opened the drawers, she saw that they were full of product.

'Sierra's half was the makeup,' Mav said. Reaching forward, he brushed an errant tear off her cheek. 'I insisted you probably had plenty of your own and didn't need any with that face anyway. She disagreed, said a woman could never have too much.'

Nina didn't speak for a long moment, only traced the flowers that were carved into the little drawers at the front of the makeup box, but Maverick was looking at her, and he could see that she was struggling with her emotions.

'Thank you,' she managed eventually. 'These—' She spread out her arms, encompassing all three gifts. 'These are the best gifts I've ever received.'

'So, why are you so sad?'

'I'm not,' she insisted. 'I'm just . . . A little . . . *overwhelmed*.'

Maverick didn't try and talk her down from the wave of emotions as she choked on her tears. Didn't he understand exactly what she meant? Hadn't he felt that swift kick to the stomach when Nina had thrown her arms around Poppy and invited her to blow out the candles? In that small moment, Maverick had looked at them, and he'd seen everything he'd ever wanted. He'd thought: *My girls* – and then he'd felt that instant punch of panic.

So, he didn't try and placate Nina now. He understood. And based on what she'd told him about her childhood, her mother, and, yes, her past lovers, the speed, the intensity, of them was probably even more overwhelming for her than it was for him. And that was saying nothing of the extremely traumatic incident that had brought them together in the first place . . .

He did reach for her though, and he did haul her across the two feet separating them and onto his lap.

Nina didn't laugh as he'd hoped. She snuggled into him and sighed as if she'd found a momentary resting place. Her slender fingers, always so anxious, toyed with one of his shirt buttons. 'I like this,' she whispered. 'I like this too much.'

'Yeah. Me too.'

He didn't say more. He couldn't quite manage it against the weight of his past, which pulled him backwards when he'd rather not remember. But he'd been here before. He'd rushed into a relationship with an unavailable woman, and it had almost destroyed him.

As much as he'd never regret Shannon, because she'd given him Poppy, Maverick didn't want to relive any of that pain, and saying goodbye to Nina was already going to be difficult enough.

He didn't give her any false comfort, only held her as she regained her composure, and when she seemed to have levelled out a bit, he said. 'You look like someone who's never had cake for breakfast.'

She laughed quietly. 'Do pancakes count?'

'No.'

'Why not?'

'They're the wrong flour to sugar ratio to be considered cake,' he said seriously, and pushing to his feet, started carrying her to the door.

'Wait! Mav! I've got to change.'

Maverick looked down and noticed for the first time that she was wearing the old 'Rage Against the Machine' shirt he'd had on the night before and a pair of little shorts. 'You looked dressed to me.'

'What if Poppy recognizes your shirt?'

'Poppy is about as interested in my clothes as she is in vegetables – i.e. not at all.' Still, he put her down and watched as she quickly lifted the shirt up and off and sent him a playful wink over her shoulder.

Maverick's mouth watered at the sight of her slender back, bare to his gaze. Because he was standing close to the door, he kicked it shut.

Nina laughed.

He went to her, said, 'I love the way you look,' as he approached because it was true, and because he didn't want to sneak up on her.

She watched him over her shoulder, her dark eyes beckoning him, her mouth set in a sexy smirk, and when he stopped directly behind her, she pressed her bare back into him, welcoming him.

His hands rose to her naked breasts and kneaded. Leaning down, he trailed his lips over the velvet skin of her neck. 'I love the way you taste,' he murmured and lightly bit down on her shoulder. 'I love the way you fit in my hands.' To make his point, he cupped both of her breasts, and when she moaned, he whispered, 'I love those little noises you make.'

'Mav . . .'

'What do you want, Nina?'

'Touch me.'

Her trust almost shattered him. He knew what she was asking, knew that it took momentous courage after what she'd been through. And then she said, 'When you touch me, it makes me forget everything else,' and he groaned aloud.

He took her mouth in a passionate kiss as he slid his hand down, past the waistband of her shorts, breaking the kiss to curse when he slipped two fingers through her and found her soaking wet.

Nina let her head fall back onto his shoulder as she arched into his touch. One of her hands snaked back to hold on to his neck as he began to move, sliding his fingers up and down her damp inner flesh. 'I'm already so close,' she whimpered.

'Fuck,' he swore again. He slipped a single finger into her, felt those little muscles closing around him. He thrust quickly, pulling almost completely out of her every few strokes to rub the nerves around her entrance.

When she started panting, he gripped her hip with his free hand as if he could anchor himself to earth, to her, and when she closed her eyes and started riding his hand, he brought his lips to her ear and whispered, 'You're so goddamn sexy.'

'Mav . . .'

'I could come just from watching you.'

She erupted on a gasp.

Her back bowed.

Her body tightened around his finger, holding him close as the orgasm rolled through her, and when she started sliding down his front, he hauled her into his arms and placed his lips gently on hers.

This kiss was tender and slow and deep, full of everything he felt but couldn't say. Things like, *I want you, I need you, I'll miss you.*

It went on, spinning them through time, and when they finally broke apart, Nina smiled, and she whispered, 'Best. Birthday. Ever.'

Chapter 16

'Please, Maverick. I promise you won't regret it,' Markus whined for the hundredth time during dinner on Thursday evening.

Models, reps from Western Wear, and Markus's people had arrived in groups all throughout the day. Although he had spent most of the afternoon walking around, scouting locations, and taking notes, Markus clearly wasn't done. 'You don't have to do anything except go about your usual routine – wearing the clothes I tell you to. And occasionally listening to some direction – turn this way, look that way, smoulder.'

'*Smoulder?*' Maverick looked and sounded genuinely horrified. 'Markus, I've told you, I'm not a model.' He sat back in his chair and crossed his arms over his chest, his food forgotten.

It was a gesture Nina had come to think of as defensive, as if he could use his arms to protect himself from whatever was making him anxious.

'Neens, back me up,' Markus demanded.

Maverick turned those blue eyes on her, silently begging.

'It pays well,' she offered cautiously, thinking it through. 'If I did it with you, we could float all the rescue horse expenses for months.'

Markus gasped. 'Wait, you'd do this? *Why?* You never agree to photoshoots!'

'Because I can't ask Maverick to do it if I'm not willing to do it, too,' she replied, looking at Mav. 'And I really want him to do it.' There was more to it than that, but she couldn't say aloud that she wanted something, some evidence, to commemorate her time at Hunt Ranch with him.

Mav looked only at her when he said, 'My participation aside, I still think you should limit your interactions with them, try not to be seen.'

Nina settled for an easy truth. 'Markus has had all the models sign NDAs already. And the photos won't come out for months. By the time they do, I'll be back in LA.'

Maverick didn't comment on that. 'I've seen some of the models who arrived today. They're in their twenties. And *models*. I'm a forty-year-old rancher.'

'Models are models,' Markus countered, clearly having thought through his argument. 'They can sell it, but anyone looking at those pictures will see the staging. You . . . You look like you belong here. So, while *my* models will sell Western Wear to people looking for top-of-the-line denim, people like your guests at Hunt Ranch, *you'd* sell it to people who know the lifestyle, people who do what you do. You'd be the face of the campaign.'

'He'll do it.' This came from Sierra, who sat at the head of the table, sipping her red wine.

Maverick threw his hands up. '*Seriously?*'

The look of utter betrayal on his face made Nina smile – she couldn't help it. But she stroked his thigh beneath the table, soothing him.

'If he does it,' Sierra continued without acknowledging Maverick, 'we want "Maverick Hunt, Proprietor" on every one of his pictures.'

Maverick stared at her. 'Sierra.'

'Mav, I'm not an idiot. They're paying us a fortune to be here. They're renting out every spare room we have for two nights. And our name in a catalogue that sells high-end denim . . . That advertising would typically cost me *tens of thousands*.' She threw back the last of her wine, stood and repeated, 'He'll do it.'

Before she could walk away, Markus added, 'You too, gorgeous.'

Sierra's spine stiffened. She turned an incinerating glance on Markus. 'Traitor.'

Maverick smirked. 'Think of all the advertising dollars we'd save.'

Nina and Poppy looked back and forth between them like spectators at a tennis match.

'Fine.' Sierra tipped her chin up. 'But I can only be available for two hours in the afternoon.' When Maverick started to argue, she only talked over him. 'You can get work done while they're shooting. I can't.'

'I think two hours is great,' Markus interceded.

As Sierra walked away, Markus turned those calculating eyes on Poppy.

'No.' It was, to everyone's surprise, Nina who spoke up. 'She's too young, Markus.'

'Some of the best start younger than her.'

'And end up skipping childhood completely. No.' She looked to Maverick for support.

'I don't like the idea of her face being plastered in magazines for thousands of strangers to see,' he affirmed. 'No.'

Nina was genuinely relieved. She had seen the life Poppy had. The kid was sweet and kind and loving. She was so carefree. And she was too young to understand what she'd be trading, too young to agree to something that momentous. Because Markus was right. Poppy, with her long, chocolate-coloured hair, naturally golden skin, and oversized brown eyes could have been one of those kids. Famous at five, floundering at fifteen, forgotten at forty.

Still, Markus knew when Nina meant no, and begrudgingly relented. 'Fine.'

'I also want a copy of the print you gave Nina for her birthday,' Maverick added.

Markus's eyes twinkled. 'Deal. I—'

Whatever he'd been about to say was cut off by the doorbell. The ring pealed through the house, somehow sounding louder than usual due to the time of night.

Maverick frowned, clearly not expecting anyone. But he rose from the table and went to answer the door.

Nina heard the tinkling laugh first. It carried through the front of the house to the kitchen. 'I wonder who that is?'

Next to her, Poppy looked up at her with big, sad eyes. 'It's Shannon.'

Nina didn't question how Poppy could possibly know that. And she didn't ask why Poppy called her own mother 'Shannon' instead of 'Mom'. Turning to Markus, she said, 'Shannon Carlyle? Is she contracted for this shoot?'

'Yeah. Her agency contacted me unsolicited.' Markus crinkled his nose. 'She's kinda old news, but I hate to say no. Especially to someone who's given her life to the business.' He looked back and forth between Nina, who looked as sick as she felt, and Poppy, who looked as if she might burst into tears. 'Why?'

It was Poppy who said, 'She's my mom.'

Markus looked at Poppy with genuine surprise. 'What?'

'Shit.' In her panic, Nina forgot to watch her mouth.

Poppy's eyes welled with tears. She looked up at Nina, and though she didn't say anything, the plea was obvious.

Nina didn't think. She didn't try and placate Poppy or tell her that her mom had the legal right to visit. She scooped the five-year-old off her chair and headed for the back door.

'Where are you going?' Markus hissed. 'Don't leave me. You know I get awkward in tense situations.'

'Tell them we went to the barn to check on Barbie,' she hissed back, and disappeared outside.

She didn't stop, didn't pause to think that she had no right to make decisions for a child that wasn't hers. She only had to see those tears . . .

She wasn't sure if it was just the shock of the moment, or confusion, or if Nina's own panic had somehow transferred to Poppy, but the kid started crying genuine tears. She flung her arms around Nina, buried her face against her neck, and sobbed with an abandon only children felt comfortable expressing.

Unsure of what to do, Nina hiked Poppy higher onto her hip as she walked. It was almost a mile to the barn, but she thought she could manage Poppy's weight that far.

She used a tone she never knew she'd had, one that was soothing. 'It's okay, Poppy. We're just going to take some time with the horses. We're going to relax and maybe groom Zeph. How does that sound? And then tomorrow, when you feel better, we'll say hi to your mom, okay?'

Poppy nodded against Nina's neck, and even though she didn't speak, she seemed to settle down a little. Her sobs quietened, then stopped altogether. But she didn't loosen her arms around Nina's neck or move her face away from where she'd hidden it.

Nina knew she'd overstepped. But she didn't regret it, *couldn't* regret it. She understood what it was to see your mother coming and feel sick to the stomach. She knew what it was to want to hide from the person who'd given you life. And she couldn't have just sat there while Poppy suffered all those sick, confused feelings.

And if anyone had anything to say to her . . . Well, then she'd deal with it.

Maverick could only stare at Shannon in shock as she threw her arms around him and kissed him full on the mouth.

'Hi, darlin',' she crooned, her high-pitched giggle zinging through the house.

'Shannon.' His voice could have frozen out a forest fire. The problem was, Shannon was pure ice already.

'You look good, Mav,' she said and turned those purposefully seductive brown eyes on him.

He didn't feel the effect of them as he once – very foolishly and a long time ago – had. He asked, 'What are you doing here?'

'I'm in the Western Wear shoot!' She laughed and, uninvited, started walking through the house – the house that he had once offered her as a home. 'I couldn't believe it when the offer came up. I thought it would be fun to surprise you both.'

Maverick followed her like a mistrustful dog might follow a newcomer in his home. 'You're supposed to give notice of visitation, Shannon,' he said, hating that Poppy would be caught off-guard.

'Oh.' She made a small sound of distress. 'I didn't think you'd mind, Mav.'

She entered the kitchen a moment before him.

Maverick braced, preparing for Poppy's dread and anxiety, preparing for Nina's uncertainty. Only, they weren't there.

Markus sat alone at the table, drinking a glass of wine he'd topped to the brim. He smiled tightly. 'Shannon? What on earth are you doing at the ranch house?'

'Oh, Markus! It's so great to finally meet you! I've been following your work for ages.' Her eyes ran over him. 'You look so fabulous!' Going to him, she air-kissed both his cheeks. 'I bet you didn't know I used to live here,' she said, laughing. 'Poppy's my baby.'

'You're a mother?' The force of Markus's surprise could have flattened a Coke can at ten feet.

Shannon either didn't pick up on it or didn't care. 'I know. It took me a year to bounce back from pregnancy,' she sighed. She held out both arms, displaying a killer body.

And a few nips and tucks, Maverick thought.

He noticed that she had yet to ask where Poppy was but didn't comment on it.

'A little birdy told me that Nina Keller is a guest at the ranch,' she said, lowering her voice dramatically. 'I was hoping I could network—'

'Oh. Thinking about going into acting?' Markus asked blandly.

Maverick didn't smile at Markus's tone. If Shannon had heard that Nina was at the ranch, then others had, too. And that was a problem for him.

Still, Shannon had made her first mistake because Markus would not forgive someone who'd use his photoshoot to get to Nina.

Even Shannon seemed to pick up on it. 'Oh, no!' She waved one hand. 'But you know how these things happen,' she said. 'The more people you know, the better . . .'

'Hmm.' Markus sat back in his chair.

Perhaps sensing that she should have played her card a little more subtly, Shannon swept her gaze around the kitchen. 'Where's Poppy?'

'Oh, she's at the barn. Something about mucking stalls . . .' Markus shrugged.

The relief swept through Mav like water over a fresh burn. Markus didn't have to say anything for him to know that Nina had stepped in and taken Poppy down to the barn. That's who she was. But because he hadn't heard a car start up yet, and assumed they'd left on foot, he turned back for the door.

'Where are you going?' Shannon pouted.

'To get my girls.' He nodded once. 'I assume you know your way back to the resort.'

He left feeling lighter, like he could take on the next day with Shannon hanging around if he had Nina to distract him and Markus to run interference.

Maverick climbed into the Jeep and started towards the resort, but when he got a few hundred yards down the road and saw Nina carrying Poppy, his daughter's face buried against her neck, a punch of love hit him, and it was so big, so intense, that it stole his breath.

He hadn't meant for it to happen. Hell, he'd even tried to prevent it. But only a dead man could have resisted her. Nina had a warrior's heart and a contrastingly gentle spirit. And he wouldn't do her the disservice by saying that her looks had no bearing; he had eyes, and the woman was sexy as hell.

Still, he wouldn't do anything about it because she had told him her ground rules already and it wouldn't have been fair to pressure her with his feelings.

Nina heard the Jeep approaching and turned. Her entire body relaxed in relief when she saw that it was him and that he was alone. Still, as he pulled up, she looked at him as if waiting for him to reprimand her.

Mav had to bite his tongue to stop himself from pouring out his heart right then. In fact, if she hadn't had Poppy as a shield, he might have done it anyway, the consequences be damned.

'Need a ride, ladies?'

Poppy unstuck her face from Nina's neck at the sound of his voice, and the sadness and dread in her puffy, tear-filled eyes just about killed him. It was his fault. He didn't know how to hide his anger and bitterness and, yes, fear, when Shannon showed up, and Poppy picked up on his emotions. She barely knew Shannon, and certainly not enough to always react so devastatingly.

He'd have to work on that. For himself, because he had to let it go eventually. Because he *wanted* to let it go. But for Poppy too, because her life would be a lot easier if she didn't have to live with Mav's bitterness and anger.

Nina offered him a small smile.

Maverick put the car in park and got out. He gently took Poppy from Nina, and when her little arms and legs tightened around him, he had to actively refrain from texting Markus and telling him that the shoot was over.

Even if he wanted it to be, he couldn't have done it. To Markus, or to Sierra, who had managed to negotiate one hell of a deal for use of the resort. And he couldn't have done it even if he'd been prepared to disappoint them. They'd signed the contract already.

He rubbed Poppy's back. 'It's okay, baby. You don't have to see her today if you don't want to. You can wait for tomorrow.'

He hated that he had to prepare her for it anyway. Shannon might have been negligent, but she had rights. And, worse, she had leverage, because if Mav refused her anything, they both knew she could legally push for more.

Poppy leaned back and used one tiny hand to brush her damp hair off her cheek. 'Do I have to?'

'Well, yeah, baby. She's your mom.'

'I don't want her to be my mom.'

Mav didn't know what to say to that.

'Why can't Nina be my mom?' Poppy continued, unhindered by his silence.

Mav didn't look at Nina or laugh it off. He couldn't. 'Nina has to go back to her home. And her job.'

'But she'd make a really good mom,' Poppy insisted, latching on to the idea. In her little sing-song voice, she started listing all the reasons she thought Nina was a good fit. 'She's pretty, she can do French braids and she smells nice and she likes horses like we do. Sisi likes her. And she let me blow out her candles.'

Unable to resist, Mav glanced at Nina.

When their eyes met, she tried to laugh it off. 'I'm qualified,' she said seriously. 'I *do* smell good.'

Maverick opened one arm for her.

She didn't hesitate. She came to them, slotted beneath his arm, and then wrapped both of hers around them. She didn't stay there long, only long enough to squeeze them both and say, 'I think any woman would be lucky to be your mom, Poppy.'

She stepped back, and because he still held Poppy, she gently took the keys from his hand. 'I'll drive.'

'The barn,' he said, knowing none of them would go back to the ranch house until Shannon had left. At least for tonight. Tomorrow, he'd start dealing with it. Start trying to move forward again.

Nina only nodded. She climbed into the driver's seat and waited for Mav to get in the other side before starting the Jeep.

○

Markus looked at the woman sitting across the table from him, drinking wine she'd poured for herself like she owned the place.

Shannon Carlyle was a stunner, one of those rare women who'd won the genetic lottery – and had been told how beautiful she was by every person she'd met. She was an even six foot, a true blonde, and had come-get-me brown eyes that oozed sex and, when she wanted, vulnerability. She'd forged a solid career for herself for years but had fallen short of being a household name. At thirty-six, she was holding on by a single acrylic.

Markus, who had spent close to a decade studying people's facial expressions, saw the exact moment she turned that practised vulnerability on and aimed it in his direction. 'I suppose I deserved that.'

Because he had paid generously for her participation, and because he was solely regretting that he hadn't seen through her interest before he'd signed her, at first he tried to be diplomatic. 'It's not my place.'

'I just wanted to see her, you know. And Mav . . . He's a good dad, but he's so overprotective. He makes me feel unwelcome.'

The moment the criticism left Shannon's mouth, Markus changed tack. He drew from his own acting past. 'I wonder why,' he said, sounding genuinely surprised.

He had been sitting opposite Poppy, so hadn't missed the look of panic on the kid's face when she'd recognized Shannon's laugh. And he hadn't missed the fact that Shannon had name-dropped Nina before she'd even thought to ask after her own child.

'I think . . .' She paused as if struggling with her emotions.

Markus had to hand it to her, she might make a go of acting yet.

'I think his ego couldn't handle it – when I broke up with

him.' She wiped beneath her eye as if checking for tear-streaked mascara. 'He was heartbroken. He called me every day for weeks.'

'Hmm.' Markus tapped his lips as if thinking. 'I wonder if your kid had anything to do with that,' he said, this time too dryly for her to miss.

Those brown eyes froze over. The emotion disappeared immediately. 'I didn't want kids. He forced me to have her.'

'Bullshit.'

'He told me he wanted her. He *pressured* me.'

'A man, even one who's only a genetic contribution, telling you he wants to keep the baby you're pregnant with, is not the same as a man forcing you to have that baby. That's an adult, having a discussion and accepting responsibility for his actions.' Markus leaned forward in his chair. 'Sugar, I might not know Maverick Hunt well, but I only had to meet you once to know who the problem was in that relationship.'

Before she could throw her wine in his face, as he could tell she was sorely tempted to, he continued. 'We're going to keep this professional. The fact that we don't like each other isn't going to affect the shoot. But I'm going to make you three promises, just in case.' He held up his first finger like a teacher lecturing a child. 'If you harass Nina Keller while you're here, I will spread filthy, filthy lies about you to all my industry contacts. She's my ride-or-die, and you're just an ugly person with a pretty face that I'm paying for.' She gasped. 'Two, if you upset that kid, I will photoshop fifteen pounds onto every shot you're in.' She outright paled at that. 'Three, if you behave and give me good work without upsetting my family, I'll give you a few more years. I'll help you network. I'll tell everyone what a pleasure you were to work with. If it doesn't stick, it'll at least give you another four or five years to float until you can land a rich husband dumb enough to put up with your bullshit.'

She took her time thinking it through.

'Come on, honey. We both know the only reason you're sniffing around Nina is because those twenty-year-olds are snapping at your heels and you're hoping to get lucky with a second career when modelling drops you flat.' He pushed. 'The only way you stay relevant at your age is if you're too famous to drop – and I can help you bridge that gap.'

She didn't deny it. 'I've worked really hard. You might not understand, and I'm not asking you to, but I gave up a really good life because I wanted my career more. And it wasn't easy.' Markus, oddly, thought she might have been genuine. 'Walking away from Poppy was the second most difficult thing I've ever done. But building a successful modelling career was harder.' She tipped her head haughtily. 'And, yes, you're right. I can feel it dying.'

He stuck out one hand. 'So?'

She took it. 'Make me shine.'

Markus nodded. 'Keep those claws retracted.'

She pushed back from the table and started for the door, one foot perfectly in front of the other in an unconscious runway walk, her child seemingly forgotten.

She paused before exiting, asked, 'When Mav said, "My girls," was he talking about Nina Keller?'

'They're a thing,' he said. 'A good thing. Don't fuck with it.'

She nodded and walked away, not even bothering to stop and say hi to Sierra, who leaned against the wall, silently listening.

They remained quiet until the door slapped shut.

Sierra came to him. She nabbed his wine glass from his hand and took a huge gulp. 'Will you marry me?'

Markus laughed. 'Honey, if we didn't bat for the same team, I'd cart you off to Vegas tomorrow.'

She sighed. 'Drat.' She sat in the chair next to him.

'People like that only cooperate when the terms and conditions are in their favour.' He sighed. 'Besides, if modelling does drop her flat, who do you think she's gonna tap sympathy dollars from first?'

'Ugh.' She plonked her forehead on the table, muttered, 'I

know.' She took a deep breath and then raised her eyes back to his. 'I try really hard not to hate her – Shannon. But I can still hate that you're right.' She looked at the dinner table, half-eaten plates of food forgotten. 'Where did the others go?'

Markus rubbed his hands together for dramatic effect. 'So, check this. The doorbell rings, and Maverick goes to get it. Poppy immediately recognizes Shannon's voice and starts tearing up.'

'Poor kid.'

He held up one hand. 'Wait for it. My girl sees the tears, scoops the kid out of her chair, and just abandons the front line!'

'No . . . Really?'

'She left me alone to deal with Cruella! My best friend. Abandoned me like yesterday's socks.' Markus nodded. 'God only knows why I'm so thrilled about it.'

'Nina took Poppy away from Shannon?' Sierra asked, her eyes wide with disbelief.

'Shannon wasn't in the room yet. But yeah . . . Just *poof*.'

'Shit.'

'It's love.' He shook his head, thought, *About damn time*. But knowing it didn't stop the worry.

'Do you think she'll stick?'

Markus didn't want to give his doubts room to grow. But he felt he had to warn her. 'She struggles with people. She doesn't trust easily.' He laughed tiredly. 'Hell, the only reason she kept me was because I refused to budge. And if Maverick knows what's good for him, he'll refuse to budge too.'

'Yeah, that's what worries me.'

'He won't fight for her.'

Sierra polished off the rest of his wine. 'Maverick will leave the decision up to her. He might – *might* – tell her how he feels. But he won't pressure her. And he won't ask her to stay because the last time he did, it blew up in his face spectacularly.'

Markus knew that. Isn't that what he'd told Shannon when she spouted that bullshit about being pressured into having the kid?

'Make me a promise.'

'After you just put Shannon in her place? Sunshine, I'd go to the moon for you.'

Markus picked up her hand and kissed the back of it. 'When it happens, we don't let them get away with being stupid.'

'I hate interfering.'

Markus burst out laughing. 'Bitch, you *love* it!'

Sierra looked stunned for a moment, as if she couldn't believe he'd actually said it. But when she started laughing, she laughed loudly. 'Oh, God, I really do! People can't be trusted to make decisions for themselves!'

They laughed until they both had tears streaming down their cheeks, and every time they made eye contact, they only laughed more, laughed harder.

Markus thought that while he and Nina might have been soulmates, he and Sierra were kindred spirits. They had the same need for planning and organization, the same obsession with success and ruthlessness in carrying it out.

Like most of the decisions in Markus's life, once he decided that he and Sierra were going to be lifelong friends, he grabbed ahold with both hands. So, when she stood and started cleaning the kitchen, which was usually Mav's chore, he pushed to his feet to help. 'Tell me your story.'

'My story?'

'Everything,' he confirmed as he threw food scraps into the bin. 'Including why you feel sympathy for that bitch?'

'That obvious?'

'You're fierce and stubborn and love your brother and niece, and yet you didn't pile into Shannon as I'd have expected . . .'

'It's one of those long, sad ones,' she warned.

Markus looked up at that. He saw the grief in her eyes, felt a little jolt of surprise at the intensity of it. But because he knew that friends didn't shy away from the pain, he topped up his empty wine glass and passed it to her.

'I think that Shannon might have actually suffered from PPD, and I make a conscious effort to withhold my disdain for her because of it. And it's hard. Because I hate her. Not just for what she did to Mav, or for abandoning Poppy. But because my baby died, and I will never understand how she could just walk away from hers, from Poppy, when I would have done anything for even a single minute with mine . . .'

Markus gave her time. He stood at her side while they did the dishes. He didn't speak. He just listened as Sierra talked, telling him things she hadn't told anyone else.

She told him that she'd birthed a stillborn baby at full term, and that the biggest regret of her life was that she'd refused to hold her dead child before they'd taken her away. She told him she'd only ever loved one man, and that she'd loved him since she'd been fifteen years old. She told him that whoever had said the opposite of love isn't hate, but indifference, had been wrong, and that you could only truly hate someone proportionate to how much you had once loved them.

Chapter 17

Although Mav's internal alarm had him rousing at four-thirty the next morning, for the first time in his life he didn't feel like he had the energy or the willpower to get out of bed. And the fact that he dreaded the photoshoot wasn't the full of it. Some, but not all.

Rather, the woman curled up against him, her head on his shoulder, her arm flung over his chest, her leg strung over both of his was the heart of the problem because even as Maverick told himself he should get up, he didn't want to wake her. He didn't want to leave her side at all.

She was almost halfway through her stay, which meant that in only two weeks, she would pack her bags and walk out of his life as if she'd never been a part of it.

Terrified of the thought, needing to remind himself that she was still there with him now, he raised his fingers to her arm and distractedly traced a pattern on her bare skin.

It was hard not to compare her to Shannon, even though he knew in his heart that the two women were as different as day and night. Nina was reserved and quiet, almost shy, and she guarded a gentle heart. Shannon was loud and flirtatious. Vivacious. And cold.

But they were both career women, working in fields that made it hard to balance family. And unlike Shannon, who had made promises and then balked, Nina had only been honest with him from the start. Hadn't she insisted on those ground rules that first night?

'What are you thinking about?'

Her sleepy voice had him glancing down at her. Her eyes were still half closed, her long lashes hiding them from view. 'I didn't mean to wake you,' he said quietly, and kissed the side of her head.

'I could hear you thinking in my sleep.' Her cheek curved against his bare chest when she smiled. 'Are you worried about the photoshoot?'

'Not really.' But he couldn't bring himself to tell her that he was worried he'd regret letting her walk away from him for the rest of his life. And he was outright terrified of telling her how he felt in case she felt pressured into trying to make it work like Shannon had. 'Shannon arriving like she did is fucking with my head,' he said, which seemed to sum everything up quite neatly.

'I'm not her.'

'Not even close,' he agreed. But because he felt that panic pressing in, he asked, 'Do you remember that day you asked me if I loved her, and I was unsure?'

'Yes.'

'I'm not unsure anymore. I didn't love her. I liked her. I liked that she was smart and successful, and for a while her glamour seemed to be a – I don't know – contrast, maybe, to the ranch life. The sex was good.' He frowned as he thought what it was to touch Nina, to feel his whole world revolving around her pleasure. 'Not intimate. But good. But, no, I didn't love her.'

It was the closest he could come to saying the words to Nina just then. But Mav knew, in that moment, with Nina in his arms, that whatever he'd felt for Shannon hadn't been love. Not even close.

She didn't pry, didn't ask what made him bring it up now. She rolled over and looked at the time on her phone. 'Are you going out to the horses?'

'Yeah. I should have been out the door already.' With a tired groan, Mav rose to a seated position. He looked down at Nina, ran one hand over her hair before leaning down and pressing his lips to hers. 'Go back to sleep.'

'Could I tag along?'

'To bring the horses in?'

'Yeah.' She toyed with the hem of his shirt that she wore. 'I want to spend the time with you while I can, you know.'

The fact that she was already living with leaving on her mind affirmed his decision not to say anything.

Nina started rambling. 'I won't get in the way. I can just start on grooming Barbie in her stall and then help with the others once you've brought them in.'

'You're never in my way, Nina,' he said, but because those bigger words threatened to spill from him, he moved to the end of the mattress and pushed to his feet. 'Why don't you go get changed. Meet me in the kitchen when you're ready?'

'Okay.' She hopped off his bed. 'Five minutes.'

The moment she left he sat heavily back down. He ran both hands through his hair and exhaled a huge breath. 'Shit.'

The single word wasn't exactly poetry, but it about summed up his situation. As difficult as it was to keep the course, Maverick knew he had to. He could admit that he was scared, and that trust didn't come easily for him, but asking Nina to stay would have been selfish. It wouldn't have been fair for the girls, for Nina, who'd have to split her time between LA and Santa Barbara. And for Poppy, who'd have a half-timer in her life – and that was *if* things worked out. If they ended, he'd have been responsible for his kid's first heartbreak.

But knowing what he had to do didn't make living with the decision any easier. Still, never one to wallow, he pushed back up and walked through to his bathroom to change.

Dressed in a white flowy dress, cowgirl boots, and a black Western Wear cowboy hat, Nina watched from the sidelines as Markus had Maverick saddle Zephyr. It was their fourth time running through it, but neither man nor horse showed a flicker of frustration.

In the golden fields around them, models, wardrobe personnel, and makeup artists prepared for their own scheduled segments. Although Nina knew that Shannon Carlyle was there, and that the woman's eyes were constantly glued on her, Nina ignored her completely.

Behind his camera, Markus cued Maverick to start again.

Mav swung the saddle onto Zephyr's back, being careful to control the downward movement as the forty-pound saddle landed on the horse. While Markus snapped dozens of pictures, Maverick went about slowly rearranging the saddle pad and threading the cinch strap through the cinch ring. He tightened it, finished it off with a Windsor knot. And when he stepped back, removed his hat, and wiped his sweaty brow with his forearm, Markus took a few last shots and then lowered his camera.

'Okay, I think we got it that time.'

Mav comically raised both hands in a prayer of thanks.

'Har. Har.' Markus's eyes were glued on his camera as he flicked through the shots. 'Wait until you see these, Cowboy. You'll fall flat.'

'I've seen your work. I already know you're good. But that doesn't mean I have to enjoy doing it.'

'True. But you'll do it anyway because you want to help a friend – and because you're terrified of your little sister.'

Maverick only sighed in agreement, making Nina smile.

'Okay, Neens.' Markus turned to her. 'You're up.' His eyes scanned her, checking, she knew, for any wardrobe or makeup changes he wanted to make. The last of her bruises had faded, and although her ribs still throbbed from time to time, she'd learned how to move to minimize the pain. Finding nothing out of place, Markus shucked his head in Maverick's direction.

She walked to where Maverick stood by Zephyr.

People stopped what they were doing to watch.

Nina didn't feel nervous. Modelling was just another type of acting, after all, pretending to be someone you weren't in front of a camera while others watched the show.

'Okay.' Markus let his camera hang from the strap around his neck as he directed. 'I'm thinking Nina in the saddle, Mav leading the horse.'

'Why don't we take the saddle off?' Mav suggested. 'Go bareback with us both on. Maybe, Nina in front of me.'

Markus's eyes rounded with glee. 'Is that safe?'

'With Zephyr – yes.' When Markus still seemed unsure, Maverick added, 'I would never put Nina in a dangerous situation.'

Nina's heart tripped a little at the words, spoken with sincerity.

It also seemed to be all the convincing Markus needed. 'Okay. Fuck it. Let's do it.'

Maverick patiently removed the saddle again and carried it to one of the saddle racks he and Benji had hauled out. 'With our combined weight, we can't move much. Zeph could manage it, but it would be a strain on her back.'

'We'll do mostly still shots. No walking but maybe slight movements to reposition her body.'

Maverick nodded.

Nina looked around. They were far from the barn and any mounting blocks, and without the saddle and stirrups she had to ask, 'How are we going to get on?'

'I'll get on her first and then help you up.' So saying, he gathered the reins in his left hand and vaulted onto Zephyr's back in one smooth movement.

Markus's jaw dropped open.

Both of them stared at Maverick.

One of the models behind them whispered, 'He's so smoking hot,' to one of her friends.

At her side, Markus asked, 'Are you a little turned on right now?'

Nina sighed, but she didn't deny it. 'Oh yeah.'

Watching Maverick on horseback had become her favourite pastime. He was so natural, so comfortable, and, she'd admit, impossibly sexy too. And in those small moments when she saw him soothing an animal, stroking its neck with his large hand as he whispered words of approval, Nina couldn't bear to look away.

When he held out one hand for her, she didn't hesitate even though she had no idea how he was going to get her on too. She went to him. 'What do I do?'

'My back's not what it used to be,' he said with a small grin. 'So, Markus if you pop a knee . . .'

Markus knelt, putting one knee at a ninety-degree angle. He jokingly bowed his head. 'Your humble servant, my queen.'

The giggle tore from Nina's throat before she could contain it. 'Markus, this is serious,' she chastised.

'Yes – your highness.'

'Oh my God, you're impossible.' She laughed. But when she took Maverick's hand and stepped on Markus's knee, the smile on her face was big and bright.

Maverick lifted her onto Zephyr's back easily. As soon as she had found her balance, he shimmied her back so that she was pressed against him, asked, 'You okay?'

'Perfect.'

She wasn't given time to adjust to the feel of the horse's bare back beneath her as Markus draped her dress how he wanted it and began directing them.

For close to forty minutes, they followed his orders, shifting their faces and bodies to the angles he wanted. Eyes looking forward, scanning the horizon. Nina's head resting against Mav's chest, one of his hands holding the reins, one of his arms around her waist. They even did one pose where she sat sideways on Zephyr's back, both of her dress-covered legs falling next to one of Mav's.

'Okay, last one,' Markus called.

Behind her, Maverick's body sagged in relief.

'Mav, put that arm back around Nina's waist again. Neens, tilt your head back and look at him over your shoulder. We're going for sexy, can't-get-enough-of-you vibes.'

Nina's body came to life as Mav's strong forearm wrapped around her waist, the dark blue shirt he wore contrasting with her white dress. She used her God-given talent to hide that burn of need as she tilted her head back to look at him.

Mav's blue eyes softened, smiled. 'This is an easy one,' he said.

On the ground, Markus shouted, 'Someone get me a cold bottle of water!' making both Maverick and Nina smile.

As they looked at one another, everyone else disappeared. The shutter sound intensified, each click coming so close to the one behind it that Nina barely heard it at all.

If Markus gave direction, Nina didn't hear it. She was too focused on the man holding her, his eyes mirroring all those emotions she felt stirring inside of her – love and lust and panic and despair. Without thinking, Nina shifted. She placed her lips on his, and when he sighed, it was her who took them deep. The kiss was sweet and long and intensely intimate.

As Nina sank into him, Mav's arm tightened around her, holding her against him. Nina's heart thumped heavily, her excitement uncontainable. And when Markus yelled, 'Okay, that's it! Perfect!' and Mav pulled back, she was mortified to realize that she'd let the moment get away from her.

'Sorry,' she whispered, slightly breathless still. 'I didn't mean to—'

'I did,' Mav said, his voice tight with an impatience she'd never heard in him before.

Beneath the impatience, she heard the pain and she regretted that she'd caused it.

'I know the stakes are different for you,' he said, *so* quietly. Tiredly. 'But I'm not going to pretend that you kissing me in front of your people doesn't make me feel like king of the fucking world.'

And with that, he slipped off the horse and held his arms out for her. He helped her down, and then before she could speak, turned and walked off.

Nina watched him go, her heart in her throat, and when Markus approached, his eyes filled with concern, she faked a smile.

'You okay?' he asked. 'That looked intense.'

Nina almost said she was fine, but it would have been a lie. 'I don't know what I want anymore.'

'Bullshit, baby.'

Her eyes snapped to his.

'You think I don't see you,' he whispered. 'Honey, I see all of you. So,' he ceded, gently, 'I know that you're scared, and I understand why. But don't pretend that you don't know what you want. You're stronger than that.'

She hated that he was right. 'I can want him and still know it's a bad idea, still not know what to do about it.'

Markus cocked one hip. 'From where I'm standing, it looked like a really good idea – a delicious one, even.' Leaning forward, he showed her the picture, frozen on his huge camera screen.

Nina's breath caught.

It was that second in time before she'd kissed Maverick, that single moment when the attraction had been pulling them closer. 'Am I that obvious?' she asked and raised a single finger to trace her face on the screen, memorizing the look of love she'd worn. 'I thought I could hide it better.'

'You're so worried about being vulnerable that you haven't even looked at him yet.'

Her eyes shifted, focusing on the shot of Maverick.

And all she could do was close her eyes and say, 'Shit.'

Markus pulled her in for a hug. 'I know you've worked for everything good that's ever happened to you. But I promise, Neens, sometimes good things just happen for no reason.'

Only mention of her work, her career had that constant simmer of panic heating to a boil. Because what if she gave up Maverick for her career, and then her career imploded anyway? And what if it didn't, but then she was miserable because she'd walked away from him – and Poppy? Because God knew she adored that little girl too. And even though the negative was so much easier to focus on, there was a selfish, desperate part of her that asked: *And what if you could have both?* And it was so big, so terrifying, that she couldn't even consider the possibility.

'And on the rare occasion the universe gives you lemons,' Markus continued, 'you make goddamn lemonade because you're going to need it for the scorcher the bitch undoubtedly has just around the corner.'

'I know that good things happen,' Nina argued.

'Do you?'

'Yes.' Nina gave him one last squeeze. 'I found you, didn't I?'

Markus sniffled and waved her away. 'Go. I'm done with you for the day.'

'Does that mean you're queen now?'

Markus winked at her. 'You know it.'

Nina laughed as she walked away in search of Maverick. She found him back at the barn, mucking out Zephyr's stall as if the devil were on his back.

She stopped a little distance away, watching him through the open door. He was so big, so strong, and, she knew, so capable. It made her want to lean on him. It made her want to tell him all of her dark truths because he would help her – she absolutely knew that to be true. In fact, that might have been the entire reason she *hadn't* told him yet. Before she'd known him well, she'd worried that he would judge her. But now, she knew she hadn't told him because she was terrified of what he might do. Not to her. But *for* her.

He sensed her. His gaze lifted, and the moment he saw that it was her, he banked the worst of his anger. The fact that he didn't want to scare her only made her love him more, but Nina didn't say that. She didn't say anything.

She walked to him and, roping her arms around his waist, nestled in. 'I'm sorry.'

The fight drained from his body in one big exhalation. Nina felt it leave him. 'I'm sweaty.'

'I don't care.'

He sighed and, dropping the rake, wrapped his arms around her. 'You have nothing to be sorry for. *I'm* sorry. I keep promising myself I won't pressure you, and then every time I'm with you I feel this urge to drop to my knees and beg.'

Nina's heart swelled until she couldn't contain it any longer. The love seemed to burst within her, flooding her system with absolute joy.

'And I know that's unfair – to you and to Poppy. Christ, you're a famous actress! I know that.'

That joy dimmed around the edges.

'I know it's a mistake as sure as I know that I was raised to fight for what I want. And even though I want to believe it might work if I asked you to stay, history has made me terrified to trust. And it's not just me this time. It's Poppy too. And I can't make decisions based only on what I want anymore. So, I'm not going to ask you.'

She nodded, unable to meet his eyes as her disappointment flared.

'But Nina—' he tipped her chin back, forcing her gaze to his anyway '—there'll always be a place for you here. With us.' Those blue eyes held hers. 'Do you understand what I'm saying?'

She knew that he wouldn't give the words to her, that he was leaving it up to her. She nodded. 'I do.'

'One day, one month, one decade. It doesn't matter. I'll be here.'

He didn't kiss her. He wrapped both of his arms around her and held her close, cocooning her in the safety of his promise.

And Nina could only internally laugh at herself because she'd already made up her mind.

She wouldn't tell him though. *Couldn't* tell him until she'd sorted out her life and weathered the upcoming storm. Because it was coming. She could feel it gathering with every day that she sheltered. And when it broke, it would hurt. It might even destroy her. But if there was one thing she could do, it was protect Mav and Poppy from her choices.

Chapter 18

That night at the wrap party, Nina sat with Sierra and Poppy as models, assistant photographers, clothing and makeup artists, and brand reps enjoyed relaxing after a long, hot day of hard work. Markus made the rounds, completely in his element being the centre of attention.

On stage, a different band than the one that had played earlier that week, sang 'Something in the Orange' by Zach Bryan. Nina hummed along as she sipped Maverick's beer, which he'd given her when he'd gone to fetch her another margarita from the bar.

As the band wrapped up the song, Nina joined the applause. 'Thank you. Thank you.' But the lead singer didn't immediately start into the next song. She said, 'We have a special treat for you tonight.'

People stopped what they were doing to look towards the stage.

'For those of you who don't know Maverick, he's one of the owners here at Hunt Ranch.' Behind her, the musicians started playing quietly. 'He's gonna be singing a song for you tonight. And, trust me, this is a rare occasion.' She ducked under her guitar strap and held out her instrument. 'Put your hands together, folks.'

People clapped wildly.

Markus howled like a wolf.

As Mav walked onto the stage and took the guitar, Poppy, who had been sitting by Sierra, chatting away about her day, came to Nina. She climbed up onto Nina's lap without pause, said, 'My dad sings good.'

'I bet,' Nina managed, but she couldn't tear her eyes off the stage, where Mav was settling in, strumming the guitar as naturally as if he played for a living.

God, he was sexy, dressed in blue jeans and a black Hunt Ranch shirt, his ball cap on backwards.

'I promised a special woman that I'd sing for her sometime, and, well, this song is one of my favourites,' he said into the mic. 'I'm a little rusty, so you'll have to forgive any mistakes.'

People laughed.

Maverick looked right at Nina, winked. 'This is "Run" by George Strait.'

Nina wasn't familiar with the song, but it was obviously popular. She looked around as people whooped and clapped, but the moment Mav started singing, they settled down to listen, almost as if they were as afraid as she was that they might miss a moment of it.

> *'If there's a plane or a bus leaving LA*
> *I hope you're on it*
> *If there's a train moving fast down the tracks*
> *I hope you caught it—'*

His voice was deep and smooth. Nina almost couldn't believe how good he was. And even then, she wouldn't have cared if he'd been terrible because he was looking at *her*, singing to *her*. And the lyrics brought tears to her eyes.

"Cause I swear out there ain't where you ought to be

So, catch a ride, catch a cab
Don't you know I miss you bad
But don't you walk to me
Baby, run, cut a path across the blue skies

Straight in a straight line
You can't get here fast enough
Find a truck and fire it up
Lean on the gas and off the clutch
Leave LA in the dust
I need you in a rush
So, baby, run
If you ain't got a suitcase

Get a box or an old brown paper sack
And pack it light or pack it heavy
Take a truck, take a Chevy
Baby, just come back'

Her throat started closing. Her eyes burned. And Poppy, seeing her tears, reached up to gently touch her face. 'Why are you sad?' she asked, her own big eyes starting to tear up.

'I'm not sad,' Nina insisted, and hugged the little girl to her. 'I'm happy.'

Overhearing their conversation, Sierra turned serious eyes on Nina. 'You should listen to the original sometime. Even Mav can't hold a candle to George Strait.'

Nina doubted that. But she didn't reply. She was too busy listening to the song, holding on to every word.

'There's a shortcut to the highway out of town

Why don't you take it?
Don't let that speed limit slow you down
Go on and break it
Baby, run, cut a path across the blue skies

Straight in a straight line
You can't get here fast enough
Find a truck and fire it up
Lean on the gas and off the clutch
Leave LA in the dust
I need you in a rush
So, baby, run
Baby, run

Oh baby, run
Baby, run'

People started cheering the moment he finished the song. 'Thank you.'
From the back of the crowd, Markus shouted, 'Encore!' and had people applauding in agreement.

Maverick passed the guitar back to the lead singer. 'One's all I've got in me, folks. I'm gonna let Jessie take it from here.'

The lead singer took the mic again. 'What'd I tell you?' she shouted. People hooted and whistled.

Before she started her next song, Jessie laughed into the mic. 'I hope you enjoyed it. He's only ever sung for us once and I had to get him blackout drunk first.'

She started strumming her guitar. 'This is "Feathered Indians".'

As the music filled the night, Maverick ambled back to where they sat, Nina and Sierra's drinks now in his hands. He passed them each one and then sat down by Nina.

Poppy immediately slipped from Nina's lap onto his. 'You sing so good, Daddy,' she praised him.

He kissed the top of Poppy's head. 'Thanks, baby.'

Nina couldn't look at him. She knew that everything she was feeling was too close to the surface just then. While the song had roused her nerves, his proximity had every one of them firing overtime. The immensity of it all was astounding.

Nina knew that roots grew when they were watered, and that family didn't have to be connected by blood. Family could be made. Luigi and Markus had taught her that. But what she felt for Maverick was different. It was more. *Everything*.

Shannon stood with a group of colleagues barely out of high school, one ear tuned to their conversation, most of which she barely understood. But her eyes were glued on the tight circle the Hunts made, their chairs turned together, keeping everyone else at a little distance.

Maverick and Nina Keller might not have advertised the fact that they were together. They weren't all over each other. But their attraction was obvious. And the kiss during the photoshoot . . . Shannon didn't care how good of an actress Nina Keller was, that kiss had been one-hundred-per-cent spontaneous. And real.

Shannon, who had always used jealousy to hone what she wanted for her own life, didn't feel that green-eyed regret when she looked at Maverick and Nina together now.

She had known Maverick had never loved her. Oh, he'd tried to convince himself he did when she'd fallen pregnant, but his willingness to step in and take responsibility had only made her feel trapped. It hadn't mattered that he was a good man, one of the best. A woman could still feel trapped by a good man.

She'd told him she was pregnant three days before her scheduled termination because, despite what people thought about her, she was a fair woman and he'd deserved to know. And the look on his face . . . The complete joy . . . It had terrified her because it had only taken one look at Mav's face to know that she couldn't hurt him by going through with it.

Maverick had told her he'd support her no matter what, but she'd told Markus the truth when she'd said she'd felt pressured. Because he'd wanted that baby so goddamn much.

So, she'd chickened out. And although she'd managed to contract a few maternity shoots during her pregnancy, for the most part, she'd been alone at the ranch house from four-thirty in the morning until six in the evening. She didn't like horses or getting dirty – and neither did her skin. And because she'd seen how hard Maverick worked for everything, she had felt like she couldn't say anything, couldn't complain when he'd finally come home, stressed and exhausted.

As her belly had grown, she'd felt the baby sucking the life out of her. And every time someone's eyes had lit up and they'd said those things people say to pregnant woman, things like: 'You must be so excited,' 'Boy or girl?' 'When are you due?' 'Do you have any names yet?' all Shannon had felt was shame. Because all she wanted was to get the baby out so that she could start getting her life back on track.

And then Poppy had been born, and that impossibly huge burst of love she'd felt the moment they'd put her child in her arms had terrified her more than the depression or dread or shame. Because she'd seen the writing on the wall. That burst of love had been so bright it had illuminated her whole future. A life on the ranch she hated with a man she didn't love, raising a child instead of pursuing the one thing she'd wanted since Harry Jensen had stopped her and her mother on the sidewalk to scout her for his modelling agency when she'd been a fourteen-year-old nobody with a middle-class future ahead of her.

So, she'd left.

But it had taken her two months to summon the strength to

actually walk away from Poppy. And, although she didn't deserve to say it, it had broken her heart. She'd had to sever herself completely because every time Maverick called and tried to get her to go visit, Shannon had felt that panic rise in her throat. She'd known, even then, that if she went back, held her daughter, smelled that infant smell, she wouldn't be able to walk away again.

Still, leaving had cast her into a depression that sometimes still swallowed her. Though she couldn't speak to anyone about it – *boo hoo, poor woman who abandoned her baby!* – she checked the Hunt Ranch Instagram every day, hoping for something – *anything* – of Poppy.

Shannon was an intelligent woman. She did not wallow in self-pity because she knew she had made her own choices. But it was only now, with her career dwindling despite the blood and pain she'd suffered for it, and not a single person but herself to care, that she realized that Poppy would have loved her unconditionally. Ironically, she might have been the only person who would have, too.

Instead, Shannon had stayed away and now she and Poppy didn't know how to interact with one another. And Shannon *tried*. But it was hard to try when the five-year-old in question would so clearly rather be anywhere else.

Seeing that Nina was walking to the bar, Shannon politely excused herself from the group and drifted to her. She wouldn't stir trouble. She had too much riding on Markus to piss him off.

She came up beside her, wasn't above noticing that while Nina Keller was beautiful, the actress wasn't built to knock people flat like she was. Nina was small and delicate while Shannon was tall and slim with perfect proportions.

The tension ratcheted up a notch when Nina noticed her. The air between them seemed to solidify.

'Don't worry. I'm not going to cause a scene,' she said by way of introduction. 'It's not my style.' Which wasn't entirely true. Drama was necessary for attention. But at the right time and place.

Nina didn't reply right away. She smiled at the bartender and ordered two margaritas and a beer, and it was only once the man had turned to sort the drinks, that she faced Shannon. 'What do you want?'

Shannon had to hand it to her. Nina Keller had a backbone. 'I was hoping you could invite me to join you,' she replied.

Nina stared at her in shock.

'Mav doesn't trust me—'

'Don't tell me that surprises you?'

'No. Not at all.' She refused to succumb to sadness though it would have been genuine and probably would have helped her cause. 'I don't want to push my way in. But I'd really like to spend a little time with Poppy before I leave tomorrow.'

'Shannon—' Nina shook her head '—you're Poppy's mom. You don't have to ask me for permission.'

'I figured if we could get along, it might put Mav at ease. Poppy . . . She picks up on his emotions, you know. It makes it hard to want to try.'

Nina's eyebrows raised, but not in judgement. Her eye flickered over Shannon, considering. 'Why don't you visit her?'

The question, the bluntness in which it was asked, momentarily shook her. But she replied honestly, 'At first, it was because I was too afraid that I'd give in to my own feelings and stay. And then because I was too ashamed. Now . . . Because I see Poppy's dread when she sees me and it's too hard.'

'Did you ever think she might dread you less if she knew you better?'

Shannon drew back slightly at that. 'No. I've seen you with Poppy, so you might not understand this, but some women aren't made for motherhood.'

'Yes. And some choose not to be. There's a difference.'

Shannon didn't bother arguing. 'Yes.'

Nina sighed. She turned to face the Hunt circle. Shannon followed her gaze and saw that Maverick was on alert. The silent messages that passed between Nina and him were impossible to miss.

'Come on then,' Nina said after a long moment. With the drinks in her hands, she started back to the Hunts' circle.

Shannon followed. Her palms slicked with sweat. Her heart beat an anxious tune in her throat. And when she saw Poppy's eyes widen with anxiety at only the sight of her, she exhaled a deep breath.

Nina frowned at her. 'What's wrong?'

In a moment of complete weakness that she'd regret later, Shannon said, 'For an intelligent, successful woman, it's galling to not know what to do.'

'Don't try to be her mom. She doesn't know you, and it confuses her. Just be yourself. She'll loosen up. Trust me on this; I have zero experience with kids, but Poppy's made it really easy for me.'

'I know it doesn't mean much coming from me, but I'm happy for you and Maverick. And for Poppy. She clearly adores you.'

'It's a little soon for that,' Nina said cautiously.

'No.' Shannon looked directly into Nina's eyes. 'If he'd looked at me like that – the way he looked at you during the shoot and when he sang – even *once*, I never would have left.'

Nina didn't deny it. She asked, 'So that's why you left?'

'In a nutshell. I'd worked too hard for my career to stay with Poppy when Maverick never looked at me like that.'

Surprisingly, Nina didn't seem judgemental. 'I understand,' she said, 'what it's like to live and die by your career. I know the terror of being a woman in a vanity industry. But I'm telling you from experience, if you don't step up, you're going to lose her for good. Poppy . . . She's five. If you started giving a damn now, by the time she turned ten she would barely remember a time when you weren't there. But if you don't step in soon, by the time she's ten she won't care about you at all.'

Shannon's throat closed at the possibility.

'Mav . . . He would never try and stop you from seeing her.'

'Oh God,' Shannon whispered anxiously, cutting Nina off as they came close.

'Look who I found,' Nina chirped brightly.

'Hi.' Shannon actually waved before she caught herself. 'I hope you don't mind if I join you for a bit.'

There was a moment of stunned silence before Mav got to his feet. 'Of course not.' He offered her the space next to Nina on the settee and then walked off to pull himself a chair from a nearby cluster.

The conversation started back up slowly.

For the first time ever, Shannon didn't try and bridge that gap between her and Poppy. She didn't even look at her daughter though she was acutely aware of those big brown eyes turned warily – maybe also a little cautiously? – in her direction.

She talked and laughed with the others, slowly relaxing though she wasn't sure she'd ever feel comfortable with them.

And an hour later when the band started playing Shania Twain's 'Any Man of Mine' and the line dancing instructor got up to lead the dance, Poppy jumped up on the chair. 'Daddy!'

She didn't even have to tell him what she wanted, Shannon noted. He just knew.

Maverick got to his feet with a resigned sigh. 'If I have to do it, you guys have to do it too.'

Sierra didn't need to be told twice. She did a little shoulder shimmy and whooped. 'I'm gonna get Markus.'

Maverick held out one hand for Nina. 'Come on, baby. You can't leave me stranded.'

'I don't know how.' Nina laughed.

'That's why there's an instructor,' he insisted and pulled her to her feet.

He didn't offer Shannon a hand or tease her lightly, but that cool, blue gaze met hers. He tipped his head towards the dance floor, said, 'Shann?'

'Yeah,' she rasped. She loved to dance, loved to lose her thoughts to music. 'I love to dance.'

'Me too!' At Maverick's side, Poppy's eyes lit up. They skimmed over Shannon, considering now.

As she pushed to her feet, she tried to keep her tone casual. 'What's your favourite song to dance to?'

Poppy considered this question seriously as they walked. But after a few seconds, she turned those big eyes on Maverick. 'Daddy, what's that one called?'

'"The Git Up".'

'I like that one,' Poppy said. 'What's yours?'

'It's called "Tik Tok". By Kesha.'

'Oh, I don't know that one.'

'I'll play it for you sometime,' Shannon said.

Poppy grinned up at her. 'Okay!'

Shannon smiled as she took her place next to Poppy on the dance floor. But for the first time ever, she stayed. And she danced. And when the song ended and another one started, and Poppy grabbed her hand and giggled, Shannon thought about what Nina Keller had told her. And she decided that maybe late was better than never.

And it would help to have a contact who was a famous actress – just in case.

Chapter 19

Two days later, while Maverick went in for a few hours to check in on the horses and prepare for the week ahead, Nina stayed at the ranch house with Poppy. Upstairs, Markus was packing his bag to head back to LA.

At first, the five-year-old had seemed content to watch TV, but after an hour, she started getting restless. Still dressed in her PJs and dragging her teddy bear along by one arm, she came to where Nina sat at the kitchen island, drinking her coffee.

Without a word, she passed Nina the teddy bear and when she took it, Poppy used both hands to pull out the bar stool next to Nina's. Seeing what Poppy intended, Nina used one foot to hold the stool in place as Poppy climbed – literally – into the seat.

'Do you want some juice?'

Poppy shook her head. 'Where did my dad go?'

'I think he's checking on the horses,' Nina replied. But because Mav had specifically asked her to keep an eye on Poppy if she woke up, Nina added, 'Maybe we can all go for a ride later?'

Poppy instantly brightened at that. 'Yeah!'

'Which horse is your favourite?' Nina asked.

'Zeph. She's Daddy's horse. The black one.'

'I know Zeph. Your dad is teaching me how to ride on her.'

'How come you don't know how already?' Poppy asked. 'You're old.'

Nina laughed lightly at that. But she replied, 'I live in the city, so there aren't many horses around to learn on.'

This news seemed to genuinely upset Poppy. '*No horses?*'

'Not many.'

'You should move here,' Poppy decided. 'We have lots for you to ride,' she added exuberantly. 'Zeph and Spud and Spirit and Diablo and Moon and Princess and Spot.'

'That's a lot of horses,' Nina affirmed.

Poppy nodded, her smile bright. 'If you lived here, you could ride them all the time.' Using one little hand, Poppy pushed her tangled hair away from her face. 'And I can ride with you.'

The childish argument shouldn't have held so much appeal for Nina. But it did. She thought about what Mav had told her – that she'd always have a place there. And she remembered the lyrics to the song. And only remembering had a warm glow rising within her and spreading throughout her body.

She thought back on what Shannon Carlyle had told her, and alarmingly found herself easily bashing through any arguments she'd made against her and Maverick working out. She and Shannon might have both been career women, but Nina had something with Mav that Shannon self-admittedly never had. That counted for something. Didn't it?

'Can I ask you a really important question?' Nina asked and turned in her chair so that she was facing Poppy fully.

Poppy nodded.

'Would it be okay if I asked your dad on a date?'

'A date?'

'Yeah. You know, when two people like each other and want to spend time getting to know each other better.'

Poppy seemed to think about this very seriously for a moment before asking, 'Can I come?' Her eyes narrowed on Nina's face.

Nina hesitated, but only because she knew that inviting Poppy would complicate things for Mav, who always thought about his daughter's heart before his own. But she also wanted him to know that she understood that, and that she would do her best to leave Poppy's heart intact. 'I think that would be so fun,' she said. 'Like a two-for-one deal.'

'Yeah!'

'What do you want to do on our date?'

'Hmm, I dunno.'

'Do you like movies?' Nina asked.

Poppy nodded her head vigorously. 'Yeah! Daddy and I like *Barbie*. Maybe we can go watch that?'

'I think that one's done in theatres. But we can see what else is playing. And then maybe we can go and get dinner afterwards.'

'Pizza!' Poppy declared.

'Pizza.' Nina smiled. 'Pizza's my favourite.'

'Mine too!'

'Okay.' Nina exhaled. Who knew that asking a five-year-old for permission to date her dad would be so nerve-racking. 'Movie and pizza date. I'll ask your dad and let you know what he says.'

'He'll say yes,' Poppy predicted. 'He loves pizza.'

Nina couldn't help the laugh that bubbled up and out of her mouth. There was no point in telling Poppy that dating was a little more complicated than that. But the little girl's simple acceptance also had her wondering: why couldn't it be simple?

A date was hardly a marriage proposal, after all. People dated and broke up every day, and though their situation was admittedly more complicated, they both deserved just one evening of simple, good fun.

Needing a distraction from her own thoughts and hoping to entertain Poppy too, she asked, 'Do you want to bake some cookies?'

Poppy's eyes rounded with delight. 'Yeah!' She hopped off the bar stool and went to the little bookshelf to the side of the kitchen cabinets. Without waiting, she climbed onto the counter and, kneeling on the granite top, fished through the recipe books until she found one with a blue cover. 'This one has cookies in it!' she declared and waved the book in Nina's direction.

'Okay.' But because she was terrified Poppy might fall, she hurried over to her, plucked her off the counter, and put her back down on the floor before taking the recipe book. 'What type of cookies are we going to make?'

'Chocolate chip.'

'Good choice.' Nina started flipping through the recipe book, hoping she'd find the recipe. She saw recipes for potato salad, beef stroganoff, and pineapple upside down cake. She even saw one for something called *Bombe Alaska* and promised herself she'd google what it was later.

When she found the chocolate chip cookie recipe, she saw the smudges on the pages and noted the slightly faded ink. 'Do you guys make these often?'

'Yeah, they're my favourite,' Poppy replied.

Nina scanned the ingredients. 'Let's check we have everything before we start.'

Maverick frowned when he walked into Sierra's office at the resort and found her white as a ghost, a single piece of paper in her hand. 'Sierra?'

'Did you know about this?' she asked quietly and passed him the paper.

Maverick knew what it was before he even looked down to confirm it. 'Yeah, I knew.'

Still, he felt the blow as surely as Sierra had. He supposed he'd started hoping that Benji would change his mind and stay.

'Benji wanted to tell you himself. And I think he had that right.'

'You're my *brother*, Maverick. You're supposed to be on *my* side.'

He could see those cracks forming in the dam wall, growing

wider with every second that passed. Her eyes flooded, and though she tried to resist the tears, once the first one fell, the rest followed.

He knew it was time, but he hated that he couldn't help, couldn't do more to take the pain away from his little sister. He rounded the desk, wrapped her trembling body in his arms, and he said, 'Honey, if I was on his side, I wouldn't let him leave at all.'

'Oh God.' The sob that tore from her had him bracing his own body against the violent shudders.

Mav didn't hush her. He didn't tell her it would be okay because he knew how heavy those empty promises landed. He held her, his hand circling her back for minutes until she calmed.

When she finally took a huge breath and stepped back, her puffy, red eyes hit him like a punch to the stomach. And when she started to apologize, he stopped her with one hand. 'Don't. You're allowed to be sad. Confused.'

'Am I?' she asked and plucked a tissue from her drawer. She dabbed her eyes, wiping away smudges of mascara. 'I was the one who ended things,' she reminded him.

'You did what you had to do to survive,' Mav said quietly. 'To move on. Do you think Benji doesn't know that?'

'I hate myself for hating him.' She sat down heavily and stared at her dark computer screen. 'Every time I snap at him or say something hurtful, I hate myself for it. And, still, I can't seem to stop. Every time I look at him, I . . .' She shook her head.

Maverick wanted to tell her that she didn't hate him, and that she only needed to keep that distance between her and Benji because she knew in her heart that he was the only one who understood – who *shared* – her pain. Pain that she wasn't ready to face yet. But he didn't. Some things people needed to unpack themselves.

Sierra picked up the piece of paper again. 'Two weeks. He gave me two weeks' notice. Came in here and spoke to me like I was nothing but his employer, said he'd received an offer he couldn't refuse.

'And I said, "Okay."' She released a watery laugh. 'And now all

I can think is that it's the strangest thing to have no words for a man you've known your entire life and loved for over half of it.'

'Sometimes you don't need words. Sometimes a person knows your heart enough to know everything you want to say but can't.'

Sierra laughed sadly. 'You're getting sentimental in your old age, Mav.'

'Maybe. Or maybe I've known both of you your entire lives, too.'

Taking a chance, he pulled out the chair opposite her desk and sat. 'Do you know when Benji asked for my permission to marry you, I asked him why? I told him, "If you're only doing it because she's pregnant, don't." I suppose I knew from experience how wrong that could go.'

Sierra didn't look at him, but he knew she was listening.

'Benji just laughed, and he said, "You know it's always been her, even when you pretended not to."'

'Why *did* it bother you so much?'

'You started chasing him when you were fifteen!' Mav laughed, remembering how Sierra had hounded his best friend. 'You were a kid. Benji was twenty. He was too old for you – and he thought so too.'

'Maybe,' she ceded. 'But I made him think about it plenty.'

'I don't want to know.'

'He made me wait until I was nineteen.' She smiled though her eyes remained *so* sad. 'Probably would have made me wait longer if I hadn't told him I was going to sleep with Kyle Channing.'

'Kyle Channing?'

'I made him up,' Sierra said. 'Got all dressed up for this imaginary date, and then made sure I left my car keys down at the stables so that Benji would see me leaving.'

'Smart.'

She accepted that with a small tip of her head. 'Manipulative, too.' She sighed. 'I would have done anything to have him, and it's so strange now, to look back and wish I'd never set eyes on him.'

'Yeah. I felt the same way about Shannon when she first left.

But then, after I had some time to heal, I realized that if we hadn't met, I wouldn't have Poppy . . .'

'I don't have that luxury.'

'No.' Mav swallowed his own pain and guilt and regret and said those words he should have said a long time ago. 'I'm so sorry, Si.'

She frowned. 'It's not your fault.'

'I asked you to come back.' He pinched the bridge of his nose when his own tears stung. 'I committed to the resort because I wanted you to come back. After Mom and Dad . . . I don't know. I guess I wanted us to stick together. I wanted you to have something here to come back to and I—'

'Mav,' she cut him off, 'I came back because it was time. The resort gave me the job I wanted,' she acknowledged. 'But even without it, I would have come home. Maybe gotten a job at one of the hotels in Santa Barbara or Santa Ynez.' Reaching across her desk, she took his hand, gave it a quick squeeze. 'You built something for me to come back to, but I chose to come home because I was ready.'

'If you hadn't come back, you wouldn't have suffered so much.'

'Maybe not. But I would have ended up with Benji anyway. I know myself well enough to be honest about that, so, please, stop accepting responsibility for my decisions.'

'I wish I could take some of that pain from you,' he said. 'You're my baby sister. I'm supposed to look after you. Mom and Dad—'

'You have looked after me. Mav, you *do*. But at some point, you're going to have to accept the fact that you're not personally responsible for everybody in your life. I'm a grown woman, perfectly able to look after myself.

'And so is Nina,' she added, abruptly changing the subject. 'Have you told her how you feel yet?'

Maverick leaned forward, placing his forearms on his knees and linking his hands. 'Not in so many words. But she knows.'

'Say the damn words, Mav.'

'She knows,' he repeated. 'And has to be able to make up her own mind.'

'You're so scared of history repeating itself,' she said quietly. 'Nina's not Shannon.'

The first flicker of irritation slashed through him. 'Sierra,' he said calmly, 'I'm going to let you have that punch given the day you're having. But if you think, for even a second, that I don't know that, I'm not above calling you an idiot.'

'So, tell her!'

'I won't use my love to blackmail her into staying.'

'Mav—'

'I've told her she'll always have a place here,' he said, cutting her off. 'Nina knows her own mind.'

'Telling her she'll always have a place here, changing the lyrics to a song, isn't the same as having the conversation,' Sierra pushed. 'It's not the same as looking them in the eye and saying "I love you!"'

'*You're* going to talk to *me* about having a conversation with my partner?' he demanded.

'Yes. Yes, I am. Because I let my person go, Mav. And it's like willingly opting into a half-lived life. I don't want you to ever feel this pain.' She stared at him, her face flushed with anger and pain and panic. 'You can't say that Nina knows her own mind and then not trust her to know what to do with the words you give her, not trust her to know that you're not pressuring her, only loving her.'

Because that settled a blanket of dread and guilt over him, he didn't argue.

Sierra came to him. She gave him a little shove, sending his chair wheeling. 'Trust Nina not to hurt you. Trust her to know her own mind.'

He sighed. 'I—'

'You're afraid.'

'I'm afraid,' he admitted slowly, and as much as he hated the words, it felt good to finally say them. 'Shannon leaving hurt. But Nina leaving . . . it might kill me. And, worse, it might hurt

Poppy.' He ground his teeth together, bracing against the thought. 'I don't ever want my little girl to feel that pain, that *inadequacy*.'

'You've done a good job of keeping things quiet,' Sierra argued. 'Sure, Poppy will be sad if Nina does leave, but only because they've bonded some. She's a child, Mav. In a week, she'd have moved on.' She gave him one last poke. 'Don't be a coward. And stop using your daughter as an excuse for not taking the risk.'

Mav exhaled a huge breath. He wanted to tell Nina how he felt. He had fought the urge constantly because every time he considered just saying the words he remembered Shannon's bitterness and her accusation that he'd pressured her. So, he'd held back.

But he hadn't realized that keeping the words from her was a different kind of pressure, a weird bargain where he only took the risk after she'd agreed to stay. And maybe that wasn't exactly fair either. Maybe the hardest part about trusting someone again wasn't only trusting that they knew their own mind and heart but trusting that they loved you enough not to hurt you too.

'I'm a coward,' he admitted after a long pause. 'But I have good reason to be.'

'You do.'

'And you're a piece of work,' he said.

'But I have good reason to be.'

'You do,' he ceded.

'Tell her.'

He nodded. 'I'll try.' But as he opened the door to leave, he added, 'Does this mean you'll talk to Benji?'

Sierra snorted.

Maverick shook his head as he walked away. The two of them couldn't go on like this, and as much as he hated to say goodbye to his best friend, maybe a little distance would help for a while. Give them both space to breathe before they circled back to each other. Because if there was one thing he knew about Benji and Sierra, it was that they circled back to one another eventually.

He was walking across the shaded parking lot, his thoughts

spinning around his family, when he saw the lost guest. The man was tall and Hollywood handsome in a tailored suit. His blond hair was perfectly styled, his green eyes looking around in confusion.

'Can I help you?' Mav asked. 'You look a bit lost.'

'Oh, thank you! I'm actually looking for a friend of mine who's staying here. Nina. Nina Keller.'

Mav's spine tingled. 'Oh. How do you know Ms Keller?' he asked, deliberately keeping his voice casual.

'I'm the producer on her new movie. *Shadowlands*.' So saying, he pulled out his phone and flicked through his pictures until he came to a photo of him and Nina on set. He held it up for Mav to see.

Mav looked at the picture, noted that Nina looked happy and relaxed as she posed for the selfie. 'Your name?'

'Alexander Cane.'

Mav took out his own phone and called Nina. Three long, mournful rings sounded before it went to voicemail, so he hung up and typed the name into his web browser. IMDb was the first result that popped up. He saw Alexander's picture, verified his information. 'I'm heading to her now if you want to tag along.'

'Where is she?'

Mav noted that the man – Alexander – skirted away from Shadow as the dog ambled over to greet him. He didn't bother pointing out that she was friendly. He got the sense that Alexander Cane was more concerned about getting dog hair on his fancy suit than anything else.

'She and her best friend are staying at the ranch house,' he explained. 'For privacy.'

The man's eyes dimmed slightly. 'Markus is here?'

Maverick wondered about that even as he relaxed. The man was obviously close to Nina if he knew who Markus was. 'Yeah. He's leaving this afternoon, but he comes out to visit on weekends.'

Maverick started in the direction of the Jeep. Whether the suit came or not, he needed to get home. He'd left Nina and Markus in charge of Poppy while he'd run through his Sunday tasks, and God knew his daughter was probably running them ragged.

'Ah, let me follow you in my car.' He indicated to a brand-new BMW in glossy black. 'That way I can leave from there.'

'Sure thing.' Mav climbed into the Jeep and started the vehicle, his thoughts still on Sierra and Benji.

He drove the mile to the ranch house slowly, enjoying the clear day and the hot country air blowing in through his open window, and when he pulled beneath the shade of the oak tree out front, he felt a little more settled.

Alexander slipped his BMW in next to the Jeep and got out. 'Are you employed here?' he asked.

'In a manner of speaking.'

'It's a nice piece of property. Must be worth a fortune.'

'I bet.'

'Says something about the owners – that they haven't sold out yet.'

Mav nearly smiled. 'I'm sure it does.'

'Not quite sure what she's doing here,' Alexander continued. 'She didn't even tell anyone where she was going. Just up and disappeared – right at the end of filming too.' He dusted the leg of his trousers. 'She has me worried.'

'Hmm,' Maverick said noncommittally. Nina's bruises were gone, but he knew the damage was still there. And it was her story to tell or to keep close.

He tried to make conversation as he led the way up the porch steps. 'You just out for the day?'

'Yeah. I figured I'd track her down and check in before heading back.'

Maverick frowned at that. That same niggling feeling set in at the base of his spine. Something about the word – track – didn't sit right.

But then he opened the door and the first thing he heard was Nina and Poppy's laughter coming from the kitchen. His unease vanished. His heart swelled.

He led the way to his girls without a word.

Alexander followed, wordlessly too.

Maverick entered the kitchen, and then just stopped and looked. Nina and Poppy were sitting at the kitchen table, rolling cookie dough into balls with their hands. They both had flour streaked on their cheeks. Poppy had a dollop of batter on her nose.

Nina looked up and saw him. Her dark eyes lit. 'Hi!'

And then Alexander stepped out from behind him, and everything changed.

The spoon she'd been using dropped from her hands to the floor with a clatter, causing Poppy to giggle hysterically.

Nina didn't react to the mess or to Poppy's giggles. She just stared at the newcomer, her face deathly pale, her eyes huge in her face.

'Nina! It's so good to see you!' Alexander took one step forward.

Nina pushed to a fumbling stand. Her hands reached for Poppy, half dragging the five-year-old out of her chair too.

'Nina?' Poppy asked, even as Nina held her close.

Maverick was so confused for a moment that he just stood and stared. He waited for Nina to meet his eyes, but she couldn't. She was too focused on the man standing next to him, on watching his every expression and movement as a prey animal might watch a predator it knew it couldn't outrun.

Realization crept up on Mav like a surprise attack in the wilderness, slowly and then all at once and violently, and when Nina finally managed to glance at him, one look between them was all it took to confirm it.

And then the rage came.

PART THREE:
STAND

Chapter 20

Los Angeles, California – June 2, 2025

Nina managed one ear-piercing scream and a violent kick before a large hand covered her mouth and nose, cutting off her air supply.

In her panic, she forgot the knife in her hand. She struggled, kicking out violently, but when he tore at her pants with his free hand, ripping the button and forcing the zipper down, her panic turned cold. And when he touched her, his fingers pushing inside of her, she knew she'd rather die than live through the rest.

Nina didn't think. She gripped her hands, preparing to claw and tear at him, and belatedly remembered the knife. She drove it backwards, into his leg, felt the moment flesh gave to blade.

He roared with equal parts fury and pain, spat, 'Fuck!' as she pulled the knife out, preparing to strike again.

But he plucked it from her fingers as if she were a child holding a toy.

She was dragged backwards, kicking and clawing, through her own house. Nina was distinctly aware of several things.

Though she would not make it outside, the front door was wide open. And it was *such* a beautiful day.

Though she could not breathe, she could smell the liquor and cologne on him, and it terrified her.

Though her phone was not on speaker, she could hear Markus screaming her name over the line.

Though she desperately wanted to live, she was probably going to die.

And when he threw her onto the floor and she saw him for the first time, only a second before Alex's fist connected with her face and pain bloomed through her skull, she thought that dying might be better after all.

Hunt Ranch, Santa Barbara County – Present Day

Nina saw the moment that Maverick's eyes flooded with recognition, but she couldn't speak, couldn't open her mouth and voice the words.

God, she could *smell* Alex's cologne, the same one he'd worn that night. And with the smell came the memories. His arm around her throat, his fingers tearing at her pants and pushing inside of her, and when she'd stabbed him with the knife, his rage. Her back ached where she'd landed on the hard floor. Her ribs, still injured, throbbed from where he'd kicked her. And that was nothing compared to the memory of that first stunning blow to the face.

She saw Alexander casually inching closer, his hands in his pockets, his green eyes taking in the kitchen. 'Nice place.'

Nina didn't understand how somebody so beautiful, somebody who had everything – a successful career, money, looks – could be so twisted. So cruel. 'What do you want, Alex?'

He held both arms out at his sides. 'I wanted to check in. Make sure you were okay.' His words were so friendly, his threat so clear.

Beneath her hands, Poppy shifted to look up at her and Nina's heart broke under the weight of her own shame.

'Hey, Poppy . . .' Nina said.

Poppy's big eyes were clouded with confusion, but she whispered, 'Yeah?'

'Why don't you go ask Markus to braid your hair? He knows a bunch of fancy braids.' Her voice was clear and strong, and she wondered how she could sound so normal when she was falling apart inside.

'But—'

'Poppy.' Maverick cut off her argument, using a tone that brooked no argument. 'Listen to Nina, please.'

Poppy seemed to want to argue. She looked back and forth between them for a moment.

Nina, remembering the promise she'd made, said, 'We'll ask him later, together.'

'Promise?'

'I promise.'

Seemingly appeased, Poppy said, ''Kay!' and ran out of the room in search of Markus.

The moment she was gone, Nina felt that first trickle of relief, and when Maverick walked around Alex and came to stand beside her, facing the threat, she felt herself calm completely. She was safe here. Today. Absolutely.

And knowing it gave her the courage to demand, again, 'What do you want, Alex?'

'I just thought I'd stop by.' His voice was *so* friendly, *so* casual. But Nina knew the monster that suave façade hid. 'We're waiting to film your last scene before wrapping.' His eyes flicked over her. 'You look good, Nina.'

Bile rushed her throat at the casual compliment. Considering he'd torn her clothes and forced his fingers inside of her, she knew as well as he did that the words were meant to fuck with her head.

Her entire body trembled with the force of her humiliation. And shame. Because this man had violated her, and instead of fighting back, she'd run.

Maverick placed one of his heavy hands on her shoulder, and Nina hated that she flinched against the contact.

He didn't move it as her breath rushed out of her.

'Get out.' The words from Nina, the cold tone they were delivered in, surprised everyone, including herself.

'Nina . . .' Alex tried for shocked hurt.

His act didn't fool her.

And it didn't fool Maverick either. He took one step in Alex's direction, moving in front of her completely. 'Now.'

Alex's eyes clouded with well-practised confusion. 'I don't understand.'

Because she needed to face Alex herself, because she wouldn't let Mav take the weight of her past in addition to everything else he carried, she stepped to his side again and took his hand. She stared down at their connected fingers when she felt the tremors of rage passing through him and into her. He was literally vibrating with it.

His anger gave her courage, each ripple of it that passed from him through her fingers charging her with strength. She forced her eyes to Alex's. She wanted him to see her vindication when she said, 'I'm going to the police.'

Alex frowned quizzically, a born actor, a practised liar. 'I'm not sure what you're on about, Nina,' he said in a quiet, coaxing voice. 'If the strain of filming has been too hard on you, on your mental health, we'll understand. Take more time to rest and think it through.'

His threat was clear, his use of 'we' pointed. But this time, Nina didn't let it sway her. 'When I tell everyone what happened, they're going to want to see that scar from where I cut you, and then they're going to match your blood to the blood on the knife currently in their evidence.

'And when the media frenzy starts and the facts come to light, how many people do you think will stand by you?'

The shift happened so quickly. Alex's green eyes turned hard and flinty. 'I'll ruin you for libel.'

'We'll probably ruin each other,' she agreed. 'But that doesn't mean I'm going to keep quiet. And it doesn't mean I'm going to settle either, so don't bother having your lawyer contact me. No amount of money is going to keep you out of prison.'

He took a step towards her.

Maverick didn't even move. He said, 'You're in my house, and I've just found out you're the one who assaulted my woman. If you take one more step in her direction, I *will* kill you. And I will enjoy it.'

Maverick's tone had a streak of fear gripping Nina's spine, and when she angled her face up to look at him, her fear turned to pure terror. He would do it. She could see the barely contained violence in his eyes, hear the cold, almost eager fury in his tone. And because she was scared, not of him, but *for* him, for Poppy, she stepped in front of him, physically preventing him from taking a single step.

Clearly sensing that he was playing in dangerous territory, Alex held both hands up and backed away. 'You know how this ends, Nina,' he said.

And he smiled at her.

Nina's spine locked with momentary terror even as her skin crawled like liquid in motion.

Alex turned, but it was only once the front door slammed shut that Maverick slipped around her and charged after him.

'Mav!' Nina ran after him, terrified of what he might do.

Markus was coming down the stairs, Poppy close behind him. 'What on earth—'

She didn't stop to explain. She opened the front door and stumbled onto the porch as Maverick strode towards the sleek black BMW that Alex had arrived in.

'Is that Alex?' Markus asked as he followed her onto the porch, his confusion clear.

Nina could only nod.

Alexander had opened the car door and was preparing to get in, but when he saw Maverick, he smiled and turned, leaning on the car arrogantly. 'Look, this is all one big misunder—'

Without a word, Maverick gripped the car door and slammed it violently shut.

Alex screamed as his hand was crushed between the door and the car. 'Fuck!' He dropped to his knees, cradling his broken hand against his body.

Maverick took a fistful of Alex's hair and yanked his head back. He leaned in close, but his words were stated clearly enough that Nina caught them. 'That's for touching my woman.'

'She's a lying slut!'

Maverick didn't acknowledge that. 'If you come here again, I will kill you.'

'I'm going to sue you for everything that you have!'

Maverick ignored him. In a perfectly calm, quiet voice, he added, 'I will bury you in a quiet spot somewhere on my acreage. Somewhere nobody would ever think to look.' He let Alex go with a violent jerk of his hand. 'Now get the fuck off my land.'

Alex scrambled to get into his car. But it was only once he was safely inside, the motor running, that he rolled down his window – just an inch – and spat, 'My lawyers will be in touch.'

He sped out, his car kicking up a cloud of dust in its wake.

Nina watched as Maverick pulled out his cell phone. 'Hey, Sandie. A black BMW is going to be heading out the gates in a few minutes. Take the plate number down. Make sure your team knows not to let it back in.'

Chapter 21

Maverick hung up.

Turned.

Until that moment, Nina hadn't been certain she would find the strength to speak out. She'd come to Hunt Ranch for the peace and quiet, to recover from her physical injuries. And even though she'd still been reeling from the trauma of the assault, she hadn't hired security because she'd understood that if she just kept her head down, kept quiet, Alex would never dare touch her again.

But he had made one fatal error: he had come to Hunt Ranch, and he had cornered her in a room with Poppy. And it had been that – the knowledge that one day, it might be *Poppy* in a room with a man like him – that had sealed his fate. Because how often did Nina think about her own childhood and wish that just one person had cared enough about her to intervene?

Still, she was so glad she'd come. Not only because she'd met Mav, but because she'd needed to rest first, to enjoy those last few weeks of her career without the shame of being a victim.

Because people would question her. Others would call her a liar. She didn't have many friends in Hollywood, and while she was sure a few women would take her side by default, Alexander was respected and well connected. Lawyers would strip her down to her bones each time they made her relive the attack. And when they locked Alex away, it wouldn't matter that unquestionable evidence would have put the nail in the coffin, her career, everything she'd worked for, would be in jeopardy. History had told this particular story too many times for her to seek false comfort.

Still, she had expected that if she ever spoke up, she would be called a liar and that she might lose her career. She had expected that she would be terrified and ashamed and devastated.

And while that fear and shame and devastation hovered beneath the surface, they were suppressed beneath a layer of bravery, of strength. Because as she looked at Maverick, standing in his own front yard, attempting to leash his rage before approaching her again, she knew that she had found something that she had never considered she might need: help.

Behind her, Markus had placed one hand on Poppy's shoulder, keeping her in place so that she couldn't run towards the trouble. The five-year-old, who had clearly never seen her dad in an outright rage before, was eerily quiet.

Nina wanted to comfort her, but she couldn't quite manage to look away from Mav. He came to her, each step filled with purpose, deliberation. He drew her face closer using both hands and took her mouth in a fierce kiss right in front of Poppy, who giggled, her shock forgotten.

When he broke away, he didn't ask her for an explanation or for the whole story. He said, 'What do you want to do?'

Nina closed her eyes as love and relief welled up inside of her. He would let her decide, always. And once she had decided, he would stand by her. And it was the loveliest thing in the world to take a stand on a foundation that was so solid beneath her feet.

She gripped his wrists with both hands, looked into those familiar blue eyes. 'I'm going to go back tomorrow. Formally report it.'

'I'm coming.'

It was not a question or a request for permission. But Nina felt that she had to deter him, 'Mav—'

Maverick gripped her neck with one hand and brought her forehead to his. He closed his eyes for a moment as if he needed to gather his courage, and he repeated, 'I'm coming.'

'Mav—'

He covered her mouth with his, stealing the words, and when he broke away, he said something she hadn't expected. 'Please, Nina.' Her heart swelled, but before she could speak, he added, 'Don't ask me to sit here and do nothing while you're fighting the biggest battle of your life.'

And even though she wasn't comfortable with it, even though she knew it was a mistake, in that moment, with Alexander so fresh on her mind, Nina didn't have the strength to fight him.

She held out one hand for Poppy, and when the five-year-old left Markus's side and took it, Markus turned around and walked inside without a word.

Nina sighed. Markus would be shocked and hurt. She knew it. She even understood why. She'd lied to him, her best friend. She'd let him worry about some deranged stalker when she'd known her attacker the entire time. She'd betrayed his trust. But she pushed all that aside for a minute to squeeze Poppy's little hand and say to Mav, 'Before you got back. Before . . .' She didn't finish the thought, pushed all thoughts of Alex from her mind. 'Poppy and I were actually chatting.'

'Nina likes you, Dad!'

'I really do,' she laughingly added. 'We were going to ask you out on a date.' She tipped her shoulders anxiously when he only stared at her. 'We decided it would be more fun if all three of us went on one. Together.'

Poppy nodded solemnly. 'Pizza and movies.'

Mav paused for a moment as if he was unsure, or maybe stunned. He rubbed his chest over his heart before crouching down to Poppy's level. 'You want me to take you and Nina on a date?' he clarified.

'Yeah! A pizza and movie date.'

'Am I allowed to kiss Nina on this date?' he asked seriously.

'Yeah, but you have to kiss me too,' Poppy replied.

'Oh, okay.' Maverick tugged Poppy forward and placed a kiss on her lips. He wrapped his arms around her and then looked up at Nina, his blue eyes glassy. 'Thank you – for getting her out.'

'Nina likes me too!' Poppy offered happily, unaware of the current swarming around her. She stepped back from her dad and took Nina's hand. 'Can we finish the cookies now?'

'Yeah.' Nina gave Poppy's hand a squeeze. 'Why don't you go show your dad and I'll run upstairs and get Markus.'

'Okay! Come on, Daddy!' Poppy ran ahead without waiting.

Mav lingered. 'You okay?'

'Not really.' She felt the tears claw up her throat then but refused to give in to them. 'I'm so sorry, Mav – for bringing him here.'

'No.' He shook his head. 'You're not doing that. You're not taking any blame – any shame – for any of this.

'He came here of his own volition, just like he broke into your house and hurt you of his own volition.' Roping his hands around her waist, he drew her close, kissed one cheek and then the other. '*You* fought him off. *You* took measures to protect yourself while you rested. *You* kept my little girl away from him and forced her to leave the room. *You* are risking everything to speak out against a man who has considerable weight in your industry when nobody would blame you for keeping quiet.'

When she dropped her head to his shoulder, exhausted at only the thought of the impending battle, he raised one big hand to the back of her head and sighed deeply. 'You're so strong, Nina.'

Nina's heart swelled. 'You make me feel brave.'

'No, I make you feel safe. You're brave all on your own.' He kissed the side of her head, stepped back.

'I have to go speak to Markus . . .'

'I'm calling Sierra in. And Benji,' Mav said. Nina's first thought was to object, but Mav caught the look of panic. He took her hand, raised it to his lips, and kissed her palm. 'They're family.

We do this as a family.'

She knew what he was offering her, and she couldn't turn away from it even though she knew she should. She nodded, but only because she couldn't find the right words to promise him anything amidst her turmoil.

Mav opened the door for her. He waited for her to go in ahead of him, and Nina saw when he glanced back as if making sure that Alex was truly gone. She hated herself for that – for bringing that danger here, to this beautiful place.

She looked towards the stairs, took one steadying breath before going to look for Markus.

She found him sitting on his bed, his head in his hands. She didn't knock, just walked in and sat beside him. She rested against him, placing her head on his upper arm, and she waited for him to speak.

It took him minutes. But when he looked up, his eyes were devastated. 'I'm going to hug you before I let my mad out.' So saying, he gave her a bone-crushing hug.

Nina returned the hug. Tears burned her eyes. 'I wanted to tell you. So many times.'

He pushed to his feet then, breaking all contact. That little distance hurt. But Nina didn't try to bridge it.

'Why didn't you?' he asked, eyes flashing. 'Christ, Nina. I would have been shocked. Of course, I would have. But I would have believed you. Me.' He slammed both hands to his chest. 'I would have believed you one hundred per cent.'

'I know.'

That seemed to take the wind out of his sails. 'What?'

'I never – not for one moment – doubted you, Markus. That's why I didn't tell you. Because you might have had my back, but your mama bear would have taken over.' She looked into his eyes. 'You would have tried to keep quiet if I'd asked, but eventually you would have snapped. You would have confronted him or made up a rumour that he had—' she waved one hand '—gonorrhoea or syphilis. And I wasn't ready.'

'Baby girl, if I'd known it had been Alex, I would have invited him over for a drink – and then castrated him with my nail file. Sloppily. *Slowly.*'

'I know.'

'Shit.' He sat down heavily again. Repeated, 'Shit.'

'Keeping it from you has almost been harder than dealing with it. I wanted to tell you so many times, Markus,' she repeated. The tears came then, each one falling from her and taking some of that guilt and shame away with it. 'But I . . . I wasn't ready to face it. I wasn't ready to fight, and Alex came,' she rambled, 'to the hospital. He told me that it was in both our best interests to forget what had happened, and I knew.' She exhaled a huge breath, closed her eyes momentarily. 'I knew that if I just kept quiet, he wouldn't hurt me again.'

'I should have known,' Markus stated. 'When you refused to bring security, I should have put the pieces together.'

She took his hand, so familiar, in hers. 'We both know how much pull Alex has. The only reason I know he'll be charged is because I hurt him. I drew blood. But that doesn't mean everyone will believe me. Alex will lie. He'll spin it, say that we were sleeping together, and that when he tried to break it off, I attacked him. He'll say it was self-defence. His lawyers will tear apart my character and find small things to splash in court.' A chill dropped all through her body. 'They'll pay my mother to spread lies about me. And it doesn't matter that he might still go away, at the end of the day, I might not have a career to go back to. Because *you know*. You know who controls this industry, and you know how wary they'll be of hiring a woman who's made an accusation like that against one of their own.'

'It's the twenty-first century,' Markus argued. 'You'll have a career to go back to – even if it's only acting for female directors,' he belatedly ceded.

'Alex is one of the biggest producers in Hollywood. His close circle of friends is responsible for most movies made in the US.'

He took a moment to mull this over. 'How's your British accent?' he asked. 'I've always wanted to live in London.' He leaned back and framed her with his hands, closed one eye. 'I'm seeing you in a Victorian-era gown. Pink silk.' He nodded. 'It's working for you, baby. I'll call you miss. And you can call me guv'na.'

Nina didn't laugh it off as he wanted her to. She took both his hands again. 'I love you. And I'm sorry I never told you.'

He sighed, suddenly serious again. 'I want to say it's okay. But, honestly Neens, I'm not sure that it is.' The anger in his eyes turned to pain right in front of her. 'I had to listen to you being assaulted over the phone. That scream . . .' His eyes filled. 'I'll hear that scream in my dreams until the day I die, and, still, nothing will ever be more terrifying than having to hang up on you to call 911 and tell the police to hurry the fuck up because he had you.

'I didn't know if they would get there in time. I didn't know if you would be alive or dead by the time I reached you. And when I finally arrived at your house, you were being carried out on a stretcher. Your face was beaten bloody. You were unconscious. But I thought . . .' He held up one finger, exhaled a huge breath as he regained his composure. 'I thought you were dead.'

'Markus—'

'And, yeah,' he kept going, 'I get not wanting it public. But *I* deserved to know. *I* would have guarded your secret until you were ready. It would have been hard not to kill him,' he clarified. 'But I would have done it.'

Nina hated that she had hurt him, and she didn't know what to say other than, 'I'm sorry.'

'At some point, you're going to have to realize that it's okay to let people in, and that not everybody is going to betray you eventually.' He sighed sadly. 'God, Nina, I have over a decade of friendship proving my loyalty and you still don't trust me.'

Nina thought that over, tried to determine if it was true or not.

Did she trust Markus? She had always thought so, but it was also difficult to admit that trusting someone meant sharing your secrets with them and knowing they would safeguard them – which she hadn't trusted Markus to do.

She thought back over their friendship, saw those little imbalances now. If anything – good or bad – happened to Markus, Nina was the first person he called to celebrate or commiserate with. Over the years, she had been there for him through countless break-ups, job loss, even his mom's death. She had held his hand and let him cry. She had come, bearing pints of ice cream and, once, when a man had broken Markus's heart unexpectedly, the materials to make a voodoo doll. She had listened. She had been present. She had been a good friend.

But had she ever, even once, called him with her own problems?

It was humiliating and upsetting to realize that the first time she had fully relied on their friendship had been after the assault, and even then, she'd been in the hospital and Markus hadn't given her a choice.

'I think,' she said after a long while, 'that growing up, I never had anyone to teach me how to trust. My mom . . . She betrayed me more times than I can count. And it's hard,' she insisted, 'to learn trust as an adult when your entire childhood was spent staying safe by learning to be wary and cautious. But I'll try,' she promised.

Markus gave her a soft smile. 'Can I be petty for one more second?'

She nodded.

'You told Mav – a man you've known for two weeks – and not me.'

'I didn't.' Nina frowned. 'He pieced most of it together, I think. But he only really caught on today when . . . when Alex came . . .'

Seeing her struggle, he took her hand. 'Okay. It's shallow and weak, but that makes me feel a little better.'

Nina smiled. 'Markus, I love him,' she said, and she felt lighter for having said the words.

'I know.' He looked right at her, his brown eyes serious. 'When are you going to trust him enough to tell him?'

Chapter 22

Benji put his phone down on the table, showing them his open web browser and a zoomed-in phone photo of Nina and Maverick kissing on Zephyr's back. The caption read: *Nina Keller Ropes in Millionaire Cowboy*.

Nina's heart raced, pushing a flush of heat through her entire body. The panic began to creep into her previous calm.

Behind her, Maverick placed both his hands on her shoulders, massaging the tension there. 'Breathe,' he commanded.

Nina inhaled a deep breath, held it for three long seconds, and released it again.

Markus said, 'It must have been someone from the shoot. A model or makeup artist who was watching . . . We could sue for breaching the NDA – if we found out who it was.'

'It could have been anyone,' Nina pointed out tiredly. 'Even some of the guests stopped to watch the shoot. Honestly, I'm surprised I managed to stay out of the spotlight this long.'

In the chair opposite her, Sierra was pale-faced and quiet.

Mav had put Poppy in front of the TV in the next room with a few of the freshly baked cookies. Eddie Murphy's distinct voice playing Mushu from *Mulan* trickling through to where the adults convened around the kitchen table.

Benji picked up his phone. 'The article was released early this morning, so he must have come straight here once he found out.'

'Which means he's been looking for you,' Maverick pointed out.

'Yeah. You know how it is. Google any celebrity and the latest news pops up first.' Benji leaned one hip against the kitchen counter. 'I'm surprised more people haven't shown up.'

Maverick paced away before spinning on his heel and coming right back.

'They will.' Nina could see the writing on the wall. She watched Maverick and all she could think was: *I did this. I brought this here.*

It didn't matter that she hadn't decided to go public, she had still brought trouble right to the Hunts' door. To Poppy.

The thought made her nauseous.

'We lock the gates.' Sierra met Maverick's eyes. 'We keep the public amenities open to resort guests, but we close to the public and further reservations until this is sorted.'

'No,' Nina managed to argue through the suffocating weight pressing in on all sides. All eyes turned to her. 'I won't have him affecting your business. He's taken enough from me already. He can't have this.'

'I respect that. I do,' Sierra insisted when Nina opened her mouth to argue. 'But it's not only you. We can't have the press hounding our guests. They come here to relax. It wouldn't be fair to have the place crawling with media.'

'It'll only get worse once Nina goes to the police,' Mav prophesied. 'How long could we close for?'

'Our financials are good. We can afford to close the restaurant and café to the public for a few weeks without hurting, maybe even a month. We keep the gates closed, cross-reference guest IDs with reservations at the gate.'

'No.' Nina pushed back from the table. 'No.'

'Nina, this isn't just going to go away,' Sierra said gently.

'I know.' She could already feel that panic and despair threatening to take her under, but she forged ahead, knowing what she had to do. 'And it isn't going to go away after a few weeks, or a month. This will be messy. The legal battle alone could last *years*.'

The patient acceptance on both the Hunts' faces confounded her. Didn't they realize what they were risking? Everything they had worked for. Everything *Mav* had worked for. Their family legacy – the one that he had worked so hard to build.

'I'll leave,' she decided. 'Tomorrow.' Grasping ahold of the idea, she continued, 'And then when I go in to talk to the police—'

'We.'

She looked across the room at Maverick.

'When *we* go in to talk to the police,' he said again.

Markus shot one finger in Maverick's direction. 'What he said.'

She didn't correct her statement. 'Mav . . .'

'Don't do it,' he said, and even though his voice was even, she could see the panic dancing in his blue eyes.

Nina's despair rose, but this time she battled through it. 'When I go to the police, the media storm will come to me in LA. It'll redirect attention away from the ranch. And you.' She looked at Mav. 'But you need to steer clear of me for a while.'

'That's not going to work for me.'

'Mav—'

'No.'

In her panic, Nina tried to fight him. She turned around to face Markus. 'You directed that shoot. You can call whoever wrote that article and inform them the kiss was staged. I can post something similar to Instagram.'

Markus looked deep into her eyes. 'Nina—'

'It'll work,' she insisted, through breaths that had started becoming erratic. 'You know it'll work.'

Nina's edges, already so frayed, began to unravel in earnest, unspooling the control she had of her body. Her hands shook, and she clasped them beneath the table, refusing to break down.

'I brought him here. I ran and I lied, and I brought him here.' When the sob rose in her throat, she swallowed it. 'To Poppy.'

Nina closed her eyes as the weight of her guilt momentarily overcame her.

'But I can keep him away now,' she insisted.

'Okay. That's it.'

She opened her eyes as Maverick marched over to where she sat. Nina could see the rage in him, but she wasn't scared. Even when he hauled her up out of her seat and into his arms, she knew he would never hurt her. And when he looked into her eyes and said, 'Enough,' in a voice that brooked no argument, she could only stare at him numbly.

'Enough,' he said again, gently this time. His arms tightened around her. His lips touched her forehead for one fleeting moment that somehow still managed to be long enough to impart comfort. 'Taking blame that is not yours to carry is not going to solve anything. We said we weren't going to do that.'

'He was in the same room as Poppy today,' she managed, her voice thick with tears. 'God, Mav. If you and Markus hadn't been there . . . If-if we had been alone . . .'

Because Nina knew what it was to be a child in a small room with a dangerous man, and she had brought Alex to Poppy's home. She might not have welcomed him in, but she had lied by omission.

And the most terrifying truth of all was that if Alex hadn't shown up at Hunt Ranch, Nina might never have found the courage to say anything.

'But you weren't alone,' Maverick reminded her, and sent his own quick thanks heavenward. 'And you won't be alone going forward either.' Turning slightly, he sat down in the chair he'd hauled Nina out of and then pulled her onto his lap.

He tried not to internalize the fact that she was distancing herself from him, tried to remind himself that she was panicking and scared. But he took her hand, linked her fingers with his. 'Do you want this – *us*?'

It didn't matter that there were three witnesses, and that he was putting his heart on a platter in front of them. He needed the words.

'That has nothing to do with being rational—'

'Do you want this?' he repeated.

She nodded.

Mav felt some of that tension drain, even as he demanded, 'Give me the words, Nina. Trust me with the words.'

'I want this. *You.*'

When she blinked, dislodging fresh tears, Mav raised both hands to her cheeks and used his thumbs to brush them dry. 'You don't let people you care about face their demons alone. It's not always that simple,' he ceded with a small tip of his head, 'but it should be. Let me—'

'Us,' Markus interjected.

'Let *us* help,' Mav finished.

Nina slumped against him and sighed. 'It's going to be rough, Mav. Imagine never being able to leave the ranch because the media are literally camped outside the gates. Or, having to tell Poppy to hide every time Jenna drives her to daycare so that her face doesn't end up plastered in tabloids.'

He didn't lie to her. He rubbed small, slow circles on her back, soothing in the only way he knew how. 'I know.'

He looked across the room to his sister, asking her for permission because the resort was half hers, too.

Sierra nodded. 'We look after our own.'

'We'll close to the public for a few weeks during the worst of it. Starting now, through the initial media frenzy. Take it day by day after that.'

'And Poppy?'

If Maverick had had any doubts before that moment, they vanished completely when Nina asked about Poppy. The simple question reminded him that he had finally found a woman who thought about his kid first. A woman who wanted his five-year-old along on a date with them, did fancy braids in her hair, and baked cookies for no other reason than to keep her entertained.

'It's summer. She's only in daycare because of the ranch. We pull her out for a few weeks.' He shrugged. 'I'd prefer for her to be close anyway.'

'If you're okay with it, Nina, I would like to debrief the staff at the meeting tonight. The more eyes watching for media, the better.'

Nina nodded.

Sierra looked at her watch. 'We have a few hours yet.'

'I think I should tell you the full story.' On his lap, Nina angled her face to look at him.

Mav's heart broke at the devastation in her eyes. 'If you need to, that's fine,' he said. 'But we don't have to know the details to believe you. We're here for you regardless.'

'I want to – to explain.'

He heard the guilt in her tone and wondered at it even as he nodded. 'Here.' He dislodged her from his lap and moved off the chair, offering her the seat again before he grabbed her a glass of water.

As much as he wanted to keep holding her, he knew his body wouldn't be able to hide his rage as he listened to her story, and he didn't want to scare her. Nina needed strength just then. Not the anger and violence he felt coursing through him.

'I dated him – Alex.'

In the chair next to Sierra's, Markus's brows shot up.

'I knew, even though I said yes to going out with him, that it wouldn't go anywhere.' She smiled grimly. 'I liked him as a person. He was funny. He had this weird way of being pushy and making it seem charming. But I only said yes because I felt . . .' she shook her head, searching for the word '. . . obligated, I guess. He had given me this huge role. The role that very well might have made me – at least that's what I thought at the time. So, I never told anyone. My plan was to go out with him and then try to work it into the conversation that I wanted to be friends.

'Except every time I tried to bring it up, he'd kinda talk over me, you know. It sounds so silly now . . . I could have avoided so much just by being firm that first time he'd asked me out.

'I don't really have a ton of experience in that department . . . I didn't know that I was leading him on.'

'You weren't.' This came from Benji. 'Agreeing to go on a date with a man is not agreeing to anything else, including sex. And the fucker knew that. I'm not saying it's a crime to try. I think that's pretty normal. But it is to assume. And it certainly is to pressure.'

Nina shook her head. 'It didn't feel like pressure the first date. He was aggressive, but mostly just in talking over me. That kind of thing. But I started to get a little offput when he didn't even give me a chance to refuse the second date. He just showed up at my house, told me he'd made reservations.

'I was in my pyjamas already, so he knew I had no plans. I felt like I couldn't say no. But I was committed to telling him I wasn't looking for anything serious. So, I went.

'And because he picked me up in his car, he dropped me home afterwards—' Mav was looking at her, so he saw her eyes glaze over as she thought back '—at my front door, he kinda spun me around and pressed in. You know, very romance novel hero.'

'Yeah. Except you didn't want him to,' Sierra observed.

Nina nodded. 'He kissed me. And I don't remember feeling anything except trapped. I was trying to move away when his hand dropped to the front of my pants . . .'

Mav could imagine her, so small, trapped against her own door by a man a foot taller than her, and it crushed him to even think about it.

'I panicked. I shoved him off me.' She chuckled mirthlessly. 'He looked so surprised,' she recalled. 'As if he'd never been rejected before.

'I told him I wasn't looking for a relationship. He pushed back, and said we could keep it casual. And I guess that's when I told him I wasn't interested – in anything. At that point, I didn't even want to be friends with him. He had really scared me.'

'What did he do – when you rejected him?' Sierra asked.

'That's what's so surprising. He didn't get mad or push and shove me. He smiled and said that he was disappointed but that he understood, and that maybe it was better if we kept our relationship professional anyway.

'We didn't see each other for months between then and filming starting up, and by the time we started on *Shadowlands*, he seemed to have moved on. He even brought his new girlfriend to set a few times, introduced us . . .

'But he watched me.

'I tried not to overthink it. I told myself I was imagining it because he had scared me. But I'd often feel my skin crawl and turn around and see him standing there, staring at me. But he'd always just smile and wave or nod, you know. Alex . . . his greatest gift is lying. I see that now.

'The last time I saw him before the attack, I kinda laughingly said something like, "I can't believe we're almost done." Something like that. And he didn't laugh or comment on how quickly the time had passed. He didn't say anything.'

She clasped her hands together beneath the table, and Mav dropped his own hand to cover both of hers.

'That's the night he came?' Markus's eyes glinted black with rage.

'Yes. And I knew. The moment I was in my kitchen, I knew that someone was there with me even though I couldn't see him. I could *feel* him.'

'And you called me,' Markus offered.

She nodded slowly. 'I called Markus. I don't even know why 911 never crossed my mind.' She frowned. 'Actually, that's not true,' she corrected. She looked across the table. 'Markus has always been my safe place.'

Markus took a comically huge gulp from his wine, making everyone smile.

Nina cleared her throat, summoning the courage to continue. Smiles vanished; everyone knew what was coming and had to prepare for it.

'He told me to grab a weapon and get outside. So, I grabbed a paring knife from the knife block and crept towards the front door.' She exhaled a huge breath. 'I even managed to open it before Alexander grabbed me from behind.'

'You screamed,' Markus reminded her in a shaky voice. 'I heard you scream over the phone.'

'I did. Once. Before his arm locked around my throat.' She smiled grimly. 'It's so strange, but before that night, I would have sworn I could put up a good fight against a man. Not win, of course. But put up a fight. But he choked me, ripped my pants open, and took the knife from me, as if I were—' she shook her head rapidly, forcing her tears to fall '—an infant.'

Her voice came in a rush. 'I managed to get one jab in with the knife – and that was when he threw me on the floor; that was when I saw that it was Alex.

'He punched me. I think that must have been what gave me the concussion because I remember thinking about raising my arms to protect my face, but I couldn't move. It was like my mind had separated from my body.

'He knelt on the floor and grabbed me by my shirt front, kinda pulled me into a seated position. And he said, "After everything I've given you, did you really think you could just use me and walk away?" And then he kissed me. And I couldn't do anything. I couldn't move my arms to try and push him off. I couldn't even feel my jaw, so biting him was out of the question.

'And just when I had accepted that I was going to be raped or maybe even die, I heard someone screaming my name.'

Maverick's vision wavered as the word 'raped' slapped through the room. But he didn't get up and pace as he wanted to. He sat completely still, trying to control himself – for Nina.

'Someone else was there?' Markus asked.

Nina nodded through her tears. 'You were.'

'Jesus.' Markus didn't try to stop his own tears. 'Jesus Christ.'

'You were screaming my name over the phone I'd dropped. And I heard you. And so did Alex.

'He realized that I had called for help. He panicked. He punched me a few more times, and I lost consciousness but he must have kicked me and broken my ribs.

'I woke up in the hospital, and you were the first thing I saw,' she said to Markus. 'And I realized I was alive, but I couldn't find any relief.' She shook her head again, frantically this time. 'I was so tired. A . . . and you kept ranting on about some deranged stalker, and I just let you. Because it was easier than trying to explain.'

'Neens . . . Oh God.' Markus reached across the table, and Nina gave him one of her hands. 'He came to the hospital.'

'I know. I told you that.'

'No. Neens, he came that night too.'

'What?' Maverick and Sierra said at the same time.

'When you were still out of it . . . He came while you were still being checked over.' Markus swore. 'He reeked of alcohol. He looked deranged. And I thought: What a good friend, coming straight from some A-list party as soon as he heard the news.' He tapped his forehead hard with the base of his palm. 'And I'm only just realizing that he had no way of knowing about the assault unless . . .'

Nina was silent, her eyes downcast.

Mav reached for her hand and linked his fingers with hers.

She sent him a fleeting smile that didn't reach her eyes, but finally said, 'When he came the next day, once the nurses forced you to go home—'

'I'm going to kill him.' Markus's face was completely serious.

Maverick agreed with the sentiment. But he gently pushed Nina to tell the rest of the story so that he could help her if she struggled recounting it to the police. 'What did he say?'

'He apologized at first. He said that he had a substance abuse issue and that he was going to seek help for it.' Nina laughed mirthlessly. 'My heart rate was so high, one of the nurses came to check on me.

'But once she left, Alex said, "I think it would be in both of our best interests if we just forgot about this." And when I had nothing to say to that, he said, "It would be a shame if we lost our chance at an Oscar because of a misunderstanding." He kept using that word – *misunderstanding*.

'I panicked. It felt like I had spent years training for this marathon, only to have someone tackle me two feet from the finish line. And all I could think, as I lay there, unable to move while my attacker sat at my bedside, was that my mother's prophecy had come true. I had ended up on my back – just not in the way I'd always feared.'

Markus scoffed. 'Fuck Lulu!'

Calmer now, having recounted the worst of it, Nina sat back in her chair. 'I believed him. I knew he wouldn't risk hurting me again or ruining my career if I kept quiet, so when the cops came, I said I didn't see his face,' she continued. 'I let him win because I was afraid. And I still haven't forgiven myself for that. I'm not sure that I ever will.'

'Don't do that to yourself,' Sierra said before Mav could interject. 'Being a woman is hard enough. Don't carry his guilt for him.'

'You're speaking out now,' Mav reminded her. 'You're risking everything you've worked for so that a monster is caught and caged.' Afraid of the immensity of emotion coursing through him, he didn't pull her into his arms as he wanted to. He just gently tugged a strand of her long hair. 'It's the most unfair thing in the world to expect a victim – a survivor – to stand up against their perpetrator, to expect them to be brave when we as a society have failed them already, to expect them to publicize their trauma and fear even though nothing might come of it.'

'But I need to,' Nina said. 'Because if I don't, one day it'll be another woman getting hurt. It'll be someone else's mother or daughter or sister or friend. And she might not be as lucky as I was.'

Her tone was hot with rage, but Maverick welcomed it because seeing her angry was so much better than seeing her sad or scared or ashamed.

'I need to do it because he *deserves* to suffer the consequences of his actions. I need to do it because I want to see the fear in his eyes when he realizes that I'm not just going to go away.'

'So, we go.' He nodded. 'Together.'

Nina looked at him. 'I don't want this to ruin you, Mav. You've worked so hard . . .'

'You've kinda ruined me all by yourself already.'

He didn't care that everyone was listening. She had destroyed him in the best way possible, and Mav knew that whatever came, they would face it together. And once the storm had passed, they would rebuild together too. He didn't know how they would make it work. Only that they had to try.

He wanted this soft-hearted, brave woman to be his.

Officially.

Permanently.

He could only hope that after the storm she wanted him as much too.

Chapter 23

'How are you holding up?' Markus asked Nina as soon as Mav, Sierra and Benji left for the weekly staff meeting.

Nina didn't tear up. She was too tired to even cry. But she replied honestly. 'Not great.' She rested both arms on the kitchen table. 'I'm scared. And angry. And in love for the first time. But, mostly, I'm exhausted.'

'Focus on the good,' he advised. 'Always. Let the anger fuel you for the days ahead but let go of the fear. We're here. He can't hurt you now.'

'He can,' she argued. 'And he will.' But she smiled, remembering how Maverick had stood by her side to confront Alex. 'But I think I'd have enough, you know. If I lost my career. Mav. Poppy and Sierra. The ranch . . .'

'You fell fast,' he said, but his tone was cautious.

Nina heard it. 'What?'

'Just be careful, okay? I really like Maverick. And God knows, the man is easy to look at. But just . . . be careful. I want this for you – but that doesn't mean I can't be scared at how quickly you're moving, too.'

Nina wasn't offended. Markus's concern came from a heart that loved her fiercely. She did say, 'I never wanted a man.' She laughed aloud at herself. 'After watching Lulu all those years . . .'

'You're not your mother.'

'I know that. *I do*. But growing up in that environment really damaged me, Markus. Men have always made me anxious. Even the few that I slept with . . . I only did it because I thought I had to prove to myself that I wasn't . . . I don't know – "frigid" sounds too cold. But it's probably close to accurate. I didn't enjoy it – sex. I didn't feel a connection or . . . or pleasure. The *idea* of intimacy terrified me. And instead of proving to myself that I was normal, the few times I tried only seemed to reaffirm my doubts. Because how could I go thirty-four years without feeling—' she slapped one hand to her chest '—*this*? This *want*. And *need*. Just the urge to be closer to someone, to be touched by someone – *him*.'

When tears burned her eyes, she refused to let them fall. 'And it's the loveliest feeling to know that I'm not broken, just locked. And that I was waiting for the person who had the key. The right person.' She exhaled a huge breath as the immensity of emotion wrapped around her. 'He's so kind, Markus. So gentle with me.'

Markus sniffled. 'Girl,' he rasped.

As she spoke, Nina realized what she had found. And it gave her courage. 'I'm going to marry him.'

'What?' he stared at her.

Nina laughed, as stunned by her declaration as he was. 'He doesn't know it yet. I only just realized it myself . . . But why wouldn't I hold on to this with both hands?'

'It's a lot to take on.' He tipped his head in the direction of the lounge where Poppy was still watching TV.

She shook her head. 'Not for me. Loving Poppy is easy. Maybe it's not maternal love yet, but I have no doubts that I can get there in time. Loving Mav is scary and overwhelming, but that doesn't mean it's not good. He makes me want things I've never thought about before.'

'Like marriage.'

Nina nodded slowly. 'Like marriage. And . . .' She swallowed the lump in her throat down. 'He makes me think about babies,' she admitted shakily.

Markus gasped dramatically. He used both hands to run a drumroll on the table. 'I can do your wedding and maternity shoots! Oh my God – long, lace sleeves on the dress. Hair, half down, half up. And you, on horseback in that white gown and black cowgirl boots. Mav on the ground, looking up at you. And when you're preggers, Mav can do that trick where he gets Zephyr to lie down. I'll dress you in a maroon – no, hunter green! – tube dress and a cowgirl hat and boots, and then you can lean back against Mav and the horse, both hands on your belly. Oh. My. God! I'm so excited. I know I said go slow, but I changed my mind. Can you expedite this?' he teased.

Nina didn't laugh it off. She could see his vision. And she wanted it. 'I mean, as maid of honour, you'd have a deciding vote on the dress.'

Markus did a booty shake in his chair. 'How soon do you think you can get this ball rolling?' he asked. 'Now that the idea's in my head, I'm not going to sleep until it's done—'

'Nina?'

Both Markus and Nina turned as Poppy came into the kitchen. 'What's wrong, Poppy?' Nina asked kindly.

'Where's my dad?' Poppy asked, but she came to Nina and climbed onto her lap with no self-consciousness.

Nina absently tucked an errant strand of Poppy's hair back into her braid. 'He just had to pop into work for a bit. He should be home soon.'

'The bad man came.'

Nina's hands paused in their task. She floundered for a moment before making a decision. Turning Poppy a little, she said, 'He did. But your dad scared him away.'

'Daddy always scares away the bad man.'

'He does,' Nina agreed.

But Markus saw her hands shaking and intervened. 'Hey,

Poppy. What do you think about me being your Uncle Markus?'

Poppy eyed him seriously. 'Do you like dolls?'

'Girl, I had a Barbie Dreamhouse growing up. My mom saved up to buy it for me when I was about your age.' He looked at Nina. 'She knew it would make me happy even though it was hard for her.'

'I have a Dreamhouse!' Poppy chirped. 'Daddy bought it for me after we watched the movie!' She hopped off Nina's lap and grabbed Markus's hand. 'Come see!'

Markus winked at Nina. 'Excuse me. I have uncle duties to attend to.'

Nina watched them go with a smile on her face.

But seeing that there were wine glasses on the table and plates in the sink, she pushed to her feet. Doing the dishes would give her something to distract herself with because although she knew that there was a future on the ranch with Maverick, and all she had to do was reach out and take it, the notion was still terrifying to her.

He might not have said he loved her yet, but he had also told her he wouldn't. He had told her that there would always be a place for her in his life, and in a way that was far more of a commitment than those three words, which were used so often and so casually.

Nina's life as a perpetual single hadn't been lonely, but she wondered now how much of that had to do with finding comfort in avoiding fear and how much of it had to do with genuinely not being lonely. Had she actually been happy, or had she been comfortable? She wasn't quite sure.

She'd had Markus, of course. But they both worked all week and some weekends and nights too. So, getting together wasn't always easy. And when they did get together, it was for a few hours here or there, brunch or a drink or dinner.

But what she did know now, after only a few weeks of being surrounded by the Hunts, was that she couldn't imagine ever going back to that solitary existence.

She liked living with them, liked that they ate dinner together every night and celebrated birthdays and bickered. She adored Poppy's happy chatter and little footsteps as they sounded through the house. She loved making love in Mav's big bed and then falling asleep in his arms.

When she was with them, she felt like she'd found a family, *her* family. And if there was a part of her that was terrified it might all just be novelty, she snuffed it. Because wasn't it better to choose happiness, even if it only lasted a short while? Nina thought so . . .

Maverick sat in Sierra's office, waiting for the management staff to join them for the weekly debrief. Although he hated making Nina's attack the centre of attention, the resort staff deserved to know what they would be facing.

For the first time in a long time, Sierra and Benji didn't snap at one another as they waited for everyone to trickle in. They didn't talk either, but Mav figured Nina's story had given them something to distract them from their usual standoff.

On the floor, Shadow sighed in her sleep.

As staff began to arrive, Mav couldn't help but compare this meeting to that first one where he'd heard about Nina, only two weeks ago. It was so strange that a life could drastically change in such a short period of time.

Two weeks for him.

Less still for Nina. Her life had changed completely in only a few minutes, when a man had broken into her house and stolen pieces of her using force.

Sierra finally looked up and did a quick headcount before saying, 'Let's get started.'

As the room fell quiet, Sierra continued, 'Today's meeting is going to be a little different from what you're used to.'

Nobody spoke, though there were a few curious expressions and raised eyebrows.

'As you all know, Nina Keller has been staying here for the past two weeks—'

The clamour immediately started again. Deb gushed, 'She's so sweet!'

Lucas, their event planner, added, 'Pretty, too,' and shot a wink in Mav's direction.

Sierra talked over them, calling attention back to her before they could continue. 'Her attacker showed up at the ranch today.'

A deathly silence followed.

Sierra spoke into the void. 'She knew who he was. A producer on her new film who didn't like the fact that Nina didn't want to date him.'

'What?' This came from Jordyn, whose feet dropped off Sierra's desk as she leaned forward in her chair.

'Holy shit,' Paul added.

'He threatened her after the attack, which is why she came here. And this morning, he came to—' Sierra made air quotes '—check up on her.'

Lucas turned beet red. 'I hope you told him to fuck off.'

'Actually,' Sierra said, smiling, 'Mav broke the guy's hand.'

There was a loud round of applause.

Paul slapped him on the back.

Jordyn gave him a single nod of approval.

'But?'

All eyes turned to Deb.

'I mean, there is a *but* – right? You wouldn't be telling us if there wasn't.'

'Tomorrow morning, Nina and Mav are going to head back to LA. To officially file a police report.' Sierra linked her hands together on the desk, Mav knew, trying to appear calm despite the storm. 'After which, we will be closing the resort gates to the public for two weeks.'

Sierra continued through the ghostly silence. 'We're expecting a media storm. And we want to keep Nina as safe as possible during it. Obviously, we also want to continue to provide our guests with the luxury and privacy they're paying for.'

Jordyn collapsed back in her seat. 'Sierra . . . The restaurant – the bar – is our cash cow.'

'I know.' Sierra sighed. 'I am fully aware of the risk we're taking, but we can survive two weeks of limited operations.' When Jordyn didn't say anything, Sierra added, 'Think of it as a two-week vacation, Jords. You'll be feeding twenty to fifty people a day instead of hundreds.'

'I mean, I'm all for the break and I'm sure my staff are too, but I don't want you guys to risk the resort. I freaking love my job here.'

Several nods followed her statement.

'We're not risking the resort. Closing to the public will hurt – yes. But we'll manage.' Sierra sighed. 'We look after our own here. And since Mav and Nina are dating—'

'Goddammit.' Jordyn fished a hundred-dollar bill from her bra and passed it to Deb.

Paul groaned. 'I'll give it to you after the meeting.'

Lucas said, 'Ditto.'

Mav had to ask, 'You guys had a pool going?'

'We did,' Deb said sheepishly.

'Dude!' Jordyn slapped his arm. 'I'm happy for you and shit, but you just cost me.' She shook her head. 'Maverick Hunt dating *the* Nina Keller. Who would've guessed?' She angled her head to look at him. 'I'd ask if it's serious, but I know you.'

'I don't do casual,' was all he said in reply.

'Oh my God, could you imagine if she moved here? And we got to see her all the time?' Deb asked excitedly. 'We'd have our own resident celebrity!'

'Let's not get too ahead of ourselves,' Mav warned, only because he desperately wanted that future but couldn't focus on it until Nina was safe.

There was a lot that needed to happen before they even had that conversation, including dealing with Alexander Cane and the ensuing fallout. And, still, he was man enough to admit that he was scared.

Nina had a life that she had worked really hard for. But so did he. If they chose to stay together, if she chose to stay with him, it would be hard. For both of them. He would never ask her to give up acting, so there would be months of distance when she was actively filming. And, yeah, he could visit relatively often.

But it would weigh on them.

And Poppy.

He could know in the depths of his soul that Nina and Shannon were nothing alike and still understand that it would be difficult for him and Nina to make an honest go of it. And if it didn't work out . . .

'It's going to be a rough couple of months here,' Sierra said, distracting him from his thoughts. 'I've put together some Dos and Don'ts of talking to media.' She reached for a wad of papers and passed them around. 'The gates will be locked, but they'll try get in anyway. If in doubt, just say "No comment," and then come and get either Mav or me.'

She picked up another stack of papers and passed them around. Mav looked down at the IMDb photo of Alexander Cane. Handsome. Successful. Wealthy. And a complete predator.

'This is the man who assaulted Nina . . .'

Chapter 24

The LAPD's assistant chief of police, Aiden Flint, was a towering, lanky man with a build that implied many late nights and skipped meals. His hair was dark brown and a little unkempt, as if he was constantly running his fingers through it. Nina thought he might have been intimidating were it not for his eyes, which were big and brown and gentle.

Those eyes studied her calmly as she and Maverick took a seat in his office.

That morning on the drive to LA, they had called Alison, her agent. And though it had been a difficult conversation, Nina had told her everything.

Alison had been shocked and hurt and enraged on Nina's behalf, but after she had worked through her own emotions, she had powered forward unquestioningly, gathering resources and contacting the assistant chief, whose children went to school with hers.

'I read the report on your attack three weeks ago,' Aiden Flint said. 'I'm very sorry that happened to you.'

'Thank you. I . . .' Nina trailed off as she thought about what to say.

Mav reached over and took her hand in his. He gave her a

small squeeze, but he didn't let her go.

'I lied,' she rasped. 'In my statement.'

Aiden Flint didn't even blink. He nodded slowly. 'We know.'

'Excuse me?' Nina asked, confused.

'Miss Keller, as of yesterday afternoon, we've been trying to contact you for an interview regarding two alleged assaults, both of which were reported by Alexander Cane.'

Maverick's hand jerked in hers.

Nina barely felt it.

Her blood ran cold, sending a shiver up from the base of her spine to the top of her head. She blinked slowly as the reality of her situation dawned like news of some fatal disease. 'He . . . I'm sorry, what did he say exactly?' she whispered.

There were no tears. Only bone-deep exhaustion.

'Mr Cane said that he went to check up on you because you hadn't been handling the stress of filming well. He stated that you got into an argument and that when you attacked him with a knife, he fought back – in self-defence. He alleges that he left the scene because he was afraid for his own safety, and that he didn't report it at the time because he was concerned for the assault's impact on *Shadowlands*.'

The assistant chief didn't pause. 'He then asserted that when he went to Hunt Ranch to speak to you about what had happened, you—' he looked at Maverick '—slammed his hand in his own car door. X-rays show that he has four broken fingers.'

Maverick released her hand to lean forward in his chair. He rested his elbows on his knees and said, 'Good,' clearly. Slowly.

Aiden Flint's mouth quirked.

Nina couldn't feel anything. She was numb down to the soul.

'Someone has already leaked the story to the press,' Aiden Flint continued.

Nina closed her eyes. Though she wasn't aware of doing it, she rocked slightly in her chair.

'What I can't figure out is why you're here without a lawyer and why you're not telling me to go fuck myself?'

Nina heard the words. Slowly, her mind made sense of them. She opened her eyes to look at Aiden Flint.

'Miss Keller—'

'Nina.'

He tipped his head. 'If you think I believe that a six-foot man had to knock you black and blue, render you unconscious, and crack two of your ribs to disarm you, you're not as smart as you look. And that's not saying anything about the state of your clothes when you arrived at the hospital.'

A warbled sob slipped from her lips. Nina covered her mouth with her hand, mortified as the tears started. Her entire body shook with the force of holding them back.

Aiden Flint opened the top drawer of his desk and fished out a pack of Kleenex. He passed it to her. 'But I am going to tell you to get your lawyer here before you speak to me. You know this isn't going to go away without a fight, and having your lawyer here will reduce the number of times you have to recount everything.'

'Just like that?' Mav asked, his scepticism clear.

'I've run into Alexander Cane before.' Aiden's eyes shuttered. 'Between the initial interview and the follow-up, my last victim completely changed her story.'

'You think he paid her off?' Mav asked.

'One can only assume.' Aiden looked at her again. 'Do you have an attorney?'

Nina shook her head. 'Only an entertainment attorney. I've never needed a personal one.'

'I can recommend someone,' he replied. 'She's one of the best. If you have nothing pressing to do today, I can give her a call and she'll come down if she doesn't have a hearing. She owes me.'

Nina nodded, and even though she could barely make out Aiden Flint's face through her glassy eyes, she had to ask, 'Why? Why would you help me?'

He took his time replying, but when he did, he said something she hadn't expected from the assistant chief of police. 'My wife . . . She has a past. She's been through some things. Bad things. Things she's still working through fifteen years into our marriage. I have daughters. And I'm a veteran cop who's seen things done to women by men . . . Things that you wouldn't believe. So, this,' he said, looking directly into Nina's eyes, 'this is personal for me. As it should be for every man who loves any woman, be it his mother or wife or daughter or sister or friend.

'But because it's personal for me, you really need a lawyer here. If *we* do this,' he said pointedly, 'we do it properly. We leave no room for doubt. We get you the best lawyer money can buy, we help her build a solid case, so that when this goes to court, he's left looking exactly like the idiot – the predator – that he is.'

Nina was too overwhelmed to speak. But because he would be able to read the emotion on her face, she looked at Maverick.

And it was him who read the reply in her eyes and said, 'Call her. Call the lawyer.'

'Today is 23rd June 2025.' Maverick remained completely quiet as Aiden Flint started the official interview only an hour and a half later. 'Ms Keller, could you state your name and address for the record?'

'Nina Marie Keller, 34 Hollybrook Drive, Hollywood.'

'Ms Keller, do you understand that this interview is being recorded?'

'Yes.'

'For the record, Ms Keller's boyfriend, Maverick Hunt, and attorney, Linda Patton, are present.'

Maverick couldn't even enjoy the title, coming from a stranger's lips for the first time. He was too tense. Too focused on Nina, who looked so small and tired just then.

She sat in the chair next to his, opposite Aiden Flint. She was dressed in a pretty white sundress that would have looked beautiful against the summer golds of the ranch but that just looked stark against the grey walls of the LAPD's Hollywood Station's interview room. Her dark eyes were sad and heavy, her shoulders rounded. But every time she spoke, her voice was strong and clear. God knew he admired her for it.

'Ms Keller, are you aware of the assault allegations made against you by Alexander Cane?'

'Yes.'

'For the record, could you please state your own account of the events of June 2nd 2025?'

Mav listened as Nina began to recount what Alexander Cane had done to her, slowly at first, and then faster as her panic began to take ahold.

Aiden Flint listened to her, only interrupting a few times to ask clarifying questions, one of which was: 'The police report says that your friend, Markus Johnson, asked a stranger to call 911 on his way to you. Is that accurate?'

'Yes.'

'Why did you call your best friend? Why not 911?'

'I grew up with a single mom who . . . entertained men a lot. She told me that if I ever called 911, the police would take me to jail. As a kid, when things would get rough, I would lock myself in the bathroom. As an adult . . . It honestly never even occurred to me to call the police. I panicked. And my best friend has always been a place of safety for me. But he – Markus – he had someone else call 911 while he stayed on the line with me.'

'We've got that recording already, but the caller had no information except that there was a break-in at your address. Do you still have Markus's outgoing call listed on your phone?'

'Yes.'

'Would you be amenable to submitting that phone to evidence?'

'Yes.'

'Would Markus Johnson be prepared to give us a statement corroborating this?'

'Yes.'

'Thank you.' Aiden Flint ended the interview for the recording, leaned back in his chair. 'Unfortunately, your phone is only going to prove that you called Markus. It'll tell us when and how long that call was. Markus's testimony will verify the content of that call.'

'Can't you subpoena the content of the call to Markus?' Maverick asked, growing impatient. 'He was on the line while she was being assaulted.'

'We can only subpoena call detail records, showing who you called, when the call started and ended, and which cell tower you were linked to, none of which we have any need for with Nina's permission to access her phone. To get anything more, a judge would need probable cause to grant us a warrant, and it would probably be a waste of time as phone companies don't automatically record calls.

'Unfortunately, in this case, calling 911 from your phone instead of Markus would have helped – 911 calls are recorded and, due to their nature, the transcripts are easier to obtain.'

'So, basically, it'll be my word against his?' Nina asked quietly.

Mav hated the defeat in her tone. He wished he could do something. Anything. Instead, he was useless. Helpless.

'In my experience, cases like this typically end up being clearer than the physical evidence would suggest.'

Aiden pushed to his feet. 'I'm just going to grab a bag for your phone,' he said, and left the room.

The moment they were alone, Linda reached out and touched Nina's hand. 'You did an amazing job, Nina. I know it's hard but try to remember that every time you recount this, you're simply stating facts from memory. Every time Alexander Cane recounts his side of the story, he's going to be trying to remember every lie he told. He'll slip up, and when he does, I will catch it.'

Nina only nodded.

Aiden came back into the room. He held an evidence bag open for Nina, who dropped her phone into it.

'Come on. I'll show you out.' It was only once they were in the hallway that Aiden added, 'That was a great start, Nina.'

'I wish I had done things differently.' Nina shook her head. 'I could have avoided all of this if I had just been honest from the start.'

Mav linked his hand with hers.

But it was Aiden Flint who said, 'Maybe. Or maybe you would be going through this exact same thing with severe injuries, having had no time to recuperate.'

'What happens now?' Mav asked.

'Typically, in cases like this, accusations aren't enough to make an arrest. Alexander Cane came in here with his lawyer, so you can guarantee he already has an answer to counter every question I'm going to ask him. So, we gather all the evidence, and as soon as I find something solid, we take him in. He'll get out on bail, but optics are everything in a case like this. And you—' he turned to Linda '—kick his ass in court when the time comes. In the meantime, as I'm sure your attorney will advise you, stay far away from Alexander Cane. Do not try and talk to him. Do not go anywhere he might be, including the *Shadowlands* set. Don't give him any reason to make another accusation.' He looked straight at Mav. 'That goes for you too.'

'Thank you, Mr Flint.' Nina tried to smile, but Mav could see how much that tiny gesture took out of her.

'I'm just doing my job. You're the one risking everything to do this.' He ran his hand through his hair. 'Where will you be staying – so that I can follow up?'

'We're staying at Nina's place tonight. And then I'm taking her home,' Mav said, but he looked to Nina to confirm. When she nodded, he added, 'We'll drive up as often as you need us to.'

'I'll keep you updated as the investigation proceeds.' He nodded to them, turned to look at Nina's new attorney. 'Help me nab this fucker, Lin.'

Linda smiled grimly. 'With pleasure.'

She held the door open for them, and it was only once they had exited the police station that the attorney said, 'Do you mind if I follow you to yours? We should go over everything again, and I should prepare you for what's in store.'

'Of course.' Nina rattled off her address again.

Linda followed them back to Nina's home in the Hollywood Hills, her nifty Mercedes easily tailing Mav's Jeep through the dense LA traffic.

In the passenger seat, Nina was completely silent. Her big, brown eyes were vacant and shadowed with exhaustion, her arms wrapped around her raised knees.

Mav knew that there were no words he could give her that would be adequate, no words that would make her feel better. So, he didn't say anything except, 'I'm here with you.'

Nina turned in his direction, purposefully showing him the emotion in her eyes when she replied, 'Thank you for . . . everything.' She shook her head. 'You don't deserve this.'

'It is you who doesn't deserve any of this. I'm choosing it,' he said firmly. 'I'm choosing you – every time, Nina.'

She tried to smile but couldn't quite manage it.

When his Maps told him he was a quarter mile from her address, he started to see the cars and news vans parked on the side of the road. The neighbourhood had not been designed for traffic of any kind, so many of the vehicles were illegally parked half in the road, making two-way traffic flow nearly impossible.

Nina put her seat back, hiding. 'Just keep driving. Linda will follow.'

'Hotel?'

'Yeah,' she rasped.

He dislodged his phone from its holder on the dash and passed it to her. 'Put the one you want to stay at in.'

She quickly rerouted them and passed the phone back to Mav, who remounted it in its holder.

But when they drove past her house, he didn't look at the dozens of people standing outside her home or sitting on her little walkway and lawn, he glanced back down at Nina. She wasn't even crying. She was pale and defeated, her eyes empty.

Chapter 25

'Once you've written your public statement, send it to me and I'll edit it or approve it. Once we've nailed it down and you're safely back at the ranch, we'll both post it. You, to social media. Me, to my firm's pages. After that, the media will pick it up and distribute it for us.'

'Okay.' Nina knew she should have said more, or maybe profusely thanked Linda for her help, only she couldn't find any remnant energy. She felt so heavy, so tired.

'This is going to be hard, Nina,' her attorney warned for the dozenth time. 'But we've got this.'

Nina nodded.

Linda smiled kindly. 'I'll be in touch almost every day. Given your celebrity status, things are going to move really quickly at first. But given that you don't want to settle, things will slow down towards the court date. They always do.'

'Thank you,' Nina managed.

'Get some rest.' When Mav started walking her to the door of the suite he'd booked, Linda waved him away. 'I know the way.'

Mav extended his hand, and when Linda returned the shake, he gently closed both of his over hers. 'Thank you. We appreciate your help.'

'Oh, trust me, this one is going to be my pleasure,' she reiterated.

Nina waited until she heard the door click softly closed, but the moment it did, she fell apart. It was as if the lock clicking into place had the opposite effect on her, unlocking everything she had held back during the interview and the follow-up meeting with her attorney.

She didn't sob. She only curled into a ball on the bed and let her pent-up tears flow freely and silently, blurring her vision.

Mav didn't say anything.

Neither did she.

What was there to say? She felt as if she had come into his life under false pretences, and she had made things so difficult for him. For Poppy. It didn't matter that she hadn't meant to fall in love with him. She had.

Her shame was so immense just then, that she was the one who broke the silence first. 'I'm sorry,' she whispered, knowing that the words weren't adequate.

Mav kicked off his boots. She heard one and then the other as they dropped to the floor. He climbed onto the bed behind her and moulded his big body to hers, one arm pulling her close, his legs folded beneath hers. He kissed the side of her hot, damp face, and he whispered, 'I'm not.' He moved his arm to trail his fingers down her bare arm. 'I'm angry and stressed and sad. But I'm also the happiest I've ever been. Because whatever happens, I found you.'

Nina thought about that, and as much as she wished she could change things, it was also exceptionally humbling to realize that the worst thing that had ever happened to her had also resulted in the best.

'What do you need, Nina?' he asked, interrupting her thoughts. 'Food? Wine? Sleep? Markus? I can call him. He'll come.'

Even the thought of food made her warring stomach sick. Sleep wouldn't come. Markus needed time to decompress with Juan, just as she did with Mav. 'I want you to love me so hard that I forget everything else, even momentarily.'

Mav's breath caught. She heard it, that little catch.

'Are you sure?' he asked, always so sweet, so concerned.

'It's what I *need*,' she whispered in reply.

Mav made a rumbling sound in the back of his throat that shot straight to her womb. He moved, making space to roll her onto her back. His blue eyes, hot with his own need, searched hers. 'How do you need to be touched?'

'It doesn't matter how you touch me, only that it's you.'

Mav smiled his full, dimple-popping smile. But it was Nina who felt lighter, as if the happiness that sparked in his eyes kindled a fire within her. She would protect this man and his family even though it would break her heart.

'Have I told you that I love this dress?' he asked, his voice low as he toyed with the strap of her sundress. 'It's so sexy. And—' he slid, first one, and then the other, strap down her shoulder, shimmied the dress's bodice down to her hips '—easy to remove.'

Nina fished her arms out of the straps and raised them to him, wanting to touch his golden skin. She started on his buttons, slowly at first and then quicker as the desperate greed in his eyes fuelled her own.

The moment the last button gave, she raked her nails lightly over his chest, chasing the quiver in his muscles.

He had barely touched her, but it didn't matter. She was ready – wet – just from the anticipation of what he would bring her.

'Tell me what you want,' he reiterated.

Nina took one of his big hands in hers and lowered it between her legs. She needed to remember that, despite what had happened to her, she had found someone whose touch to her most vulnerable self did not take, but gave.

'Here?' Mav asked, and when she nodded, he slid two fingers through her. He closed his eyes when he felt how wet she was, said, 'You make me wild, Nina. Touching you makes me want to take you ruthlessly, even while knowing what you've been through makes me want to be gentle and go slow.' His eyes opened, burning into her, *through* her. 'You tear me up inside.'

Nina swallowed. He had loved her fast and slow – but *ruthlessly*? It was a testament to her trust in him that the thought turned her on instead of scaring her. 'Take me ruthlessly,' she said.

Mav's eyes snapped to her face again. They darkened with intensity even as he said, 'I never want to scare you.'

'I'll tell you if it's too much.'

There was one moment of perfect stillness.

And then Maverick flipped her over. Nina's brain took a moment to process the new position on her stomach. But before she could move, he gripped her hips with both hands and dragged her backwards and up so that she was on her knees and elbows, her ass in the air.

Her heart thumped. But not with fear; with adrenaline, surprise, and anticipation.

When he unbuckled his belt and lowered his zipper, he did it slowly. The sound of his metal buckle sent a shiver through her, even as his zipper being lowered unravelled her.

She didn't turn and look back at him because she liked not knowing what he was going to do. And that surprised her. For someone who had never let her body take over, this ability to simply allow herself to *feel* was new and overwhelming and right. And it was because of him. Only him. Because she trusted, absolutely, that he would never do anything to hurt her.

Mav lifted the skirt of her dress and let it fall over her shoulders, exposing her thong-covered ass to his gaze. She thought he might pull her underwear to the side or take them off entirely, so Nina gasped in shock when he gripped the flimsy lace in both hands and tore it as if it were a piece of paper.

He tossed the scrap of fabric onto the floor, leaving her completely bare.

She fought a wave of self-consciousness, but it disappeared the moment Mav gripped her hips in his hands and said, 'Look at you. All ready for me. So fucking perfect.'

Oh. My. God. Nina had not known the power words had in the bedroom until that moment. But only those few from Mav were enough to have her body tightening mercilessly. Her upper thighs were soaked. Her core ached to be filled. 'Mav,' she begged.

'You wanted me to be ruthless,' he reminded her, and instead of entering her from behind as she'd been expecting, he slid his hard length between her legs, stopping when the head of his penis nudged her entrance.

Nina's breath rushed out of her as he began to thrust, teasing her, his hands at her hips easily controlling her body's every movement. It didn't matter that he wasn't inside of her. Every nudge against her pushed her higher, the pointed absence of him somehow more erotic in that moment.

Nina felt that familiar wave gathering. She pressed her hips backwards, asking for more, but Mav just chuckled and kept torturing her, his hands reclaiming control of her restless hips easily.

Her core pulsed.

Each breath came in time with it.

And just when she was braced to go under, he stopped.

Nina's eyes flew open as the orgasm started receding immediately. 'Mav,' she whined.

'Ruthless doesn't have to mean violent,' he said, and she could hear the smile in his voice.

'But—'

Before she could say more, he started again, slower now, each press of him against her meant to build that wave back up. 'Watching you like this makes me so fucking hard,' he said hoarsely. 'I could come just from looking at you.'

Nina moaned loudly when she realized that he was torturing himself too, delaying his own release with hers. She was so wet that she could hear the slap of him against her, and somehow that only made it hotter.

Her hands gripped the comforter.

She buried her face in the bed, smothering her wanton cries.

But when he stopped the second time, she groaned at the loss.

Her arms and legs shook, as if her suppressed release needed to escape her body through different means.

Mav didn't continue right away. He demanded, 'Look at me,' and when she turned to look at him over her shoulder, he leaned down, angled his head, and licked through her once, his wet tongue dragging sensation everywhere it touched.

'Mav,' she begged, as her body danced on the edge for the third time. 'Please.'

'Please what?'

'Make me come.'

He entered her in one powerful thrust. Nina didn't have time to brace as the orgasm he'd been teasing exploded through her. She cried out as her body pulsed around him, taking him deeper, holding him closer.

Mav didn't even move.

He held himself inside of her as she came down from the tide, and the moment he felt her body quieten, he let go, spilling inside of her without a single thrust.

He released her hips and collapsed beside her on the bed.

They took a long moment, both of them lying on the bed, facing the ceiling. But it was Nina who moved first, sprawling over him, a well-loved woman in the afterglow of self-discovery.

She knew what she had to do. What she *would* do.

Maverick, with his kind, gentle heart made her want to be stronger. He made her realize that while he constantly went out of his way to protect and help people, nobody did the same for him. His parents were gone. Sierra and Benji, though they loved him fiercely, were both just trying to survive their own storm. Poppy was protective of him, sure. But Nina loved him enough to give him the gift he'd given her daily since they'd met, even when she'd been a stranger. So, she'd protect him. And she could only hope he'd forgive her when the time came.

Mav levered up to kiss her forehead. 'Was that okay for you?' he whispered.

Nina smiled. She said, 'Ruthless.' And although she was decided, she needed this night to say goodbye. Because Mav would be hurt. He would feel betrayed. He might never see that she had done it *for* him – because she loved him. He might not take her back when it was over.

So, she'd take tonight.

And tomorrow . . . Tomorrow, she would do what she had to do.

She fell asleep on his chest in minutes as the day's events caught up to her. Maverick memorized the feeling of her slight weight pressing into him. He closed his eyes and inhaled the familiar coconut scent of her hair, and when she stirred, he wrapped both of his arms around her because she had once told him that it made her feel safe to sleep that way.

Nina shifted. She sighed in her sleep and then settled again.

Mav stayed like that, holding her while she slept, for over an hour. But when a glance at the clock showed him that it was nearing seven, he gently rearranged her and slid off the bed.

He picked up his phone from the nightstand and carried it through to the lounge that sat just off the bedroom, making sure to turn off the light on his way out.

He grabbed a bottle of water and the room service menu before he sat down on the couch and unlocked his phone.

There was a text from Sierra:

How did it go?

And one from Benji:

Tell Nina not to go online.

Mav frowned at that, but because he didn't want to be angry when he was still basking in the afterglow of her, he didn't open his web browser either. It wouldn't serve a purpose. He believed Nina absolutely. He loved her indefinitely, and that was all he needed to know.

He called Sierra so that he could update her and say goodnight to Poppy.

She answered on the first ring with: 'How is she?'

Mav ran one hand through his hair. 'Not great, but she's holding on,' he said honestly. 'She passed out about an hour ago . . .'

'I can imagine.'

'Yeah. She's a trouper.'

'And the police? What did they say?' Before he could answer, Sierra continued, 'Benji told me that Alexander Cane accused her of assaulting him. Apparently, it's all over the news.'

'Yeah. But the assistant chief of police believed her. Apparently, this isn't the first time he's run into that fucker.'

'There was another woman?'

'Yeah, but she changed her story a few days after reporting it.'

'He paid her off,' Sierra said.

'Probably. Which also means she would have signed an NDA, so she won't talk.'

'Do you know who she is? Maybe we can find her, ask her to help us . . .'

'I don't.'

'Let me look into it. I have a friend who works in admin for the LAPD. If the report's not public already, she'll get it to me.'

'I don't know. Dragging someone else into this feels *wrong*.'

'So, we ask. But let her decide what she wants to do. We can do that much for Nina, Mav. Numbers matter in situations like this . . .'

'Fuck.' But because he knew she was right, he closed his eyes momentarily, said, 'Okay.'

'Stay positive, Mav. We have to believe that good will win. Otherwise, what's the point?'

'The cop put us in touch with a really good lawyer. So, that's something.'

'How long until you come home?'

'We're going to head back tomorrow and then come down when we're needed.' But because he was already dreading the months ahead, he felt that he had to warn her. 'It's going to be a long haul here, Si.'

'Yeah.'

'I'm sorry in advance.'

'You can't choose who you love, Mav. I know that better than anyone. And even if you could, I wouldn't choose anyone else for you. Seeing you and Nina together . . .' She sighed. 'We'll pull through. We'll find a way to make the resort work – even if we have to become a social media hub.'

Mav shuddered at the thought. But he could live with it if it meant having Nina there with him. 'It'll die down.' *Hopefully*.

'Yeah . . . Mav . . .'

'What?' he asked, sensing her tone.

'We shut the gates today. Security called a few hours ago to say that news vans were pulling up outside.'

'We knew this would happen.' But he hated it. Hated them, for what they were doing to Nina, who had already suffered so much, and for threatening his family's livelihood, which they'd all worked so hard for. And for what? So that the general population could be apprised of the intimate details of one stranger's life?

It sickened him.

'Yeah,' Sierra agreed.

'Do me a favour: keep Poppy close.'

'I'm offended that you'd even ask.'

'Sorry.'

'You're forgiven, but only because you have a lot on your mind.'

'Is she awake?' he asked.

'Yeah. One sec.' Sierra shouted through the house, 'Poppy! Your dad's on the phone!'

Maverick heard Poppy's excited squeal and her little footsteps running. When she took the phone, she was breathless. 'Hi, Daddy!'

'Hi, baby!' he greeted her in the same tone and smiled despite the day they'd had.

'Where are you?' she asked.

'I'm in Los Angeles with Nina, remember? But I'm coming home tomorrow.'

'Okay!'

'Are you having fun with Sisi?'

'Yeah! We made steak. And then we watched *Trolls* in the fort Uncle Benji built.'

Mav's eyebrows shot up at that. 'Oh? Uncle Benji's there?'

'Yeah. He's sleeping in the spare room because you're not here. But he says the bad man won't come, so don't worry, Daddy.'

Mav's heart ached. His voice was tight when he said, 'I won't worry,' even though he would. 'Uncle Benji and Sisi will look after you. But make sure you listen to them, okay?'

'I'm good, Daddy,' she reminded him.

'The best,' he affirmed.

'I'm going to go finish *Trolls* now.'

'Okay.'

'Oh, wait,' she said. 'Can I speak to Nina first?'

Mav smiled. 'She's sleeping, baby. But we'll see you tomorrow, okay?'

''Kay!'

Poppy hung up before he could speak to Sierra again, but Mav didn't call back. He shot Benji a thank-you text and then put his phone down and closed his eyes, exhausted.

'Mav?'

He opened his eyes, asked, 'Hey. Did I wake you up?'

Nina shook her head, but he knew immediately that she had heard at least part of the phone call. 'Poppy wanted to speak to you.'

'I heard. I . . . can't.' She shook her head. 'I'm so sorry, Mav.'

'For what exactly?' he asked, because he didn't blame her for anything.

'For going to Hunt Ranch!' her voice came out loud and panicked. 'For getting involved with you when my life was a mess! For endangering . . .' She took a deep breath, rasped, 'For endangering Poppy.'

'Nina, come here.' He held out one hand for her, and when she took it, he tugged her onto his lap. 'Life is messy. Almost always. But I'd rather do it with you than alone. And you never endangered Poppy. Alexander Cane did.'

'It's not that simple,' she insisted.

'Yes—' he brushed her long hair behind her ear '—it is. But you have to be willing to accept that you are a victim – a survivor.'

He hated when her eyes welled with tears. 'I don't want to be weak.'

'Being a victim doesn't mean you're weak. It means something happened to you. And being a *survivor* – that means you're still moving forward despite it.' When she started to argue, he talked over her. He asked, 'Take yourself out of it, Nina. Put any other woman in your place.' Though he hated the thought, he pushed, said, 'Put Poppy in your place.'

She bit back a sob.

'What would you tell her if she was in your shoes?' he asked. 'One day, when that little girl is a grown woman, we might be having this conversation with her. So, what will you tell her? As her dad, I need to know what you'd say to her.'

'That it's not her *f-fault*,' she managed eventually. 'And that she didn't do anything wrong.'

'Exactly.' He wrapped his arms around her, felt his heart settle when she nestled against him. 'It's not your fault. You didn't do anything wrong.' And because he could feel her pulling away, he added, 'I'm with you. I'm not going anywhere.'

Chapter 26

They slept cocooned in each other, arms and legs entwined. But when Maverick woke up in the morning and Nina wasn't there beside him, his blood ran cold.

He found her sitting in the lounge of the hotel suite, her long hair falling down both sides of her face to her hips, her big eyes sad. He knew before she said, 'We need to talk,' that she was pulling back.

But he sat. He rested his forearms on his knees, linked his hands, and lifted his eyes to hers. When she struggled to speak, he forced a smile, gave her an encouraging nod. But he didn't touch her. He was too afraid that if he did, he might do something crazy. Like refuse to let her go. Kidnap her.

'I have to do this by myself, Mav.'

Of all the words she could have broken him with, those weren't the ones he would have guessed. Because if she'd said she didn't love him or didn't want a life on the ranch, he would have understood. But Mav, who had been raised with all the love and support in the world, and who had continued to give and receive that love and support, didn't understand why she'd need to stand alone.

'Why?'

'Mav . . .' She reached for his hand then. 'You don't know.'

'So, *tell me*,' he demanded quietly as the first of his panic slipped through.

'You don't know what it's like, to be hounded by the media day in and day out. To have them take pictures of your everyday moments – going to the grocery store, blowing your nose, or . . . or sharing a kiss on a horse – and blow them up into a consumable product, into an . . . an event!'

'I know what I'm getting into. I have my eyes wide open.'

'The fact that you'd say that is only proof that you have no idea. Mav, I *know* you. You'll hate every moment of it.'

'You think I don't know that?' he asked. Because he did. He understood – and dreaded – that inevitability. 'I *know*, Nina. But I'm prepared to do it – for you.'

'I'm not prepared to ask you to do it.' And then she said the only thing that could have destroyed him at that moment. She said, 'For Poppy.'

Mav hated what she was doing even as he loved her more for doing it. Because it would be Nina who would think about Poppy's – about *his* – wellbeing over her own. Still, that deep, dark insecurity that existed in him had him saying, 'If you are only trying to protect us – don't. I can look after myself, and I sure as fuck can look after Poppy. But if you don't feel the same way, if you don't want that life, I'll understand. But I need you to be honest with me, Nina. Am I showing up, am I *fighting* for you as a friend or as a woman who wants more from me?'

'It's not that simple!' she insisted.

'It is.'

'I can't give up everything that I've worked for.' She engaged that skill that had made her famous then. Mav saw it click into place. It didn't matter that he knew she was acting, it still devastated him when he saw her resolve. Because it was unmovable. 'I *won't* give up everything that I've worked for. I'm sorry, Mav.'

He knew she was evading even as the pain of her rejection tore through him. He thought he had been here before. But he hadn't. This was more terrifying than Shannon abandoning him with an infant. This was the end of a future he'd wanted with every cell in his body.

'I never asked you to,' he reminded her. 'I'm here, Nina. I showed up, to help you fight for what you want.'

'Mav, you've known me two weeks. Two of the lowest weeks of my life.'

'Yeah, maybe. But I've been searching for you for a lifetime, and that has to count for something. And if I can love you as much as I do at your lowest, God only knows how much I'll love you at your best.'

'Mav,' she urged, her tone slipping.

'Nina.'

'I'm asking – *begging* – you to go home, to give me time to sort my life out. Please.'

Arguing wasn't going to change her mind. He could see that she had made her decision, and that she was sticking to it. If anything, the more he resisted, the more committed she seemed, and Mav would rather cut off his own arm than make her feel trapped and miserable. He'd unknowingly done that to a woman once before and still regretted it, and Nina already had so much to carry.

'Call Markus,' he said, because he'd be damned if he'd leave her alone like this. 'Once he gets here, I'll go.'

He waited for her to nod before pushing up off the sofa and walking through to the en-suite shower. He ran the water cold, stripped, and stepped under the unforgiving spray, hoping that the frigid water would freeze out his anger and despair and grief. But it only left him cold and numb.

He knew in the deepest part of his soul that they were destined. He even knew she loved him too. But how could he justify staying when she'd begged him to leave? How could he try and show someone who'd never been loved by a lover that *making* love to someone and *loving* someone could be completely different and that the precise test of real love was sticking through the bullshit that life threw in your face?

Mav had no fucking idea.

And if there was a small, insecure part of him that had known this would happen, that reminded him he had been expecting it, he tried to ignore it. Because even as she broke his heart, Mav understood why she was doing it. Hell, he even admired her for it.

Nina could hear the water running in the shower and had to actively stop herself from going to him, from slipping inside the shower and pressing her body to his, from taking his mouth and then begging him not to leave, from apologizing for causing that pain in his eyes and then never letting him go again.

Fuck *Shadowlands*, because that conversation with Mav had been her best performance yet.

But as difficult as it was, she knew that she was right, and that she was doing the right thing. For Mav, who had worked his entire life to make Hunt Ranch the serene escape it was. For Poppy, who didn't deserve to be indoctrinated into the world's deceit because of Nina's mistakes. For Sierra, who would have stood up for Nina for no other reason than Maverick had asked.

Despite all of Mav's points – and he had made some that had her heart beating overtime – Nina couldn't ask him to sit with her through police interviews, press conferences, Instagram wars, and media harassment. It wouldn't have been fair, and she loved him enough to want to spare him.

Because he would stick if she hadn't been the one to put her foot down. Nina absolutely believed that to be true. And, when it was all over, she really hoped she'd be proven right.

And if there was a not-so-small, niggling part of her that knew she feared trusting him, feared relying on him too much, Nina forgave herself for it. Because she had absolutely meant what she'd said: Maverick didn't know what he was taking on.

Tomorrow, when she made her official statement, the war would truly start. And all wars had casualties. It didn't matter that this one would primarily involve words, twisted into lies and arguments that masked the truth, people would get hurt. Nina was already one of them.

But she'd be damned if the Hunts would be, too.

Still, when Markus arrived, dressed in neatly pressed, pleated khaki pants and a white linen shirt, it took every ounce of her God-given talent to remain composed.

'What's going on?' he asked, his dark eyes searching her face.

She could hear Mav rummaging around in the bedroom as he packed. 'I asked him to leave.'

Markus nodded slowly. He didn't tell her she was an idiot or argue with her. This man, who knew every corner of her soul, the corners that Maverick was still learning, said, 'I don't agree with you. But I've got you.'

Nina's eyes burned, but she refused to let the tears fall until Maverick had left. Still, holding them back made her think about how often she had cried in the past month, and how often she had cried in front of Maverick. It wasn't because she was a particularly sensitive person either. It was because he made her feel safe, and in doing so gave her the space to be vulnerable.

He came out of the bedroom, looking like every woman's dream on legs. Nina promised herself that one day, hopefully soon, he would be hers again. Forever.

She didn't say that.

Instead, she walked into his arms and gave him a hug, trying to impart every thought in her head and feeling in her heart through only that contact.

Mav didn't shy away. He squeezed her back, and he said, 'Call if you need me.'

Nina nodded, but the moment he stepped back, severing contact with her, she felt bereft. As if she'd been stuck in a raging river, desperately holding on to a fallen tree branch for days, and she had just willingly let it go, succumbing to the rapids.

He turned to face Markus, and although she couldn't see his face, she could see her best friend's, so she saw all the messages passing between them. But when Markus held out his hand for Mav's, Mav only said, 'Seriously?' and pulled Markus into a bone-crushing hug.

And Nina walked away, because she knew that if she didn't, she would cave.

Markus went to Nina the moment that the door shut behind Maverick. 'Are you sure about this?'

The words came then. 'He would have stayed, Markus. He would have put everything on the line for me, and I won't let him do that. When this is done, when the nightmare is over, I want Hunt Ranch to go back to. I want Poppy to not be traumatized. And—' she sighed '—I guess I want Mav to know that there's more to that broken woman who showed up in his life in pieces. I am strong. I am brave. And I am independent. Or, at least, I was. I just need to get back there.'

'I can see that arguing would be futile,' he said, and although he didn't agree, there was a part of him that understood too. Because she was right. The court battle would be long and messy, and it would hurt.

'I'll listen anyway,' Nina replied.

So, Markus asked the difficult question. 'How much of this has to do with Lulu? How much of you is terrified because you're not comfortable depending on him?'

Nina replied honestly. 'About thirty per cent. But most of me only wants to save him from himself. Because he thinks in black and white, in right and wrong, and we both know that this entire drama is going to be played out in the grey.

'I don't want to hurt them, Markus. I love them.'

His phone vibrated, and when he looked down at the screen and he saw the message from Maverick –

Keep me updated on everything. Please.

– he knew that for the first time since he'd met Nina, his loyalty was split. And he was alarmingly okay with that.

Nina had said that only thirty per cent of her reasoning had to do with her mother, but Markus knew that it was more. Because trust wasn't something you just learned overnight. It was taught through *years* of relationships, of friendships and love affairs and familial connections, starting and running their course and ending, and Nina hadn't had much opportunity to learn that.

Still, he picked his bag up off the floor and tossed it onto the sofa. 'I see you shovelled out the big bucks?' he said as he took a turn about the two-bedroom suite.

'Mav did. I should go down and put the room in my name.'

'Ah, no. I'll put it in mine. You need to stay incognito.'

Nina sighed deeply. 'Can you do something for me?'

'Always.'

'Can you help me put my house on the market? Find a realtor, get my things out of it . . . I'd do it myself, but it's swarming with media.'

Markus's eyebrows rose. 'You want to sell? Are you sure? That's the first big thing you ever bought for yourself . . .' More, he knew she loved that house.

'I'm sure. It's not . . . *home* anymore. Since the attack . . . I only realized yesterday when we drove past it that I'd already let it go.' She shrugged. 'I'm going back to the ranch when this is over. If Mav forgives me . . .' She didn't finish the thought. 'If he doesn't, I'll still want a new place. Maybe with some land . . .'

'Okay. I have a friend who's a realtor. I'll give him a call.'

'Thank you.'

He could see her exhaustion and, beneath the resolve, her

heartbreak. 'What can I do to help?'

Nina laughed sadly. But there was only one thing that would help, so she said, 'Play "Run" by George Strait.'

Markus pulled out his phone. He found the song on Spotify and pressed play.

He hit pause almost immediately. 'Maverick changed these lyrics,' he stated.

Nina nodded. 'Yeah. I've listened to this song like a billion times now. It's keeping me going.'

'Girl.'

Nina nodded. 'I know. You don't have to tell me. I know.'

So, Markus didn't. He went and sat beside where she'd plopped on the sofa, took her hand in his, and hit play again. And then simply sat by her side and listened to George Strait sing 'Run'.

Chapter 27

At noon, Maverick pulled up to Amanda Black's address. Though the assistant chief had refused to give him any of her details, whoever Sierra's friend in the LAPD was hadn't been quite as discreet.

He looked at the house for one long moment, knowing that what he was about to do wasn't smart. Hell, it wasn't even fair. The last thing he ever wanted to do was make another woman feel unsafe. But he had to try. For Nina.

The house was a small but neat hacienda style in East Hollywood. There was a red front door and flower beds full of flowers lining the pathway up to the porch. It was cheery. Homey.

He got out of the Jeep and walked to the front door, steeling himself for the rejection.

A dog started barking from inside the house, and before he'd even pressed the doorbell, a woman stepped out onto the porch.

She was small and blonde, only a fraction taller than Nina. Her eyes sized him up, not warily, but questioningly. 'Can I help you?'

'Amanda Black?'

'Yes.'

Mav exhaled a deep breath. He didn't know what to say, or how to start. All he knew to be true was that he loved Nina and would do anything for her, so he started with: 'Have you heard the news about Nina Keller?'

Amanda's eyes cooled immediately. 'I have no comment.' She turned to go.

'I'm not media!' he called after her, but he didn't follow. He stayed well away from her front porch because he didn't want to scare her. 'I'm dating Nina.' And because that wasn't exactly true, he corrected with: 'I'm in love with her.'

That seemed to give her pause. Amanda stopped at her door and turned to face him. 'Look, I read about what happened – about what Alexander Cane said about her.' She laughed bitterly. 'Only an idiot would believe that bullshit. But I'm sorry. I can't help you. Legally.'

'You signed an NDA?'

She was silent for a long moment before ceding, 'I settled the matter privately.' She ran one hand through her long, blonde hair. 'Not a day goes by that I wish I hadn't. But I can't take it back.'

'I would never ask you to. I've seen how it weighs on Nina, and I understand that sometimes it's easier to just let go. I just . . . I'm looking for something – *anything* – that might help. I promise that I will only share the information you give me with Nina's attorney, and that she will keep your identity confidential if that's what you want.'

Her blue eyes raked over him. 'Why? Why would I trust you?' she asked.

For Mav the answer was easy. 'Because I love a woman who's living what you lived through, and I would never do anything to hurt her, and – by default – hurt you. Because *I know*. I've seen the terror and despair and hopelessness.'

She nodded, though she remained stoic.

From somewhere inside, a little boy called, 'Mom!'

Amanda Black glanced back at her house. She was quiet for a long moment.

Maverick held his breath.

'Look, I won't promise anything. But if you give me Nina's lawyer's details, I'll reach out and speak to her confidentially. That's all I can give you.'

Maverick felt a small glimmer of hope. 'Thank you.' He took out his phone and pulled up Linda Patton's cell number. He rattled it off as she plugged it into her phone, and when he was done, he added, 'Let me give you mine too.' When she just stared at him, he explained, 'Nina . . . She struggles to tell me everything. But if you ever feel like you need to talk to someone who's been through what you've been through . . . I'll ask her. I think it would help both of you, you know. To not feel so alone.'

Amanda didn't speak. Her eyes shone with unshed tears. But after a long moment, she nodded, and Maverick gave his number.

He didn't step onto the porch or try and reach out and shake her hand. He stayed back, giving her space, said, 'Thank you. I really appreciate it. And I'm sorry.'

And then he left.

He drove straight home, and forced his Jeep through the press camped outside the Hunt Ranch gates. He parked beneath the big oak tree and climbed out, and even though everything had changed he still felt that instant relief the moment his booted feet hit his own land.

He inhaled a huge breath of fresh air and felt his heart settle. In the house, Shadow barked.

Mav leaned into the truck to get his duffel, and by the time he turned around, Poppy and Shadow were out the door and sprinting to him as though he'd been away for years instead of a single night.

'Daddy! Daddy!'

She jumped and he caught her with one arm, raised her onto his hip easily as Shadow danced around his legs. 'Hi!'

'I missed you so much!'

'I missed you too,' he said, and he kissed her forehead.

He had too. It was weird, being away from her. Every time he had sat down over the past twenty-four hours, he had felt like he had forgotten an item on his to-do list, only to realize that he didn't have any list while he was away.

'Did you have fun with Sisi?'

'Yeah. Lots!' She used one small hand to brush her hair back from her face. Her small face puckered into a frown. 'Where's Nina?'

'She has to look after herself for a little while, baby. But she'll be back.' He knew he shouldn't get Poppy's hopes up, but he needed something to hold on to. He needed to believe that Nina would make her way back to him – to them.

'Oh.' Poppy's eyes welled instantly. 'Is she sick?'

'No, she's not sick. She just has a sad heart, and she needs some time to fix it.'

'But, Daddy, you know how to fix everything!'

Mav chuckled at that, even as he wished he had that childlike confidence. 'Cookies don't work for everyone.'

'Oh.' Poppy considered this seriously for a minute before asking, 'What about cake? Nina likes cake.'

'How about, next time she comes to visit, we can make her a cake? See it if helps?'

Poppy nodded. ''Kay.'

He carried her up the porch stairs and set her down when he saw Sierra leaning against the front door. 'Poppy, if you take this inside—' he put the duffel on the ground '—there's a present in there for you.'

Poppy did not hesitate. She lifted the bag, which was comically too big for her, and half carried, half dragged it inside so that she could rummage around in it.

The moment the door slapped shut behind her, Sierra said, 'So?'

'I know, okay. I know everything you're going to say. Hell, I even agree with most of it.'

'So, what are you going to do?'

'Give her space. Because she asked. Show up for her when she'll let me. Be here for her if and when she's ready to come home.'

'Okay.'

Mav raised his eyebrows at that. 'Okay? That's it? No argument? No calling me an idiot?'

'Nope.' But she looked at him, her eyes filled with obvious concern. 'How are *you* doing, Mav?'

He exhaled. 'Not great.'

'Shannon all over again?'

'Worse,' he said. 'So much worse. The only thing keeping me from full-blown panic is knowing that she's trying to protect me – and Poppy. That's what she said. And I can't even be mad at her because the fact that she thought about my kid at all – and during the worst time of her life – only made me love her more.'

'But?'

'There is a not-so-small part of me that is terrified that she won't come back.' He cleared his voice of emotion. 'And I'm not so sure what to do about that.'

'I think you make sure you've told her how you feel about her, and then you give her the time and space to decide what she wants,' Sierra said slowly. 'I think, as hard as it is for you to truly believe it, you acknowledge that Nina is not Shannon. You know that in your heart, Mav. Otherwise, you never would have let yourself fall in love with her.'

'I didn't *let* myself do anything,' he insisted. 'She just knocked me clean off my feet. Those goddamn eyes . . . I didn't stand a chance.' And strangely, he felt better having admitted it. 'I wanted her from the first, but I didn't want to need her. And then before I had even acted on the want, I somehow ended up needing her.'

'I know it's hard for you,' she said. 'But you have to trust her to know what she's doing. She'll come back.'

'I hope so.' Mav sighed. 'But I hate not being there. I hate not being able to help her or comfort her. It feels like I've abandoned her when she needs me most, and that goes against everything I've ever believed in.'

'So? What are you going to do about it?'

'We need to rearrange my schedule indefinitely going forward. If she reaches out, I need to be able to pick up and leave at a moment's notice. I won't pressure her on the relationship because I know she doesn't need that stress right now. But I'm also not going to sit here, twiddling my thumbs, while she faces that fucker alone.'

'I'm way ahead of you.' Sierra cocked one hip. 'I asked Benji to stay on and help until things blow over.'

Mav's eyebrows rose at that. 'Thank you for doing that for me. I'm sure it wasn't easy.'

'I don't know . . .'

Maverick waited silently for her to continue.

'Part of me hated having to do it. And part of me was relieved that I had a legitimate excuse to ask him to stay. And as much as I know it's fucked up, as much as I can't talk to him without snapping, I also selfishly feel safer knowing he's here when you're not.' She shook her head. 'What type of person does that make me?'

'Human.'

Sierra laughed. Leaning forward, she linked her arm with his and tugged him through the front door. 'What can I do for *you*, Mav?' she asked, redirecting the conversation.

'Can you help me open an Instagram?'

'Seriously?'

'Yeah.'

'*Why?*' She led him through to the kitchen. 'Mav, given your relationship with Nina, being online right now isn't a good idea. It's *brutal*. And it's only going to get worse.'

'I know. But I don't know how else to let her know that I'm here for her. I want her to know that I'm not afraid of the scrutiny.' He went to the fridge and pulled out two beers, twisted the cap off the first and passed it to Sierra before opening his own. He sat at the kitchen table.

Sierra held one palm out. 'Phone.'

Mav passed it to her, because even though he hated being online, he wanted to support Nina there too. Hating being online didn't mean that he was ignorant of the fact that most of the world operated there now, and he wanted to be there for her in every way possible.

Sierra was quiet for a few minutes as she worked. And when she spoke, she said, 'Okay, I've downloaded the app, and I used your work email and laptop password so that it's easy to remember.'

'How do you know my laptop password?' he asked.

'HuntRanch123. Seriously? You're about as mysterious as white bread.'

He smiled despite himself.

'What do you want your handle to be?'

'My handle?'

'Your public username.'

'Maverick Hunt,' he replied.

'Maverick Hunt will appear below your handle anyway.'

'So, what's the point in the handle?'

Sierra hesitated perceptibly. 'I have no idea. Just run with it.'

'What's yours?'

'Corporate_Cowgirl.'

'Huh. Okay . . . Make mine . . . NK_Fanboy.'

Sierra laughed. 'Really? What if the media get ahold of that?'

'Yeah, I wanna make her smile, even when I'm not there. And fuck the media. Let them come. The more there are here, the less there are hounding Nina in LA.'

'Aw, Mav,' she sniffled mockingly. Her fingers flew across his phone as she continued the set-up. 'Okay. What do you want as your profile picture?'

'There's one of Barbie saved on my phone. She doesn't want us public, and I can respect that. But she'll know that it's me, know that I'm here for her even if I have to keep my distance . . .'

She scoured his messages. 'Got it. That'll also be your first post.'

'Does it have to be?'

'No, you can opt not to have it display on your grid.'

'Nina's making a public statement on Instagram today. I want that to be my first post.'

'Let me follow her.' Sierra concentrated for a moment, but when her eyes clouded, he knew that Nina and Linda had already posted the public comment.

'Read it to me,' he demanded hoarsely.

'Mav . . .'

'I can handle it.'

'The post just says "Public Statement" but there's a link in her bio to the full statement.' Sierra took a deep breath and began.

To my colleagues, fans, and fellow victims,

As many of you know, false assault allegations have been made against me by Alexander Cane, the producer on my new movie: Shadowlands. *While I'm not usually one to post about my personal life, I've recently (with the help of many friends) found the courage to speak up.*

On June 2nd, Alexander Cane broke into my home in the Hollywood Hills. He physically and sexually assaulted me and then fled the scene once he realized I had been on the phone with @PhotoQueen immediately prior to, and during, the assault.

I was taken to the hospital with a severe concussion and two fractured ribs.

During my hospital stay, Alexander came to see me. He apologized and told me he had a substance abuse problem, and that he was seeking help for it. He then advised me to remain quiet regarding what he repeatedly called a 'misunderstanding' if I wanted to win an Academy Award for my role in Shadowlands.

I ran.

I'm ashamed to admit it now. But I was scared. I still am. For my personal safety, of course. But also, I'm afraid of losing everything that I have worked so hard for.

Though it shames me to admit it, I also didn't want anyone to know what had happened to me. It's hard enough to stop seeing yourself as a victim, as weak, helpless ... But it's impossible to stop other people from seeing you differently once the world knows ...

So, I lied.

I told the police that I hadn't seen my attacker, and I went to recuperate at the beautiful @HuntRanchResort, where slowly, I began to feel safe again.

... Until Alexander Cane tracked me down there two weeks into my month-long stay.

He arrived at Hunt Ranch after a photo was leaked online, revealing my location. He threatened me. And it was only after I told him that I was filing a police report that Alexander decided to file his own assault allegations. Fake ones.

I thought that nothing would be worse than the trauma of that initial assault. But I was wrong. It is far more painful to be accused of the very crime that happened to me – and by none other than my perpetrator.

However, I am committed to seeking justice. My legal team and I are working to clear my name and reveal the truth.

I appreciate the love and support from my fans and community during this difficult time.

To my Shadowlands *colleagues ... 'Sorry' doesn't come close. I'm absolutely devastated. We all worked so hard ...*

I don't know what's going to happen. But I do know that I'm refusing to settle. Because if I walk away, I absolutely believe that one day soon another woman will be living the hell I'm currently living. And I refuse to let that happen.

Still, I ask that you please respect my privacy as I navigate this difficult process from here in LA. I am sad and tired, but I am also resolute and strong. I have to believe that the truth will prevail.

Thank you for standing by me.
With love,
Nina

Mav's heart ached. 'Fuck, I should be there,' he said. Because he could imagine Nina as she sat down and struggled to put her pain into words. He could imagine her braving the after-effects, and even though it comforted him to know that she had Markus, he wanted to be the one to hold her, to comfort her. Because it hurt him every time she hurt.

'Most of these comments are supportive,' Sierra pointed out. She smiled. 'Markus's comment is pinned. It says, "@KingCane, I hope you currently feel the fear I felt listening to you assault my girl over the phone."'

'Did he post anything – Alexander Cane?'

Sierra clicked through to @KingCane's profile. 'He's made his account private. That's good.'

'It is?'

'Fuck yeah. It means he's being torn a new asshole by her fanbase.'

'Good.' Mav nodded.

'Okay, so I'm going to use an app to share Nina's post. And I'm going to copy and paste that link into your bio.'

'Thanks.'

Sierra paused. She cackled like a hyena.

'What?' Mav asked.

'Nina followed you back.'

It was the stupidest thing in the world for him to feel a little more connected with her because of it – but he did. So he'd be grateful. 'Okay.'

'No . . . You don't get it. She only follows forty-five people. And she has three *million* followers, which means . . .' She angled the phone for him to see the screen, pulled down the page to refresh it. The 'Followers' number jumped up by two thousand people immediately. She did it again. This time, it jumped by five thousand.

'You'll be Instafamous by the end of the day, Mav,' she prophesied, and passed him back his phone. 'Make sure you post Markus's professional photos on there. It'll give Hunt Ranch bookings a huge boost.'

'Maybe a few that don't feature us,' he said, but only because he knew Sierra worked hard on the ranch's marketing and advertising. 'But I didn't do this for us. I did it for her. So she knows . . .'

Sierra looked at him for a long moment. 'You know, I don't think I've ever said this to you before, but I'm really proud of the person you are, Mav. And Mom and Dad would be, too.'

'Yeah.' But he pulled her in for a hug, knowing that she had her own demons to battle. 'Of both of us.'

It was stupid and reckless of her to follow Mav back online – Nina absolutely knew that. But she had promised herself that she wouldn't text or call him, knowing that if she did, she would cave and ask him to come back. So following him back felt like a silent plea: *Thank you*, *wait for me*, and *I love you* rolled into one.

She actually laughed when she saw that his handle was 'NK_Fanboy,' and when he didn't post anything, but only shared her public statement as his first post, Nina felt the warmth and certainty of his love spread through her.

Chapter 28

Two days later, Nina was woken up at seven a.m. by a call from her attorney. 'I'm sorry for the early call,' Linda began, 'but I wanted you to hear it from me: the LAPD arrested Alexander Cane last night on suspicion of breaking and entering, sexual assault, and grievous bodily harm.'

Nina's brain, still cloudy from sleep, struggled to process the momentous news for a few moments. But once it had, several emotions sped through her, one after the other. Shock: how was this happening so fast? Relief: if he was in prison, he couldn't hurt her or anybody else. Loneliness: because all she wanted to do was call Mav and tell him to come and pick her up.

The last few days had been the loneliest days of her existence. Even with Markus's infallible support, it felt as if, now that she had found Maverick, every day without him felt off. Empty. Lonely. Terrifying.

'That's good, right?' she asked, pushing all thoughts of Mav to the back of her mind.

'Yes. To be honest, I was wondering what Aiden's next step was going to be. Yesterday, he told me that the fingerprinting from your house came back.'

'From over three weeks ago?' Nina asked.

'Hey, that's record time in the LAPD. Their backlog usually takes two to three months. Anyway, Cane was arrested a few years ago for a DUI. He contested the field testing and got off, but his prints were in the system. Nina . . . They were all over your house.' She cleared her throat. 'And on the pants the doctors cut off you.'

'But he admitted to being there,' Nina said, refusing to feel relieved. 'Can't they argue that his prints were there from when I allegedly let him in.'

'Yup. But it's *where* they were found that was incriminating,' Linda stated. 'The outside and inside doorknobs of the *back* door.'

'Which is where he must have broken in from . . .'

'If you let him in as he claimed, you would have let him in the front door. His prints would have at least been on the doorbell. But they weren't. Instead, they were all over the *outside* back doorknob.'

'I had opened the front door before he grabbed me,' Nina remembered.

'Which is why his prints weren't on the front door at all. That's strike one against his statement already, and Aiden will use it to trap him. And, uh, I know it's hard to hear this, Nina, but the pants were really helpful too.'

Nina swallowed the bile that rose in her throat. 'How?'

'His statement said he went there to talk to you, and you got into an argument. He stated that you pulled a knife on him and that he overpowered you, but nowhere does he mention touching you *intimately*. Your statement said that he grabbed you from behind and ripped your pants open, and the fingerprinting pattern corroborates that. He's left-handed. We know that from the bruises on your face, the majority of which were on the right cheek and jaw. And the thumbprint on the button of the pants was from his right hand, which corroborates that he had his left around your throat. His concierge doctor is going to be subpoenaed too, so we'll know more about the knife wound eventually.'

'So, could this send him away?'

A long silence prevailed, and when Linda broke it, she said, 'I think it's more accurate to say that this is probable cause for an arrest and questioning in relation to your allegations. It might still be his word against yours, but this will be brought up in court and it *will* make a difference, Nina. We're on day two and it's already looking bad for him; that's great news.'

Nina's heart sank. 'But it's not concrete.'

'Nothing's concrete in the courtroom anymore.' She sighed. 'Hell, we're even having to submit video evidence for testing prior to court these days because AI doctoring has gotten so good. But, Nina?'

'Yeah?' Nina rasped.

'*I'm* good. I'm one of the best. And I will catch him every time he slips up. And when he does, I'm going to cast so much doubt on every word out of his mouth that a jury will have no choice but to believe you.'

'I trust you,' Nina replied, and considering she couldn't summon the strength anymore, it was damn reassuring to have someone so confident and competent in her corner.

'Aiden picked up Alexander from a red-carpet event he was attending,' Linda continued.

Nina almost smiled. 'Not very private.'

'If there's one thing Aiden is a master at, it's optics. Better yet, Alexander was drunk. He threw a punch. Aiden's going to add resisting arrest and assaulting a police officer to the charges.'

'Will he stay there – in jail?'

Linda's tone was cautious. 'I want to say yes, but my job is to prepare you.' She sighed. 'His defence team is good. Some of the best. He'll probably get out on bail even though we're pushing the violent felony angle.' Before Nina could speak, Linda added, 'But this is good news! It'll go towards his character testimony.'

'Okay.'

'There's one other thing I'm legally required to ask you.'

Nina closed her eyes. 'Shoot.'

'His team reached out yesterday. Obviously, they can see where this is going because they wanted to know if you'd go for an alternate dispute resolution.'

'You mean settle out of court?'

'That's what they're calling it, but I have to warn you, because this is a criminal case now, it would require you to recant your statement. We'd essentially be pulling the rug out from under the criminal case, and, although Aiden would try to protect you, there might still be legal repercussions for you.'

Nina hated that she was even remotely tempted by the offer. Not by the money – millions – she would receive, but by the possibility of ending this. Now. If she settled, she could be back with Maverick on Hunt Ranch in a few days. She could start piecing together what was left of her career. She could move on. 'I hate that I'm even considering it,' she whispered over the line.

'You'd be a fool not to.'

Because she needed the strength just then, she pictured Poppy. All that innocence and joy and *brightness*, and it was enough to remind her why she was doing this. 'But I can't let him get away with it anymore. We know there was at least one other woman before me. And if I don't do something there'll be more after me too. And the damage is done now. My career is either over or it's not, but changing my story now would only do more harm than good.'

'I'm hearing "No"?'

'No,' Nina said firmly. 'We finish this.' And because it felt really good to say it, she added, 'Let's bring the fucker down.'

'Atta girl.' She exhaled a huge breath. 'Now, I'm going to ask you to do something and it's going to be really unfair . . .'

'I'm ready,' Nina said, and her voice was firm with conviction.

'In California, victims of a serious felony are given reasonable opportunity to be heard prior to pretrial release.'

Nina felt sick to her stomach. 'You want me to speak?'

'It'll be a quick statement. We'll draft it beforehand, and you can read it off the paper tomorrow at the bail hearing. But given how important optics are going to be in this case, I'm going to advise you to do it. But it has to be your choice. Because it'll be hard, Nina.'

'Everything about this is hard.'

'I know.' But Linda didn't say more, only waited.

'I'll do it,' Nina said even though just the thought of speaking about the attack in front of all those people made her feel sick to her stomach. It wouldn't be acting, where she pretended to play out a horror that ended the moment the cameras stopped rolling, a horror that wasn't hers. This nightmare would continue indefinitely.

'I'll draft it and send it to you in a few hours. You can edit it how you want and send it back to me for final review by the end of the day. His bail hearing is tomorrow at nine. I can pick you up – if that's easier?'

'Ah, no. Don't worry about me. Markus will want to drive me.'

'If you need anything, let me know. I understand how hard this must be for you, but I promise you that we are making excellent progress.'

'Thanks, Linda.'

'I'll see you tomorrow.'

'Yeah. Bye.'

'Bye.'

Nina hung up the phone.

Because she was still in bed, she flopped onto her back and sighed. Her stomach roiled, forcing bile up her throat. Her skin crawled with anxiety.

She had to physically resist the urge to call Mav. Because he would have come, instantly and without question. And because she had a few hours before Linda sent her the draft statement, she shut her eyes, curled into the foetal position, and tried to find momentary peace the only way she knew how: sleep.

It was Markus who called Maverick once the bail hearing time was set.

Maverick answered the phone immediately, his: 'What's happening?' pulling a tired chuckle from Markus.

'Alexander's been arrested and his bail hearing's tomorrow morning. Nina's going because Linda asked her to give a public statement.'

Frustrated, Mav ran one hand roughly through his hair as he paced the barn's breezeway. 'Fuck.' *I should be there*, he thought. And instead of saying it, he said, 'Fuck!' again, this time loud enough that Zeph popped her head over her stall door to check what all the fuss was about.

'So, here's the thing,' Markus continued. 'I think you should be there,' he said, as if he'd read Mav's thoughts.

Mav stopped pacing. 'She specifically asked me to give her space,' he explained. 'Christ, Markus, you think I don't want to be with her while she goes through this?' he demanded. 'I'm going crazy knowing I'm not there for her. But my hands are tied.'

'Mav, do you trust that I know what Nina wants? What's best for her?'

'Of course.'

'She doesn't have any experience relying on other people. The way she was raised . . .'

'Yeah,' Mav sighed. 'I know.'

'Why do you think she visited Hunt Ranch instead of staying with me? Why do you think I couldn't stay but only visited on weekends?' Markus demanded. 'Why do you think I had to stage a freaking photoshoot just to spend more than those weekends with her?' He sighed deeply. 'I've been Nina's best friend for years, and she still can't lean on me. And not because she doesn't want to or need to, but because she very literally doesn't know how.

'She needs you to be there tomorrow, Mav. As the one person

who knows her better than you, I'm telling you that she won't get through it without both of us there . . .'

'Markus, I don't know what to do.' Because how could he show up when she'd asked for space? He already felt uncomfortable about creating the Instagram account, but the way he figured it, she could have just ignored him there if she'd really wanted to. But she hadn't, he reminded himself. She'd followed him back, and even though they hadn't messaged each other online, he'd felt connected to her the moment she had.

'I know that,' Markus insisted. 'But I won't let myself feel guilty for it because I know her. And because it's been my job for the last decade to teach her how to accept love. Please, Maverick. Please come.'

He'd have had a hard time staying away without the push from Markus. But with Nina's request still on the forefront of his mind, he said, 'I'll be there. But I won't approach her in public unless she makes the first move. She set boundaries, Markus. I have to respect them – even if I hate them.'

'I think that's fair,' Markus ceded. 'I'll ask Linda to get you a pass. If you coordinate picking it up with her in the morning . . .'

'Yeah, thanks.'

'Okay. Bye.'

'Bye.'

The next morning, Maverick left the ranch at five a.m. so that he could be on time, and because he'd gotten there early, he'd driven around for close to forty minutes before parking and making his way to the courthouse.

Due to the celebrity nature of the case, the judge had restricted public access; however, that didn't stop the media from crowding the courthouse steps.

The moment they spotted Mav, they descended like vultures on a carcass.

'Mr Hunt, could you verify your relationship with Nina Keller.'

Mav didn't say a word.

'Mr Hunt, is it true that you assaulted Alexander Cane?'

Mav desperately wanted to say, 'Fuck yes,' to that – but heroically refrained.

Even though he could see Nina, Linda, and Markus sitting at the front, their backs to him, he took a seat towards the back of the courtroom as he waited for the bail hearing to begin.

He felt so out of place among the suits, dressed in his blue jeans, boots, and baseball cap, but he swallowed down the skin-crawling claustrophobia and waited patiently until the case was called.

The moment it was his heart started racing. He didn't look at Alexander Cane as he was brought out. He looked at Nina's back, and he saw the way her shoulders rounded and her gaze dropped. It was like she was carrying an immense burden that visibly weighed her down.

He didn't move through the bond discussion, didn't flinch when the state pressed the judge to deny bail and argued that Cane, with his vast resources, was a flight risk.

He listened intently to Linda's statement, which provided a brief but powerful depiction of the events of that night and called the judge to see through Alex's polished façade to the predator beneath. Linda recalled snippets of Alexander's statement, and then pointedly undermined them by comparing the physical size difference between Nina and Alexander Cane. She closed with a poignant reminder that the days of forgiving men in power for crimes against women were over.

It was only when the judge said, 'At this time, I would like to hear from the alleged victim, if she's able,' that Mav leaned forward in his chair. He held his breath as Nina slowly stood. His heart broke when he heard her breath sawing through the courtroom.

For the longest time, she didn't say anything at all, only stood there, all eyes on her, her rapid breaths telling him she was on the verge of a panic attack.

'I'm so s-sorry,' she stammered.

The judge nodded kindly, said, 'Take your time, Miss Keller.'

Come on, Nina, Mav thought. *You've got this.*

As if she'd heard the frantic thought, she turned to look over her shoulder, right at him.

Her eyes widened when she saw him.

Their gazes held.

Mav gave her a single bolstering nod, and mouthed, 'Breathe,' as he mimed taking a big breath and expelling it slowly.

Nina's eyes welled, but she nodded. He saw her shoulders rise with the huge inhalation. And then she turned to face the judge again.

'If you'd prefer, I can take your statement in as written?'

'No.' Nina shook her head. 'I'm ready.'

Still, she took another minute to breathe. And then she began:

'Your Honour, my name is Nina Keller.' Though she started off a bit wobbly, her voice grew as she continued, 'I am the victim – the survivor – in this case, and I am here today to express my concerns regarding the potential pretrial release of Alexander Cane on bail.'

She took a long moment to compose herself. 'On June second, Alexander Cane broke into my home. He waited for me, and when I arrived home, he attacked me and then violated me in ways that I am still struggling to come to terms with. I truly believe that if I had not been talking to a friend on the phone at the time of the attack – a friend who called 911 on my behalf – I would not have escaped without being raped. Or worse.

'The trauma I experienced that day has affected every aspect of my life. I struggle to sleep. I've developed intense anxiety and a fear of public places. Due to Alexander's involvement as a producer, I haven't been able to work or fulfil my contractual obligations on the set of *Shadowlands*, the film I'm currently acting in.

'I can no longer stand to be touched, even casually, by anyone other than my closest friends.

'I am a shadow of the woman I used to be. On some days, the woman I was only a few short weeks ago, one who was strong and successful and *happy*, seems like a figment of my own imagination.

'Knowing that the person who inflicted such harm on me could be released and possibly come near me or my loved ones is exceptionally damaging to my mental health, especially considering he has done so multiple times already. He came to see me in hospital after the assault, and the second time when he came to the place I was recuperating at afterwards. Both times, he attempted to talk to me about what he called a "misunderstanding", but that to me was a trauma that I will be dealing with for the rest of my life.

'As such, I respectfully ask that you consider the impact of this case on my life and the potential threat of Alexander Cane to my – and other women's – safety and wellbeing. I urge you to deny bail, or if bail is granted, to impose stringent conditions that will ensure my safety.

'This is not only about me and my personal safety but also about ensuring justice and preventing further harm to others. I hope the court will act in a way that reflects the severity of Alexander's crimes.

'Thank you for your time and consideration.'

The judge nodded. 'Thank you, Miss Keller.'

Nina sat back down.

Mav exhaled his own breath. He wanted to stand up and shout, 'That's my woman!' in front of everybody. He wanted to pull her into his arms and never let her go again. But knowing that she had asked for space, he didn't do any of that.

He listened to the defence attorney's statement, which undermined everything Nina had said.

'Your Honour, the allegations made against my client are a complete farce, a desperate attempt by a woman who craves celebrity and attention, a woman who *my client* romantically rejected *months* prior to the alleged incident.

'Yes, Alexander Cane did go to Ms Keller's house that night; however, he did not go there with the intention of harming her. Quite the opposite, in fact. My client went to Ms Keller's house to check up on her when rumours circulating on the *Shadowlands* set indicated that her mental health was suffering from the stress of filming.'

Maverick's stomach roiled with literal sickness as the lies poured into the courtroom. His eyes flickered to Nina, and although she sat straighter now, she looked brittle. Breakable.

He wanted to go to her. He wanted to hold her and tell her that everything was going to be all right. But he couldn't because she had drawn that line clearly. And that crushed him.

'Unfortunately for my client, when he arrived at Ms Keller's residence, she attempted to seduce him, and when Alexander Cane informed her that he was in a committed relationship, Ms Keller flew at him. She attacked him with a knife, Your Honour, leaving my client no option but to fight back despite Ms Keller's significantly smaller stature.

'And as for afterwards . . . Put yourself in Mr Cane's shoes. A young, attractive, *powerful* man, suddenly caught in a scandal not of his own making, a scandal eerily resonant of those many #MeToo movement claims that were exaggerated or false and that unforgivably diluted the immensity of sexual assault claims for women everywhere as a result. Is it any wonder that he feared for his own safety? Is it any wonder that he ran?

'Your Honour, if my brief summary of that night is undermined in any way by the frequency of false allegations like the one that Nina Keller has made against my client, all you have to do is look at the man himself. Mr Cane is a respected member of the community, an upstanding citizen with no history of sexual or violent crimes.

'And Ms Keller . . . Ms Keller is a woman who grew up in a broken home where she was systematically deprived of love and attention. She is an actress of the highest calibre, as proven by her extensive list of accolades and awards. She is a woman who is paid millions of dollars to *lie* for a living.

'That being said, it is a travesty that we are here at all today, Your

Honour. My client deserves to go home and recover from the toll that these allegations have taken on him, and to recuperate with the help of his family and friends. He deserves to be within the comfort of his own home as we prepare to defend his innocence.'

Maverick, who had been raised with a clear sense of right and wrong, didn't understand how anyone could defend someone who was so clearly guilty. He knew the defence attorney was being paid a fortune, but how could he sleep at night knowing that he was putting a predator back on the streets? Did he not have a wife or sister or daughters?

Maverick stoically sat through the flight-risk discussion, his nerves so on edge that he didn't hear the courtroom door open or see Amanda Black until she walked past where he sat, her purse clutched against her chest like a shield. A man who he assumed was her husband walked beside her, his hand pressed supportively to her lower back.

Mav's heart stopped beating as she stopped and took two rapid steps back.

The movement seemed to garner some attention from the judge, who raised his eyebrows at the interruption.

All eyes shifted to Amanda then, including Linda Patton's. When she saw Amanda, she sprang to her feet and hurried to where the other woman stood.

She whispered something, and Amanda shook her head. But she passed the attorney a piece of paper.

'Ms Patton, if you're quite done,' the judge said, clearly frustrated.

'Yes, Your Honour.' She led Amanda Black and her husband to where Nina and Markus sat, ushered them into the bench row.

Up to that moment Mav hadn't, not even once, looked at Alexander Cane. He was afraid he wouldn't be able to control his rage. But he did then. He couldn't help himself. And when he saw Cane's red-faced, eye-popping fury, Mav outright grinned.

Perhaps he sensed Mav's taunting gaze, but Alexander shifted his eyes to Mav's, where the message 'Fuck you,' was as clear as day.

Mav recognized the unguarded hate that nestled in the other man's irises, but he didn't let it bother him. It was completely mutual.

'Your Honour, I apologize for the interruption; however, I would like to submit a second victim's statement – this one written – for your consideration.'

The judge only waved her forward and took the piece of paper. He scanned it. The only indication that what he read was highly disturbing was the way his bushy eyebrows gathered.

He was quiet for a long moment once he had put the piece of paper down.

The proceedings began again. Mav listened intently as the judge summarized the list of charges. He noted that rape had been added as the presumptive charge and finally understood what he had asked Amanda Black to do.

Maverick felt sick with shame. Even though he couldn't take back asking Amanda for help, and even though he knew that she had ultimately made the choice herself, he hated that both the women had to put their trauma out in the open to get justice.

Still, the judge set bail at a measly four hundred and twenty-five thousand dollars and required that Alexander Cane submit all his travel documents prior to release.

He ended the hearing by saying, 'Due to the highly disturbing nature of the charges against you, Mr Cane, I'm also granting temporary restraining orders to both Ms Keller and Mrs Black. You are not to contact – or go within five hundred feet – of either of them until your next court date, after which the facts and evidence will be reassessed.'

The moment the hearing concluded, Amanda Black and her husband stood to leave. They hurried down the aisle as if they were terrified of being stopped and questioned.

Mav pushed to his feet and stepped out in front of them.

Amanda Black smiled at him.

'I'm so sorry – for asking for your help,' he said. 'It wasn't right.'

Amanda shook her head. 'Honestly? It feels like this weight has been lifted, and I had gotten so used to living with it, I had completely forgotten it was there.' She surprised him by leaning forward and giving him a huge hug. 'Thank you for being so kind and understanding. You gave me a chance to finally lay this all to rest. Linda . . .'

'She's great,' Mav said, and gave her a squeeze before stepping back.

'She is. She's pushing to have my NDA nullified due to the criminal nature of the case. I might have to give back the money.' She laughed. 'But the craziest thing is that I haven't spent a dollar of it. Every time I thought about using it – and, trust me, there were times I needed to – I remembered where it came from, and I couldn't stand for my big expenses – my home and my kids' education – to be tainted by *him*, by what he had done.'

Her husband reached out and touched her, only casually, on the elbow, but it was enough to bolster Amanda. She smiled. 'We're going to send him away this time, aren't we?'

All Mav could say as she started to walk away was, 'Fuck yeah, we are.'

He gave her one last wave and then turned to leave without looking back at Nina. Because as much as he hated to go, he knew that the line between showing up for her and not respecting her wishes was blurrier than he would have liked.

Chapter 29

Although she could feel Alexander's eyes searing into her, Nina did not look at him. She was scared, yes, but she also didn't want to give him any sort of power over her. She turned around to look for Mav instead and saw him embracing the small blonde woman who had submitted her own victim's statement.

'She's the other victim Aiden told us about. Maverick somehow got her details and went and spoke to her,' Linda said, seeing the direction of her gaze. 'Gave her my name and number.'

'What?' Nina whispered, completely shocked. 'Why didn't you say anything?'

'I didn't think she'd show, and I didn't want to get your hopes up. She's terrified of the NDA she signed.'

Nina looked at the woman. She was small, maybe only a little taller than Nina herself, with an angel's face and dimpled smile. She couldn't have been more than twenty-six or seven now, which begged the question: how old had she been when Alexander Cane had raped her?

Nina's throat burned because if she, with her unlimited financial resources, fanbase, and thirty-four years, had struggled to come forward and tell the truth, how difficult must it have been for the other woman, who had been so much younger when her choices had been taken from her? How scared and ashamed and alone must she have felt looking down the barrel at Alexander Cane and his team of lawyers *after* he had already reduced her by so much.

And, still, through all of that, Nina couldn't tear her eyes away from Mav as he smiled down at the tiny blonde. Because in that moment, she finally understood: trust wasn't built on words, which could be so easily undermined, forgotten, or taken back. Trust was built on actions, on what you *did* over and over, on showing up for the people you loved again and again, for the big things and the small things, the good and the bad.

Luigi's had taught her family, but she had never let any of the crew there get close enough to rely on them completely. Markus had tried to teach her trust over the years, but she had resisted leaning on him fully. Looking back now, she thought she might have been too scared that if she did, her only friend would start to see her as a burden. Like her mother had.

And then the assault had happened. And she had been so tired, so broken, that she hadn't really been able to resist all those small things Mav did that had given her some light and hope back. Things like six a.m. riding lessons and inviting her to stay in the ranch house and buying her a makeup box for her birthday and holding her while she slept.

She hadn't lied to him when she'd said he'd met her at her lowest. But instead of steering clear of her, he had shown up for her, again and again, even when she'd been a stranger and, now, even when she'd tried to push him away.

Nina had been on the verge of a full-blown panic attack before her statement, but then she'd thought of him, and in thinking of him, she had sensed him there, behind her. Only one look back at him had steadied the ground beneath her feet. Maverick showing up hadn't taken away her fear; it had just reminded her that whatever happened, she trusted him to stay with her, to wrap her in his arms when she was scared and pick her up when she fell.

The absolution with which she believed in him was astounding.

Nina wanted to touch him.

She needed *him* to touch *her*.

Only, when she managed to refocus her attention on where he'd been standing, he was gone.

Her heart, already so unsettled, lurched. Her anxiety reared. 'Where did he go?'

'What?' Markus frowned. 'Who?'

'Mav . . .'

He turned around to search the crowd.

But Nina didn't hear him. And she didn't stop when he called for her to wait. She pushed through the crowd, elbowing her way through the people flocking to the doorway so that she could catch him before he left.

In her rush, her mind consumed with reaching him, her heart filled with the irrational panic that she might not, she didn't notice the people giving her curious looks and whispering about her among themselves.

The moment she was in the hallway, she looked both ways and, not seeing him, started running for the exit, her ballet flats slapping the cold floor with every step.

She burst out the courthouse doors and into the bright LA sunlight like a bird escaping a cage, her chest heaving with every breath, her eyes searching the grey concrete steps wildly.

Photographers swarmed her immediately. Cameras were pushed into her face. Voices rose in a mighty clamour, the questions merging and becoming indecipherable.

Through the crowd, she saw him. He was already across the courtyard, about to turn onto the street. 'Mav!' she yelled.

He didn't hear her over the noise of the press, only kept walking.

Nina ignored all of the questions still being thrown at her. At the top of her lungs, she yelled, 'Quiet!'

Silence descended, as if the news crews were completely unused to being addressed with the same blatant disrespect they used on others. Nina could have laughed at the unanimous look of shock had she not been so focused on the man walking away from her.

Before she could yell again, a kid, a young man with a patchy beard and a small recorder said, 'I've got you.' He shoved the tiny device into her hand. The moment his own hands were free, he cupped them around his mouth and whistled.

The whistle was loud. It pierced the beautiful day. People on the sidewalk stopped to look in the direction it had come from. Others glanced over their shoulders.

Nina was watching Maverick walk away, so she saw the exact moment he registered the sound.

He turned.

Even though she was too far to see the look in his eyes, she knew that their gazes met. She could feel that connection, and it was so strong and vital.

Still, she raised one hand, almost tentatively, and waved, and when he turned and started making his way back to the courthouse, she passed the recorder back to the reporter. 'Thank you.'

The kid beamed.

The others started shouting questions again. And this time Nina answered them as she walked.

'Miss Keller, what is the nature of your and Maverick Hunt's relationship?'

'He's my boyfriend,' she replied, her eyes glued on Mav as they got closer and closer.

'Miss Keller, is it true that Alexander Cane sexually assaulted you?'

'Yes,' she rasped.

'Nina, what do you have to say regarding Alexander Cane's assault allegations against you?'

'I'm five-four and one hundred and ten pounds. Do the math.'

A round of chuckles followed that.

'Miss Keller – what now?'

Maverick had reached the other end of the pile of people

so that now they were separated by twenty-odd reporters and cameramen.

The question 'What now?' ricocheted in her head. *What now? What now? What now?*

'It's going to be a long, ugly process,' she replied. 'But I'm strong. Resilient.' Her eyes locked with Mav's, and he smiled. 'And my support system is infallible,' she finished.

Nina's heart didn't race or lurch or swan dive. It settled, calmed. Found peace. Because he was exactly what she needed – always.

She had expected him to keep his distance. She had even hoped he would. But her expectations had been grounded, always, in her own experience of the world. Nina, who had grown up without trust and love and communication, had fully expected Maverick to let her battle her demons alone. Except here he was. And, she knew, here he would be until this nightmare was over. He would keep showing up for her, even to his own detriment. And if he was going to show up anyway, she wanted him at her side, his hand linked with hers in the courtroom imparting all the strength and comfort she couldn't summon for herself.

The reporters started making space for him to pass through.

Maverick held her gaze until they were standing face-to-face.

Every single person was eerily quiet, as if they had agreed to capture this moment by tacit agreement.

Nina wondered what to say.

But she didn't have to.

'I'm so fucking proud of you.' Mav's voice was husky with emotion.

Nina nodded though her eyes blurred. 'I did it.' Her voice shook, but she said the words proudly and for the world to hear. Because even though the road ahead would be long and bumpy, she had half dragged her broken body, half been carried, up the biggest hill already. And it had been the most difficult thing she had ever done – and probably would ever do.

'Yeah, you did,' Mav affirmed.

He didn't try and touch her, didn't say anything that might give away the relationship he thought they were still hiding.

It was Nina who said, 'What are you doing here, Mav? You hate the city.'

He looked at her face for a long moment, trying to decide what she wanted, and Nina let him see the answer in her eyes. She nodded, desperate to finally hear the words. She didn't just want them. She *needed* them.

Mav exhaled a deep breath of relief. 'I do hate the city. But I love you.'

Hearing the words from him for the first time was unlike anything Nina had ever known before. It wasn't joy or relief or excitement, but some strange emotion that contained all three of them in staggering quantities.

Nina grinned. Her heart, so heavy only moments before, flew. She indicated the reporters, said, 'They want to know: what now?'

All the microphones swung in Maverick's direction. 'You know what I want,' he said. 'I'm just waiting until you're ready to trust me with your heart.'

The reporters swung back in her direction, making her laugh. 'I'm ready,' she said, and there was no doubt. There was some fear, but Nina finally accepted that she was allowed to be scared. Trusting somebody else with your heart was terrifying, but maybe it was supposed to be, maybe that was *why* it was so special too.

Mav smiled his dimple-popping smile. 'Yeah?'

'Yeah.' Nina had never seen anything more beautiful than the denim-clad cowboy standing in front of her with the city at his back. 'I love you, Mav. I need you like I need my next breath. I don't feel safe enough to live free when you're not with me.'

He put his hands on his hips and exhaled a deep breath of relief. 'Sounds like we're on the same page.'

Nina nodded, waiting.

'I just have one question?'

'Okay.'

'Please, for the love of God, could I kiss you in public now?'

Another round of laughter followed.

'I want the world to know you're my woman, Nina.'

Nina didn't reply. She walked straight into his arms and pressed her lips to his.

Everyone cheered. Reporters, spectators who had stopped to watch the unravelling scene, Linda and Markus, who stood on the steps above them, watching.

Mav took her deep. His hands gripped her hips and pulled her close, sealing the last of that space between them. His tongue swept into her mouth and gave, uncaring of the fact that the world was watching, and when they finally pulled apart, Mav didn't step back. He kept her close, his arms wrapped around her, his big body sheltering her even when she hadn't asked.

Nina closed her eyes and revelled in the safety of his arms. She breathed in his familiar scent and rested for the first time in days.

If either of them had been paying attention, they would have seen Alexander Cane and his attorneys standing on the other side of the courthouse steps, completely forgotten by the media just then. They might have looked at Alexander's face and seen his outrage and his hate. His madness.

PART FOUR:
LIVE

Chapter 30

As summer spread into fall and fall into winter, the temperature changed, becoming cold even by California standards. Like the weather, the legal battle began to cool after months and months of heat.

Mav grumbled aloud as his big hands fumbled to take a screenshot of the latest news snippet of Nina's case. The caption read: 'Things Not Looking Good for Alexander Cane,' and the article detailed how the prosecutor had revealed damning holes and inconsistencies in his statements.

Mav posted the screenshot to Instagram and included a link to the article, just as he had done for every court milestone, and then he closed the app and temporarily deleted it from his phone so that he and Nina could escape the ensuing chatter.

It didn't matter that Cane was clearly guilty or that he had hurt Nina, Amanda Black, and two other women who had since come forward; he was still a man with connections and power, and the predator wielded both with merciless force.

The *Shadowlands* film had been wrapped up using a body double for the last scene, something that had hurt Nina irreparably. She'd had to stand by and watch as the project she'd put her entire self into had been finished by someone else. The movie was in post-production, but Nina's agent had said that there were whispers, rumours that Alexander Cane was being pushed out of the film due to his bad press.

Nina had told Alison that she was taking a year off to deal with the legal battle and the aftermath, but Maverick knew that she was also scared. She was worried that she might not be cast in the future, and she had removed herself from the equation completely to come to terms with it.

Mav hadn't fought her on it because he'd known she'd needed the break. But he wasn't worried about her career either. He had seen all her films now, and he knew she'd have her choice of projects when she was ready. But knowing it – *believing* it – and trying to convince her of it were two separate issues.

And even then, he barely had the bandwidth to focus on it. The trial and online war were brutal.

During the first few weeks, Mav had made what Sierra had called a 'rookie mistake' and started reading the comments on Nina's first post after the assault. Although most of them were supportive and encouraging, there were many that tore her apart, calling her a liar, an attention seeker, a slut, and worse. Reading them had left Maverick in despair for days.

He didn't understand how anyone, but especially someone who hadn't been in that room with Nina as Alexander Cane had violated and hurt her, could be so casually and thoughtlessly cruel.

It was taking its toll on Nina, too. She struggled to sleep. She never felt like eating. And the result was that her already diminutive frame had shed weight she couldn't afford to lose in the first place.

And still, she powered forward.

Maverick did, too. He showed up for her, again and again. He went to every attorney meeting and court date and held her hand through it. He attended interviews Linda organized and stood on the side of the set as the interviewers made Nina relive her trauma over and over again. He drove her to and from the ranch every time.

He was exhausted.

So, he had absolutely no idea how she must be feeling, but he did know one thing: if he had loved her after only two weeks, whatever he felt for her now couldn't be measured with something as simple as a word.

He was in awe of her strength. He marvelled at her innate and consistent kindness. He deeply appreciated that she still found reasons to laugh because it was something he had started struggling with through his own exhaustion. And every time she went out of her way to help Poppy with even the most minuscule of tasks, he had to fight his urge to drop onto his knees right then and there.

But he had waited. He hadn't wanted to give her anything else to think about. He understood that even good things could be distracting and exhausting, and he wanted Nina to focus on herself. On staying strong and healthy and whole.

But now, with things so clearly about to wrap up, he wanted to take that step.

Sierra came into the kitchen just then. She wore rhinestone-studded bell-bottom jeans, a cherry-red top and matching boots, her long blonde hair tucked beneath a black cowgirl hat.

'You coming to the barbecue tonight?' he asked, in lieu of a greeting.

She nodded tiredly in response, but Mav could see that the additional burden of his half of the ranch was beginning to weigh on her, too.

He waited for her to look up at him. 'I'm sorry I've been so preoccupied recently. I feel like you've been handling my portion of the resort . . .'

She frowned. 'Mav, you don't need to explain. Jesus, the last six months have been hell on us all, so I can only imagine what Nina – and you by default – are going through.'

He nodded. 'Yeah, it's been rough.'

'How's she doing?' Sierra asked. 'When I ask her, she just smiles and says "Good," but I know she just doesn't want me to worry.'

'She's tired, Si. But I think she's holding on.' He laughed softly, but it was at himself, at how wrapped up in her he was. 'I woke up this morning to an empty bed, and figured she was just up before me. But when I popped my head into Poppy's room to check on her, Nina was passed out in the bed with her.'

'Poppy's having nightmares again?'

'Yeah. And if she cries in the night, even when I insist that I've got it, Nina gets up and she comes with me.' Mav took a moment to steady himself before adding, 'I always hoped I'd find someone. I always wanted what Mom and Dad had, you know . . .' At Sierra's nod, he continued, 'With Shannon . . . I knew I was making a mistake even though I truly believed it was for the right reasons. But with Nina . . . I've found this woman who's going through her own hell but still finds the energy to get out of bed and snuggle my kid when she has bad dreams.'

'I'm happy for you, Mav. Nobody deserves to be happy more than you do.'

'Yeah . . . So, I was actually hoping I could talk to you about that . . .'

Both of Sierra's brows rose.

'You know Mom and Grandma's rings were being stored in the safe . . .'

Sierra's eyes watered with emotion instantly. 'You're going to ask?'

Mav reached into his pocket and pulled out the ring box with their grandma's ring. 'I just have a feeling that we're close to done with Cane, and I don't know . . . I guess I want to give us something good to hold on to through the end. But if you want this,' he held up the box, 'I'll find something else. I was thinking maybe a ruby.'

'No. Take the rings,' Sierra said hurriedly and swiped her eyes.

'I have no need for them. If I did, they wouldn't have been sitting in the safe for so long.'

'I'll take Grandma's,' he said. 'You take Mom's. I know it's yours.' It was the ring Benji had once asked him for.

Sierra didn't deny it. 'You don't think Grandma's is too simple?'

Mav opened the box. The ring *was* simple. A thin, yellow gold band with a small princess-cut diamond in it. 'No. Nina barely wears jewellery as it is.' He outright grinned. 'And I think she'd appreciate something from the family more than a big, fancy stone.'

'Mav . . .' Sierra sniffled. 'I'm so freaking happy for you right now.' She shook both her hands as if she needed to physically expel some of it from her body.

'She has to say yes first,' he reminded her, though his own heart thumped with excitement.

Sierra rolled her eyes. 'She will.'

Whether it was the talk of marriage or merely because Benji had already been on her mind, Sierra sobered. 'Have you heard from him recently?'

There was no need to ask who she was referring to. Benji had left three months prior when the worst of the media frenzy had died down. Though they were prepared for swells of media attention at each court milestone, for the most part, things had smoothed out at the ranch. Operations were back to normal, though the media attention had put them on the map. Last Mav had checked, they were booked out nine months in advance.

'Yeah. He texted me pictures a few days ago. He and Diablo are working a wrangler job for a ranch that runs along the Colorado River in Moab, Utah. He seems good . . .' Though he didn't mention it, Benji texted Mav every week, and he always opened the conversation with the same three words: 'How is she?'

'And Skye is handling the job okay?' Sierra asked, redirecting the conversation back to Benji's replacement at Hunt Ranch.

'Yeah. She's solid.'

'Good—'

The conversation trailed off at the sound of footsteps coming down the stairs.

Nina and Poppy walked in, both of them dressed up in jeans, boots, and wool-lined jackets for the Winter Wonderland Barbecue. Nina had braided Poppy's hair, but her own hip-length hair was covered with a knitted white beanie.

Poppy ran straight for him. 'We're ready!'

'I see that,' Mav stated, but he had a hard time tearing his eyes away from Nina. She looked tired, and it only made him marvel because she was still the most beautiful woman he had ever seen.

She smiled and came to him too, slotting at his side as if she'd always belonged there. The ring burned a hole in his pocket. 'We had a hard time deciding which boots to wear,' she explained.

'Understandable.'

Nina looked across the room at Sierra and clearly caught his sister's slightly maniacal grin. 'What?' she asked, looking back and forth between them.

'Nothing,' Sierra basically sang.

Nina frowned.

Mav shot Sierra a pointed look and tried to redirect Nina's attention. 'We ready to go?'

'Yup.' When he took her hand, she took Poppy's. 'We're going to have to do lots of dancing if we're going to keep warm tonight.'

'I love dancing,' Poppy said with a small sigh. 'Shadow, come!' she said, calling the dog to her side.

Sierra followed them out of the house and closed the door behind them. 'Your grandma used to say: "Dancing feet make a happy heart."'

'I have a happy heart!' Poppy chirped, and everyone laughed.

They piled into the Jeep. As they started down the ranch road to the resort, Mav looked back in the rear-view mirror and met Nina's gaze. She winked at him. He winked back. And when he turned his eyes back to the road, his thoughts were preoccupied with the question he wanted to ask as soon as they were back home – and the answer he hoped he'd receive.

The Wagon Train was bustling.

Guests danced and ate. The cold December air was alive with music and laughter.

Nina sat next to Sierra as they watched Mav and Poppy dance together. The song that was playing was fast and upbeat. Poppy was jumping up and down, all sense of rhythm forgotten. But Mav didn't care or get self-conscious, and when his daughter held out a hand for him, he took it and twirled her in a circle, making her laugh.

Sierra and Nina were both quiet for a long moment, each enjoying the crisp night, the music, and the scent of the hot mulled wine drifting to them from the bar.

But it was Sierra who broke the silence. 'Watching them always makes my heart ache.'

Nina turned to look at her. She wanted to say 'Me too' but refrained, sensing that their aches were for completely different reasons. She kept quiet, giving Sierra space to talk.

'I look at them, and it breaks my heart that my mom and dad never got to meet Poppy or see Mav as a dad.' She closed her eyes, whispered, 'God, Nina, they would have loved being grandparents. They would have *lived* for it.'

'I'm sorry I never got to meet them.'

'They would have loved you – for how happy you make Mav. But for who you are too.' Sierra watched her brother and niece a moment longer. 'He needs someone who is strong enough and kind enough to help him carry all the burdens he takes on. He needs someone he can lean on too, and you . . . You're really good for him.'

'I hope so,' Nina said, but she felt her heart swell. It was important, she realized. Sierra's approval was important. Because she had been looking out for her brother since their parents had died – just as he had been looking out for her.

'He makes me really happy.' Nina marvelled at the immensity of that. 'Before I met him, I thought I was happy. I had this job I loved and was good at it. Successful. I had one amazing friend and a few good acquaintances and colleagues. My life was comfortable. But after the assault . . . Everything I thought I knew about life was stripped away. My job was on the line. I couldn't tell my one true friend the truth. I felt like I had nothing. Like I *was* nothing.

'And then I met Mav. And everything fell into place. I discovered the difference between complacency and happiness. And the worst thing I've ever lived through ended up being fate's way of making sure I ended up in the right place at the right time with the right person.'

'I'm so happy for you – all three of you.'

'Me too,' Nina said, and despite the exhaustion and fear and anxiety, she meant it.

When the band ended the song, Sierra and Nina joined in the applause.

Nina glanced back towards the dance floor and saw that Mav was making his way to her, his hand holding Poppy's, his blue eyes fastened on Nina's face.

As he reached their group of chairs, the band started playing 'Run'. Mav held out one big hand for her.

He didn't say anything, only waited for her to slip her hand into his before pulling her to her feet and leading her to the dance floor where couples were beginning to sway.

Nina placed one hand on his shoulder as he brought her other to his chest and placed it over his heart. She sank into him, felt his familiar scent wrap around her like an embrace.

They slow danced to their song, and it was only when it was halfway through that Nina pulled back to look up at him. She didn't say, 'I love you.' She had said it many times before. She said, 'You make me happy, Mav.'

And he replied, 'You make *me*, Nina. Happy. Whole. In love. Everything I've ever wanted to be, you make me.'

Her eyes burned even as her body responded, pulling tight with need. 'Mav . . .'

'What do you need?'

'Take me home.' She pressed her body to his, roped both arms around his neck, and whispered, 'Please.'

They turned to look for Sierra and Poppy at the same time, saw that the two of them were at the overladen food table, piling their plates with food. 'It doesn't look like they'll notice if we slip off . . .'

'Text Sierra anyway. We'll come back for them when they're ready.'

Mav smiled at her as he pulled out his phone. 'This is actually good timing; I want to speak to you about something . . .'

Nina frowned at his tone. He sounded . . . She didn't know. Off. Anxious maybe. 'That's sounds ominous.'

'It's not.' But his face paled a bit. 'I hope.'

'Mav . . .'

He silenced her concern with a kiss. 'Wait until we're home.'

Nina felt relief spread through her. As certain as she was of their love, the kiss calmed her even as his casual reference to 'home' settled her racing heart. They didn't quell her curiosity though.

They bundled into the Jeep, laughing when Shadow leapt onto Nina's lap and licked her face, refusing to be left by Maverick for even a moment.

In the Jeep on the way home, she asked, 'Did we get a new rescue?'

'Nope.'

'Did you win the lottery?'

'Also, no.'

'Did Poppy get into trouble at school?' The thought had Nina leaning forward in her seat. 'Whatever happened, it wasn't her fault.'

Maverick laughed. 'I fucking love you. But no. Poppy is still an angel child.'

'Okay, I'm stumped.'

'It's a surprise,' he teased. 'You have to wait and see.'

She groaned exaggeratedly, but the truth was she liked this casual teasing. So much of their relationship had been governed by heaviness already; it was nice to just be in the moment, laughing and joking about whatever surprise Mav had in store for her.

He parked the Jeep under the big oak tree.

Nina got out of the car, but she took a moment to let her head fall back as she looked at the thick branches spreading outwards and into the night. 'We should hang a swing here,' she said, feeling inspired.

Mav closed his car door at the same moment that Shadow started growling. The dog lowered to her belly and started inching towards the house, her teeth and gums exposed.

Nina stopped moving immediately. She had never heard Shadow growl, and the low, feral sound had rivulets of fear streaking through her. 'Mav?'

'Stay here,' he said calmly. Too calmly.

Alarm coursed through her at his tone. Nina rounded the hood. When he started to walk towards the house, she grabbed ahold of his arm, stopping him. 'Mav? What's wrong?'

He folded her into a brief hug. 'Nina, I need you to stay here, okay?' When her body tensed, he took her face in both hands, looked into her eyes. 'Something's wrong.' He took his phone out of his pocket and closed both of her hands around it. 'Call the cops. Do *not* come inside. For any reason. Until I come and get you.'

'Mav—'

'Nina.' He talked over her and pressed a kiss to her forehead. 'I need you to stay here. Promise me,' he demanded.

She couldn't voice the words, so nodded.

'It'll be okay.' He took one step back, and then two, depriving her of her safety net even as he walked towards Shadow and the dark house, towards danger, protecting her always.

Chapter 31

Mav's booted foot crunched over the glass of the porch's broken lightbulb, announcing his presence to whoever was in his house. But he didn't let it stop him. This was his home. His land. The house where his family slept – and that was sacred.

Still, because he didn't have his gun or a death wish, he crouched low as he approached the front door. Reaching up, he turned the knob and pushed the door open.

As it swung wide, he glanced inside.

Next to him, Shadow made that ethereal sound again. 'Stay,' Mav ordered, knowing the dog would obey.

He entered slowly, making sure to keep quiet as he crouched low.

The cloying smell of overripe cologne clung to the air, just as Nina had once described it to him. To say that he was surprised would have been an understatement. Alexander showing up at Hunt Ranch with the criminal trial pending wasn't just plain stupid. It was madness – and that's why Mav knew that this was the point of no return.

Still crouched low, he moved along the interior of his house, making sure to be absolutely quiet as he clung to the walls.

His gun safe, a modern biometric one that only his fingerprint could open, was kept in his room – he just had to reach it. And soon. Because all he could think about was that Nina was a sitting duck outside.

Mav's heart thumped with adrenaline. His hands, surprisingly, were steady. His eyes, adjusted to the dark, scanned the lounge and the hallway leading to the kitchen, and seeing nothing, hearing nothing, he crept to the stairs.

He took them slowly, quietly, and when he came to the hallway, he deepened his breathing and softened his footsteps.

He opened his bedroom door, stepped inside, and flipped on the switch. He took two hasty steps towards the closet where his gun safe was.

And then stopped.

Because there, lazing in the chair in the corner like a king on his throne, a black nine-millimetre in one hand, was Alexander Cane.

Mav had run into plenty of wild animals on the ranch. He saw the shy bobcats every now and then and, once, had faced a black bear at thirty feet when he'd rounded a trail corner on Zeph's back and almost run into the damn thing. But none of those encounters had filled him with the same wariness facing Alexander Cane did. It was unpredictability that made animals dangerous, but better an unpredictable animal than an unpredictable man.

Alexander grinned, and it was feral. Unhinged. He waved the gun nonchalantly. 'No Nina?'

It said something about Alexander that he looked better than ever, almost unaffected. As if the havoc he'd wreaked had had no impact on his mental or physical health. Unlike Nina, Amanda Black, and the other women, whose lives had been turned inside out by the man sitting in front of him like a king on the precipice of full-blown insanity.

'You're breaking the terms of the restraining order,' Maverick said calmly, trying to use reason. If Nina had called the cops, they'd be about ten minutes out by now. All he had to do was stall. 'If you leave now, we'll forget all about this.'

'Hmmm, tempting.' He laughed gleefully, like a sadistic child who'd just killed a puppy, Mav thought. As if to prove his train of thought, Alex cackled. 'And you think I'm stupid enough to believe you'd just let me walk?'

'No.' Alexander shook his head mock-mournfully. 'Unfortunately for you and your family, you fell victim to a home invasion gone wrong.'

'Use your brain,' Mav said patiently. 'Do you really think, after the scandal you've been involved in, that the cops won't look to you first?'

'Maybe. But they'll have nothing to tie me to it. As we speak, I'm having a romantic dinner with a beautiful blonde who wants to be a movie star.'

In a desperate attempt to stall, Maverick said, 'Your fake alibi won't hold up. We have cameras at the front gate and on every building on the property. So, unless you walked here, we have you on video.'

'You're lying,' Alexander spat. 'Just like that whore!'

'Nina never lied.' The words were spoken quietly but firmly.

'Yes, she did!' he screeched. 'She wanted me! She led me on!' He pushed to his feet and started pacing. He tapped the gun grip to his own forehead. 'I fell into her trap – just like you! Can't you see what she is?'

'I do see *who* she is. She's brave and strong and kind and generous.'

Alexander cackled again. 'See, the only difference between us, is that I can see the truth so clearly. *I'm* strong enough to end it.'

'Alexander—'

'No. Shut up!' He paced constantly, that same wild animal. Caged.

Mav took a deep breath. As Alexander worked himself up, Mav worked to calm his own heart rate. He bought time. He waited for an opportunity to strike back.

'They don't believe me,' Alexander said, his eyes glinting with panic and fury. 'They don't believe that she led me on, that . . . that she paraded herself in front of me like a bitch in heat! She used me. She *wanted* me, and it was only once we'd cast her that she changed her mind. Manipulative bitch!' He waved the gun about erratically. 'Dumb, manipulative bitch. They're all the same.'

'Why don't we sit down?' Mav suggested quietly. 'Talk about it?'

Alexander's eyes snapped to him. For one single breath it looked as if he might consider it.

But the moment passed.

The Joker-like grin spread. 'Oh, you'd like that, wouldn't you.' Raising the gun, he pointed it at Mav. 'We're done talking. Where is she?'

'She's at a ranch barbecue, just down the road,' Mav lied.

'You really think I'm stupid?' He laughed. 'Why don't we test that theory? I'll put a bullet in you, and then while you lie on the floor bleeding out, we'll wait and see if she hears it and comes running . . .'

Mav's muscles shortened as he prepared to duck and then dive. His only chance was if the first shot missed, and he could tackle Alexander to the ground where he would have the size advantage.

As if he'd sensed his thoughts, Alex smiled maniacally.

He hitched the gun one inch higher.

Time slowed.

Mav could hear the blood rushing through his ears. His eyes never left Alexander's. And because he was so focused on the predator in front of him, he didn't register the sound of footsteps coming up the stairs or see Nina when she appeared in the doorway.

It was only when she said, 'You don't have to hurt him, Alex. I'm here,' that Mav felt true fear.

He went from calm and ready to panicked and frantic the moment Nina entered the equation. Because if he died, he was just dead. But if she died, his body would keep living without a heart. 'Nina—'

'Oh, no. This is perfect.' Alexander waved her into the room with the gun. 'Tell him the truth,' he spat. 'Tell him how you led me on and then forgot about me the moment you got what you needed from me.'

Nina looked into Mav's eyes, and even though she said, 'I led him on,' her eyes frantically said everything else. *I love you. I'm sorry. I'm scared.*

'No, you didn't,' Mav argued, drawing Alexander's attention back to him. 'He's insane. He's a predator with a narcissistic bent. And he's going to spend the rest of his life in prison.' Turning to Alexander, he taunted him. 'What happened to you? Huh? Do you struggle to get a hard-on, Alex?'

'Shut up!'

'Mav,' Nina begged quietly.

'Oh, I think I hit a nerve,' Mav mocked, even as he braced to take Alexander down.

'You know nothing!'

'Is that why you have to hold a woman down to get her to have sex with you?' Mav asked, deliberately pulling all that contained fury towards him.

A roar filled Mav's ears, and he wasn't sure if it was from Alex or the blood in his own head.

Alexander turned the gun on Nina.

Mav didn't think.

He lunged.

He heard the shot as he took Alex to the ground. Alexander might have been toned, but he didn't lift heavy shit on a ranch all day. Mav pinned him down easily.

There was one sickening moment where he turned around, his heart completely still, but the instant he confirmed that Nina was all right, standing in the corner, pale and in shock, he unleashed the full force of his rage on Alexander.

There was no mercy left in him. Mav let the fury come. He alternated left and right hooks to Alexander's face until the man's eyes rolled back in his head and his skin was a canvas of bloody, swollen flesh. And, still, he didn't stop. With every thwack of his fist on bloody flesh, he reminded himself of what this man had done to his family, to other families, and he felt nothing but sick satisfaction.

After a full minute, his arms were numb from wrist to armpit.

'Mav.'

He threw one last punch as Nina's shell-shocked voice punched through the adrenaline.

'Mav,' she said again, and this time she fell to her knees and wrapped her arms around him. 'Stop.'

He slumped against her.

As the adrenaline drained from his body, he felt the searing pain for the first time.

Nina released a warbled sob and clawed frantically at his shirt, pulling it from his jeans so that she could look.

He knew it was bad. He could feel the blood draining from him, leaving him light-headed.

'Oh, my God. Mav!'

'Don't worry. I'm gonna be okay.'

'What do I do?'

Her hands shook. He could see them trembling . . . Or maybe his vision was wavering.

'Mav!'

Why did she sound so far away? he wondered.

He felt more than knew he'd fallen onto his side, his head at an awkward angle, and even though he couldn't move, he kept his eyes open and on Nina's face. Because he didn't want her to be scared. And through the numbness and confusion he also knew that if he died, he wanted her to be the last thing he saw in this life.

She was so beautiful.

As his blood stained the floor beneath him, he started to lose touch. Shadow was barking furiously. Nina was crying, but he suddenly couldn't remember why, and when he tried to raise one hand to touch her face, it simply fell back to the floor with a heavy thud.

He frowned as she hurriedly removed her jacket, groaned in pain when she put her entire bodyweight on the wound.

His vision went seconds before he heard her scream. 'We're here! Hurry!'

'This is the county sheriff!' a voice called through the house.

'We're here! Hurry!' Nina screamed.

Blood soaked through Mav's shirt and squelched between her fingers. 'Mav!' She tried to shout his name, but it only came out a croak. 'Mav, wake up!'

He didn't move. He didn't so much as flutter his eyelids.

The sound of footsteps pounding up the stairs reached her ears seconds before a swarm of armed police officers burst into the room.

'Help me!' Nina rasped. 'Please! Please help me!'

'Jesus.' An elderly man, with a badge pinned to his shirt, dropped onto his knees beside her. 'Mav!' He slapped Mav's face gently. 'You there, son?'

Mav's lashes fluttered.

'He's breathing.'

Nina felt cold and numb. It was as if every drop of blood from him leached the life out of her too. 'Help him. Please.'

'Paramedics are right behind me.' He placed his hands over hers, pressed down heavily. 'I've got him. You can move your hands now.'

Nina's arms didn't budge, and despite her best efforts she couldn't make sense of where her arms ended and her hands began. She started crying. 'I can't move.'

'That's okay, hon. You're just in shock.' His voice was quiet and soothing, his big hands pressing down on hers oddly comforting. 'We'll hold him down together.'

'Mav,' she rasped.

There was no response.

Her entire body started shaking violently, but still, she couldn't let go.

'He's the toughest person I know,' the sheriff said gently.

'Yeah.'

Nina was so focused on Mav's face, his jaw slack, his skin leached of colour, that she barely noticed the other cops checking Alexander over, and when the paramedics hurried into the room maybe a minute later, she couldn't feel her body at all.

'GSW takes precedence,' the sheriff said, his tone leaving no room for argument.

The paramedics knelt, one on either side of him. 'We're going to have you both move in three, two, one.'

The sheriff moved, taking Nina's hands with his.

The paramedics took over.

'Come on. We're going to let them work and then we'll meet them at the hospital.'

'I'm staying.' Nina's tone was resolute. The numbness spreading throughout her body momentarily retracted as the heat of her rage warded it off. 'I'm staying with him,' she repeated.

'GSW to abdomen,' the paramedic said calmly. 'Haemorrhaging from truncal trauma. We need to get him to the ambulance, apply a haemostatic to try and reduce blood loss for transport.'

They rolled Mav onto their stretcher as if he were a child, not a grown six-four man.

'Where are you taking him?' Nina asked.

They didn't reply, only moved past her, calmly carrying her heart on their stretcher as if he were just another day on the job.

'Ms Keller.' The sheriff tried to stop her from following, but when Nina only shook him off and hurried after Mav, he followed. 'Ms Keller, we'll follow them. But there's nothing you can do for him.' When she didn't stop – couldn't stop – he caught her wrist in his hand, gently pulled her up short. 'I know this is hard to hear, but you have to let them work. You'll only get in the way and distract them.'

'What do I do?' she asked as a sob tore from her throat. 'What the hell do I do?'

And he didn't lie to her. He said, 'Pray.'

Chapter 32

Nearly six hours later, Sierra sat next to Nina in one of the chairs in the hospital waiting room. Poppy had cried herself to sleep on her lap. Markus, who had left LA the moment Sierra had let him know what had happened, sat with Juan on Nina's other side. They were all eerily silent, too scared to make idle conversation, too exhausted to care.

Nina was still covered in blood, in Mav's blood, because in the chaos nobody had thought to find her clean clothes. She was pale, her big eyes smudged with fatigue. Sierra didn't think she'd spoken a word since they'd arrived.

Sierra almost hadn't believed it when the front gate had called her to say that the police were responding to a 911 call from the ranch house. She hadn't thought. She'd grabbed Poppy and shouted for José to give her a ride. They'd reached the house in minutes, just in time to see Alexander Cane loaded into an ambulance, his face beaten and bloody.

When she'd asked a deputy what had happened, he'd only said that Mav had been hurt and that the sheriff had driven Nina to the hospital so that she could stay with him.

Sierra had followed straight away. She had called Markus. But it had only been when she'd arrived and spoken to the sheriff that she'd found out that Mav had been shot.

Shot.

Her big brother, so strong and infallible . . . Shot.

Had she not had hours to come to terms with it, she still might not have believed it.

She'd called Benji without thinking because he would come. Mav needed him. *She* needed him.

And, still, if there was one thing Sierra was very, very good at, it was turning off. She didn't cry or rant, though both were threatening. She simply went numb. She felt nothing, only stared blankly at the white wall in front of her.

Another hour passed.

A doctor came out. Nina shot upright in her chair. But he circumvented their little group with an apologetic smile and made his way to a family sitting on the opposite side of the room.

Next to her, Nina collapsed back in on herself.

'I'm sure we'll know how he is soon,' Sierra said, sensing that Nina was on the edge of her threshold. 'Surgeons don't spend this long working on dead people.'

Nina released a warbled sob at that. She spoke for the first time, and she said, 'He jumped in front of that bullet for me. He . . .' Nina had to pause and breathe through her sobs. 'He took the bullet for me, Si.' She buried her head in her hands. 'Oh, God. What have I done?'

Sierra's heart broke. She had no doubts that Mav had jumped in front of a literal bullet; it was who he was. But because she knew the fear and confusion Nina must be feeling just then, she replied, 'You've given my brother everything he ever wanted, Nina. Don't diminish what he did for you with misplaced guilt.'

'Amen,' Markus said quietly, and took Nina's blood-stained hand in his.

The doors opened again, but this time it was Benji who ran in, his shirt damp with sweat, his eyes crazed and bloodshot. He stopped when their eyes met, said, 'Sierra?'

'We're still waiting,' she replied, knowing everything he wanted to know from only her name on his lips.

He exhaled a huge breath and linked his hands behind his head as if he needed to take a breather, as if he'd run from Utah instead of taking the quick two-hour flight.

Sierra hated that she was relieved to see him, hated that she needed him to take over because she could feel her panic chipping slowly away at her own walls and she didn't know how much longer she could hold them up for.

Benji didn't ask questions or force Nina to relive what had happened.

He simply took charge.

He dropped his small duffel bag on the floor and knelt to unzip it. He pulled out an ancient Wrangler tee, one that Sierra herself had worn many times, and he came to crouch in front of Nina. 'Hey.'

Nina's eyes instantly welled. 'It's my fault—'

'No.'

'He came for *me*,' she insisted. 'Alexander came for me.' Her words came in a rush of anxiety then. 'And I've survived the last months by telling myself that the assault was the worst thing that would ever happen to me – but it wasn't. Not even close. Benji . . . There was so much blood.' She looked down at her hands where blood had dried in the fine cracks of her pale skin. 'I don't know how a person can survive losing so much blood.'

'Have you seen the size of that guy?' Benji teased. 'He has a lot swimming around in there. He'll be fine.' When Nina didn't reply, only nodded, he continued gently, 'No news is good news right now.' He unknowingly repeated what Sierra had said only moments before he'd arrived. 'It means they're still working, and that's what we're going to hold on to. Okay?'

Nina nodded.

''Kay, arms up,' he ordered. When Nina only stared at him, Benji grinned. 'I won't peek. Sacred rule of brotherhood.' As if to prove his point, he held the shirt up in front of his face, waited for Nina to tug hers off and then open the bottom of the one Benji held. He waited until her head was through before tugging it down her torso. 'Mind if I toss this?' he asked, holding up Nina's blood-stained shirt.

'No.'

He pushed to his feet, walked to a nearby trash can, and threw the bloody shirt straight into it. When he came back, Sierra said, 'I'm pretty sure they have separate trash for bloody items.'

'What they don't know won't hurt them,' came his succinct reply. He cocked one hip. 'What does everyone need? Coffee? Food?'

Just the thought of coffee made Sierra want to throw up. It didn't matter that it was close to two a.m., her empty stomach was too sick to handle the caffeine.

'I don't think I could stomach anything right now,' Nina said, speaking Sierra's thoughts.

'Markus? Juan, I'm guessing?' Benji leaned forward to shake Juan's hand.

'We're good, thanks,' Markus replied.

But because she knew Benji, and she knew he needed something to keep his thoughts from focusing on Mav, she said, 'Could you take Poppy for me while I go to the restroom?'

He came to her immediately, gently took Poppy's weight with a practised ease, and when Poppy stirred, and said, 'Daddy?'

Benji kissed the side of her face and replied, 'Not yet, honey. I'll wake you up when you can see him.'

Poppy yawned. ''Kay,' she murmured, and then buried her face against Benji and promptly fell asleep in his arms, her legs dangling.

When that near-constant grief rose up within her, choking her, Sierra pushed to her feet. She refused to let the memories of her lost dreams pull her under, especially now when Mav needed them both.

So, she let the past lie. And she walked away.

Nina was so consumed with thoughts of Mav that she didn't hear the exchange or see Sierra walk away. Nor did she see when Sierra returned and took her place at her side again, like some tireless watchdog.

Time was irrelevant. Every second may as well have been a year, and it didn't matter how long it took so long as whoever came to speak to her told her that Mav was alive and fighting. Because if he had even a small chance, he would take it. Mav always fought for what he wanted.

Thirty minutes later, an exhausted-looking doctor came out.

Nina shot to her feet because they were the only ones left in the waiting room.

He took those steps towards them, and for a long moment Nina could only look down at his soft-soled shoes as they padded across the linoleum floors, because she was too afraid to look at his face and read the news there.

'Sierra Hunt?'

'Yes,' Sierra said.

'And Nina.' The surgeon smiled at her. 'He said your name the moment he started coming out of anaesthetic.'

Nina slowly raised her eyes to meet the doctor's, and what she saw there had her knees close to buckling. 'He's alive,' she said even though she had clearly heard him say that Mav was coming out of anaesthesia.

'Yes. And he's doing great. We took a while because we had to do a full exploratory laparotomy and cardiac evaluation to assess the extent of his injuries. The bullet did some damage, but we're confident that we found and repaired it all.' He passed her a bag. 'These were on him when he came in.' The surgeon grinned. 'Personal items I'm sure he'll have some use for.'

'Thank you.' In her relief, Nina didn't look at the bag or its contents. She threw her arms around the doctor, uncaring that she was a mess of blood and sweat and that she was blubbering all over him. 'Thank you so much.'

He patted her on the back.

'Can we see him?'

'He's in recovery now. But he should be fully awake soon. A nurse will come and get you.'

She exhaled in relief. 'Thank you,' she repeated.

The surgeon grinned. 'My pleasure.' He rubbed the back of his neck awkwardly. 'This is so unprofessional, but do you think I could get an autograph?'

Nina laughed for the first time in what seemed like forever. Tears streamed freely down her face, and she didn't even bother swiping them. 'You just spent six hours saving my world. Yes. Of course. Anything.'

He passed her a blank piece of paper and a pen, and after a glance at his name tag, Nina wrote:

Dear Doctor Bently,
  Thank you for saving my heart!
  Love,
  Nina Keller

He smiled when he read it. 'This is awesome. Thank you.'

'Thank *you*,' Nina said sincerely.

'The nurse will be with you shortly,' he reminded her. And then he left.

Nina spun around. Every single one of them was crying, even Poppy, who had just woken up and wasn't even sure what was going on, and Juan, who had never even met Mav before. None of them spoke; they just met in a huge group hug.

Nina knew that they had all been listening as intently as she had to the surgeon, but she said, 'He's alive. He's going to be okay.' And because she needed to hear the words aloud again, she repeated, 'He's going to be okay.'

When she broke away from the group, Benji was frowning down at the bag in her hand. Nina's gaze began to drop, but before she could look at what he had been staring at, he snatched the bag from her, 'Ah, I'll hold on to this!'

'. . . Sure. Thanks, Benji.' When he crossed his arms, hiding the plastic bag, Nina frowned. 'Are you okay?'

'Yup.'

Sierra snort-laughed, and when Nina glanced at her, she only shrugged.

'What did I miss?' Nina asked.

'Nothing,' they replied at the same time.

'Guys—'

Nina's attempt to pry it out of them fell flat the moment she saw the nurse approaching. She hurried over to her. 'He's awake?'

'Yes.' The nurse smiled. 'We can take you two at a time, but only for a few minutes each.'

Nina turned to the others because even though she wanted – needed – to be there, she respected that they were his family and that they needed to see him too.

'I just have something to give him,' Benji said. 'I'll be quick.'

'I'll go with you,' Sierra seconded. 'That way, Nina and Poppy can stay longer once we're done.'

Nina nodded. She took Poppy's hand and gave it a squeeze, said, 'We can see him soon,' even as she watched Benji and Sierra walk away with the nurse.

Chapter 33

Mav forced his eyes open when he heard the door, and when Sierra and Benji walked in, the first thing he asked was, 'My girls?'

'All accounted for,' Benji replied. But he held up a plastic bag that contained Mav's wallet and the ring box he'd had at the barbecue. 'Thought I'd give you this before you see Nina.'

Mav smiled even though it took effort. 'Thanks.'

'I'm best man, right?'

'Who else?' Mav replied, but his heart settled knowing that Benji had come. 'Can you stay awhile?' he rasped. 'I'm going to be out of commission for a bit . . .'

Benji's voice was raw when he replied, 'Christ, Mav. As long as you need. You know that.'

Mav's gaze tracked to his sister. Sierra's characteristic neatness was gone. Her hair was a mess, her clothes crumpled, her makeup smudged. 'You look like shit,' he said, knowing that the casual ribbing would settle her more than any assurances that he was fine.

'You look like death warmed up,' she returned instantly, making him smile. She came to him, and she hugged him awkwardly over the hospital bed. 'Don't ever do that to me again,' she warned, her voice hitching with emotion. Lowering her voice just for him, she added, 'I won't survive any more, Mav.'

Because he understood some of her grief, the loss of their parents, he said, 'I won't.' And because he knew that he could never understand the rest of her grief, the loss of a child, he added, 'I'm here for you, Si. Always.' It was a promise, even though they both knew life always had her own plans.

Sierra squeezed his arm one last time and then stepped back from the bed. 'I'll go get Nina and Poppy.'

Benji lingered as Sierra walked out. 'You scared the shit out of us, Mav.' He cleared his throat. 'But I'm sure as shit glad to see you awake.'

Mav's mouth was dry, his lips cracked and sore. But he had to ask, 'Have you heard anything – about Cane?'

'No. Don't worry about that now. He's not walking away from this.'

'But you'll keep an eye out? Just in case?'

'Of course.'

'Sierra—'

'I know. I've got her – always. Don't worry.'

Mav sighed tiredly.

'You ready?'

'Fuck yes.'

If last night had taught him anything, it was that waiting was a waste of time. He wanted to look at Nina and call her his wife, and in the early light of a new day he couldn't quite remember why it had seemed so important to wait for the right moment. He loved her. He needed her. All he could do was hope that she was done waiting too.

Because time was a fickle bitch. He knew that more than anyone else. But his own fears, his insecurities, had made him cautious when, really, he should know to be greedy against the clock, to hoard moments and memories as if each one might be his last, *their* last.

In his haste, and still drowsy, he fumbled, trying to open the Ziplock bag.

Benji took it from him. He removed the ring box and closed it in Mav's hand. 'Okay.' He turned to go, paused in the doorway. 'I'm happy for you, Mav.' And because he was still a best friend, he added, 'But I still don't know what she sees in you, you ugly fuck.'

Mav braced against his own chuckle. 'Don't make me laugh.'

Benji tapped the doorframe on his way out.

Maverick didn't even have time to get himself together before Nina and Poppy walked in, their hands linked together, their eyes heavy with equal concern.

His heart settled. 'There they are.'

Unlike Nina's, Poppy's eyes brightened immediately. 'Daddy!'

She ran to the side of his bed and tried to scramble up by swinging one leg onto the mattress. She gave a few hops before Nina came to her and with a quick reminder to be careful not to jostle him, gave her a boost onto the bed.

Poppy crawled up the bed. Even though she was careful, she tugged on his IV, pulling it painfully in the back of his hand, and when she curled up by his side, both of her knees jabbed his side, sending fire down his entire body.

Mav didn't care. He gently rearranged her before placing a kiss on Poppy's forehead.

'Daddy, we were really scared,' she said solemnly. 'Everyone was crying.'

He knew that she probably didn't quite understand the gravity of what had happened, and instead of explaining, he thanked God that she still had enough childish innocence left in her to think him infallible, to think he would always be around to love and shelter her.

But he met Nina's eyes, noted that they instantly filled. 'We were really scared,' she reiterated.

Because he could feel that little distance between them, and because he understood Nina, and knew that she was protecting herself with it, he said, 'Nina, I would fight to stay with you every time.'

She didn't argue. 'I know that. I do. Absolutely.'

'I want a lifetime with you.'

Tears streamed down her face. 'Me too.'

'Come here,' he said, and held out his free hand for her.

'Yeah, Neens! Come here!' Poppy emphasized, breaking through the tension and making them both laugh.

The moment his hand closed around hers, he closed his eyes. It didn't matter that he knew she was safe and had seen her with his own two eyes. Touch, tactile confirmation, was what he had needed.

'I was so scared, Mav.' She ran her free hand through his hair, soothing him. 'Nothing . . . *Nothing* has ever terrified me more.'

He knew she was comparing his near death with her assault, and he hated that she had felt that fear again. But he didn't give her false comfort. He said, 'I know. I felt the exact same way watching him turn on you. Why do you think I did it? Why do you think I jumped in front of you?'

She tried to smile, but she couldn't quite manage a reply through her tears.

It was Mav who said, 'You – *both* of you – are my life, my entire reason for existing. I didn't jump in front of that bullet to only save your life, Nina. I jumped in front of it to save mine too.'

A warbled sob left her lips.

'Nina, why are you sad?' Poppy asked, her little voice confused. 'Daddy's fine!'

Nina nodded, but it took her a long moment to find her voice. 'I know, Poppy. I'm just happy.'

Mav took a deep breath. His hand, holding Nina's, began to sweat. 'There's actually something really important I was going to ask you last night, before . . .'

Nina frowned. 'I remember. What is it?' she asked. 'I'll sort it for you.'

He laughed even though it was excruciating. 'I really hope so.'

He briefly unlinked their hands to fish the ring out from beneath the blue hospital sheet. Once he had it, he held the box in his open palm, giving her the choice to take it or not.

Nina's eyes rounded with shock. 'Is that . . .'

'Yes.'

Poppy asked, 'What is it?'

'A promise,' Mav replied. 'A promise to love and cherish Nina for my entire life – just like I love and cherish you.' He briefly touched his nose to Poppy's, making her giggle.

And then they both turned to Nina, waiting.

She just nodded.

'Give me the words, Nina.'

'Yes. Of course. Yes.'

Mav's heart soared. Shifting Poppy's weight, he used both hands to pop the top of the box because of course Nina would say yes without even looking at the ring. 'It's small,' he warned. 'But it was my grandma's, and I want you to know . . .' He sorted the words in his head, sensitive to Poppy and Shannon. 'Nobody but my grandma ever wore it.' He hadn't ever even considered giving it to Shannon because he had known she would have been disappointed by it. 'If you want something different—'

'Don't.' Leaning over the bed, Nina kissed him, ending the discussion. 'I love it.' She spread her left hand in front of him. 'Make me that promise, Mav.'

He slipped the ring on her finger and then collapsed onto the bed with equal parts relief and exhaustion.

It was Nina who reached out and brushed her hand over Poppy's head. 'How do you feel about me being your stepmom?' she asked.

'Can't you just be my real mom?' Poppy countered.

Nina looked at him, clearly unsure of how to answer.

'I think,' he said cautiously, 'that anybody would be lucky to have two moms.'

'Maybe we can come up with a special name instead of "mom"?' Nina suggested, always kind, always considerate. 'Like Neens. Or Bonus Mamma?'

Although Shannon hadn't done much to deserve it in the past, over the last six months she had surprised Mav by calling to speak to Poppy every few days. She had even visited once every month, had paid to stay at the resort so that she could spend a few days close to Poppy. Mav wasn't sure what had brought about the change, but he appreciated that Shannon was finally trying.

'I like "Bonus Mamma",' Poppy said without hesitation.

Nina grinned. 'Then you can be my Bonus Baby.'

Poppy sighed happily. 'This is the bestest day.'

And even as his entire torso throbbed with pain, Mav said, 'Yeah. Yeah, it is the bestest.'

He patted the side of the bed because he needed to touch Nina, needed to hold her.

Nina eyed the bed sceptically even as she gently climbed up. 'Do you think it'll hold us all?'

'We'll find out,' he said in reply.

The bed didn't so much as creak as Nina's slight weight settled at his other side.

Unlike Poppy, whose elbows and knees were a hazard, Nina was painstakingly careful not to jostle anything. She curled up on her side next to him and placed her head on his shoulder. 'Am I hurting you?'

'No. You're exactly where you're meant to be.'

Whether it was because it was three in the morning or because of the stress of the night, Poppy was asleep within minutes. Nina lifted her head to look at the five-year-old, and when she saw her eyes closed, her mouth slightly open, she said, 'She's out.'

'Understandably.'

Nina watched as Mav closed his eyes, but because she knew that he was fighting his body's need to go under, she whispered, 'Sleep. We'll be here when you wake up.'

'I don't want this moment to end yet,' he argued tiredly.

'It won't end,' she said. 'We'll spin it out over a lifetime, Mav.'

His arm briefly tightened around her. 'I'm surprisingly happy for a guy who just got shot.'

Nina chuckled quietly, but because she wanted him to know that she had dreamed of this future with him, she said, 'Hey, Mav?'

'Hmm?'

'Do you remember on my birthday when Poppy told me to make a wish as I blew out my candles?'

'Yeah,' he whispered.

'I didn't have time to think it through, and I wished the words that were in my heart at that moment, words that my mind hadn't had time to process yet.'

He managed to crack his eyes open to meet hers. 'Give them to me.'

Nina rolled slightly so that she could place a kiss gently on his lips. And she whispered, 'Ask me to stay.'

Author's Note

I'm not going to talk about sexual assault, powerful predators, or the fact that reporting such crimes should be the victim's choice. Because if you're reading this, you're probably a woman. And you know. You've been taught about such things, you've been trained how to be careful since you were young enough to conceptualize sound.

This book came together with the help of a small but mighty tribe:

Alicia (@theromanticbibliotheca), who always provides me with honest feedback and early typo catches.

Kerry (@readkerryread), who has been an ARC, now beta, reader for me going on five years.

Nicolette (@sippingbookswithsampson), my number one hype girl!

@msgoddessreads for always providing me with those little insights that make a big difference.

Kyri Bailey (@bailey_read_books), @Kindlecraze_creation, and Sann (@Sann._.readz) who also beta-read for me – and provided me with such valuable feedback!

Ashley Warren (@scribemindstudio), who helped me smooth out my writing.

George Green, Grace Marshall, and the incredible HQ team for believing in my story.

And last, but never least, to every reader (ARC and otherwise) who spent their valuable time reading *Night Rider*. Being a writer is a difficult, often thankless job, but every time you talk/post/DM me about my books, I remember why I routinely do this. So, thank you!

Thank you!

Much love,

Sloane

Dear Reader,

We hope you enjoyed reading this book. If you did, we'd be so appreciative if you left a review. It really helps us and the author to bring more books like this to you.

Here at HQ Digital we are dedicated to publishing fiction that will keep you turning the pages into the early hours. Don't want to miss a thing? To find out more about our books, promotions, discover exclusive content and enter competitions you can keep in touch in the following ways:

JOIN OUR COMMUNITY:

Sign up to our new email newsletter: http://smarturl.it/SignUpHQ

Read our new blog www.hqstories.co.uk

X: https://twitter.com/HQStories

🅕: www.facebook.com/HQStories

BUDDING WRITER?

We're also looking for authors to join the HQ Digital family! Find out more here:

https://www.hqstories.co.uk/want-to-write-for-us/

Thanks for reading, from the HQ Digital team